SHELTER
FOR NOW

BOB HOWARD

Cover art by Lorena Martin of Premade Ebook Covers

DEDICATION

This book is dedicated to my dear and supportive friends Ivan and Christina Martinez and their wonderful children, Kenneth, Tanalee, and Theo Robert Martinez. It means the world to me that their two older children, Kenneth and Tanalee, enjoy my books. When Theo is older, I hope they will encourage him to read them, as well.

Bob Howard

CONTENTS

Bob Howard

ACKNOWLEDGMENTS

When I started Shelter for Now, I had a working title and some really different ideas. I wanted to go places that other zombie apocalypse authors haven't gone, but I have also kept in mind everything my readers have suggested. The number one request has been for shorter chapters for those people who like to finish a chapter before going to sleep at night. So, Shelter for Now has twice as many chapters as Exist for Now. I have connected with many of you through social media, and I got to meet some of you on a trip to Columbus, Ohio this last summer. I would like to thank all of you for your encouragement and support. When I write, I think about whether or not you will like what I'm creating.

I always like to mention the people who give their valuable time to proofread the material. Whether it is a little or a lot, every little bit helps. Unless you've tried to help a writer, you can't imagine how rough it is on beta readers. Rob Kilburn, Cori Anderson, and Stacie Turcotte all gave much appreciated input on this project. Of course my wife and my daughter, Dawn and Julie, have put some long hours into the book. I'm grateful to all of you.

Lorena Martin of Premade Ebook Covers is the best! When I give her an idea of what I would like the cover to be, she comes back with a variety of samples and choices, as well as suggestions on what might work better. I'm very glad we discovered her work.

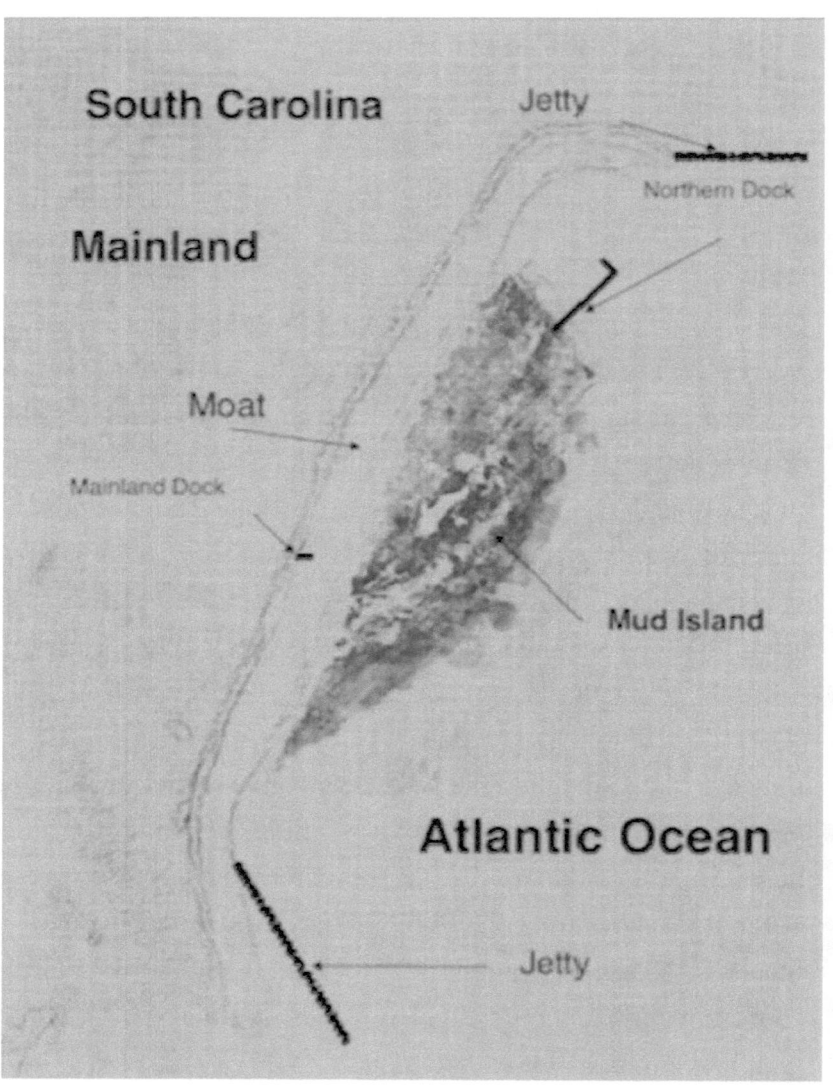

South Carolina

Jetty

Northern Dock

Mainland

Moat

Mainland Dock

Mud Island

Atlantic Ocean

Jetty

1 EXECUTIVE ONE

The White House was a bee hive of activity as the Secret Service and White House security personnel ran from room to room organizing the different groups that would be departing together on board the incoming squadron of Marine helicopters. One by one they were touching down on the White House lawn, quickly loading with passengers, and lifting off just as quickly.

The White House had far too many guests present on the evening of the infection outbreak who were listed in the Presidential Succession Act. After the President, there were eighteen positions of power identified as next in line should the person above them be unable to survive. Of those eighteen, there were twelve at the White House for President Freeman's birthday. They had all insisted upon staying despite the increasingly horrifying news that was coming in from around the world. None of them wanted to be the first to leave as long as the President was staying, and he wasn't going to let anything ruin his birthday party.

When it became obvious that the city itself was as much in chaos as the rest of the world, the guests began making their private phone calls. Security personnel were sent to gather up the family members to be brought to the White House. As the sun went down, more and more vehicles were arriving at the security checkpoints that would allow access by the families and friends of important guests.

The process broke down when other important Washington power-brokers began arriving. People who felt they had contributed enough cash or other resources to the last campaign went to the White House with complete confidence that they and their families would be welcomed with open arms.

The East wing entrance checkpoint was choked with people demanding entry in a matter of minutes, and when vehicles arrived carrying the families of the various Secretaries in the line of succession, people wouldn't let them through. As the chaos mounted it became obvious to the security officers that they would have to close the gates and stop anyone else from entering. Just as they were closing the gates, the infection that had been spreading wildly throughout every major city in the world began surging down the streets around the White House.

The sound of gunshots on the front lawn of the White House caused an automatic response from security guards, and Secret Service agents began well rehearsed procedures to ensure the safety of those they were sworn to protect.

There were still Senators, Congressmen, and an assortment of dignitaries who were arguing with each other when the first infected dead wandered in among them and savagely bit the extended arm of the Ambassador to France. The infected appeared to be a young woman who had not showered in days. In reality, she had been as sophisticated as the Ambassador, but when she had been dragged down in the street a few blocks away, she had been bitten several times and died quickly. Her body had been trampled by the crowds of people trying to escape, and her clothing made it seem like she lived on the streets.

The ambassador had been shaking his fist in the face of an armed guard through the closed iron gate and informing the man he would never work another day in Washington, DC. At first he felt angry because he had been interrupted. Then he felt surprise and confusion and asked the filthy young lady what she thought she was doing.

Then he felt the pain burning in his arm. When he started to scream, the people pushed in all directions just to try to put some distance between themselves and the creature that was pulling away a large piece of the man's forearm using her teeth. Some of them continued to try to get through the closed gates while others understood it was time to find another way to escape.

A security guard opened the gate just a few inches to allow someone to get through, and the crowd of normally distinguished and civilized people reacted. When they grabbed the gate and pulled it open so fast that they pulled the guard with it, the crowd surged forward pushing the infected young woman ahead of them. Secret Service agents did as they were trained and shot her repeatedly in the chest. The crowd around her tried to push backward in the opposite direction, and it created an open area all around the woman's body.

There was a moment when everyone paused. It was almost as if there was a video playing, and someone stopped it at the moment when the agents opened fire. Everyone stayed where they were except the woman who had been shot. The bullets had punched her in the chest and knocked her down, but she got back up. A second volley of bullets included one that struck the infected woman in the forehead, and this time she didn't get back up. The agents all figured it out at the same time. It didn't take a word of explanation for all of them to realize the target had moved from the chest to the head.

Inside the White House, the Secret Service had their lists of groups that would be taken away in a helicopter next. The President's group had already been lifted to safety, followed shortly by the Vice President and his family. The first Marine One helicopter banked away from the city in the direction of Andrews Air Force Base to rendezvous with Air Force One. The President had his wife and two teenaged daughters with him. They had not been able to locate his son or the Secret Service detail assigned to protect him. Even though he was in his mid-twenties, the President still thought of him as a kid, and he made the agent in charge swear they would find him and bring him to the shelter.

The helicopter carrying the Vice President and his family appeared to be heading north, but the flight plans were known only by the pilots and copilots.

The President pro tempore of the Senate, Harold J. Thornton III, watched from inside the White House until it was his turn to be escorted to a helicopter. The Secret Service agent who came for him said the President was safe in an undisclosed location, and so was the Vice President. He had to admit, he had been at least a little disappointed to find he hadn't moved up the chain of succession by at least one spot. He wondered where the Speaker of the House was since the Speaker was one step above him in the chain.

The agent didn't have much information for Senator Thornton. He only knew that the Senator was going somewhere to the south, and his family had already departed for that location. He was also told that government intelligence units were referring to the crisis as an extinction level event caused by a contagion. The Senator never cared for biology classes, but he was pretty sure it was serious.

"Whatever," he said out loud. "Just get me out of here."

******

President Freeman's helicopter landed at Andrews Air Force Base only to find the base to be under siege. Air Force One was fueled, and preflight checks had been done. All they had to do was move the President from the helicopter to the plane, but across that short distance was a barrier of gun fire and the infected.

Secret Service agents and Air Force Security Police were laying down heavy fire toward a huge crowd of infected dead that had somehow breached the secure area between them and Air Force One. It appeared that many of the infected were wearing hospital gowns, and had possibly been in treatment at the base hospital before anyone knew the contagion was so lethal.

Malcolm Grow Medical Clinic was closer to the Air Force One hangar than the helicopter crew would have liked. When the Air Force decided where to locate the hangar, they had in mind that the President would be closer to medical treatment if the need arose. It wasn't located in the immediate vicinity of the hangar, but it was close enough. Now it was keeping them from moving the President to his means of escape.

The Marine Captain flying the helicopter was a combat veteran, and he was not someone who would hesitate to make a split second decision. On his command, the President and his family were escorted back to their seats and strapped in. The big

Marine helicopter went upward like an elevator, and it immediately banked to the right.

It barely traveled one hundred yards before it sat down on the main runway directly in front of a private passenger flight that had just been fueled and was moving slowly toward the terminal. The flight crew was on board, but it had not yet been boarded by passengers.

Marines and Secret Service agents knew exactly what the Captain had in mind, and as the helicopter landed, the doors were already opening. The President, his family, and his staff were escorted quickly to the Boeing 737 that had already come to a stop. Stairs were being driven out to the side of the plane and were in place just ahead of the presidential party.

When the President arrived at the top of the stairs, the pilot was at the door waiting for him.

"Welcome to Executive One, Mr. President."

Executive One was the designation given to any private aircraft that was used to carry the President when Air Force One was not in service.

The Boeing 737 was a comfortable plane, but President Freeman surveyed the passenger cabin with distain. It just wasn't Air Force One. He thanked the pilot and went to a seat, thinking the entire time that they would find a way to transfer to his more familiar surroundings as soon as they could.

The plane taxied toward a runway as soon as the last person was on board and the stairs were removed. Through his window the President could see the big blue and white plane where he wanted to be. It was also rolling forward and heading toward a runway.

President Freeman motioned for one of the agents to come to his side, and he told the young man to inform the pilot that they should coordinate with Air Force One to rendezvous at the best location for them to transfer over to his plane. He was not going to travel all the way to their shelter in first class. To him it was just too undignified.

The agent went forward and spoke with the flight crew. There were only four flight attendants on the plane, and they were doing the best they could to get everyone situated. The agent returned with the information the President wanted to hear. If he had come back with anything else, he would have sent him back with the message that it wasn't a suggestion, but the young agent said they would arrive in Pittsburgh in just about an hour, and they could make the transfer then.

The pilot had been slightly offended because his 737 was a fine plane, and he was pleased to have the call sign of Executive One, even if it was under such unusual circumstances. He would follow the orders of the President, but he told his copilot that he would vote for the other guy the next time. He told the navigator to prepare a flight plan to Pittsburgh even though there was no one they could call to file the plan with.

Pittsburgh came into view before the President had a chance to finish his third bourbon and water. For some reason, he found even that to be somewhat annoying. He didn't recall ever having to finish a drink quickly on Air Force One just because they were going to land.

The Captain of the Boeing 737 made the usual announcements about landing and said which gate they would approach. President Freeman considered everything the pilot said to be unnecessary. All he wanted to know was that Air Force One would be there too.

As soon as the President complained about this new demonstration of incompetence, the pilot announced that Air Force One was on approach and that there was a change of plans. They would stop parallel to each other on separate runaways and escort the President and his party directly to Air Force One because the airport terminal was no longer safe.

The view of the airport from Executive One was slightly obstructed by smoke, but every passenger on board could see that Pittsburgh had not escaped what was happening in Washington. In every direction they could turn, the skyline was accented by the orange glow of fires, and one of the brightest of those fires was the main terminal of the airport. As the sun had set the fires appeared to grow larger.

Stairs were being driven to both planes even before they came to a stop, and the doors were hardly open before the President was rushing out of the private flight.

Normally the pilot would have been even more insulted by the President's lack of courtesy, but even he was beyond caring. From his view in the cockpit, he could see that the faster everyone got off of the plane the sooner he could get back in the air. The turmoil up by the main passenger terminal was enough for him to know that it wasn't safe to hang around any longer than he had to.

It wasn't until the passengers had all disembarked that the copilot asked the pilot where he planned to go. He realized that they had a perfectly good airplane with plenty of fuel, but they had no destination.

"Any idea where Air Force One is going?" he asked.

"I heard one of the Secret Service agents say something about a shelter of some kind in Columbus, Ohio. Any chance they'd give us a break because we got them this far?"

"Wouldn't hurt to ask, but let's just go to Columbus first. If we radio them and ask, they're just going to say they don't know what we're talking about."

"If they answer at all," said the copilot.

They didn't bother to ask the tower for clearance to take off because the tower had gone dark, and they couldn't raise them on the radio. The pilot watched for incoming traffic and fell in behind Air Force One as soon as it taxied onto a runway for take off.

******

The airport at Columbus, Ohio didn't do any better than the airport at Pittsburgh. Large fires raged through the business district downtown and through the upscale neighborhoods on the northeast side of the city near John Glenn International Airport. It was totally dark outside by the time they reached Columbus, and power had failed across the city. Entire neighborhoods were in darkness, and the blue and red lights on police cars were more visible from the air.

The pilot and copilot of Air Force One established radio communication with the crew of the 737 that had carried the President out of Washington. They realized the Boeing passenger liner was still following them when they also noticed there was no other air traffic approaching Columbus. All they knew was there had been distress calls from flight after flight until there was just silence.

The two flight crews agreed that the 737 should bypass Columbus to see if Rickenbacker International Airport to the south was doing any better, and then they could decide which was better for them to approach. The pilot of the 737 checked their fuel and saw they had plenty left to be able to make another detour and radioed that he would check in as soon as they had Rickenbacker in sight.

Air Force One was trying to raise the tower at John Glenn, but they were only getting static. Some of the automatic systems were still working, but there was no voice contact. The pilot and copilot were happy to see the Instrument Landing System antennas located along the runways were still functioning, and they were able to set the proper glide slope for the big plane on the longer of the two runways.

The pilot radioed the passenger Boeing 737 and informed them that the ILS was working at John Glenn International, so they were going to land. They said they would wait for them on the ground if Rickenbacker wasn't a good choice for them, and they would be escorted to safety along with the presidential party.

The plane lowered its landing gear and raised its nose about five degrees as the pilot adjusted to match the glide slope. Just as he was about to touch the wheels to the runway, the copilot began yelling into his microphone to abort. There were people on the runway. The glare of the runway lights was bright because of the surrounding darkness, so the pilots didn't see them until the last second.

The plane was already low, and they got a glimpse of the people in the glare of their landing lights. It made their skin crawl from a mixture of surprise at the close call and the bodily injuries they could see. Many of them resembled victims that had already walked away from an explosion. Missing limbs and wounds that had organs exposed were easy to spot even though the plane accelerated and began climbing again.

The pilot and copilot had pale faces and wide eyes. Behind them the navigator gripped the armrests of his chair almost to the point of breaking through the leather. Neither one had to ask the other if he had seen the people or their injuries. They both knew they hadn't imagined any of it.

As the plane raced by just over the heads of the people on the runway, the jet wash from the big engines blew them from their feet as if they were made of paper. Many of them were unable to get up again because their legs were mangled by the blast at the knees and ankles, but they still crawled.

The flight crew didn't know they had nearly landed Air Force One on the heads of a horde of the infected. They had seen the infected at Andrews Air Force Base and in Pittsburgh at a distance, but they had been far enough away that they had not yet experienced the feeling of fear that people on the ground had been through. From their perspective they had been injured people, and they didn't know they were already dead.

In the comfort of the private quarters in the tail of Air Force One, President Freeman was swearing at the top of his lungs. He had chosen to stand just as the plane was landing, and the sudden upward tilt and thrust had tossed him over a table into the laps of Secret Service agents who had followed the advice of a flight attendant who had asked the President to stay in his seat as they landed. Being the President, he didn't believe the laws of physics applied to him.

The agents did their best to be sure the President wasn't hurt by the fall, but they could do nothing to prevent injury to his pride. His considerably large ego made him want to lash out at someone, so he shouted for all to hear that those idiots flying the plane would be grounded, and that the closest they would ever come to flying again would be at an amusement park ride.

The plane banked to the east and did a tight turn to line up on the shorter runway. It was about two thousand feet shorter than the first runway, but the pilot and copilot felt like it was long enough. They needed seven thousand five hundred feet, and it was eight thousand feet long. It was shorter than they liked, but it was enough.

They established a glide path on the second runway and descended for a second time. Since the runway was shorter, the pilot brought the plane down sooner than he had on the first runway. His lights and the runway lights illuminated the area ahead enough for him to see what appeared to be shadows on the runway, but this time he didn't abort the approach. His wheels touched the asphalt, and he began applying the brakes.

"If there's someone on the runway, they can move," he said out loud.

In the next few seconds, he learned there were definitely people on the runway, and they didn't move. The plane almost seemed to hop from one moment to the next. First there would be a bump on the right side, and then there would be one on the left.

In the back of the plane the President's wife and two teenaged daughters were all screaming. They couldn't see the infected that were being crushed under the landing gear, but they felt the bumps and jolts.

Finally, they could feel the plane coming to a stop, and the pilot turned to the left and headed for a large patch of concrete that could be used for a landing pad. If they had any luck at all, besides being able to successfully put the plane on the ground, they would be able to contact a military unit in the area with helicopter support.

They had tried since leaving Washington to raise the cargo plane that had left before them carrying the President's limousine. They didn't know if it would be waiting for them on the ground or if it had crashed along the way. It appeared more and more like getting a convoy into downtown Columbus was going to be difficult.

There was a loud pounding on the cockpit door, and the copilot went to see who it was. When he saw through the small eyepiece that it was the President, he didn't hesitate to open the door.

President Freeman burst into the cockpit and let loose a barrage of insults and obscenities. The crew was stunned, especially in light of what they had to do just to put the plane on the ground. Among other things, he threatened their continued ability to get jobs as pilots.

When he stormed out of the cockpit, the pilot, copilot, and navigator didn't speak. For a group of professionals who took great pride in flying Air Force One, there was no greater insult than to have the President show such behavior toward them. As combat veterans and professionals, they went back to work trying to find a way to get him from Air Force One to his destination.

Outside the massive airplane runway lights switched off one at a time. The crew saw the lights going dark, and the darkness was advancing toward them. The lights on the plane were all that they had in only a few minutes as the darkness closed in behind them. The entire runway was black, and the timing could not have been worse as a radio call came in from the former Executive One.

"Air Force One, be advised we are almost on approach. Please confirm that you are off the runway."

They knew the Boeing 737 would have them on radar, but in the darkness they wouldn't be able to tell if they were out of the way. They also would not have guessed Air Force One had landed on the shorter runway. They would assume the President's plane had used the longer runway because they were a bigger plane.

"Executive One, we are on the short runway and have near zero visibility. The longer runway is occupied. We're moving off the runway onto a taxiway but do not have the identification of that taxiway. Green taxiway lights went out with the runway lights. We will locate an apron and be out of your way before you reach our location. You are clear to land."

Even though the 737 was no longer carrying the President and not really entitled to be called Executive One, the crew of Air Force One knew how they felt and kept their spirits up by addressing them that way.

Air Force One made a slow and careful turn onto the taxiway and straight into a horde of infected dead that had been drawn to the noise and lights of the plane. The pilot continued forward, and the plane rocked slightly as the wheels rolled over them.

"What are we going to do once we get stopped?" asked the copilot. "It's not like we can open the door and get out."

"We're safe inside the plane, so my guess is that we should sit tight until sunrise. The military should be able to get to us then."

The pilot knew his voice didn't convey much confidence, but worrying about getting out of the plane wasn't high on his list of things he wanted to do in the dark.

There was bright light on their port side, and they all gathered around the window. The 737 was coming in for a landing. It was a good thing they didn't try the longer runway, but in the glare of the big headlights they could see dozens of shadows moving on the asphalt.

"Executive One, be advised that the people on the runway are not alive. Do not pull up. Landing is your only option."

The crew of Executive One couldn't believe they were going to land on top of so many people. They committed to the landing earlier than usual because the runway was shorter, so their wheels were firmly on the ground when they reached the mindless horde of infected.

Warning lights illuminated almost immediately as the infected were scooped into the engines. On both sides of the plane, fire shot from the engine nacelles, triggering the automatic fire suppression systems. Smoke trailed behind them, but they would be safe as long as they stayed on the runway. Despite the fact that it at least gave the appearance they were killing people, the pilot kept steering in a straight line.

When they came to a stop, they could see Air Force One on a taxiway, and the big 747 was surrounded by the infected. It had the appearance of the tarmac at an airshow with hundreds of tourists trying to get a closer view of the plane, but in this case, they were trying to get closer to the living people inside.

The pilot of Executive One turned onto the taxiway and put its lights directly onto the President's plane. The noise from his engines and the bright lights were enough to draw the crowd toward them, but there was still no way to stop the siege of either plane. The infected seemed to be everywhere.

"Air Force One, I recommend that we both power down and go dark. If we do, they may move away by morning. Do you have ground support inbound?"

"Negative to the support. I agree with going quiet. I don't know what they will do if we don't make any noise, but it's worth a try."

Both cabin crews shut down their engines and started switching off the lights. In the darkness of Air Force One the pilot informed the passengers of the situation and asked everyone to remain as quiet as possible. It was unlikely that the infected would be able to hear casual talking or other sounds inside the planes, but the slightest amount of light from inside may be enough to keep them at the planes longer.

The passengers and crews settled in for a long, sleepless night.

2 TUNNEL

The railroad business at Union Station was growing faster than the city of Columbus, Ohio could handle, and there was an inevitable result. By the end of 1873 there had been dozens of collisions between locomotives and horse drawn wagons. In most cases the wagons would get their wheels stuck in ruts between the rails. Sometimes it was just a stubborn team of horses that became frightened by the vibrations in the tracks and refused to move another step. Whatever the reason, people, horses, and mules were dying on the railroad tracks. Even pedestrians were occasionally the victims of progress. To the casual observer the cause was simple. There were too many tracks next to each other.

The station was already providing services for forty-two passenger trains every day, and according to the owners of the railroad companies, they planned to nearly triple that amount over the next twenty years. Many of the passengers were just passing through on their way to the frontier, but some stayed, and Columbus grew along with the railroads.

Only a decade before, the leading cause of death for people from Ohio was the Civil War. When it ended in 1865, Columbus found itself at the crossroads of the eastern trade centers and the expanding west. Commerce was going to make Columbus important, and the City Council wanted to decrease the possibility of trains hitting pedestrians and wagons on North High Street.

At a special meeting on February 16, 1874, the Council passed an ordinance that would allow for the construction of a six hundred foot long tunnel under the North High Street railroad tracks.

It was an expensive endeavor, and the money was expected to come from the sale of municipal bonds, but they could not sell enough of them to raise the capital to build the tunnel.

The brick kilns in Nelsonville, Ohio manufactured and delivered all of the bricks required to build the tunnel, but the city of Columbus defaulted on its payment. The owners of the Nelsonville Brick Plant angrily loaded their bricks back onto trains for shipment south. They told the City Council there would be no further deliveries to Columbus until payment for this shipment was settled. After all, they owed one hundred and twenty men their salaries for the time spent making enough bricks for such a long tunnel.

The Council tried asking the railroads to build the tunnel, but the owners of the railroads had problems of their own. They had overestimated their own worth, and their investors were demanding repayment for the loans they had taken out to lay thirty-three thousand miles of tracks after the Civil War ended. They told the civic leaders of Columbus it was not their problem.

To make matters worse, inflation caused a depression that became known as the Panic of 1873. Worldwide depression followed, and Columbus, Ohio found itself desperately searching for a way to finance the tunnel or at least pay for the services they had already contracted. Word spreads fast when a city defaults on payments, and their credit was in jeopardy.

Their salvation came from an unlikely source. The federal government was investing heavily in Civil War restoration projects and had shown no interest in helping Columbus with its little problem. If money was going to go anywhere, it was going to go to cities in the south that had been burned to the ground.

When the City Council was approached by a man who claimed to be from the government in Washington, and who was prepared to pay for the tunnel, they were skeptical. However, they couldn't look a gift horse in the mouth, and they needed the money bad enough to agree to some unusual terms.

The man said he worked directly for the Office of the President, and that President Ulysses S. Grant had authorized him to take over the construction of the tunnel. In return, the City of Columbus would not monitor the construction in any way. Laborers were to be sent from other cities, and the operation would be under the direct supervision of the military. They also needed ten times the amount of bricks than what the city had previously ordered. The owners of the Nelsonville Brick Plant were ecstatic to have such a big order while the rest of the country was entering a depression.

The City Council called a special meeting to discuss the offer from the federal government. Some of the members were suspicious about what the city would need to do in return for such a windfall, but even they had to admit they were so desperate for help financing the project that their concerns were not going to stop them from accepting the offer. It was a unanimous vote in favor of letting the federal government build the tunnel.

By the end of the week work crews were arriving along with supplies. North High Street was closed to all wagon and pedestrian traffic at the railroad crossing, and a fence made of canvas was erected around both excavation sites. Security protected the privacy of the construction from start to finish. As loads of bricks were delivered, the work crews received them outside of the area even though the delivery drivers hoped to see what was going on inside. When they asked why so much brick was needed, they never got an answer.

Even more suspicious was the fact that the crews worked in shifts around the clock every day of the week, and when they weren't working they were sequestered in a private encampment built near the construction site.

After only a few weeks the laborers loaded their equipment onto freight trains and left, but the canvas enclosure remained in place. An entirely new crew of workers arrived along with covered wagons and crates. They disappeared behind the canvas and never came back out through the same side where they entered. Six hundred feet away they would eventually emerge from the opposite entrance. No one paid much attention to how many wagons of supplies were carried into the tunnel because of the distance between the two entrances, nor did anyone question what was in the crates.

Two months after the canvas barriers were put up, they were removed. The man who said the President had sent him to Columbus hardly took the time to say goodbye. He simply told the City Council the tunnel was ready for traffic, and he left. The Nelsonville Brick Plant most likely survived the depression because of the large brick order, and Columbus had their tunnel without any debt to pay off.

With much fanfare and celebration the mayor held a ribbon cutting ceremony and then rode on the first wagon to officially use the tunnel. Behind him was a long line of dignitaries in wagons waiting to follow him through, and one by one they descended below ground.

Even the mayor was surprised by what he saw. The entrance was much larger than he had expected, and the surface of the road was wide enough for two wagons to pass each other going in opposite directions without difficulty. Oil lamps burned at regular intervals, and although visibility was limited, they could see far enough into the distance to allow the wagons to move at a reasonable speed without running into the pedestrians who chose not to use the raised foot path along the right side of the tunnel.

When he emerged into the daylight on the opposite side, he was satisfied with the accomplishment. Despite a questionable beginning, the tunnel was open, and there would be no more collisions between trains and wagons.

******

Maybank described his shelter to the survivalist group and was met with plenty of skepticism. Most of the members felt like a survival shelter on an oil platform was the equivalent of painting yourself into a corner.

"You won't be able to leave," said Jerry. His shelter was being built under Fort Sumter, and it was an ambitious undertaking. It was one of the biggest shelters being built for the survivalists using taxpayers' money.

"Why do I need to be able to leave the shelter?" asked Maybank. "If we have to use our shelters, we won't want to leave them."

Jerry started to say something else, but he was interrupted by the leader of their group.

"You aren't supposed to leave your shelter. Once the end comes, you're supposed to get inside and stay there," said a man with long hair.

Titus Rush wasn't an imposing figure, but he was well respected by both his peers and by the government. When he spoke, he didn't have to ask for everyone to give him their attention.

"I'm not saying I'd put a shelter on an oil rig, but no matter where you put it, whether it's on an oil rig, under a Civil War fort, or inside an island, the idea is to stay inside where it's safe."

Everyone knew that Titus had selected an island as his location for a survival shelter. Some of the members didn't like the idea of having the Atlantic Ocean blocking fifty percent of the escape routes, but Maybank had him beat by locating his shelter several miles out into the Gulf of Mexico.

Maybank picked up on Titus' theme of self-survival.

"Yeah, Jerry. If an apocalypse happens, I'm going inside and staying there. I'm not leaving for anybody."

"Okay, everyone, let's move on. Martin, why don't you tell us about your location?"

One of the oldest members of the survivalist group was Martin Sullivan. He was a bit self-conscious speaking in front of more than two people at a time even if they were old friends, but he got to his feet and cleared his throat.

"Well, I decided to put mine in the middle of a city. It's coming along pretty well."

Martin hoped there wouldn't be any questions, but more than one person raised their hands as he started to sit back down.

"Martin, you know we need more than that," said Titus.

"How do you build a shelter in plain sight in the middle of a city?" asked Maybank. He was glad to get the attention off of himself.

Martin reluctantly stood back up and said, "It's not as hard as you think. The Army Corp of Engineers just told the city that they were restoring an old tunnel that was built around 1870. It turns out that President Grant was a survivalist, too."

Someone yelled, "All politicians are survivalists, Martin."

That drew scattered laughter from the room. There was no shortage of dislike for politicians in the group, but when they had been approached by the government with the offer to build their shelters meeting all of their design specifications, they couldn't turn down the government's money. It meant they could build their dream shelters the way they wanted.

"What do you mean by that, Martin?" asked Titus.

Martin did better answering direct questions, so he went on just a bit more relaxed than he had been.

"President Grant believed another war was just around the corner. He didn't know if it was going to be another civil war or an invasion from another country, but he believed something would happen. Because of his close ties with Ohio, he knew that Columbus was trying to build a six hundred foot long tunnel in the middle of the city."

The group was a bit entertained by Martin's explanation, so there were a lot of good natured questions. Someone asked why in the world did they need a tunnel that big in 1870.

"To keep trains from running over wagons," said Martin.

This time he had to wait for the laughing to die down after answering the question because he had replied as if the answer was obvious.

Another survivalist said, "You won't have any shortage of places to put backdoors. Did you have the government buy up all of the buildings around it?"

That made Martin smile, because it was also his idea to have his shelter connected to a rather famous network of not-so-secret tunnels that snaked around under the campus of the Ohio State University.

The North High Street Tunnel was only a few miles from the University, and the only hurdle was getting the exclusive rights to connect to the tunnels. Martin didn't want anyone else dropping in unannounced once the shelter was complete.

All they had to do was make sure money was placed in the right hands, which wasn't hard to do since colleges and universities are always being given money by grateful alumni. As a matter of fact, when a rather large donation from an anonymous donor was given to the University in return for ownership of the tunnels, no one had the slightest concern. The University needed access to the steam pipes and electrical conduits that ran through the tunnels, but they were assured that would be no problem. As long as they had access to make those repairs, the school didn't care who owned the tunnels or what they wanted them for.

New tunnels and doors appeared in places where there had previously been none. The doors had special locks that prevented curious campus work crews from learning what went on behind them. The work was also done practically overnight.

One campus maintenance man told some of his friends that he went into a tunnel one day and made some repairs. He went back the next day, and there was a new tunnel at the very spot where he had been working.

Titus seemed like he was puzzling over something.

"Martin, the main shelter is somewhere under Columbus. Why did you need for it to connect to the tunnels under Ohio State's buildings?"

Martin grinned, "Because it puts the shelter closer to the airport."

"You lost me there," said Jerry.

Martin said, "It's simple. When I told the money men from the government where I wanted to put my shelter, they said they were worried that their VIP's would have a hard time getting to it. They said they wanted two out of three plans in place: a helicopter landing, vehicle access, or air access."

"What about foot access?" asked Titus.

"I asked them the same thing," answered Martin. "They said with any of the other three choices there would still be at least some foot access to be considered. You still have to be able to get from a plane, a car, or a helicopter on foot into the shelter. They said a lot of people would die right outside their shelters just making it the last few feet."

"So you chose connecting to the airport so the VIP's could land in a plane or a helicopter and then travel underground all the way to the shelter. Why didn't you choose a location closer to the airport?"

"Because the tunnel at North High Street Railroad Station already has a shelter in it. All I had to do was make it better. The best part of the project was the fact that the tunnel wasn't used very long. It was poorly lit by oil lamps, and when it rained, it didn't drain well. It smelled so bad that people preferred taking their chances on the thirteen sets of tracks that ran across North High Street. They closed the tunnel after only a few years."

"You never told us what Grant had built except the tunnel," said Titus.

"Well, no one ever figured out there was anything but a tunnel, but it was made like a six story building, and most of it was under the tunnel. The rest of it stretched out toward the present location of the Ohio State campus. The floors were all well furnished, but a lot of moisture got in after the tunnel was sealed off. By the time it was opened and dried out, there wasn't anything of value besides the shelter itself."

"I like your idea better than Maybank's," said Jerry.

Maybank didn't like the attention coming back around to him, so he asked a logical question about Martin's shelter.

"There's almost ten miles between the airport and your shelter, Martin. Are they building an underground railroad for you? You can't expect a VIP to walk ten miles through tunnels."

"They're working on it," said Martin. "According to the officer in charge of building my shelter, they want another access point along the way. If a VIP lands at the airport in a plane, they want to be able to use a helicopter from there to several different landing zones. That way they can fly closer and then enter the main tunnel for the final leg of the trip. You should see the way stations they put in the tunnel. Supply depots with weapons and ammunition every mile or so."

"Who do they plan to bring to your shelter," asked Titus, "the President?"

3 MUD ISLAND

Living inside Mud Island had been my plan from the start. When I saw the shelter the first time, I decided to give up my apartment in Charlotte and set up house in the middle of nowhere on the coast of South Carolina. It didn't hurt when I saw I owned a seaplane, a Boston Whaler, and a houseboat all parked by the island, but then I found that my Uncle Titus had left me a really cool underground shelter that was well supplied and equally as well furnished. What I really didn't expect was everything that happened in the next year and a half.

Before the outbreak of the infection I was always a loner with no real plan for the future. My idea of a good day was fast food, preferably delivered, video games, and no interruptions. Now my idea of a good day had changed a bit.

A good day had become a day when no one died, and we had been having good days all through the summer months. Probably because we were following the advice of Uncle Titus and staying close to the safety of our shelter. He said to never leave the shelter, and we weren't exactly following his advice before this summer.

As a matter of fact, we weren't going to follow his advice once the weather got colder.

I tried to remember what the first day of the infection had been like, but it was such a distant memory that I was having trouble skipping over everything that had happened in between to get to the beginning. It was easy to remember the part about sitting in a tree, because that's exactly where I was again. The difference this time was that it was part of our plan, and it was also a lot colder than it had been back then.

The Chief had been laying out our plan to head north for the last few months. To say that he was fine tuning the details was an understatement. I had heard him saying more than once that we had to stop relying so much on luck and start thinking of strategies in advance.

That was why I was in a tree again. This time there weren't any mosquitoes, and the climbing had been much easier. I studied my forearms and wondered about how much they had changed since I started lifting weights. They had been much thinner, and they hadn't been suited for climbing trees.

"Okay, Ed. Let's see how fast you can get down from there."

The Chief was a few yards from the base of the tree, and I was on the ground almost before he could start his stopwatch.

"Not bad," he said appreciatively. "You broke your old record climbing the tree, so I'm not surprised you can get down faster without breaking an ankle."

"Did you happen to notice I picked a tree without low hanging branches?" I said with pride.

The Chief gave me his trademark smile and nodded.

"All we need to do is find you some walls to climb for practice, and you'll be able to get away from the infected wherever we go. Now let's see you go up that tree again, but instead of coming back down, I want you to jump over to another tree."

A rustling in the branches above caused both of us to tense up, but we relaxed when we saw Tom peering down at us. He had just jumped from another tree onto a thick limb about ten feet away. Then he rocked forward and backward as he tried not to fall off. Both of his arms were pinwheeling in the air as he tried to get his balance.

"It's not as easy as the Chief makes it sound, Ed."

The strain in Tom's voice was obvious, and he gave up trying to stay on the limb without grabbing at the trunk of the tree. One more inch forward the next time he rocked, and he was going to join us on the ground.

A second rustling of the trees from a new direction caused us to tense up again. This time it wasn't above us but was coming from the dry underbrush filling the gaps between the trees.

We saw the bushes moving before we saw an arm poke through, and then the infected stumbled and fell the rest of the way.

Tom moved further out onto the limb to be able to see the surrounding area.

"He doesn't have any friends with him," he called down to us.

Before the infected could push itself up onto all fours, I crossed the short distance between us. I had a short hatchet in a loop on the side of my jeans, and I pulled it to the top of an arc and just let the weight make it swing down toward the side of the creature's head.

I was proud of myself because I let the hatchet rotate as it descended, and the blunt side crushed the skull of the already dead thing that never gave a thought to what was happening. The hatchet did its damage without getting stuck in the head of the infected.

"That's the kind of training I had in mind," said the Chief. "With Tom as overwatch, one of us could move in for the kill while the other covered him. That infected gave us a practical lesson. When we go north, we need to work like that as a team."

Tom landed next to the Chief, and the two men walked over to where I was inspecting the infected dead that was face down in the brush between two trees.

The Chief seemed to block out what little bit of sunlight was coming through the brown leaves that still clung to the branches up above. Tom was the same height as the Chief, but he had a build that suited his former profession as a baseball player. The Chief was just plain massive, especially in the chest and shoulders.

"Anything interesting about this one?" asked Tom.

"He's thinner than usual," I said. "I don't know if he was a thin survivor who was recently bitten or if he's been walking and decaying at the same time."

"Judging by the smell, I'd say he's been ripening for a long time," said the Chief. "What was that Cassandra said about reaching a saturation point where there would be fewer living getting bitten and fewer replacements for the infected we eliminate?"

I thought a moment and added to what the Chief had said.

"Cassandra said the doctors on her ship had calculated that the human race would be wiped out in less than two months, whether it was by being bitten or killed by other survivors."

"Any way you do the math," said Tom, "it means we're eventually going to face off with someone or something that's trying to kill us. If we start winning the war against the infected, the survivors are going to start showing up more often as they search for a safe place to stay."

Cassandra had arrived during the summer as the only survivor on a hospital ship. The doctors had given her information that we, the Mud Island survivors, hadn't heard. The virus that had spread across the world was being passed on in the bites of people who were supposed to be dead, but things got really complicated when they had learned the virus had also managed to get into the food chain.

Our own doctor, affectionately known to our group as Bus, had started a serious regimen of testing everything. He tested the water, the air, plants, and even the insects. His biggest fear was that mosquitoes could carry the virus. If that happened, it would be almost as bad as the radioactive fallout that had caused a fellow group of survivors to seal themselves inside the shelter at Lake Norman in North Carolina. We would be forced to seal ourselves inside the shelter on Mud Island or move permanently to a colder climate where mosquitoes couldn't go.

So far Bus hadn't found a trace of the virus in mosquitoes, but every blue crab he tested had produced positive results in concentrations so high that we had no doubt that being pinched by a blue crab could spread the disease. Bus had found it to be ironic that you could be scratched by an infected dead and survive, but being pinched by a blue crab would kill you.

One of our community members, Jean, had been scratched badly by an infected, and she had been seriously feverish for a couple of days, but not only did she survive, she went on to have our baby boy she had been carrying at the time.

Bus had eventually confided in the rest of the group and told them he had at least some small hope that Jean had passed along an immunity to the virus to our son, but we might never know for sure.

Other tests gave elusive results. Shrimp that were caught at low tide tested positive for the virus. Fish that were caught in the deeper water at the end of the houseboat did not carry the virus even though some were large enough to feed on the shrimp. Despite those results, fresh fish hadn't been on our dinner table yet.

I noticed the sea gulls had been feeding on the shrimp, and from time to time we would see one catch a small blue crab. It didn't appear to make the sea gulls sick, but when Bus shot one and tested it for the virus, he found it to be infected. As long as the sea gulls didn't start attacking people, we didn't really care if they were infected. They weren't on our menu either, but we made a note to expect chickens to be carriers, too.

I flipped the infected over onto its back, and I had to stop myself from gagging. Bus had told us it was important for us to learn as much about the infected as we could, and that meant tissue samples.

We all carried Zip Lock bags for just this type of opportunity, so I pulled mine out of my pocket along with a knife.

"I hope Bus appreciates this," I said to no one in particular.

The Chief and Tom retreated a safe distance away. Not that they weren't safe while I got Bus his precious tissue samples, but the smell was awful.

Bus had told us it was important to get tissue from the base of the skull, and if possible to get some of the spinal fluid.

"Great," I said out loud. "Next time I need to remember to hit them in the back of the head."

They were covering their mouths as well as their noses, but I could tell they were trying not to laugh.

"Is there a rule that says I have to do this just because I'm the one who killed it?"

That didn't help. They both started laughing. That made them uncover their mouths and start gagging. I was fine with that until I started laughing with them. I was pretty sure it would take at least a week for me to get the taste out of my mouth.

There was more rustling in the underbrush as Kathy, Jean, Colleen, and Cassandra all emerged from the direction of the water that separated Mud Island from the mainland. In the middle of the group being protected by the women was Tom's daughter, Molly. She had been inside the shelter for the longest stretch of any of us, and she had begun asking to go out on patrol with the rest of us.

Tom had said no without hesitation, but even he had to admit Molly needed some fresh air and sunshine. He had agreed as long as she was well protected, and this group of women was about the best protection she could have.

They were formed up around Molly with their M-4's slung but ready. Molly had asked for a rifle of her own, but that was where Tom had drawn the line. She had a machete and a knife, but he wasn't ready to see her with a gun.

"How is everything back at the moat?" asked the Chief.

We called it the "moat" because it was the first line of defense that protected us from the outside world. The swamps that filled most of the area under the trees were good at slowing down the infected, but the moat was good at completely stopping them.

Even the alligators weren't as good as the moat. While they were busy hauling away one infected, ten more would slip by, only to disappear when they walked into the moat.

Jean said, "Everything checked out fine. There were footprints down by the southern jetty, but they led straight into the water."

"What's that smell?" asked Kathy.

They all knew what was causing the smell, but it was her way of joining in on the fun.

"I think that's my husband," said Jean. "Well, not actually my husband, but I have a feeling that smell is going to come back home on my husband."

"I'm glad we got the shower working in the houseboat," said Colleen.

"I hope everyone's enjoying themselves," I said.

I finished my assignment and sealed the bag. For good measure I slipped it inside a second bag. Then I peeled off my gloves and tossed them onto the body of the infected dead. It would be easier to replace them from our supply room than it would be to get the smell out of them.

Jean watched with suspicion as I put the plastic bag in my pocket.

"I hope that doesn't leak, Eddie."

There was generally some good natured laughing, but as it died down the Chief asked the women to finish giving their report.

As the weather got gradually cooler, the Chief had started organizing the training exercises, but he also set up a rotation of patrols. While one group was training, the others would be out checking the swamps around Mud Island for signs of either the infected or survivors.

The numbers of infected and living were both decreasing, but there were no guarantees. The infected didn't migrate, but they did tend to gather together and follow each other. If the footprints by the southern jetty were made by the infected, there were likely to be more of them in the area.

"It was a small group judging by the number of footprints," said Kathy.

"Did you trace the footprints back to the trees to see if you could tell which direction they had been going?"

The Chief was very curious about any patterns the infected dead might display. The area from Mud Island all the way south to Georgetown was virtually a wasteland now. If anyone had survived within that four hundred square miles, it hadn't been for long.

We had seen a massive horde walking down Highway 17 toward Georgetown in the early days of the infection, and when the citizens of Georgetown destroyed the bridges over the Waccamaw River and Great Pee Dee River to stop the horde, it caused the infected to spread out in all directions. Those that didn't get stuck in the mud and swamps or washed away in the rivers had wandered off into the woods. Sometimes they popped out of the trees along the moat and were swept quickly away on the current, but sometimes they just turned around and walked back into the trees.

The Chief and Hampton had followed a group once to see if they could determine any rhyme or reason to the way they wandered, and they had eventually found their way back to Highway 17. We might never know the answer why, but the group had walked out onto the paved surface and turned to the north. It was as if they knew they wouldn't have any place to go if they went south.

Kathy nodded affirmative to the Chief. She was just as curious as him.

"They came out of the trees from the south. I noticed the prints weren't very deep even in the soft sand, but they had been made by adult sized feet. My guess would be that they were from infected that had been dead for a long time. They didn't weigh enough to make normal prints."

We all knew that emaciated infected dead meant there wasn't much chance that there were more survivors to the south, but it also meant the infected were going to the north, possibly for the same reason. We had to at least consider that they were going north because there were no living people to prey on to the south.

"Why do they walk into the water?" asked Molly. "Why don't they just stay on the land?"

Molly had just asked the question we were all trying to answer, and we all hoped the infected weren't walking into the moat because they somehow knew there were living people on Mud Island.

Tom walked over to his daughter and got down on one knee. He didn't want her to grow up in a world where most of the human race had been eliminated, but he had to be honest with her because that was the world we were living in.

"We don't know why they walk into the water, but it's probably because they don't know the water is dangerous. They don't really know anything."

Molly furrowed her brow as she thought about her father's answer. Explaining the lack of reasoning ability shown by the infected dead was tough enough when you were talking to an adult. Explaining it to a twelve year old was not impossible, but it was not something you had to do a couple of years ago.

Molly came to her father's rescue just as he was turning to the rest of us for help.

"Daddy, I think dogs are smarter than the infected."

Tom was relieved.

"That's it exactly, Molly. Some animals are smarter than others. People know what will hurt them, and even though dogs are smart, sometimes they do dumb things like run out in the road. The infected won't even try to move out of the road. We don't know why they try to hurt people, either."

"It's time for us to get back to the shelter," said the Chief. "If we leave now we should make it back inside before dark."

Practice had a way of forming habits, and our habit was to do what the Chief said. We gathered our weapons and automatically lined up into two columns with Molly in the middle. Even though we were sure there were no infected nearby, we always assumed there were.

When we walked onto the beach near our dock, the motor of the Boston Whaler was already idling. Hampton waved at us from the boat and watched as we followed the Chief's training to the letter.

Cassandra and Kathy stepped out of the columns and took up positions as a rear guard, watching the trees on all sides to see if we were being followed. The Chief watched with satisfaction, knowing that we were much more disciplined than we had been a year ago.

******

The trip back to Mud Island was much faster now that we were working together as a team rather than a bunch of survivors who happened to get more lucky breaks than we deserved. Even the simple act of docking the boat and getting organized before hiking a mile across our island was done in less time.

The walk through the dense trees along the path back to our shelter door wasn't something we took for granted. While we were on the mainland practicing our combat skills, something could have washed up on the beach and wandered up into the middle of the island. In the early days of the infection it had been much more common than now, but there were still the occasional strays that came out of nowhere.

There was also a new menace to consider. The population of blue crabs had multiplied during the summer months. There were so many that they had become much more aggressive, targeting fish that were normally too big or too fast to become prey to the bottom feeding crabs. They were also coming further up the beach than before, and we weren't too surprised when they began foraging in the trees hunting for food. All of us were wearing tough military boots to be sure we weren't bitten or scratched as we walked through the deep grass.

One of the other natural enemies of the blue crab was the sea gull, but those tables had turned, too. More than once we had seen a gull carrying a blue crab intended to be a meal only to have it work out the other way around.

When we reached the shelter entrance, I dialed in the combination on the lock and swung the huge door open. We all piled inside, and I sealed it behind us. The door wasn't quite as big as the famous door at the military super shelter named Cheyenne

Mountain, but it was as big and thick as the vault door on any bank.

Doctor Bus was waiting for us inside, and as he helped us stow all of our gear, he told us he had some news to report from our friends at Fort Sumter.

Captain Miller and his men were getting ready for their own mission that would have a direct impact on ours. He planned on sending twenty men with us when we traveled north, but they were either going to need to find transportation, or they were going to have to stay behind. Our plane could carry our group, but that was all.

While we were gone, Captain Miller had contacted the Mud Island shelter to let us know that he and his men were starting inland with the hope of reaching the Charleston Air Force Base, and they planned to leave as soon as they could get the Chief to give them some intel about the availability of small planes or helicopters. A quick flyover by the Chief with someone getting some video was all they would need.

They were leaving in advance of us by several days because it could take them a long time to reach the base. It was only thirty miles from Charleston to the Air Force Base, but they didn't plan to travel by land the entire distance. Instead, they were going to go up the Ashley River on the USCG Cormorant until they reached the train tracks that crossed the river. From there they would go the last few miles by land.

The USCG Cormorant was a Coast Guard ship known as the Marine Protector Class. The Chief had liberated it from the Charleston Coast Guard base and then used it to stop an assault on Fort Sumter by a group of Cuban gunboats. It was later used to transport Captain Miller and about one hundred US Army soldiers from Mud Island to Fort Sumter.

"Radio them back and let them know we can take off at dawn tomorrow morning, Bus. The plane is fueled up and ready to go, so all we need to do is gather up a few things for the trip. I'll take my usual copilot with me."

The Chief sensed Kathy would be agreeable to going along, and he saw that she was already packing her gear. She gave him a sideways smile. Words weren't necessary when it came to who would go with the Chief. If something happened to the plane, we all knew who gave the Chief the best chance of surviving on the ground.

They stowed most of their gear by the entrance to the shelter so they wouldn't have much to do before leaving in the morning. If all went well, they would be over the Air Force Base and back at Mud Island before noon.

The once quiet shelter had become much more populated than it had been when the infection began. I had been by myself when it started, and it had been too quiet. Now there were nine adults and two children living in the shelter, so it had more of a community feel to it.

When Hampton, Colleen, Cassandra, and the baby arrived, we knew we couldn't leave things arranged the way they had been. For some reason we could never quite understand, the master bedroom was located in the center of the shelter. Everyone had to pass through the room if they were going up to the kitchen and living room, and they had to do the same to go downstairs to the other bedrooms, armory, sick bay, or anywhere else. We decided that the bathroom in the master bedroom was conveniently located for everyone to share, and we had spent a day relocating to one of the storerooms in a lower level. Supplies that were more commonly used by everyone were moved to the master bedroom.

When we were done and surveyed our new living quarters, we were surprised we hadn't decided to make the move sooner. We finally had the privacy we had always wanted, and everyone didn't have to tip toe through the room when Josh was sleeping.

I started to sit down at the big table in the dining area when I noticed everyone else had gathered on the other side of the kitchen. They were huddled together like a crowd waiting for a bus, and they were glancing at me as if I was an infected dead.

There are times when everyone is a little slow to catch on, but I was being particularly dense. I had apparently gotten so used to the smell on my clothes that I had even forgotten about the plastic sandwich bag in my pocket.

"I think I'll go take a quick shower, and maybe I'll burn these clothes."

I eased back out of the seat and headed for the lower levels. By the time I got back, everyone had settled in around the table except Tom and Hampton. It was their turn to cook, and it was a spaghetti night.

The Chief and Kathy were talking about their plans for the next day, and everyone else seemed to be talking at the same time about everything under the sun. I let my eyes wander around the table, and I wondered if anyone else in the world was enjoying supper the way we were.

I saw that Cassandra and Colleen were talking about Hampton as he was busy at the stove. Both were showing their appreciation for a man who knew his way around the kitchen.

When I thought about it for another moment, I remembered that there were at least two more places where people were able to sit down at a table and safely enjoy friendship with a meal, and we were responsible for them being able to do so. The shelter at Fort Sumter had been the safe haven for over one hundred US Army soldiers and a handful of civilians, and the shelter under Ambassadors Island in Lake Norman, North Carolina was populated by close to the same number of people. They were forced to stay inside the shelter for the time being due to radioactivity, but they were safe and probably as content as we were.

All in all, we had been doing a good job striking back against the infection that had left most of the world in ruins and most of the population dead. When I thought about it like that, things were better than they could have been for some of us.

4 JOHN GLENN INTERNATIONAL

Sunrise of the following day didn't give the Secret Service much hope that it would be a good day. What they hadn't seen in the darkness of the night before was the devastation on and off of the runway. It was a miracle they had landed two big planes on either of the runways. The number of planes that had run off onto the aprons or into the grass was staggering.

Several planes had landed safely and then pulled off the runways to avoid being hit by other planes. When the pilots of those planes saw Air Force One sitting on a taxiway at the end of the runway, they immediately assumed they would be safe. They powered up their engines and taxied closer.

From Air Force One, the President, the passengers, and the crew all watched in dismay as throngs of the infected dead followed the slowly rolling jet aircraft. From every direction, the infected responded to the noise, and as they gathered around the first plane to start rolling, another pilot got the same idea and began rolling his plane forward, too. Before long, there were six passenger planes moving closer to the President's plane, and there were at least a thousand infected dead on the tarmac. The crowd appeared to be growing by the minute.

The pilot of Air Force One tried using his radio to get the others to stay where they were, but they wouldn't listen. At most, there might be an armed Air Marshal on those flights with one weapon. The civilian pilots all knew there would be an arsenal of weapons on Air Force One, and they knew it would take an arsenal to save them. At the very least they expected the President would receive reinforcements, and they hoped any rescue attempt would be extended to them.

An armored personnel carrier of some kind appeared from a distant hangar but directly in the line of sight of Air Force One. The co-pilot saw it emerging from its hiding place, but it was so far away that he wasn't really sure what it was. He just knew that it was moving at a constant speed straight into the massive crowd of the infected.

The pilot joined the co-pilot and faced where he was pointing. He recognized the vehicle and told the others the Army had arrived.

As it came closer, the vehicle's details were easier to see. It sat high off the ground on eight huge wheels that made it too high for the infected to climb onto. There was a single machine gun mounted on top near a hatch, and they could just make out the man sitting in the opening. He wore a helmet and a reflective visor, but he wasn't bothering to use the machine gun.

The vehicle rolled through the horde of infected as if they weren't there. The big tires crushed everything in its path, and everything that was standing on two feet in between the front tires was either knocked out of the way or swept up underneath the body of the vehicle.

Unlike the Army vehicles used in the Middle East during recent years, this vehicle was not the familiar brown color of desert sand. Instead, it was a deep Army green.

The pilot told the others in the cabin, "That's a Stryker. Nineteen tons of pure pain to anything in its path. The gun is a M2 .50 caliber machine gun, but I don't think he plans to shoot his way out of here, or he would have been shooting already."

The Stryker drove through the growing horde of the infected straight up to the front of Air Force One. It came to a stop just below the nose but not too close for the crew to lose sight of him. The man in the helmet stood up straight and appeared to ignore the crowd that gathered around the vehicle once it came to a stop. There was an other world appearance to the area behind him where the path he had driven was paved with bodies. It left a trail like someone had driven through a cornfield.

The man extended his arms over his head, and the cabin crew saw him lower his hands to cover both ears. Then he held out both hands in fists and started holding out different numbers of fingers.

The crew understood his signal. He was telling them to use their radio to talk with him, and it was not on a channel they normally used.

The co-pilot dialed the radio to the channel indicated by the man and made immediate contact with the Stryker. He listened through his headphones and then gave an affirmative to the Stryker that he understood.

"He wants us to power up and follow him slowly."

"No problem," said the pilot. "This was exactly what I was hoping for."

In the back of Air force One the President felt the vibrations, as did everyone else. They all got out of their seats, hopefully thinking someone might be able to explain why they were moving.

The President told the head of his security detail to go find out what was happening. After his outburst toward the flight crew on the previous evening it was better for everyone if he stayed off of the flight deck..

The Secret Service agent wasn't gone more than a couple of minutes. He knew the President would expect an answer quickly.

"Mr. President, there's an Army vehicle in front of us, and we're following him toward the hangars on the other side of the long runway."

"It's about time," he answered.

The agents who stood ready to keep the President from harm exchanged silent eye contact. During the night they had quietly agreed that they hoped the Army didn't show up at night when it would be harder to see. They were badly outnumbered, and although their primary mission was to ensure the safety of the President, they wouldn't mind if it meant they would be saved too.

As Air Force One followed the Stryker, Executive One turned onto the same taxiway and fell in behind the 747. The President could see the runway from the port side windows.

"What's that imbecile doing?"

"That's Executive One, Sir. That's the 737 that flew you out of DC last night."

"Does he think that gives him the right to follow me? There's a big crowd of those monsters following him. He's going to bring them right to us."

The First Lady had come in from the sleeping quarters and was listening to the exchange between her husband and the respectful agent. She put her hand on her husband's arm and said in a low voice that she thought it was reasonable for the crew of the 737 to hope they could be saved, too.

President Freeman had won the world's biggest popularity contest when he had been elected President, but the agents around him knew very well he wouldn't win any popularity contests if the voters really knew him.

As if to accent the point, the President flew into another outburst of rage when the 737 behind them made its turn and opened up a better view of the planes that were lined up behind Executive One. The size of the infected horde had made air shows into a national event with so many of them gathering around the planes.

The morning was clear of clouds, so the sun illuminated the runway and gave them a good view. Six passenger flights had joined the procession and were all moving in a straight line for the taxiway. The infected weren't just following the planes, they were going where living people were, and they were converging from all directions.

The Stryker continued to roll slowly in reverse toward the cluster of hangars at the end of the main runway, seemingly unconcerned about the other flights or the infected. They reached the end of the taxiway, made a slight turn to the right, and then resumed their original course toward the same hangar where the Stryker had first appeared.

It didn't take long for them to cross the wide runway, and eventually the Stryker backed into the dark opening of the hangar door. The pilot kept his eyes on the man sitting in the hatch who continued to move his arms in a motion that meant to keep coming forward. When the man held up a hand for him to stop and then crossed his arms above his head, the pilot pressed on the brake pedal and began to power down.

Air Force One was sitting with the forward half of the plane inside, and everything from the wings back was outside in the bright sunshine. The other planes came to a stop and waited for some sign of what to do. The passengers and crews couldn't see too far into the darkness of the hangar, but each flight crew assumed they were part of a massive effort to save the hundreds of lives that were trapped inside the planes. The flight crews had started talking over the radio, but none of them had heard from Air Force One.

The Stryker moved a little closer to the front of Air Force One, and the man in the helmet gave the signal to use the radio again.

The co-pilot listened without speaking and then put the headset aside.

"He said to get everyone ready to disembark."

"I don't suppose he gave you a clue how we're going to get off the plane," said the pilot.

The co-pilot just shook his head. All they could do was leave it in the hands of the Army.

Word was given to the Secret Service to begin preparations to disembark, so they made sure everyone was ready. Weapons were prepared, and the family was surrounded by their security details. As a precaution against bites, the agents had bundled the family in extra layers of clothing.

Without any further instructions, the agents didn't know what else to do, so they had everyone gather down the aisles leading to the main cabin door. The President and his family were the closest to the door, and the other aisle was reserved for the staffers and the few lucky reporters who had managed to make it to the plane.

Normally, there would have been many more people along for the ride, but the sudden switch to Executive One at Andrews Air Force Base had caused some to be left behind in the confusion. He didn't know, nor did he really care that everyone had gotten off of Executive One, but many had been left standing on the tarmac. When Air Force One closed its doors and pulled away, they found Executive One had already done the same.

Both aisles sat and waited. Along the body of the plane outside, hundreds of hands reached upward. The pilots sat and stared into the darkness of the hangar wondering where the Stryker had gone. They had been so busy they hadn't noticed when it had backed away from the plane.

They heard something happening before they saw what it was, and the cabin crew rushed to the side windows and stared into the darkness for a clue. It was the deep, scraping noise of metal moving against metal.

"Over there," said the pilot.

He pointed out the left side window and then moved over so his co-pilot and navigator could join him. He was drawing their attention toward a spot that was roughly in line with the main cabin door where the floor was moving so much to trip the infected. As dark as it was, some of the infected seemed as if they had found a way to climb up the side of the plane, but the crew saw it was an illusion. They were rising upward, but not under their own power. The floor was rising underneath them.

A square platform approximately twelve feet long on each side was ascending next to the plane. The infected dead that were standing on top of it were losing their balance and falling back to the concrete floor below. It continued to rise until it was even with the top of the main cabin door, and when it lurched to a stop, three more of the infected went over the side.

From the windows where the pilots were watching and from the windows in the front passenger section, they could still see four of the infected standing on the platform. They were staggering and still trying to get their feet under them in order to walk, but one by one they managed to get their balance.

The pilot rapped on his window, and all four turned in his direction. Their reaction to seeing a living person only a few feet away was immediate, and they walked toward him.

The Secret Service agents saw the remaining infected go over the other side of the huge platform, so the agent in charge had the flight crew open the main cabin door a few inches. He was surprised to be facing another door only inches away.

There was a slight gap between the two doors, and the agent understood it hadn't just been a platform. It was an enclosed elevator. He reached across and pulled aside a large lever, and the door opened. The compartment inside was well lit, and a pair of US Army soldiers in battle dress uniforms snapped to attention.

"Sir, if you could please have the President and his party enter the lift, we should get going," said one of the soldiers in a crisp military voice.

The agent was dumbfounded but not so much that he didn't understand what was happening. This had all been planned in advance. All they had to do was get the President to the airport in Columbus, and someone else would take care of the rest.

One of the soldiers boarded Air Force One and gave a quick explanation to the agents. He said the capacity of the lift was twenty, so they would go down in shifts.

While they were in the process of boarding, he told them that down below was a deep shaft. The lift would only descend until the platform roof was level with the floor, then they would disembark into a tunnel where a vehicle would be arriving for them.

"I have a question," said the agent in charge. "While the lift is in the air, isn't the shaft exposed, and aren't those infected things falling into the open shaft?"

"Yes, Sir, but the shaft is actually close to two hundred feet deep, so whatever falls in while we're up here is going to be well below where we stop."

The agent thought it over for a few seconds and then asked, "How long will it take to fill a two hundred foot hole with bodies if you have about a thousand bodies walking into that hole?"

"Don't worry, Sir. It's my understanding that someone already thought of that. By the time we get everyone down, there will still be plenty of room in that hole."

"Someone already thought of that," the agent said more to himself than to the soldier. "I want to meet the guy who thought of that….or maybe I don't."

Once the lift was full, it was closed shut and began to lower. The lights inside were kept on, and it was much like riding down a few floors in a slow elevator. When it bumped to a stop, there was a knock on the other side of the door before it began to open.

The occupants of the lift stepped out onto a passenger loading platform that would have been normal in any underground railroad station. There were comfortable benches along the walls on a raised area above a set of tracks, and the tracks disappeared down a brightly lit tunnel.

One of the agents walked to the edge and leaned out to peer down the tunnel. He wasn't sure what he would see, but the tunnel curved away in the distance. Just as he leaned backward he saw motion, and it was coming down the tracks at high speed.

The passenger train came to a smooth stop in front of the raised passenger boarding area. It was painted the same blue and white colors as Air Force One, and it had the Presidential Seal on the side of the first car.

For the first time since this strange event began, the President smiled with satisfaction. He had hardly believed that the president of the most powerful country in the world had been forced to run from his own home whether it was from a disease or an enemy attack. As far as he was concerned, the people guarding the White House were incompetent, and he planned to have everyone replaced when he got home.

He saw the flight crew standing away from the rest of his party and motioned for the pilot to come talk with him.

"Yes, Mr. President?"

"You knew about this all along, didn't you." It was more of a statement than a question.

The pilot was confused by the statement and how the President had come to that conclusion, so he didn't have time to answer. It wasn't exactly an apology for his earlier behavior toward the flight crew, but knowing President Freeman, it was the closest he would ever come to an apology.

President Freeman turned away from him without dismissing him, so the pilot was left standing there not knowing what to do. He was relieved when the doors of the train slid open because the President didn't hesitate to hustle his family into the first car.

The agent on the train stopped a surprised aid from boarding and said the train was filled to capacity, leaving at least half of the people in the sitting area or standing on the platform. It seemed the capacity of the train had been somewhat overestimated. Either that, or the presidential party took up more space than they needed. The lift had gone up for a second time, and a steel gate had closed across the opening where the lift had been.

Less than a minute later the first of the infected dead flew downward past the entrance. The lift had gone above the floor of the hangar, and the open hole was catching its fair share of the infected that came too close to its edge. A few minutes later the bodies stopped falling as the lift once again filled the hole. The train hadn't returned for a second load, so more people from the plane were squeezed into the passenger loading area.

"Maybe we should get them to wait before going up for the next group," said the co-pilot.

"I was thinking the same thing," said the pilot, "but what about Executive One and all of the people in the planes behind them? How are they supposed to get their planes into position for the lift to reach their doors?"

"We can't just leave them up there."

"I don't think President Freeman is too worried about them," said the pilot.

Before the pilot could make his way through the crowd that had unloaded from the lift, the gates closed again and the lift ascended upward.

The bodies fell past them for a second time but this time in even larger numbers. That could only mean the crowd of infected up above had become larger.

Just as the crew was starting to worry that the elevator shaft would become full, the rain of bodies stopped again. A minute later the door to the lift swung open, and more grateful people squeezed out into the passenger waiting area.

The pilot caught the soldier by the arm and asked, "What about the other planes up there? We can't just leave those people up there to die."

"I'm sorry, Sir. I don't have any orders about them. That was the last trip up to Air Force One, Sir."

The soldier disappeared into the crowd just as the train reappeared from the tunnel. There was some pushing and shoving as people tried to be in the next train to leave. It was still too crowded when the train pulled away. The little underground railroad station wasn't intended for such a big crowd.

Just as the train left the platform, there was a scream, and that caused people to push harder. Someone fell off of the passenger platform, and an angry husband or boyfriend threw a punch at the offender who caused the fall.

In the melee that followed no one noticed that passengers inside the train were trying to pull the doors open from the inside, and there was a smear of blood on the window.

The pushing, shoving, and punching went on for several minutes until the soldier and several Secret Service agents managed to restore order. People were separated from each other, apologies were exchanged, and everything settled back down as they waited for the train to return.

******

Outside the hangar up above, the crew of Executive One tried again to raise the crew of Air Force One on the radio. There wasn't enough light inside the hangar for them to see the lift that had extended from the floor all the way to the main cabin door of the big 747. They didn't know they were sitting behind an empty plane, and that there was no plan for their rescue.

The Stryker they had seen leading the planes to the hangar emerged from the darkness and drove up to the nose of Executive One. The pilot put his headset on and was immediately greeted by a sergeant who gave him the bad news.

"What do you mean you can't help us?" he yelled into the microphone.

Before he could even get an answer the Stryker had moved on to the next plane in line.

"What did he say?" asked the co-pilot.

"He said they were sorry and that they had only planned for the arrival of Air Force One. He said they would bring reinforcements, and we could use the opportunity to get away from the planes or take off."

As the first Stryker went from plane to plane, five more of the military vehicles emerged from the hangar and began systematically clearing the crowd of infected dead from around the planes. They moved slowly and they stayed close to the planes, shooting outward. The vehicles themselves were used to dispose of the infected that were close to the planes, crushing them under the huge tires.

It became obvious after only a few minutes that they wouldn't be able to clear the entire area. The Stryker vehicles were laying down a devastating barrage of fire that would have been enough against conventional ground forces, but the infected just kept coming. The crowd was far too numerous for them to clear.

The lead Stryker radioed Executive One and suggested that they should try to take off and fly to Rickenbacker International Airport. The sergeant said there was a military reserve unit there that was run by the Navy and the Marine Corps, and they had received instructions to proceed there as soon as possible.

The sergeant wished them good luck, and to the horror of the passengers on the planes lined up behind Executive One, the Strykers began driving toward the southern exit of the airport.

In the passenger planes behind Executive One, the flight crews were having the same discussions with their passengers. Passengers were yelling threats, and some were demanding action. Some were even demanding to be allowed off of the planes. Where they hoped to go was anybody's guess.

The first plane in line behind Executive One began to power up and make a slow turn toward the grassy area between the hangars and the end of the runway.

It was clear that the pilot intended to reach the runway and take off, but all of the flight crews watching from the other planes were holding their collective breath. The ground in the grassy areas was green and well tended, but the runways were slightly elevated to allow them to drain well when it rained.

Executive One didn't have the weight of hundreds of passengers, so they could probably make it easily, but the heavier planes were going to be in trouble if the landing gear passed over a soggy patch.

The front end of the passenger jet reached the tarmac, and the front wheels were having difficulty making it over the lip of the runway, but the plane lurched forward and upward. The rear wheels reached the edge at an angle because the pilot began turning, and the big tires easily climbed onto the pavement.

There was cheering on each of the passenger planes as the first plane began rolling forward and gaining speed for take off. If not for the Strykers, there would have been far more infected walking on the runway, but they had thinned the crowd just enough. The remaining infected were also following the plane as it moved across the grass.

The next plane in line began to turn, and his dilemma was clear. He could either use the same path the first plane had taken and risk getting stuck in a rut created by the first plane, or he could try a new, untested path.

The pilot radioed the other planes that he was going to cut a new path because someone had to find out if the grassy areas were going to be overall a safe bet. An answer came from the last plane in line that he was going to make a sharp turn and use the taxiway they had followed earlier.

There was a concussive explosion near the end of the runway that rocked all of the planes. The plane on the grass came to a stop when the pilot reacted to the fireball in the distance, and he lost their forward motion. The single wheel strut dug into a soft section of wet ground and sank deeper. The front end of the plane dipped lower, and the pilot desperately applied more power, but the rear wheels had too much traction. The front landing gear collapsed under the strain, and the nose of the plane dropped toward the ground. The passengers and crew were still safe from the infected, but they weren't going anywhere.

In all of the planes the passengers and crews moved to the side of the plane facing the place where smoke and fire engulfed the wreckage of the plane that had just attempted to take off. No one had seen it coming, but the plane had slid sideways over hundreds of bodies at the end of the runway. When the front gear had lifted from the ground, the slide became worse, and they were no longer facing forward when they reached the end of the runway.

Aboard Executive One the flight crew didn't have hundreds of passengers screaming at them. They were left with their solitude and the certainty that there was nothing they could do to save their own lives, but the pilot had one idea left.

There was just enough room for the 737 to turn and begin slowly moving in the direction of the main terminal.

5 CHARLESTON AIR FORCE BASE

At sunrise the Chief and Kathy were ready to leave on their brief trip to the Charleston Air Force Base. It had become our practice to all be up before dawn. In part it depended upon how much Josh decided to let us all sleep, but even though we were safe in a shelter where nothing could do us harm, we were anything but soft. We had become as hard as the outside world, and we knew that would keep us alive longer.

It was a group effort getting them ready, and we all had breakfast together before we carried the rest of their gear up to the outer door. A quick check of the security cameras spread around Mud Island showed it was a quiet day outside. It was clear enough for us to see that there were some new tracks in the sand down by the beach, but they appeared to go no further than a few feet inland before turning back toward the water.

The tracks made us decide to send a full patrol with the Chief and Kathy rather than just two extra people, so we all geared up for a trip to the dock. Molly graciously accepted her role as big sister to Josh. She agreed to stay behind with him so Jean could go with us. Jean had been cooped up inside longer than the rest of us and was dying to get some real exercise. The last time Bus had taken a turn watching Josh for us, so Molly didn't complain. Besides, she would undoubtedly spend most of the time on the radio talking with Sam at Fort Sumter.

Molly had grown a lot in the last six months, and when she turned twelve we had thrown her a big birthday party. She had tested her limits a bit by asking if she could drink with the adults, but her request was met by so many disapproving glares that no one even had to speak for her to know what the answer was. She tried again when she asked if she could go to Fort Sumter to visit with Whitney and Sam, and she added we could let her stay there for a week or two.

It didn't take a genius to know she was really talking about spending time with Sam. He was close to her age, and every adult in the room knew their hormones were just about to boil over from puppy love. She was forced to concede that the best she could hope for was to visit, but staying for a week or two wasn't going to happen unless the Army placed her and Sam under a twenty-four hour armed guard.

We all gathered at the main door just as we had in the past, and as soon as it was opened, we went out as if there were infected dead waiting for us on our doorstep. Going out combat ready was what the Chief had called it.

We took up our positions guarding the outside of the door until everyone was clear, and the big door was sealed in place.

I had been through that door dozens of times since the first day, but I never lost my respect for the builders of the shelter. The door was set back in the side of a steep bank of trees, moss, and rocks. It was recessed just enough for it to fit in with the earth that had fallen away from the roots of the trees, and the embankment had been undercut over time by wind, rain, and possibly animals seeking shelter. The back wall of the recessed area was the door, and it was so well disguised by the natural elements found on any barrier island that you could sit in front of it without ever knowing it was a door.

There was a big locking wheel in the middle of the door that blended in with the dried branches and vines growing down through the overhang above. Once you knew it was there, it was easier to see, but to the unsuspecting eye, it was practically invisible.

When I had seen the door the first time, it didn't seem to be as well hidden, but as time had gone by and our creative minds played with new ideas, we had found more and better ways to camouflage the door.

The entrance was located almost in the center of Mud Island, but the beach side where the door was located was less dense with trees. During the winter months you could see almost all the way to the water. The leaves had been falling for a couple of months, so any infected that might have washed ashore overnight would be visible from a distance.

On the other side of the embankment that hid the door to the shelter, Mud Island was not very hospitable. The gradual rise from the beach side was over twenty feet, but it was too steep to climb from the opposite side. We considered that to be fortunate because we never had anything unexpected dropping in from above.

Whether we headed north or south from the shelter entrance, the terrain was similar. The trees became thicker in both directions, and the island leveled out to only a slightly higher slope at the center. When we had witnessed the migration of infected dead from the beach toward the moat, they had been forced to spread out to get over the middle of the island. A Russian ship had exploded in the moat at a time when the beach had been heavily populated with the infected, and we had watched them being drawn to the sound of the explosion like moths to a flame.

We had to walk about a mile, and we had worn a path from the door to the northern tip of the island because that was were we docked our plane and our boat. There was also a barge and a houseboat tied to the dock, but they were more of a distraction than they were useful. The houseboat was habitable, and we kept a modest amount of supplies in it. Our hope was that anyone who found the houseboat would think that was all there was to the island, and they wouldn't follow the path that led into the trees.

Along one side of the dock sat our most prized possession. It was a bright yellow and white seaplane known as a de Havilland Beaver. It was noisy, but it was durable. The Chief was a very skilled pilot, and if these were normal times, he would probably fly the plane every day just for fun.

As soon as we arrived at the dock the Chief stepped onto the wide float and squeezed through the door into the pilot's seat. I was always amazed at how easily he did it when I considered his size. The door always seemed so much smaller than him.

I pulled open the cargo door and fastened it to a hook on the wing strut so it would stay open. Everyone else who was carrying gear for their trip took turns stepping onto the float and stowing the gear. Kathy gave Tom a hug and kiss then climbed through the cargo door to the other side of the plane.

While we were going through our routine of loading the plane, Cassandra and Hampton cautiously approached the houseboat. It was still tied to the end of the dock where it wouldn't block our visibility of the jetty that protruded from the mainland.

The jetty was what protected the entrance to the moat that separated Mud Island from the rest of the world. When the houseboat had been tied to the side of the dock and blocking our view of the jetty, something had dislodged one of the massive granite boulders from the jetty, and sand had quickly formed a reef that made a virtual footpath from the mainland to Mud Island.

By moving the houseboat, we were able to see the jetty and the entire houseboat through a hidden camera, and even though we had seen no movement on the camera, Cassandra and Hampton approached it as if it was occupied.

On their signal everyone else made sure they were not inside anyone's circle of fire when they opened the door. A quick check showed that it was vacant, and we were clear to get the Chief and Kathy on their way. We untied the mooring lines and gave the plane a shove. It turned easily from the dock as the Chief started the incredibly loud engine. He rotated the plane and circled the houseboat as he headed out to sea. A few moments later, and he was lifting the plane into the air and climbing to his cruising altitude.

"If no one has any objections," said Tom, "I think we should do a patrol of the island while we're out here. Is everyone wearing thick boots?"

Everyone smiled and gave a thumbs up, but it was no laughing matter anymore. The blue crabs were still around even though the weather had gotten colder. If we were going to patrol the beach, someone was likely to get one hanging onto a boot.

We formed up with Tom in the lead and left the dock in the direction of the beach. It wouldn't take long for us to walk the two mile stretch along the ocean, and the exercise would do us some good.

******

It had become the Chief's practice to always take off by going straight out to sea. That way he would be able to gain altitude before coming back toward the mainland. He had taken a bullet twice in our last plane. The first time he managed to land the plane safely, but the second time had been anything but pretty. He and his passenger survived the crash, but the plane had been destroyed.

They passed over the spot where the Mercy Ship had sunk during the summer, and they could just make out the shape of it under the water. Where it sank, the hull was still partially hung up on a reef where it had become a constant reminder of the global scale of the infection. The ship had begun its journey to escape the infection off the coast of Africa and reached its final resting place on the coast of South Carolina.

After making a wide turn and climbing to a safe altitude, the Chief headed inland straight toward their destination. The Charleston Air Force Base was a joint command connected with the US Naval Weapons Station at Goose Creek. In the early days of the onslaught of the infection, the Mud Island survivors had tried to connect with the Navy but found the base was being overrun by the infected dead. They had arrived at the base just as the military was evacuating onto ships.

They had never made a close inspection of the area around the Air Force Base, but the lack of radio contact with anyone in the area had not been encouraging. The base was home to a squadron of the C-17 Globemaster III, the workhorse of the Air Force. They were not the largest transport planes in the world, but they were certainly massive in size.

When the infection became an epidemic, the military would have tried to position its assets around the world as strategically as possible. The Chief speculated that the C-17's would have been scrambled to the bases in the Middle East to retrieve our troops. They would be needed at home if we were to ever reclaim North America from the infected dead, but he couldn't imagine how the men and women in the US Armed Forces could be coping with their concerns for their families. The fact that they hadn't seen the C-17's in the air over South Carolina in the last year was not a good sign.

When the Chief expressed those feelings to Captain Miller at Fort Sumter, the Captain had given him some reason for hope. Logistically, it would be a monumental task to remove eight to ten thousand troops from Afghanistan alone. Captain Miller explained that the United States had troops in about one hundred and fifty countries, and the total number was over a quarter of a million people. That didn't include ships at sea.

Captain Miller reassured the Chief that not seeing the military didn't mean they weren't gathering their forces somewhere. As a matter of fact, his theory was that the US military had found safe haven in a colder climate, such as Greenland, and they were preparing to take back their country.

That feeling of encouragement from Captain Miller wasn't much for the Chief to lean on, but if he was going to believe in one thing, it would be his faith in his own military training. He had to hang onto the belief that the reason he had survived was the same reason why the US military would also survive.

"A penny for your thoughts," said Kathy.

The Chief snapped out of his private thoughts, and it dawned on him that he had been on autopilot. The same way people had driven to work in the past without remembering the drive, he was so focused on what the military was probably doing that he had been going through his motions as if they were a practiced routine.

"Was I that far gone?"

"Worse. You didn't even hear me the first time I asked."

"I was thinking about how this is all going to end one day. Are we going to become extinct, or are we going to fight back and win?"

"We don't have much choice. We have to fight back, and we have to hope we're not the only ones who are doing it," said Kathy.

"Captain Miller's carrier group screwed up because they underestimated the capability of this infection to escape captivity, and it got them all killed."

Kathy shook her head.

"It's more likely that they overestimated their ability to keep it contained. I think that's less likely to happen again because other squadrons and carrier groups know what happened to them by now. We learn from our mistakes. The infected won't learn from theirs."

The Chief was about to admit that Kathy had a point when he saw they were already approaching their destination. The Charleston International Airport was within view, and just beyond it was the Air Force Base.

Their goal was actually next to a private terminal that sat to the east of the Air Force Base not far from the airport. Kathy began scanning with her binoculars trying to locate Charleston Helicopter Services, and hopefully there would be helicopters on their landing areas. The trip would be wasted if they had all flown out of the area.

The building wasn't hard to spot because the terminal for private jets was the next building to the north. At least six expensive jets were parked by the terminal. One had burned to the ground where it was parked.

Kathy lowered her binoculars just a bit to the south and spotted the helicopters. There were two sitting near the building, but they were executive models that wouldn't be able to accommodate twenty armed soldiers. That wasn't good news for the survivors.

"Two executive style helicopters on the landing pads to the right of the building, Chief. They might be four or five passenger models."

"Not good enough. We need to find the big ones. I had hoped they would have landed up here by the private terminal as a way to get civilians moved to the airport more quickly. Shuttle services would've been big on that last day."

Well over a year later it was still alarming to see so much devastation. The runways were dotted with bodies that had been crushed by the big tires of rolling aircraft, and small fires had burned everywhere. Scorch marks that ended in trails of debris were evidence of how many small planes must have crashed because they couldn't run over the infected that had crossed the runways.

The terminal gates at the Charleston International Airport were almost all damaged in some way, most likely because planes had pulled away while the flexible gates were still attached to them.

"Time to circle the Air Force Base. Let's hope for friendly survivors who don't shoot for fun."

The Chief cut across the helicopter service building and followed a course roughly parallel to the main runway of the Air Force Base. The base shared the runway with the private terminal, but there was a shorter runway crossing it at an angle. It was used mostly by the smaller private planes, and it had the most debris blocking it from further use.

When the de Havilland Beaver reached the perimeter of the base, the Chief made a wide turn and came back across the roofs of the hangars and maintenance areas at the northern end of the base. If the Air Force had tried to evacuate a combat contingent or establish some sort of command and control center, it would have been from this area. Up ahead he could see where the C-17 Globemasters were usually parked, and the area was clear. If the base had been secured against the infected, there would be about two dozen of the big planes lined up on the tarmac.

A row of aircraft between the hangars caught the Chief's eye, and he knew they had hit the jackpot. At first glance he wasn't sure what model helicopters were partially covered by tarps, but then he realized it was because they were new, and he recognized them.

Three had been towed into a secure area between the buildings and camouflaged. They would only need one because each could carry twenty-two men and their gear. The range was five hundred and thirty-nine miles, which was right at the limit the Chief had hoped for.

"Will those do the trick?" asked Kathy.

Before she even asked the question they had sped past the buildings, and the plane climbed into the sky again.

"Get some pictures for me when I make the next pass. If I'm not mistaken, those are Sikorsky helicopters that were just delivered to the Navy within the last year. I read about them not long ago. Their service record isn't long enough for me to say they're any good, but they're new, and they hold enough people.

They also come equipped with an optional fuel cell, and if I was buying them for military use, I would have chosen that option."

They lined the Beaver up to make a pass down the length of the three helicopters, and Kathy leaned over for pictures. She put the setting on video so they could study the results one frame at a time.

When the Chief banked away from the buildings, he checked with Kathy to see what she thought, and she was shaking her head.

"The area around the helicopters was crawling with infected."

"Military or civilian?" asked the Chief.

"Why's that matter?"

"If they were civilian, it means the military got out with whatever they could. Civilians would have flocked to the base begging for help."

"I didn't see any uniforms," said Kathy.

"I hate to say I'm relieved, but it would be nice to know the Air Force got out to a safe zone in a place where the infected wouldn't survive long."

"Is that why you want to hit Columbus?"

"I want to hit Columbus for several reasons," said the Chief. "It should be cold enough for us to eliminate the infected in large numbers, but according to Bus, that's the most likely place to find the President. If he made it, then there would be some command and control. We could contribute by giving the military the locations of the other shelters, and they could populate them with troops the way we did at Fort Sumter."

"I've been meaning to ask you about that list," said Kathy.

The Chief was busy bringing the plane around for another pass at the helicopters, but this time they were coming straight at them from the opposite direction. Kathy leaned over to get the video, but this time the Chief saw the infected that seemed to be confined to the area.

"Was there a fence or barrier at the ends of those streets between the buildings?" he asked.

"I think so, but Captain Miller's people should be able to deal with the problem. It didn't appear to be too many to handle," she replied.

"Unless the buildings are full," he said half to himself.

"They would be," said Kathy. "I heard what you said, and I would bet the buildings were full. People who made it to here would have stayed for a while at least, thinking the Air Force would come back for them."

"I agree. Besides, they probably didn't have much choice once they got here. It would have been overrun with the infected in minutes after the military pulled out. Try getting Captain Miller on the radio. He has his intel. Let's hope his people can handle those Sikorsky's."

******

Captain Miller had good news for the Chief when his radio operator received the report. He had at least six men who were trained on helicopters similar to the VH-92A. They were all combat veterans from the 1st Air Cavalry who had become separated from their unit on the first day of the infection, and he planned to take all of them along in case he needed backup pilots.

While the Chief and Kathy were getting the location of the helicopters, Captain Jim Miller was busy with his plans to travel to the Air Force Base. The first order of business was to prepare the USCG Cormorant for the trip, and based on the Chief's last experience with the Ashley River Bridges, he had to be well under way before low tide.

The morning had begun before sunrise with a small skirmish on the surface of the shelter at Fort Sumter. His men had attempted to reason with the current occupants of the fort, but they weren't cooperative. Captain Miller couldn't help but wonder about a group of survivors that thought they could use force against an armed military unit.

They had used the hidden loudspeakers to alert the survivors to their presence and offered to discuss giving them permanent safety. In return they only asked that the survivors lay down their arms before the Army would disclose their location.

The survivors took up defensive positions around the fort and waited. Unknown to them, tear gas charges had been strategically placed around the fort and could be remote detonated. The goal was to take control of the surface, not to kill fellow survivors. However, they did forfeit their one opportunity to be invited into the shelter.

When the tear gas canisters were detonated, the survivors were forced into the open in an attempt to escape the burning gray clouds. Some of them ran for the docks and took the boats they had tied up near the Cormorant while others tried to stay in the fort. They found themselves running straight into soldiers wearing gas masks who were armed with M4's.

They expected to be shot, but instead they were escorted from the fort to their waiting boats. As a parting favor, Captain Miller's men even warned them not to cross the harbor toward Patriots Point. From what they had seen since the summer, it was occupied by someone who didn't accept visitors.

The next chore was to have a crew quickly make the Cormorant seaworthy. Since they had used it the last time it had been lightly coated with radioactive dust and had been inhabited more than once by survivors who thought it was a safe place to stay.

The cleaning had been done by soldiers in Hazmat suits, and they had the dependable Coast Guard ship ready as the sun appeared on the horizon. Her fuel tanks had been filled, and the soldiers worked as fast as they could to ensure their small raiding party had everything they needed for their trip to the Air Force Base.

Captain Miller chose to take the same twenty men with him who would go on the mission to Ohio. He wanted them to have some extra time in the field before making the trip, and even though the Charleston Air Force Base wasn't too far from their starting point, it would be a good idea for the men to remember what they would be facing outside. They had been safe inside Fort Sumter for months, and their senses had been dulled.

The USCG Cormorant pulled away from the dock on schedule, and Captain Miller told his men in the wheelhouse to get them upriver past the Ashley River Bridge as quickly as possible. They turned the ship in a tight circle and gave it every bit of speed that they could.

As they passed White Point Gardens and the Coast Guard Base where the Cormorant had originally been stationed, they saw that the city was changing. It didn't seem to take long for the lack of landscaping to make a city more void of life instead of empty. There were groups of the infected walking through the tall grass, and their attention was drawn to the Cormorant as it churned the water with its powerful engines. The infected walked toward the railing along Murray Blvd. and reached with their arms toward the ship.

Captain Miller called for one of his best marksmen to report topside with his sniper rifle. It wouldn't hurt for him to get a little practice while they made their trip up the Ashley River. He passed the word to the soldiers who were keeping a constant watch on the shoreline through binoculars that he wanted the snipers kept informed of potential targets, but to tell him personally if any survivors were spotted.

The sniper took careful aim with his M24 Sniper Weapon System and started dropping the infected dead with ease despite the swaying of the ship. At first it seemed like the other soldiers were all appreciating the expertise of their friend, but they were more amazed by the sheer number of infected that were lining up along the railing. Some were tall enough to fall over the top rail, and some were short enough to go under it. Regardless of the reason, they were falling into the river in large groups.

"Where are they all coming from?" asked one of the men.

"I don't know," said Captain Miller, "but from what the Chief told us about how many fell in at the Coast Guard Base there really shouldn't be this many."

One of the men was nicknamed "Preacher" by the others because he could quote scriptures even though he wasn't shy about killing in combat. Someone asked him if there was a scripture about the dead rising up and trying to bite the living. It wouldn't have bothered anyone if he had made one of his famous quotes, but he just sat and stared like the rest of them. He had seen things in the Middle East that he never wanted to see again, but the sight of the dead reaching out at them as the ship skimmed past was something that numbed his mind. It was like he kept dreaming but couldn't wake up. His silence bothered everyone.

Captain Miller tapped his sniper on the shoulder and asked, "Are you hitting the ones you're shooting at, or are you just shooting into the crowd?"

"I'm hitting what I'm shooting at, Captain, but it's like shooting fish in a barrel."

"Save your ammo. We'll be going under the bridges in a minute anyway."

6 GREAT OAK

The bridges came at them fast, or at least that was how it felt to the soldiers. It was the Cormorant that was charging toward the Ashley River Bridges at top speed. As a precaution the soldiers were lined up along the side rails and were ready to rush forward when the helmsman cut the ship's forward speed. They had sped passed James Island Expressway Bridge as if it wasn't there. It was so high above them that an infected that was able to hit them would need to be a precision diver.

The idea was to go under the bridges at low tide with plenty of room to spare, but just in case the clearance wasn't what they hoped for, putting weight on the bow as they cut their forward speed should cause the ship to dip downward at the right moment. If they did it too soon, the bow would rise higher after the dip, and they would clip the bridge with their mast. If they didn't do it in time, they were likely to still have enough room, but they didn't want to leave anything to chance.

The signal was relayed from the wheelhouse, and the soldiers rushed forward. The sudden decrease in speed added to their momentum as they charged toward the bow, so they were almost out of control, but they had taken the added precaution of tying a safety line from the first man to the last and then to a cleat in the stern. If anyone went over the bow, they would only hang far enough to get wet.

Captain Miller wanted to preserve radio communications between the Cormorant and the Chief at all costs, so he added one more safety precaution by bringing along a replacement antenna. If they lost their main array, they would just keep going while he had a maintenance crew installing a new antenna.

The first bridge turned out to be good practice for the second. The tide was low enough that they wouldn't have needed to put weight on the bow, but then again the first bridge was a higher span than the second.

There was also a new complication. For a second time the question came up about where all of the infected were coming from. The middle span of the second bridge was crowded, and the sound of the Cormorant's engines was drawing them to the railing as they approached.

Captain Miller saw that there were no infected wandering around on the first bridge where he could see them, and the only thing he could figure was that it wasn't possible to predict their numbers or movements. The world had changed, and it would continue to change.

"I need at least four snipers up here, like yesterday," he shouted below.

His men were good, and he was reminded how good they were by how quickly they arrived. Apparently, they saw what was happening on the second bridge and had already retrieved their M24's. By the time the Captain had yelled for them, they were on their way.

They took up their positions along the edge of the top of the wheelhouse so they could use the roof as a steady platform. They sighted in on the infected, and the Captain gave them the order. All four had a target ready, so the shots from the four rifles sounded almost as if they were one shot.

Four of the infected flew back from the railing and out of sight. None of the snipers waited for a second order, and a second volley of four shots split the air. They weren't as synchronized this time, but they were just as effective.

They fired repeatedly for the next few minutes, and the crowd of infected along the railing of the bridge was visibly thinner. All of the shots were to the head, and the infected were punched backward away from the side, so none were going to fall onto the deck of the Cormorant if they were lucky.

Captain Miller didn't have to say it, but he was still tempted. He saw the snipers begin searching for specific targets instead of just taking the first available shot. They were only shooting at the infected that were getting closer to the railing.

A raised concrete edge ran from one side of the bridge to the other, and it was hardly wide enough for a pedestrian to walk on, but the infected would not have been aware of the path. As they walked toward the railing, they were so focused on the ship approaching the bridge that they walked their shins straight into the concrete. The end result was that they would reach out for the living souls on the ship at the same moment that they would collide with the concrete, and since they had no concept of falling, there was no attempt to grab the top rail. Their bodies would simply fall forward and keep falling until they went over the bridge. Captain Miller's men were determined to keep any from making that fall.

As they would collide shin first into the concrete and fall forward, a bullet would hit them between the eyes with just enough force to keep them from coming over the railing. Some were punched backward, and some were pushed to the side, but none came over the edge.

Before they knew it, the Cormorant was passing under the bridge, and just as the Chief had experienced when he had gone under the Ashley River bridges, the infected up above didn't have a clue that they should cross to the other side. Instead, they started falling over the side the ship had already passed. Without the snipers pushing them back from the railing, they were free to continue their forward motion and go head first toward the water. More than a few began an end over end spin and hit the water at odd angles.

Captain Miller watched the infected fall for a few moments and then turned back to congratulate his men for doing such a good job. He was surprised to see one of the snipers holding up a score card with 7.5 written on it with a black felt pen.

The sniper said, "The Romanian judge gave the last high dive a 7.5 because the difficulty factor was low."

Captain Miller turned away toward the quarterdeck of the Cormorant and was just about to choke. He wanted to laugh so bad that it hurt, and he was pretty sure the sniper knew it, but everyone else was practically rolling on the deck of the boat.

Being clear of the first bridges meant they could pour on the speed. They had a couple of miles to go before reaching the next major bridge. The Chief had briefed him about all of the bridges, and he had explained this one would only be a problem if there happened to be a horde on the center span. The bridge was higher than the last two, and the rail was so low that any infected walking on it was likely to fall off on its own.

The Cormorant rounded the bend in front of the Citadel at full speed and straightened out for a fast run to a much bigger curve before the next bridge.

Captain Miller had known several Army officers who had graduated from the Citadel, and aside from the Academy at West Point, and Virginia Military Institute, he knew the Citadel to be a school that produced some really fine military men and women. He felt a bit sad wondering if any of them had the sort of luck that had come his way. He hoped so, because he was going to need all the help he could get fighting back at the infected dead.

When they came out of the big bend in the river they saw that the infected wouldn't be a problem, but they were surprised to see several smaller boats over at the public pier that ran along the west end of the bridge. The men in the boats all stopped what they were doing and waited, as if they were unsure about what they were seeing.

After a year of seeing people with guns and infected dead everywhere, the men couldn't decide if the military ship was a threat or not.

The spotter in the wheelhouse stuck his head out of the door and got Captain Miller's attention.

"Sir, they're crabbing. Those big wire cages are crab traps."

"Thank you, Taylor. Relay word to give them a wide berth and don't slow down."

The men in the boats kept their eyes glued to the Cormorant as she cruised under the bridge and past the pier. One of them held up his middle finger to indicate his displeasure with the wake the Cormorant was about to send their way. Captain Miller hadn't thought about private boat traffic, so he also didn't think about the wake. He didn't want to watch, but he couldn't help checking to see what damage they had done. The crab traps that had been stacked high in most of the boats had gone overboard, and more than a few of the men were indicating their displeasure.

Captain Miller thought to himself that they would slow down on the way back if they were still using the Cormorant, but if all went well, by the end of the day they would be leaving her alongside some railroad tracks upriver.

It wasn't hard to recognize their next landmark because of the fire that must have raged for days next to a marina. Bus had told him about how they had found the de Havilland Beaver and several other planes tied up at a pier, and that the place was right next to another pair of bridges. These were lower than the last one, and there was only one place to pass under them.

A map in the wheelhouse identified the bridge as the William C. Westmoreland Bridge, and there was only one narrow place where they could go through. To their advantage was the fact that after a year, there wasn't a reason for an infected to be on this pair of bridges. As a matter of fact, there wasn't much reason for a living person to be on it, either. Both spans of the bridge, one going east and the other going west, were so long and had so few on or off ramps, that there was too much risk involved with crossing it.

The Cormorant reduced speed and curved over toward the deepest channel that passed under the bridge. They kept watch upward trying to spot movement, but the two bridges were more like auto salvage yards than bridges. Wrecked and rusting cars of all types choked the lanes.

They were on their final leg of the trip that would allow them to travel on the water in relative safety, and it was only a matter of minutes before they saw the railroad tracks crossing the river ahead. The plan was to anchor the Cormorant near the train tracks and to raft ashore, but as the Chief had said many times, they needed to have a Plan B.

Captain Miller had always enjoyed discussing strategies with the Chief, especially since the Chief was so experienced, but even more so because the Chief had the confidence to tell an Army Captain what he really thought. If the Chief thought Captain Miller was wrong, he didn't hesitate to tell him. For that reason, Captain Miller and the Chief agreed that Plan A would end at the railroad tracks across the Ashley River. Plan B would be a direct result of the reconnaissance flight being done by the Chief and Kathy.

The Cormorant began reducing speed as it approached the tracks, and the details of its construction were confusing to the Captain and his men.

One of his Sergeants asked, "Sir, is that a fixed span, or does it open?"

"I think it opens, Sarge, but I can't tell if it slide, rotates, or lifts. The one thing I can tell you for sure is that it's old. It hasn't had much maintenance over the last few years."

There was one thing about the United States Army that no one could ever say, and that was something needed to be painted. As a matter of fact, the same could be said for all of the US military branches. If it had rust on it, someone needed to paint it.

The center span of the train tracks at the middle of the Ashley River was in serious need of painting. If not for the occasional patches of gray paint, it was so rusty red that it could have been the surface of Mars.

"The control house above the tracks is occupied, Captain."

When the warning was called out from a spotter in the wheelhouse, several weapons were aimed in that direction. The lethal deck guns trained toward the control house could have shredded it in seconds.

Captain Miller focused binoculars on the building and saw that there were several windows from which the bridge operator could monitor what was happening below. He could see an uncountable number of infected dead moving past those windows.

"Everyone stand down. I don't think Plan B will involve taking control of that structure."

He studied the building a bit more just to be sure. It was about the size of a cargo container commonly seen on any interstate highway or stacked on container ships. Its function appeared to be the logical location for the controls that would open the bridge for ship traffic, but the Chief had agreed with the plan not to take the Cormorant further up the river where it would become dangerously shallow.

******

The Chief brought the de Havilland Beaver down to the water directly astern of the Cormorant and began coasting. Captain Miller had already launched a raft and let it trail out behind the ship with a mooring line. As soon as they were close enough Kathy hopped out onto a float and caught the raft. They anchored the plane and then used the raft to board the Cormorant.

The videos showing the helicopters behind the hangars were good news for the entire mission, but the number of infected dead in the area was bad news. They not only needed to find the best way to get to the Air Force Base, but now they needed to find a way to clear out dozens of infected dead without attracting more into the area.

That was always the problem. Whenever you would find yourself in a situation where you had to dispose of a large number of the infected, you always had to make noise. When you made noise, more infected would be drawn to the area.

They watched the videos several times inside the wheelhouse of the Cormorant. Spread out on a table around the phone was a collection of high resolution photographs of the Air Force Base that the Chief had pulled from the seemingly endless supply left behind in the shelter by Uncle Titus.

"When you guys arrive at the part of the Air Force Base where the helicopters are parked, you'll have to get rid of the infected, but then you'll have to get the helicopters operational. You have only a fifty-fifty chance that they are fueled, and even if they are, they have to warm up."

"That's where we're in luck, Chief. The Navy VH-92A should be warmed up just like any other aircraft, but when they decided to buy those things, the short warmup period was a big selling point. System performance is better when you get the engine running a little hot, but these things will at least get us in the air faster than the old Sikorsky models."

"Okay, so how can we get you guys in, get the birds started, and get you back out fast enough?"

"I have an idea," said Kathy.

Captain Miller and the Chief were caught off guard by her interruption.

"Oh, don't tell me I'm not allowed to play with the big kids," said Kathy.

The Captain glanced at the Private who was at the helm, and saw the Chief was searching for a place to hide, too. They had both reacted like a woman couldn't have solved the problem even though they both had seen Kathy in action. Not to mention the fact that both of them had complete respect for women in charge. The Chief had made that quite clear when he gave the shelter at Lake Norman to Iris Mason.

They were both trying to hide their embarrassment as they stood back from the maps and photographs to give Kathy some room. Over the next few minutes, she showed them a plan that was so simple that they would never have thought of it. Now all they had to do was get to the Air Force Base.

Part of Kathy's plan changed everything else. They weren't going to go straight to the US Navy VH-92A helicopters. That would amount to nothing more than a full frontal assault, and they had told Captain Miller all about how badly that had worked out for a well armed group of survivors near Charlotte. That group killed a lot of the infected, but by the time it was over, so many of the survivors had died that they had replenished the ranks of the infected almost as much.

Instead, they were going to divide into two groups. One group would be designated as pilots, and the other group was designated as combat. The pilot group needed to go to the farthest opposite corner of the airfield to their original target, Charleston Helicopter Services, and retrieve the executive helicopters they had seen. The rest of the plan was all about diversions. The hardest part was going to be getting the main population of the infected dead to leave the area by the hangars where the VH-92A's were parked.

They decided they would try for all three of the Navy helicopters because they would have two pilots in each one. Each pair of pilots would need to take two soldiers with them to act as their flight crews, and the two executive helicopters were perfect for that part of the job.

Captain Miller gathered his men out on the deck of the Cormorant and explained the plan. The men were all excited about seeing a little action after being holed up inside Fort Sumter for so long.

The Chief used the mooring line to bring the de Havilland Beaver in a little closer to the Cormorant, and then the first group of passengers crossed the short distance to the cargo door of the plane. Once everyone was on board, he didn't waste any time getting the plane in the air. He turned the plane downriver for the take off and then made a sharp turn back in the direction they had come from. The rest of the soldiers cheered when he wagged his wings as he crossed over the USCG Cormorant.

It didn't take five minutes to reach their first objective. One single boat ramp with a floating dock on the end was the perfect place to land a seaplane. It stuck out into the Ashley River at the back of a neighborhood and had large mudflats on both sides. Past experience told the Chief that they would be able to back out and regroup if it turned out to be too heavily populated with the infected.

The Chief expertly turned the plane sideways to the dock, and the first of his passengers were able to jump over from the float and grab the wing to steady the plane. As soon as all six of them were unloaded and had taken up defensive positions, the Chief pulled away from the dock and went back for a second load.

They left two soldiers with the Cormorant anchored in the middle of the river. Other than the infected occupants of the bridge control house, the area was deserted.

After three more trips carrying gear and passengers, they had their flight crews totaling twelve men and their combat group of eight people, including Kathy and the Chief. Two of the soldiers designated for combat had gone up the steep ramp from the floating dock and gone ahead to scout the area.

From the ramp of the floating dock to the place where the dock met dry ground was over fifty yards. As a boat landing on the river it was much longer than what they usually found, so it was safer than most. If they discovered the neighborhood to be heavily populated by the infected, they would be able to retreat to the floating dock and scuttle the ramp. The infected would fall toward them as they mindlessly moved forward, but the ramp was long enough to create a gap too big for the infected to cross. It would be close, but the dead would fall into the river.

On a signal from the scouts, both groups moved together up the ramp and ran as quietly as they could until they reached the end of the dock and then spread out in the trees that bordered the neighborhood. They could see from their hiding place that there was a long street lined on one side by apartment buildings and on the other side by more trees.

"Chief, when you flew over this spot, did you happen to notice what was on the other side of those trees?" asked Captain Miller.

"More apartments and more trees. We have too far to go for us to do this house by house. We're going to have about a quarter of a mile to a main road. When we reach that road we have to cross four lanes and a grass median, so we're going to be visible, but there's some good news."

"Which is what?"

"If there are any infected dead walking around, they're probably all on this side of the road. The other side of that four lane highway is nothing but wide open fields at the end of the main runway used by Charleston International Airport."

"That's good news? Why is that good news?"

The Chief ran one hand across his full beard. He wasn't so sure the Captain would like his answer.

"I haven't seen one of those things that was able to run. Once we get to the end of that road in front of us and then run to the next one, they should all be behind us. All we have to do is stay faster than them."

The Captain stared at the Chief for a few moments and then studied the expression on Kathy's face for a long time. He decided on the spot that he would never play poker with either of them because they both kept their faces totally blank.

The street in front of them was a two-lane neighborhood road that went straight for a quarter of a mile to the four-lane road they needed to cross. A mailbox in front of a house said it was Great Oak Drive. It could have been any street in any other neighborhood now. Overgrown grass and shrubs made every neighborhood a little more lower class than they really were. This particular neighborhood was somewhere around middle class, but it sat only a little more than a mile from the end of the runway that served the airport and the Air Force Base. That meant property values were never really going to go up, and most of the land surrounding it had remained undeveloped for that same reason.

From a cluster of trees at the end of Great Oak Drive, the soldiers waited for their two advance scouts to return. Their position was so well concealed that they were able to catch glimpses of the two men from time to time as they left cover to move closer to the four-lane highway. They were equipped with a communications called the H-250/U Handset, so they were able to give reports back to the main group as they moved.

The H-250/U was considered to be a luxury to the squad of soldiers because they depended upon the continued operation of the military satellites circling the Earth. A couple of years after the infection spread across the country, they weren't surprised that the satellites were still doing their jobs, but they didn't take them for granted. They knew that at any time they could go silent. When they did, they would have to rely on old fashioned methods of communication, such as hand signals. Of course, they could also run and yell.

At the moment the scouts were running, and from what the Captain could tell, they were doing everything they could not to yell. They had reached the four-lane road, but after only a minute of observation they had turned and begun running straight down Great Oak Drive. Apartments and homes they had carefully and quietly passed undetected, they were now running past with total abandon.

There were no reports coming over the H-250/U, and Captain Miller suspected that the satellites had chosen this moment to fail. Suddenly, heavy winded voices broke through in his headset.

The Chief saw the Captain had the same expression he was sure he wore on his own face. Something had two of Captain Miller's best men running faster than Olympic track stars, and they weren't even bothering to give a report. Whatever it was they saw, it had to be something they could only describe face to face.

The squad still had its back to the water, so the escape route wasn't cut off. There was no need to retreat to the dock until they knew what it was that had the soldiers running like the Devil was chasing them.

The winded report in their headsets was coming through in clipped phrases. The Chief was sure he heard, "Won't believe it." There was also, "God help us."

Kathy nudged the Chief and pointed to the end of Great Oak Drive. When he shifted his eyes to where she pointed, he could just make out some motion on the other side of the trees. He focused his binoculars on the spot and could see that there was definitely something moving out on the four-lane highway, but he couldn't tell exactly what it was.

The scouts crossed his field of vision, and he also saw that they were drawing the attention of infected dead that didn't detect them as they went by the first time. They had been so careful and quiet as they moved toward their objective that they had managed to sneak by the infected without being seen. Now that they were running at full speed down the middle of the street, they were also drawing everything out into the open.

Despite the fact that they definitely had company, there still wasn't anything obvious that would make them run the way they were, and they quickly outdistanced the shambling newcomers that were walking out onto Great Oak Drive. Even when an infected stepped out from behind a car directly in their path, they didn't slow down. They didn't really even pay any attention to it as they swerved around it and kept running.

When the two scouts dove into the trees where the others were waiting, they both had so much momentum that they slid like baseball players stealing second base.

Everyone was ready for them to begin giving some kind of report, but they didn't have to. All they had to do was see what was coming down Great Oak Drive from the direction of the four-lane highway. It was a massive horde of the infected making its turn from the right onto Great Oak Drive.

"I remember when we saw the same thing on the road near Mud Island," said the Chief. "That horde stretched for miles."

"We didn't see them from the air," said Kathy. "Something caused them to come out onto the road after we flew over. If we're lucky, it's a smaller horde than it appears to be."

One of the two men got his wind back and managed to make a report between big gasps for air. He was in good physical condition just as all of Captain Miller's men and women were, but the sprint he and his partner had made was worth using a stopwatch for.

"Captain, we got a good view down that highway, and that's not something I want to see again. The pavement on both sides of the road and the median were full."

"Why didn't we see them?" asked Kathy.

The Chief was staring off into space as if he was seeing something but couldn't quite make out what it was.

"Kathy, do you remember on the day it all started that there was a reporter from a local station broadcasting from the upper decks of the Atlantic Spirit?"

"I was a bit too busy to notice, Chief. You remember where I was, right?"

"Oh, yeah. You were down on the dock doing what you could to keep the infected busy."

Kathy gave him a mock frown. There was no doubt in the Chief's mind that the Atlantic Spirt at least had a fighting chance of saving its passengers because Kathy had taken charge on the big pier that led to the passenger terminal. As a Charleston City Police Officer she had organized the helpless people trying to get into the cruise ship terminal and managed to create a blockade that stopped the horde of infected.

The Chief went on without skipping a beat.

"The reporter was receiving updates from the entire Charleston broadcast area, and I heard her say the Red Cross had opened an emergency shelter at the North Charleston Coliseum. It would hold over ten thousand people, but from what we could see downtown, no one was going to shelters. Everyone was trying to get away."

"But some people thought a shelter would be safer, especially people who were already near one," Kathy finished for him, "and the North Charleston Coliseum would have seemed like a safe shelter because of law enforcement and military support."

"How far is that from here?" asked Captain Miller.

"About two and a half miles," said Kathy, "but guess where people would have gone if not to the Coliseum. The airport is on the same road as the Coliseum. That road would have been a death trap. People unable to reach the Coliseum would have been trying to come back the other way, but they would have already been boxed in by thousands of people behind them. Some would have tried for the airport on foot while others would have come back to that four-lane highway."

Captain Miller checked with his two men and asked, "They saw you?"

Judging by the number of infected dead blocking the street a quarter of a mile away, the answer was obvious, but knowing for sure would help them to decide what to do next. They either needed to retreat or find a way around that horde. Fighting them wasn't an option. They could see hundreds of them already on the street and overflowing onto the yards and driveways of homes and apartment complexes, and they didn't have enough ammunition for that many infected.

Both of the soldiers nodded emphatically that they had been seen, and they said the wailing and groaning had started immediately.

Once they started the groaning, all of them had turned their attention in the direction of the two soldiers, and the parade began.

"Captain, we weren't even out in the open when they spotted us. There were just so many of them on the road shoulder to shoulder that they were bumping into each other. One of them fell down practically on top of us."

"That explains your sudden ability to run faster than a rabbit," said Captain Miller.

Kathy groaned.

"The Chief is rubbing off on you, Captain."

Captain Miller just grinned, but it was true. One of the qualities that he liked in Chief Barnes was his ability to take the crisis out of a problem with a little humor, and he found himself using the same practice with his own men.

The Chief reached inside a deep pocket and pulled out a map. He unfolded it quickly and found their location.

"We have two choices, folks. We can go back the way we came and try to get to the Air Force Base with a new plan, or we can all do a little running today."

He laid the map out flat where they could all see it, and he put his finger on the boat landing. Then he traced a line from the place where they had tied up the plane to where they were hiding in the bushes.

They could all see that Great Oak Drive was a long, three-sided rectangle that intersected with the four-lane highway in two places. The horde was advancing on their position down the right side of the rectangle where the soldiers were hiding.

"That horde is acting like someone put up a detour sign out there on the highway," said the Chief. "All we have to do is gather in the street in a group where they can see us and let them get a little closer. Then we're going to run like hell across the bottom of the rectangle and up the left side. When we reach the four-lane highway we're just going to keep running straight for the runway of the airport. It's only about a mile."

"What happens if some of them don't take the detour?" asked one of the soldiers.

"That's why we're going to gather out in the open," said Captain Miller. "We need to get their undivided attention so they'll start groaning louder. Those things do love a parade. I have to give them that much."

"Well, let's make sure this one gets lots of attention," said the Chief.

They all got up and walked straight at the oncoming wall of infected dead. As they stepped from the cover of the trees onto the paved surface the rest of the hidden soldiers watched them like they had lost their minds, but they hesitantly did the same. The

Captain waved them all to come in close so he could explain what they were about to do and then asked the Chief and Kathy if they had anything to add. The groaning horde was getting closer and louder.

Kathy said quickly, "The groaning should draw some of the infected into the open on the other side of Great Oak Drive. They've probably been hanging around all over the place between buildings, under cars, on porches, and anywhere else they could fit. We're also going to meet up with some that will be trying to join the parade from the other direction, and we have to run straight through them. When we start running we're going in columns of two using machetes only. Don't get bogged down. If you can't kill one, swing at the knees."

Everyone listened and nodded the affirmative. The Captain and the Chief took the lead and ran. The rest formed up on them into columns, and they settled into an easy trot before reaching the first corner.

Behind them, the groaning seemed to increase in pitch when they ran. It was almost as if the frustration of the horde became apparent when they saw their prey out distancing them. They had been closer to more living people than they had seen in a long time only to see them run away at the last moment.

In front of them it was as they had expected. It was clear at first, and when they rounded the corner on the bottom left side of the rectangle formed by Great Oak Drive, they could see a quarter of a mile straight ahead to the second intersection with the four-lane highway. There were only three infected dead walking out into the street, but any hope of it being an easy plan went out the window as they all saw another dozen emerging onto Great Oak Drive from an area of dense trees.

Everyone who didn't already have their machete in their hand pulled them from their belts. At their shelter under Fort Sumter they had converted one large storage room into a training area. They were all well trained by the Army, but the old world training was different. The new training was all about not getting bitten, speed, and numbers. They had practiced how to move when the numbers weren't good, and it was obvious they were going to be using that skill.

They were all wearing tactical combat gloves, but they had been warned not to keep an arm extended too long after a strike because a bite would hurt even if it didn't break the skin.

The columns only had to go a quarter of a mile before reaching the highway, so they ran right past the first of the infected that came out onto Great Oak Drive. Behind them the horde was making a lot of noise, but the distance was growing.

The Chief and the Captain were the first to make contact, and it only slowed their forward movement by a few steps. The infected were spaced out with no pattern, often knocking each other over as they lunged forward with outstretched hands. The first ones were down and out of the way, but eventually there were too many on one side for the squad to be methodical. They managed to stay in columns, but they got spread out, and that made them vulnerable.

"Form up," yelled Captain Miller.

The Chief was punching the infected in the face rather than just using his machete. His punches were faster, and he was knocking them over into each other. There was a pile up off to the right when he shoved one hard enough for it to leave its feet.

They kept moving forward so well that they were surprised to find themselves fighting their way into an intersection. The green and white street sign said it was the intersection of Great Oak Drive and Dorchester Road.

To their left were scattered groups of the infected, but one block to their right was a horde that had to be in the thousands. They were in one column, but that column was four lanes and a median wide. The column was forcing itself onto the other intersection of Great Oak Drive, so there was a tremendous logjam of infected, but gradually they took notice of the small group of living flesh only a block away.

"Keep moving forward," yelled the Chief.

One by one the soldiers crossed the intersection trying not to trip on the bodies of the infected that were dropped by soldiers in front of them, and one by one they disappeared into the dense growth of trees.

They burst out onto the other side of the trees onto a dirt road, but more importantly they were less than a mile from the end of the runway. Behind them they could hear the infected trying to get through the trees, but with so many of them trying at the same time, it would slow them down even more.

They broke into a run.

7 CHAIN REACTION

The underground train that carried the President and his family was much more comfortable than a typical subway car. It had been anticipated years earlier that the First Family would be safely carried out of the nation's capitol during a time of extreme crisis, and then transported to a shelter where they would live in the manner to which they were accustomed. To get there, they needed to be transported in something special, so it had all of the amenities they would have expected if they had stayed home.

Secret Service agents were assigned to various locations in the train. Some were monitoring electronic communications while others were in strategic positions to ensure there would be no last minute or unexpected problems. All of them knew that there was a shelter somewhere at the end of the railway that was impervious to attack, so they were content to believe they had done their jobs by getting the President and his family to safety, even though they would feel much better once they had them secure in the shelter.

Preliminary information received through secure channels about what they had left behind was not good. They were told the Vice President may not have made it to his shelter, but the information was not yet confirmed. Other officials in a direct line of succession to the Oval Office had not been heard from, and the only cabinet member who may have survived so far was the Secretary of Education. They didn't know where she was, but one report said she was with a military unit that had made it to sea.

A steward assigned to keep the President comfortable prepared a Bloody Mary at a small bar. One of the agents had suggested to her that the President had been a bit volatile, and it might help to settle his nerves. When she handed it to him, he flashed a smile for a split second. She recognized it as the closest thing he ever came to showing gratitude to the service personnel.

Outside the train, the tunnel walls seemed impossibly close to the windows, and he complained that they should have made the tunnel wider. Lights set back in the walls of the tunnel flashed by at intervals giving them the impression that they were traveling at a high rate of speed.

A chime sounded and a neutral but pleasant female voice announced that all passengers should be seated for a brief stop. The voice went on to explain that they were approaching a way station where they would disembark and enter a tunnel that was a ninety degree turn from their present direction.

The President asked one of the senior agents why they didn't just build a straight tunnel. The agent explained that he had been told there were two reasons. One was the logistical location of the tunnels. They were using tunnels that were under the main campus of Ohio State University, and they hadn't been able to do it any other way. They had tried to use existing tunnels in some places, but the university still needed them. They tried to go deeper, but they quickly discovered the underlying strata was dotted with an unexpected cave system and sinkholes. Their only option had been a ninety-degree turn. The second reason was strategic. If they were attacked through the tunnel, it could be defended easier with turns that would create bottlenecks for the attackers.

The train slowed until it came to a complete stop. They had boarded through doors on the left side, but this time doors on the opposite side opened to allow them to exit onto another platform similar to the one at the beginning of their trip. It was brightly lit and had several rows of comfortable seats. On the wall behind the seats there was another Presidential seal. Just the sight of it made everyone feel that much safer. They exited and saw a second train waiting with a new crew of service personnel standing expectantly at the open doors.

As soon as the passengers were transferred and comfortably strapped into their seats, both trains left the way station. One continued to carry the Presidential party to safety, while the other train was automated and programmed to return to the first station for a second load of passengers.

Secret Service agents and service personnel for the President take their oaths and positions seriously. A sense of honor and pride will make them loyal no matter how insensitive their wards may be. Staff who served under more than one President often told new staff about prior administrations and compared them to each other, and this one had not been the worst according to senior staff. Out of loyalty, any member of the Secret Service or the service personnel would have stepped forward immediately if they had been bitten by an infected dead. They would not have placed the President or his family at risk in order to protect themselves. The same couldn't be said for reporters.

In the case of Sally Parsons, White House Correspondent for a major news network, she wanted to be the first to break the news through any outlet she could find that the President and his family had been spirited away from the crisis and flown to safety in Columbus, Ohio. She wanted to be the one so she could get the exclusive for her network. While the rest of the world was wondering where the President was, she and a few other reporters crammed into an underground subway all had the same idea that they could be the first to break the story.

Getting out of the melee and into the Presidential helicopter had been difficult, but she was just cute enough and managed to catch the eye of a young man ready to be her hero. When she had extended her hand to him, he grabbed it out of reflex and pulled her into the crowded aircraft. After that, she had just stayed as inconspicuous as possible. She wasn't entirely sure when the gash had appeared on her forearm, but it was really becoming ugly, and it was also making her feel strange.

Through the night of sitting in the dark aboard Air Force One, Sally managed to borrow a light jacket from another man. When she had her chance to squeeze into one of the lavatories, she inspected the injury and saw the curved rows of puncture wounds. She couldn't remember being bitten, and she kept telling herself that it had to have happened some other way. She convinced herself that anyone would know if they were bitten, and since she didn't know for sure, it couldn't be a bite. She also decided no one else needed to know. She would find a doctor when they got wherever it was they were going, and she would tell him she caught her arm on the metal door of the helicopter.

When the President's blue and white train whisked away into the tunnel, the crowd left behind in the first station was still too big for the platform. People along the front were trying not to fall over the edge onto the tracks, and they were having to hold onto the people behind them. There was a constant pull from that direction, and all it would take was a big push from the people farthest from the tracks for the people up front to start falling. Despite the risk of falling, they didn't want to lose their place on the next train, so they struggled to stay where they were.

One heavyset man leaned a little too far from the edge, and the crowd seemed to sway in his direction whenever he lost his balance. It pulled back away from the brink for a moment, but the man grabbed a woman a little too hard, and a man who might have been her husband punched him. The surge of people in that direction caused Sally Parsons to be half pushed and half pulled toward the front just as the train arrived. She was already more dead than alive and her body was just being carried by the tidal wave of people desperate to be in a safer place.

People on the tracks were too busy trying not to get run over by the approaching train to worry about losing their place in line, and when the doors opened again the car was quickly filled to capacity. The doors closed, and the train pulled away. Even before it disappeared into the tunnel ahead, something was happening inside. There was pushing and shoving on the landing, but there was terror inside the train.

Sally Parsons was dead, but the infected dead that used to be Sally Parsons was in a crowded train car with more people than it was intended to hold, so she didn't have to chase anyone. The only man who could have ended the biting before it got started made the mistake of putting the infected dead version of Sally Parsons in a headlock. She bit deeply into the exposed area on the inside of his upper arm, and her teeth found the brachial artery. He reflexively pushed her away, and her teeth pulled out a sizable portion of it. Even if the bite had not been infectious, he was going to bleed out in about fifteen to twenty-seconds.

His quick death allowed her to attack the next person more easily, and in the confined space of a train about the same size as a subway car, the man who had tried to stop her was now trying to push himself into a standing position from the floor. Moments later they were both going from one victim to the next, and there was nowhere for any of them to go.

The train raced through the tunnel at high speed. When a soft chime sounded and a voice told all passengers to be seated and prepared to stop, the result was a chorus of groans, but there were no living passengers to heed the warning.

The train slowed, and several of the infected fell forward into a pile. When the door opened to reveal the brightly lit way station landing, the infected either fell through the open door or tripped over the bodies that were half in and half out of the door. The end result was a pile up on the landing and very quickly over the edge onto the tracks.

The train was programmed to leave for the return trip to the first station automatically when the door sensors detected no more passengers disembarking or standing in an open doorway, so the doors remained open, and the train stayed where it was as the infected tried to untangle themselves. The infected dead that had managed to climb to their feet and keep from falling onto the tracks had found their way over to the open doors of a second train that sat only a short distance away, and they promptly tripped and fell through that opening.

Six of them, including the former Sally Parsons, managed to leave the first train and board the second, and after the sensors on the doors of the train detected no more movement for several minutes, it too began following its programming. The doors slid quietly shut, and the train went forward to its next destination.

Before the train completely disappeared into the second tunnel following the path the President had used only minutes before, several more of the infected stumbled onto the landing. With the door no longer obstructed, the timer on the sensors began counting. The doors closed again, and for a second time the train began its return trip to the first station. This time it made the trip back with four passengers that did not have the chance to disembark. Infected dead that were still trying to get to their feet fell between the seats where they remained for the entire trip.

The way station landing remained brightly lit for a few minutes and then dimmed. To save energy, they were only programmed to stay on as long as there were trains at the landing. The infected dead that were left behind either on the tracks or on the landing had nothing to attract them but their own groans. When the lights went out again, they just stopped and stood still because that was what the infected dead tended to do. The distant sounds of the train moving toward the shelter began vibrating through the tracks, and one at a time the infected moved toward the tunnel following each other's groans.

Two trains were traveling away from the station. One was carrying infected dead back to the landing by the elevator. It was overcrowded with people who were still hoping for a chance to live. The second train was carrying infected dead to a shelter that was supposed to be the safest place in the world for the President of the United States.

******

Above ground Air Force One still sat partially inside and partially outside of the hangar. The Stryker that had appeared to be coming to the rescue of hundreds of passengers in the planes on the runway was nowhere to be seen. It was now obvious to the pilots of those planes that they were on their own.

One plane was already in flames at the end of the runway, having tried to take off through the throngs of infected dead. A second plane had attempted to reach the runway by cutting across the grass. Its nose landing gear had become stuck in the mud and then collapsed under the weight of the plane that was pushing too hard to get itself free.

Hundreds of passengers sat in the plane at a steep down angle, and no one had an idea of what to do next. The infected dead wandered around the plane, reaching up and touching it as if they knew what was inside. Some of the passengers were screaming that they wanted out while a few others were trying to come up with a plan of escape.

Across the devastation of John Glenn International Airport, the pilot of the plane that had formerly been Executive One was trying something different. They didn't have anywhere to go even if they could take off, so they were going to try for the terminal in the hopes that someone had found a way to take control of the crisis.

"Over there," said the copilot.

He pointed at a terminal gate that was extended but did not have a plane docked at it.

"At least we'll be able to walk out of the plane instead of jumping or sliding down a ramp. If there's a problem inside the gate we can also just get back in the plane and close the door."

The pilot applied just enough forward power to start the plane rolling toward the gate. Without an airport tow truck he would have to do it the hard way. The nose had to be turned slightly to the left, but that was no problem while the plane was rolling. The gate was extended far enough for him to coast the plane into position between two other United Airlines flights that hadn't been able to leave when the infection started to spread.

He finished the slight turn and eased back on the power to begin coasting. It was going to be an easy task on the first try if no infected got in front of his wheels.

The navigator had opened the flight deck door and left it open since there were no passengers on board. There was no sense in keeping the four members of the flight attendant staff separated from the flight crew. There was one male attendant, and the other three were women. He gratefully accepted cups of coffee from the youngest member of their crew. He saw that she was wearing a grave expression and didn't make eye contact.

Her name tag said, "Addison". She had shoulder length blonde hair that was pulled back into a ponytail and neatly tied with a bow.

"It's going to be okay, you know."

She didn't lift her head when he spoke, but she stopped for a brief moment as if the sound of his voice was unexpected. Then she started handing out the cups again.

"No, sir. I don't know that. I'm only twenty-one years old, and I had never seen even one person die before today. Now I have no idea how many I've seen, and God knows how many I can see walking around out there that are supposed to be dead."

The navigator hadn't expected the response. He had hoped that hearing someone say things would be fine would be enough for her, but he could tell she had a good grasp on exactly how bad things were. Worse, she had a good idea of how things were likely to turn out.

There was a slight jolt as the pilot applied the brakes a little harder than intended, but he had managed to get the door of the plane right up against the extended terminal gate.

"How're we doing out there?" he asked no one in particular.

"Not so good."

They wondered why the copilot had said that and saw he was watching something out his side window. The pilot and navigator moved up behind him to see what was there while Addison stepped out of the cabin to observe through a window from a starboard side passenger seat.

The copilot had been right. It wasn't so good. A quick glance out the port side window told the same story.

They were parked between two planes very similar to their own 737, but both were full of passengers. Each plane had the telltale signs of the worse case scenario. The windows from the front to the back of both planes were smeared with a brownish, rust color. Hands and faces were pressed against the dirty glass, spreading the smears even more. If they were closer, the crew of Executive One would be able to see the eyes in those faces were a smokey, milky white color with a bright red ring around the corneas.

The senior flight attendant stepped into the flight deck and said in a sober voice that the doors on the other planes must be closed, but the terminal gates were open. She had been able to get a good view through a small tube shaped window at eye level on the forward door, and there wasn't anything moving on the other side.

"Why do you think the forward doors of the other planes aren't open?" asked the pilot.

"I don't know, I guess because they aren't trying to get off the planes."

"I hate to tell you this, Anne, but I don't think those things know there's a forward door, let alone whether or not it's open."

They gathered at the door and none of them were convinced they should open it until everyone had the opportunity to study the view through the small window. In the end, they knew they either had to open the door or try to fly the plane to some other place where there were no infected dead.

The pilot unlocked the door and eased it open just a few inches. It was quiet, but the reaction was immediate. The smell that came in on the air through the small gap was enough to make all of them want to be sick.

No one had to say they wanted the door shut again, but they didn't have another choice. The pilot slid the door shut and then went to the galley. He grabbed linen towels and soaked them in water. As he passed them out, he told them to keep their mouths closed and breathe through the towels.

His next stop was to retrieve the contents of a special safe on the flight deck. He uncovered the hidden safe and pulled out a black box. Inside was an automatic pistol and two magazines of ammunition. As he shoved in one of the magazines, he thought back to the day when the airlines had decided the pilot and copilot could be armed. He had been against the decision.

The copilot remembered his own weapon and uncovered the safe by his seat. He had also been against the decision, but hind sight was always 20/20.

When they were ready to open the door again, the pilot slid it open, and they all covered their faces. They noticed that the overhead lights were flickering which gave the appearance of moving shadows up ahead. They stayed bunched together and moved slowly into the retractable passageway. Mike was the last to go through the door, and as a precaution, he slid it shut behind them.

"Why'd you close the door?" asked Addison.

Mike, the male flight attendant whispered, "If we have to come back in a hurry, I don't want to find something has wandered inside."

"Not to mention the smell," said Anne. "It would be good to keep it out of the plane."

The passenger loading gate was about thirty yards long with two turns. Airport security called the turns defendable points, but to the Captain the turns meant they could peek around the corner before giving away their position. When they got to the last corner before the main passenger concourse, he motioned for everyone to stay where they were, then he slowly leaned forward.

The concourse was surprisingly empty. He wasn't sure what he expected, but he didn't expect the place to be empty. There was no sign that there had been a panic or stampede of people trying to escape from the infected.

Once again he motioned for the others to stay where they were, and he tiptoed quietly toward the place where the passengers would have checked in. The smell was worse, but he still didn't see the source.

It wasn't until he reached the door to the passenger waiting area that he understood. From his vantage point behind the check-in counter he could see the doors to the other boarding areas were all closed. The doors all had panic bars across them, which meant they opened outward. Someone had looped chains through the door handles and effectively sealed off the passenger waiting area.

On the other side of each door, movement could be seen through the smeared glass windows. That would explain the smell.

The pilot of Executive One said a quiet prayer of thanks to the unknown person who had sealed those doors and wondered what had happened to them. When he was finished, he went back to the group waiting for him in the corridor.

He spoke in a low voice even though nothing would be able to hear him but his friends.

"It's one of those good news and bad news things. The passenger waiting area is sealed off from the other corridors, and nothing can get in with us. Of course the bad news is that we can't get out."

"Can we see it?" asked Anne.

"I don't see why not, but stay really quiet. I think the infected are behind every door."

They went single file out to the passenger waiting area, and they were ready to turn and run if there was even the slightest threat.

There was a waiting area with rows of uncomfortable chairs facing large plate glass windows on each side of the concourse. Waiting passengers could watch planes coming and going through those windows, and the crew of Executive One found themselves going in the direction of the view facing the place where they had spent the night. When they got to the windows, they could see Columbus in the distance and the smoke rising from many buildings. They could also see the plane that was still sending up plumes of smoke from its wreckage at the end of the runway, and to their horror they could see the forward door of the 737 that had gotten stuck in the mud was open.

The nose of the plane was resting on the ground where it sloped upward toward the runway, so the door was only a few feet above the heads of the infected that were crowded around it. They were reaching upward toward a man who was trying to climb the door to reach the top of the plane. Where he planned to go from there was anybody's guess.

Anne screamed and Addison almost passed out when they saw the man slide from the curved side of the plane and fall into the outstretched arms of the infected. Someone reached out and grabbed the door to pull it shut again. It stopped almost completely shut, but there were fingers in the way. They saw the door open and slam shut a few more times until it was flush to the fuselage.

Until the door was shut, they had been too distracted to notice that another 737 had moved into take off position at the end of the same runway where the other plane had crashed. The only thing anyone could try to do was stay at the airport or leave. Both were bad choices, but someone else had decided it was time to go.

They watched the plane roll forward and build up speed. The runway was dotted with infected that were wandering from one place to the next, and the big plane was cutting a path through them. The tail shimmied to the left and right as the plane bounced over a group of infected that had grown too large.

From the place where the seven survivors from Executive One were watching, everything was moving in slow motion. The 737 was almost as far as it could go before it would run into the wreckage of the last plane that tried to leave. The right wheel lifted into the air first because the tail shimmied to the left, and the right side bounced a few feet higher into the air. Then the left wheel came up along with the nose landing gear, and for a moment the plane was level and climbing.

It was like any other take off once the plane was level, but the pilot and copilot of Executive One saw the problem first. The vertical stabilizer and rudder on the tail were out of position to the right, and they were not moving back to the center. To their trained eyes, they knew that the pilot of the plane was fighting to keep the plane pointed straight ahead. It was trying to yaw to the right, and the pilot was fighting to make it yaw to the left.

In the end, the pilot won the battle and made the plane come back to the left, but as the nose climbed higher, the plane leaned over and pointed the right wing toward the ground.

The crew of Executive One watched as the plane made a giant, sweeping turn to the right over the airport and was almost upside down as it disappeared into downtown Columbus. The fireball that erupted was somehow larger than it should have been.

******

When the Presidential train reached the platform at the end of the line, it came to a stop in front of a tremendous door that resembled the door of a bank vault, except larger. The President had never been to Cheyenne Mountain, but he had seen enough pictures to know he would be safe inside this place. He expected more of a military presence, but he was safe, and that was what mattered the most to him.

The platform outside the door was decorated with brightly colored tiles and murals depicting historic locations in Washington DC. Considering where they had come from only an hour earlier, this was an incredible sight, and for the first time since leaving the White House, the President wore a genuine smile on his face.

Secret Service agents escorted the President and his family into the shelter, followed by the lucky few service staff members and flight crew of Air Force One who had ridden with him in the first train. Everything was spotless and smelled clean, and they were all impressed. Not one of them would have guessed they were going to be inside a shelter on this scale, and the mood had changed from one of hopeful desperation to one of total relief.

The automated train closed its doors and pulled away from the passenger platform almost unnoticed. It disappeared down the dark tunnel on its way back for a second load of passengers.

"How long are we supposed to stay on watch out here?" asked one of the Secret Service agents. He had waited until he was sure the Presidential party was out of earshot.

"You know the drill, Jack. We have to make sure some of the reporters get inside so they can document all of this for the history books."

"Can't we just wait inside until the train gets back? You have to admit, not much gets under my skin, but that dark tunnel gives me the creeps."

"I agree, but the boss said to wait out here. If the reporters don't get any pictures of him, it's going to be our fault. Besides, someone will want a picture of this big door and your pretty face standing guard next to it."

It seemed like it took forever, but eventually the headlights of the next train filled the darkness. The agents who had remained outside exchanged worried glances with each other. They should have been relieved to see it returning, but every instinct told them not to let down their guard.

When the train came to a smooth stop in front of the passenger platform, they could see their instincts had been correct. There were streaks and smears of something on the glass and the colorful sides near the doors. The train also wasn't as packed with reporters as they had expected.

The doors slid open, and the first passenger to step out didn't exactly step out gracefully. As a matter of fact, she fell flat on her face as one foot went through the narrow gap between the train and the platform. The unnatural angle of the leg and the sound of bones breaking was sickening. If not for the stained appearance of the train, every agent watching the spectacle would have rushed forward to help the woman, but they held their positions and took aim on the infected that were trying to climb over the fallen woman.

There was a whining sound that seemed to be rising in pitch and growing louder by the second, but the noise was almost completely muted by the steel and stones surrounding the vault door. Only a few feet into the shelter it sounded more like a loud hum.

Outside the shelter it was like a scream that didn't stop. If the agents inside had been able to hear the intensity of the sound, they would have ordered everyone to retreat to safety, and they would have closed the tremendous, impenetrable door.

Several agents of the Secret Service detail moved into a defensive position between the train and the open vault door, keeping their sidearms aimed at the infected as they backed toward the safety of the shelter.

As the volume of the scream rose to a deafening level, it drowned out everything so completely that when the order finally came to close the door, no one could hear it. The sound seemed to be coming from everywhere at the same time, and it was like nothing they had ever heard.

The floor seemed to be moving, and the agents were having a hard time keeping their feet under them, but they also couldn't believe their eyes. The walls of the tunnel were swaying, and the train was rocking from side to side. The lights on the passenger platform went out, and for a few moments the only light was the light escaping from the inside of the shelter.

Then the entire world became light and sound for seconds that stretched into minutes. There was also searing heat that followed the bright flash of light and the ear splitting explosion. Everything in the area outside the shelter door was incinerated, and a wave of fire and superheated air shot through the open door of the shelter and raced down the main corridor in search of more oxygen to burn.

******

In the quiet moments before the 737 slammed into the street above the shelter, the only witnesses to the crash were the infected dead. Like every other city in the country, the number of people downtown had an effect upon how rapidly the infection had spread, and traffic had brought the city to a standstill. Where cars were abandoned there were also trucks and trains unable to move, and the dead wandered among them.

The propane tanks lined up on the freight train sitting on the railroad tracks near the old High Street Station were a common sight to the citizens of Columbus, and safety studies had shown there was a low risk of rupture or fire when propane was transported by rail. There were, however, no studies that considered the effect of a propane car being hit by a 737.

The studies talked about fire, and anyone hit by the fireball caused by a propane explosion would not survive. The studies also talked about fragmentation. Anything thrown through the air by the explosion would become killing missiles.

The worst part of the explosion, according to the studies, is the overpressure shock wave that travels ahead of the flame front at supersonic speeds. If a study had been done to measure the shock wave caused by a 737 hitting a propane train, it would have concluded that the force would travel downward into the ground with a spectacular result. It would create an ear splitting sound followed by a concussive wave that would collapse the surrounding area for blocks around the center of impact.

8 SIKORSKY

The experience Kathy and the Chief brought to the group was
not so much a greater skill as it was their acceptance of what had
to be done. If that meant outrunning a horde of the infected, then
that's what they would do. They had about two or maybe three
miles of open ground in front of them, and that would be a piece
of cake to the soldiers assigned to Captain Miller's squad. The last
thing Kathy and the Chief wanted to do was slow them down, so
they set the pace.

When they started running, the sound of the horde was similar
to a train rolling slowly on a set of rusty railroad tracks. The
groaning, the dragging of legs, the trampling feet of the infected
that were still capable of walking faster than the others all
combined into one continuous noise that scraped at the nerves. By
the time they had covered a half mile, the sound of the horde was
fading, and they could see that the infected had slowed their pace a
bit. It wasn't that they had lost interest. It was more that they were
no longer worked into a frenzy.

About a mile into their run they reached the end of the paved
runway, and the Captain called for a brief stop for everyone to

catch their breath. The horde had tried to funnel itself down a narrow dirt road, so it hadn't even gone a quarter of a mile yet. Those infected that had chosen to follow by walking into the trees along Dorchester Road had gotten so spread out and tangled up in the uneven brush that they would take a full day just to reach the runway.

"Captain, you still have all of your pilots, right?" asked the Chief.

"That's affirmative. You have something in mind, Chief?"

"He always has a plan B, remember?" said Kathy.

Kathy was also curious about alternative plans from the start because the Chief hadn't voiced his thoughts about them.

"I know we talked about trying for one or two of the helicopters, but there's no reason we can't try for all three. I've been thinking that we might want to take a larger group to Columbus."

"How large?" asked Kathy.

"Everyone except Molly," he answered, "and we can drop her off at Fort Sumter. I'm sure she won't mind spending some time with Whitney."

"You mean Sam, don't you?"

They both knew Molly would jump at the opportunity to spend some time around the only eligible boy she knew. They just had to sell Tom on the idea. As for Whitney, she was a typical teenage girl, so she already had a crush on a dozen or more of the young men in Captain Miller's squad.

"Your plane's big enough for your crew, isn't it?" asked Captain Miller.

"It is, but if we take along that many soldiers and the Mud Island gang, we could use the third helicopter for supplies. We may also be coming back with more gear or more people."

"I get your point," he said. "Well, first things first. Getting flight crews to the helicopters isn't going to be much of a problem. It's getting the helicopters prepped and into the air that should be fun."

The Chief wasn't concerned, and Captain Miller had seen that relaxed expression before. It was the one that said he had an ace up his sleeve, he knew something no one else did, or he was going to do something crazy.

Kathy saw it too, and she poked him in the ribs.

"We have to start running again in just a minute. Would you care to show us your hold cards now, or are we going to have to beg you?"

The Chief was the only person Kathy had ever known who could be so cool and calm while a horde of the infected was falling all over itself to gain ground on them.

"I was studying the high resolution pictures back at the shelter, and I think those helicopters have been here long enough to have been prepped already. The rotors need to be extended after they're rolled out into the open, but face it, that's a job that can be done with the infected walking around because the work is done high enough above them. You just need to be careful and not drop any tools."

"Go on," said Kathy. "I think both of us want to know what you have in mind."

"It's simple. I'll use one of those executive choppers to drop all of the pilots and maintenance people onto the roofs around the three VH-92A helicopters. I'll get someone on the outside of that fenced area who can open the gates. Then I'll fly over to the flight line and set down. They will definitely follow me. As I draw them out I'll keep backing away. There's plenty of room out on the flight line. I can draw out the ones that want to follow. Your guys can get on top of the Sikorsky birds and start working, and a couple of people can secure the doors on the buildings inside the fence."

"You always make it sound easy," said Captain Miller.

"This one is easy when you compare it to some of the other dumb things we've done," said Kathy, "or are you forgetting how we met?"

Captain Miller had to admit. When he saw a seaplane circling Fort Jackson and dumping fuel on the heads of thousands of infected dead, he didn't think he would ever see anything crazier in his lifetime. Compared to that little trick, this plan was like earning a Boy Scout merit badge.

"No, I remember that night quite clearly. If not for you guys, we wouldn't be out here running from a couple thousand infected dead with one thing on their tiny little minds. As a matter of fact, we could even be back there in that nasty crowd ourselves."

"Speaking of which," said Kathy, "when you can smell them, they're getting too close. We might want to get the rest of this show on the road before they grow new brains and figure out what we're doing."

The Captain signaled to his men, and everyone got up for the next leg of the short marathon run. This time they had to run along the stretch of runway that passed within one hundred yards of the main concourse of the Charleston International Airport, and so far they didn't have a clue if they were going to run into any resistance.

Kathy nudged the Chief and said in a low voice, "You're up to something. I can tell."

He tried to act innocent at first, but she was staring him down.

"Okay, I'm up to something, but I'm not ready to tell you what."

"I don't care if you're ready or not. You're going to do something crazy, and I want to know what it is."

"It's not too crazy," he said.

He tried to come across as reassuring, but it wasn't working any better than acting innocent.

The Chief sighed.

"How about letting me tell you about it right before I do it? I want to test a theory."

"You mean you'll tell me what it is when it's too late to stop you."

"Something like that, but I'll promise you this much. If you really don't think my theory will work when I test it, I'll stop."

"Why doesn't that make me feel any better?"

The soldiers had all passed them, and they found themselves alone for a minute. Face to face at the end of the runway, in a wide open field, about to do something crazy again, Kathy had that feeling she sometimes got when she was with the Chief. The Chief was like her father, and she had some strong feelings for Tom, but she couldn't help wondering what would have happened if the Chief was a few years younger. Of course it was just possible that she wished he had someone significant in his life, too.

The Chief would never hear it from her, but she had often wished she could risk the radiation around Lake Norman just to bring Iris Mason back to Mud Island. She could really see Iris and the Chief as a couple.

Of the four shelters they had been to so far, the one at Lake Norman was the one they wouldn't be able to go back to until the radiation covering it had a chance to dissipate. Of course that would all depend upon whether or not the Oconee Nuclear Plant was still leaking radiation, and how much of it had been deposited over Lake Norman.

Kathy doubted they would be going to the shelter in the Gulf of Mexico anytime soon, but she also doubted there was a woman in that shelter who was right for the Chief, either.

"What?" asked the Chief. "Why're you looking at me like that?"

Kathy opened her mouth to say one thing, but something entirely different came out.

"Ever think about settling down, Chief?"

He gave her a little bit of a chuckle, but he knew her well enough to know there was something else being left unsaid.

"You might want to save that topic for a better time, like when we aren't on the menu."

He hooked a thumb back toward Dorchester Road for emphasis. Kathy glanced back that way out of reflex, and it might as well have been every infected dead in South Carolina coming after them.

"Point taken," she said.

They both started trotting to catch up with Captain Miller's men, and it didn't take them long to see why the soldiers were running faster than they had been before. The airport was far from deserted.

It hadn't surprised them at all to see the wreckage of planes at the airport. As a matter of fact they had ignored the debris for the most part because they knew what the first days had been like. It only took a moment for them to admit it was bad enough to be on a cruise ship, but being at an airport was no better than being at a hospital on the first day. As much control as they thought they had at airports, they had no control over people trying to escape who had already been bitten.

Airports were where people expected protection, but even more importantly they expected to escape. People who got onto airplanes to get away from the spread of the infection didn't understand there was nowhere to go even if their plane did take off. Ironically, some of the wreckage was from planes that had landed at the airport. They had arrived despite the warnings from the control tower that the place they were trying to land was no better than the place they had come from.

There was also no way to leave the infection behind when you were traveling with hundreds of strangers. Even if a pilot listened to all of the airport control towers that were shouting their warnings and landed in a remote, isolated place, the odds were good that they had already brought the infection with them.

The infected that had managed to pick their damaged bodies up from the rubble along the runway had long since wandered away in search of the living. Where they had gone was anybody's guess, but there were more living people inside the airport than anywhere else nearby, so that was where most of the infected dead had gone.

People inside the airport felt like there had to be a way to keep the infected from getting inside, and wherever they could they had blocked doors and stairwells. For a while at least, they survived, but it was only a matter of time. In the end, the places they barricaded the most were the places where they died because they had barricaded bite victims inside with them, and the places where they died became the places they would remain forever.

The airport terminal was filled with the infected. Every square inch of glass shorter than six feet high had a body pressed against it. Whether it was a hand or a face, there was an infected pushing at it with one goal in mind, and the urge to reach a living person was the strongest incentive to break out that they had experienced since that first day.

The Chief and Kathy had experienced something similar when they had flown to Guntersville, Alabama. They had discovered a country club full of the infected, but the infected had been unable to escape because they didn't have the incentive to break the big glass windows.

Spider webs of cracks were climbing up the glass where the weight of bodies was the greatest. Fortunately, the waiting areas and concourses in airports are seldom at ground level, and it was obvious that there was going to be a little extra time to get by the airport if the glass broke too soon.

As expected, the first window shattered quickly, and the horde of infected pushing on the glass fell in great heaps of bodies at the base of the building. Those on the bottom were crushed and would never be a danger again. Those on the top of the pile were so tangled with the rest of the infected that fell with them, that it would be a long time before they began pursuing the living who were now sprinting past them.

The few that were immediately dangerous were the ones that fell on top then rolled down the sloping piles of bodies. Some even rolled until their momentum practically stood them up on the concrete loading zones.

"Keep going," yelled Captain Miller. "They won't be able to catch up with us."

A second window shattered with a high pitched wail as stress caused the glass to explode outward. It was almost worth stopping to watch because it was directly above a small horde of infected that had broken away from the pile under the first window. The infected that were already eagerly groaning and walking toward the soldiers just disappeared under the new avalanche of bodies.

The smell was awful. The airport must have been filled to capacity when everyone inside died. Without air circulating through the building and decay happening twenty-four hours a day, the gases had built up to a staggering level. It was probably close to blowing out the windows without any help from the infected. When the windows finally shattered, the invisible burst of wind from the building felt almost like being punched with a solid wall of air.

No one laughed at the soldiers who gagged. To do so meant opening your mouth, and no one wanted to get a taste of what the wind carried. A glance toward the building was enough for everyone to know they needed to run faster.

One plane was still attached to a retractable loading platform, and a baggage cart was underneath the plane. Even as the population of the world was dying, people were still trying to check baggage through security.

A second plane had backed a few feet away after loading, but someone had driven a baggage cart straight into the path of the starboard side landing gear. The plane had continued to back away from the terminal, and the tires had blown.

The people on that plane must have thought they weren't going to survive because of the careless baggage cart driver, but judging from the devastated faces pressed against the windows, they were already going to die. Someone on the plane had been bitten.

The third plane at the terminal had given its occupants a more certain death. Professionalism had unraveled due to the panic of the airport maintenance crews, and fuel had ignited everything around the plane. It had burned furiously until everyone inside had died, and then it had burned a while longer.

"We need to move," yelled the Captain, and everyone picked up speed.

The helicopter landing area was about two hundred yards past the terminal, and everyone knew it would take time for the infected to cross that distance, but they didn't know how much time they would need to get one of the executive helicopters into the air. There was always the possibility that the reason they hadn't been used to escape was because they needed lengthy maintenance.

If that turned out to be the case, they had two choices. They could abort the mission and begin trying to circle back to the railroad tracks where they had left the Cormorant, or they could continue on foot across the Air Force Base and try to liberate the Navy helicopters by force.

The Chief and Kathy pulled up even with Captain Miller.

"We thought we would have more time to get a bird in the air," said the Chief. "Those infected are going to be on us before we can even warm one up. Any ideas?"

"That's been on my mind the whole time. If we don't need to get inside the building, what are the chances we can get on it?" asked Captain Miller.

The building they were heading for had a flat roof and was only one floor.

"I agree with what you're thinking, Captain. Get everyone on the roof and have them start eliminating the infected that are the closest. Leave four on the ground with me, and they can join you guys if it gets too busy on the ground."

"I'll go to the roof," said Kathy. "I don't know anything about helicopters, but I can shoot."

They crossed a short stretch of overgrown grass and ran up onto a concrete landing area. Two small taxiways for private planes led to the landing area, and both had the evidence of failed escape attempts parked half on and half off of the concrete.

Most of the planes were intact, but aside from the fact that the Chief didn't have any stick time in a jet plane, there weren't many places to land them. He had no doubt that every airport in the country was like this one, and he didn't want to get one of the planes into the air if he didn't have a place to set it back down.

The squad split into two groups as they approached the building. The Chief ran straight for the nearer helicopter of the two and quickly inspected the inside. There were no signs that there had been an infected trapped inside. He pulled the pilot's door open and climbed into the seat. As he expected, the helicopter must have been in the process of getting ready to escape when something had happened to the owners. The bird was ready, but the people who planned to use it didn't make it.

One of the soldiers wheeled a cart up to the side of the helicopter while a second opened the battery well. The Chief eyed the electronics and let out a low whistle. The only thing he had ever flown was a really basic two seat bird that was nothing special. This thing was as foreign as the space shuttle to him.

He turned in the seat and surveyed the passenger area. Wide brown leather seats, deep carpeting, rich wood trim on everything, a TV, and what had to be a bar stocked with a variety of liquors.

"Probably got delayed because there wasn't any ice," he said out loud.

Outside the popping of M4's had started. It was a bit sporadic, which meant they were only shooting at the infected that had crossed an invisible line. The Chief started locating the buttons and switches for everything he recognized and would worry about the rest later.

He found what he figured was the power switch and was rewarded by more indicator lights than he could believe. One of them was the ignition, and when he started the engine he also felt more at home behind the controls. He had something on his mind that he had read about a year or so before the infection, and he didn't know if it would work, but he had to try.

There was a rap on the window of his door, and he jumped, but it was only the soldier who had wheeled the battery cart up to the helicopter.

"Sir, this craft is a Sikorsky S-76D, and she's a real sweetheart," yelled the soldier. "She had lots of juice in the battery, and the warm up time is minimal. You can go ahead and start the rotors spinning."

The Chief gave him a thumbs-up and hit the switch. He saw the soldier back away from the front of the craft in the direction of the rear and then head for the building. A moment later he saw eight of the soldiers crossing the landing circle toward him. Seven piled into the leather seats in the passenger area while one joined him up front.

When he lifted the helicopter from the landing pad, everyone felt like they were inside a big ride at the fair. Even the rest of the soldiers on the roof of the building got a little sick as the body of the craft swung from left to right. It did a half circle to the right as it rocked and then began a slow turn back to the left.

"Sir, are you sure you can fly this thing?" said the soldier in the co-pilot's seat.

"Piece of cake. It's just a fancy Black Hawk, right?"

The soldier didn't bother to answer. The Black Hawk was a great aircraft, but not just anybody could fly it.

The Chief got the Sikorsky pointed in the right direction and gave it just a slight amount of forward tilt to gain momentum. He didn't need to waste time with altitude because they weren't going far, and the sleek executive helicopter crossed the runways, taxiways, aircraft parking areas, and grass dividers in seconds. Before they knew it they were hovering above the building next to the narrow street where the Navy choppers had been stashed.

The Chief felt a rush of air, and the noise level went much higher at the same time. For the first time he realized just how good the noise dampening material on the helicopter had to be.

One of the soldiers had dropped a line out the door and disappeared out of sight in one smooth move. A second had positioned himself to move and drop over the side without hesitation.

The co-pilot climbed into the back, gave the Chief a quick wave, and followed the last man out. As soon as he was gone the Chief rotated in place and headed back the way he had come.

He hoped he could land on the roof to pick up the second load because the ground landing pad was no longer an option. It had become occupied by a few dozen of the infected. Not every roof was able to support an extra seven thousand pounds, and he didn't want to wind up in the lobby of the helicopter service.

Given that the weight of the soldiers was already a strain on the building, the Chief carefully hovered and then lowered the craft toward the roof. He held it one to two feet above the surface of the building as the next group loaded themselves and their weapons into the helicopter. He rotated again and turned toward the other side of the base.

On the way across he took a moment to check on the status of the horde of infected and the large contingent of former occupants of the airport passenger terminals. He saw that the Army and Kathy had been fairly effective at reducing the numbers, but the tremendous horde from Dorchester Road was almost to the airport terminal. They had made much faster progress than he had expected so he added some speed to the second trip.

The first group of soldiers had the top of the building secure and had watches set at all sides. The second group joined them quickly, and the Chief went back for the final trip.

One end of the airport was a mass of infected walking steadily in the direction of the terminal, but the Chief knew their goal was the one story building where Kathy and the remaining soldiers were carefully taking aim at the leading edge of the horde. From his view, even he was amazed by the sheer number of the infected.

The wind from his rotors buffeted the last of the soldiers as they sent Kathy through the door ahead of them. Even as they were getting off a few more shots, they had insisted on being gentlemen when the helicopter approached. She argued with them, but it didn't do any good.

As soon as the last boot came through the door, the Chief angled the helicopter in the direction of the Air Force Base and began the last trip across. It was only a matter of seconds before they were once again in position and dropping the soldiers down the rope.

"You are landing," yelled Kathy. "Is this where you do something crazy? If you are, I'm going with you."

The Chief grinned as he answered.

"I wasn't going to waste time trying to talk you out of going with me. As a matter of fact, I would have been surprised if you had gotten out."

With the door closed and the passenger section empty, Kathy had a chance to fully appreciate the helicopter they had acquired. She had climbed into the copilot seat, but she was turned around as far as she could to take in all of the luxury.

"Did we really live like this before it all ended?"

"Some people did, but I doubt many of them fully appreciated what they had. They didn't know that real life is like living from paycheck to paycheck. You can lose it all overnight."

"When are you going to tell me the plan?"

"There isn't really time to explain it, so let me just tell you what I'm doing as I do it."

Kathy watched the top of the building fade away as the Chief lifted the executive Sikorsky into the air and immediately took a hard turn to the right. The Chief had gotten used to the controls and how well the aircraft handled, so he was in his element. She could see that he was enjoying himself, and that he couldn't wait to do whatever it was he planned to do.

Behind them the Army pilots had lowered a rope from the building onto the side facing the flight line. A large chainlink gate had been erected between two buildings creating an alley, and the three Navy helicopters had been towed into that alley. Kathy saw two of the pilots going down the rope together.

She was just about to ask the Chief what they were doing when the Chief swung the Sikorsky around to face the gate from about fifty yards away. He hovered for a moment and then carefully lowered the helicopter toward the asphalt surface of the flight line.

The Chief started to say something, but Kathy beat him to it.

"You aren't doing what I think you're doing, are you?"

"I wouldn't doubt it," laughed the Chief.

From their point of view in the helicopter, they could see the broad chainlink gate straight in front of them, and two of the pilots were almost to where a lock secured the gate against the weight of the infected dead.

Ever since the arrival of the helicopter on the first trip to the top of the building, the infected had begun moving from the buildings and alleys that surrounded the Navy helicopters that were covered with tarps inside the fenced area. They had eventually come to the heavy duty fence and had begun piling up against it. The weight of the horde pushing from behind was crushing the infected in front. The fence bulged in several places, but it was holding.

The pilots had to avoid being grabbed by the hands that were reaching through the fence, but they were much quicker than the emaciated infected. One slipped a long metal bar through the lock and then drove the lower end of the bar into the ground where it met the post where the gate was latched. Both pilots put all of their weight onto the other end of the bar while one of them swung something that could have been the biggest wrench Kathy had ever seen. It hit the lock, and it snapped apart.

Both pilots hit the ground but were up and running as fast as they could toward the rope as the gate swung outward. Just like the windows bursting at the airport terminal, the force of the horde pushing from behind caused the infected in front to be trampled to the ground.

The Chief was only about two feet from the ground when he started easing forward. The gate was completely open, and the infected that didn't fall to the ground had begun staggering toward the noisy helicopter.

The Army pilots were already safe on the roof and had pulled the rope up with them. They wanted to stay and watch, but the Chief had simply told them no matter what happened, be ready to get down into the alley and shut the gate from the inside.

"Do you still need for me to explain the plan?" asked the Chief.

"No, I think I figured it out," she yelled back. "What makes you think it will work? You know damned well that all you're going to do is blow them over and keep them busy."

That was when the Chief got that trademark smirk on his face that he always got when he knew something that no one else did.

He eased forward until he had the undivided attention of every infected dead within the enclosed area, and then he began backing away very slowly. More and more of the infected stumbled through the gate as most of the infected that had been pushed to the ground managed to get to their feet. He didn't know how many there were, but he knew it was hundreds.

On top of the building where he had dropped Captain Miller and his soldiers, they watched in amazement as the alleys between the buildings emptied. They saw the opportunity the Chief had told them to watch for, and one by one they dropped over the sides of the building and closed the big doors on the buildings. If there were more infected dead lingering inside, they wouldn't be able to come out while they prepped the helicopters.

The Chief backed the executive Sikorsky away only when the downdraft of the rotors blew over the weak bodies of the infected. He didn't want to knock them down. He wanted to draw them away far enough for the gate to be closed again. Then, he had something else in mind.

Kathy saw out her window that they had backed all the way out onto the asphalt flight line where the Air Force had previously parked the big Globemasters, and the horde of infected had followed.

"Here we go," said the Chief.

Kathy wished she was watching from somewhere else. Not because she was afraid, and not because it was the biggest mess she had ever seen, but because she would have liked to have witnessed it from a distance. It must have been spectacular from above.

Still only two feet from the ground, the Chief made the nose of the Sikorsky dip slightly forward. The helicopter rushed at the wall of approaching infected dead, and the tips of the rotors brushed the crowd of infected the way a string trimmer brushes at a crop of tall grass along a driveway. Dozens of the infected went down onto the asphalt minus their heads, and some lost more than that.

The Chief felt the front wheel roll on the pavement and immediately rocked the helicopter backward and upward so the rotors were away from the ground that had only been a few feet away from them for a few seconds. He backed the helicopter away from the horde and got it into a controlled hover a few feet above the ground. Once he was stable, he rotated to the left and got ready for a second pass.

"Wait a minute," yelled Kathy at the top of her lungs.

The Chief backed the helicopter away from the advancing horde by a few more feet. From above where he brought them into a hover again, it resembled an alien crop circle in the horde. The advancing infected dead had already started closing the circle around the bodies of those that had fallen under the spinning blades.

The Chief was grinning at Kathy like a kid who had found out he had a really cool toy, but Kathy had her mouth hanging open. She didn't know what she wanted to say, but what came out was a simple question.

"How the hell did you know that would work? I've seen lots of movies, and no one ever gets their head chopped off by getting too close to a helicopter."

"I guess I should have explained first, but I had to see if it was possible myself."

"You mean you didn't know if it would work?"

"I've never tried it before, if that's what you mean. When would I have ever tried it?"

In the distance ahead of them Kathy saw the big chainlink fence swinging into the closed position again. She knew they had secured the area for the Army to begin prepping the three Navy helicopters.

"Hang on just a second," said the Chief. "Let me do that again, and then I'll explain."

He would never have admitted it to Kathy, but when he approached the first time, he was a little afraid. If it didn't work and they didn't crash, they would be lucky. What he hoped for was what they got, but a small part of him thought they would wind up doing a hard landing that probably wouldn't kill them but would certainly strand them in a bad place.

The Chief dipped the nose for a second time, and this time it was a little smoother. He felt like he was more in control as he actually let the front wheel touch the ground before he rolled forward, using it as a guide as the rotors began cutting another swath through the horde. When the front wheel bumped into a body, he pulled up and backward for a second time.

"Those things are unbelievable," he said. "This thing shreds them, and they keep coming. Okay, let me tell you why I thought it would work."

The Chief backed them a little further away this time, realizing he had to give Kathy a moment. She was tough, but he had to admit, it wasn't every day you got to use a helicopter like that.

"When they trained us to do night drops from Blackhawks, one of the first things they drilled into us was never to approach a Blackhawk from the front. They made us watch a training video of a pilot who landed facing the base of a hill. He got out of the chopper, and then he went up the hill. His own rotors picked him off as he walked up the hill."

"That's awful," said Kathy.

"Yeah, I know, but I'll bet a lot of people don't walk into the spinning blades of helicopters because of that video. If he had seen a video like that, he'd still be alive."

Kathy was still trying to digest what she had seen and heard. She had seen it work, but she knew it was precision flying. It could be done as long as he didn't try to go too deep into the horde at one time. If he went in too far, the rotors would wobble. It was anybody's guess what would happen after that.

The Chief went on explaining, "It's simple math. From the pavement to the tip of the rotor it's just over eight feet. The manual says ninety-seven and a half inches. That means I only need to tilt the front of the helicopter three feet to take down everything but a short zombie."

"A what?" Kathy's head whipped to the left hard enough to crack.

The Chief feigned a confused expression.

"You said zombie," said Kathy.

"No, I didn't."

"Yes, you did. You said you could take down everything except a short zombie."

"No, I did not call them zombies. They aren't zombies. I already explained that to you."

It was obvious to Kathy that the Chief was going to keep denying what he said.

"You haven't heard the last of this," said Kathy. "Finish your explanation."

"That's all there was to it. All I had to do was roll forward with the front gear on the ground and the rear wheels no more than a couple of feet in the air, and anything over five feet tall is mincemeat."

Kathy gave him a grin that was a lot like the one he liked to give her, but she also figured something out. He had deliberately called them zombies to get her to lighten up a little, and it had worked. He had distracted her just enough to keep her from thinking about what they had just done and what they still had left to do.

"I don't know how your mind works sometimes, Chief. You're a psychologist and a warrior wrapped up in one body."

She saw that he had the same half smile as he began methodically easing into the dwindling horde and then backing away. Each time he left behind more devastation, and each time the horde was smaller. Finally, he put all of the wheels on the ground. They both climbed out and used rifles to drop the few stragglers that were still trying to reach them.

When they were done, they flew the short distance to the chainlink gate where they were greeted by Captain Miller and his Army pilots. All they could do was laugh, but they heard more than once that none of them had ever seen anything quite like that.

9 PATROL

While the Chief and Kathy were away on their mission to liberate a helicopter from the Air Force Base, we didn't have the luxury of just sitting around and waiting for their return. We had learned that Uncle Titus had been correct about keeping our heads down and staying inside the shelter in order to guarantee survival, but there was something he didn't consider. Survival wasn't enough.

If all I wanted to do was survive, I would have just shut my door and never opened it for anyone. I had everything I needed in the way of supplies, but people aren't meant to be alone. Some individuals could live their entire lives without ever being around another living soul, but you had to be tired of people to get to that point, and I wasn't tired of people.

Cassandra was the member of our group who came up with the idea about the Mercy Ship being a hazard to other survivors, and that we should put some kind of marker above it that would warn off other ships. We were getting ready to do a routine patrol when she brought it up, and Doc Bus was quick to recognize the symptoms he had seen in Jean, Kathy, and the Chief in the past.

As a group they shared the guilt of surviving when over five thousand others had died on the Atlantic Spirit. At least they had each other to lean on, and when they expressed their feelings to each other about escaping from the ship, they were able to reassure each other that they didn't have any other choice. Dying just because that was what everyone else was doing wasn't an option.

The Chief and Jean had left behind friends when they abandoned ship, but that didn't mean they had abandoned their friends any more than Kathy had when she chose to stay on board the Atlantic Spirit when it sailed away from the cruise ship terminal in Charleston.

Kathy had told us once that she had some bad nights thinking about her fellow officers who had stayed behind in Charleston and died. She said there were over four hundred police officers in the Charleston Police Department and that in the entire history of the Charleston PD dating back to 1878, there had been less than two dozen officers who had died in the line of duty. The Chief had made her feel better when he pointed out that the people who had sought shelter on the Atlantic Spirit were just as much her responsibility as the people in the city. He told her she just played the hand she was dealt.

Jean was the same way. She had worked with some of the nurses on the Atlantic Spirit for a long time. The doctor they worked for wasn't the kind of person who inspired her enough to feel guilt, but she was close with the rest of the staff. She handled her guilt better than Kathy, though. There was no explaining why, but maybe it was because she knew she couldn't do anything for the others. She knew that there came a time when you had to take care of yourself, and on that given day, she had done what she could to keep herself alive.

Cassandra didn't know she was experiencing survivor's guilt, but Bus pulled me and Jean aside and pointed out that Cassandra had to live with knowing the Mercy Ship was right out there in the water, but she couldn't tell exactly where. A marker might warn other ships, but it would also give Cassandra a visual place to direct her feelings. It was much the same as paying one's respects in front of a grave stone.

Doc Bus suggested that it would be a small thing to do considering the mental effects on a member of the Mud Island family. So, we agreed we would discuss it once we returned from patrol. It would take some careful planning because it meant finding a buoy that could be anchored at the site.

Hampton pointed out that there were plenty of channel markers around Georgetown that could be relocated to the spot, and they could be positioned in a way that kept people from getting too close to Mud Island. Warnings that there were sunken ships and hidden reefs would be one more layer of security.

We were all putting the final touches on our preparations to leave the shelter on patrol, and we had to keep our minds on what we were doing because it was already dangerous enough outside, but the idea of moving a channel marker from Georgetown was an instant reminder that Hampton had left behind people he had grown up with, and he too was bound to feel the effects of survivor's guilt if he returned home.

Needless to say, we were forgetting one of the things the Chief had reminded us about every time we opened the door to our shelter. We needed to have our heads on straight, or someone was going to die. Maybe that was why we forgot to take one last glance at the security camera views of the shelter door. We didn't have our heads on straight.

I spun the big locking wheel and opened the door.

"Gloves.......everybody make sure you have your gloves on," yelled Jean.

There was somewhat of an alcove outside the shelter door. From a distance it was like any other natural erosion on the side of a hill. Tree roots were exposed, and a casual observer would think it was a good place to get out of the rain. Few people would get close enough to see the big door in the darkness at the back. This time the alcove was filled with the infected, and they had blue crabs clinging to them. The only thing that saved us from having them flood inside was the fact that the door opened so quietly. Before they could react, I was already closing the door.

"Where the hell did they all come from?" yelled Bus.

"We'll worry about that later," yelled Hampton. "Right now we need to push them back enough to get the door closed."

For the next few minutes we pushed them back on each other while avoiding the pincers of the blue crabs and the grasping hands of the infected. When we finally had room to close the door again, I took advantage of the opportunity and spun the lock into place.

We were all relieved and more than a little guilty when we considered that everyone was supposed to check the cameras. We still had to deal with where they had come from, but it had been too close. After all, we had spent months trying to establish a perimeter around Mud Island that we considered reasonably safe, only to have them show up on our doorstep.

"They must have been trapped somewhere nearby and just got free," said Tom, "and I'm glad we were the ones surprised by them instead of Kathy and the Chief. At least we had the numbers to deal with them."

Tom and Kathy had grown even closer throughout the summer months, and his concern for her had just gone up a notch.

"We had the numbers," I said, "but we got lucky. I'm going to put up a sign on the door that says to check the cameras before opening."

"Better yet," said Colleen, "why don't we have an alarm system? You said your Uncle insisted on the latest technology when they built these shelters."

"I never could figure that out," I said. "He had visual equipment put in, but he didn't even bother to put a string of cans or trip wires outside."

"Well, while we're putting out a marker for ships to avoid that reef, why don't we get what we need to put an alarm system around the island?" asked Cassandra. "We could even bug the woods on the other side of the moat, and then we could stop patrolling it every day."

"Sounds like a plan," said Tom, "but first we have to go out the escape tunnel and deal with those door to door salesmen."

We all gathered up our gear and started for the escape tunnel in the room that used to be the master bedroom. Since we had turned it into an upper level storage area, we had to keep a clear path to the exit, but that was no problem. We even built a set of steps up to the hatch that was recessed into the wall so it would be easier to climb in.

The tunnel that ran to the surface was much longer than it appeared to be when we would crawl through it, but it was well lit and didn't make anyone feel claustrophobic.

As we passed through the living room on our way to the hatch, I asked Molly to turn on the outside monitors at the door and at the escape hatch.

"Uncle Eddie, I was just about to ask you why everyone was going outside when there were so many infected out there."

"Because we were dummies and didn't check the cameras first. What about the emergency exit?"

Molly switched to that camera view, and we were surprised to see so many infected. The camera for that view was located across the moat, so it showed a good angle back toward Mud Island.

"The place is crawling with them," said Tom. "Where are they all coming from?"

Molly switched the monitor to the view that showed all of the cameras, and it was like it had been back at the beginning of the infection. Every angle of the island showed the same thing.

"The Mercy Ship," said Cassandra. "Some are wearing crew uniforms."

She sounded like someone who was having the same nightmare every time they went to sleep. She sounded like she was resigned to live with seeing the entire crew again, even when her eyes were open.

"It's not just the crew," I said. "There were hundreds of people on the beaches that night, and most of them died out there in the water."

"But that was months ago," said Colleen. "How are they getting here now?"

"Longshore drift," said Hampton. "The current was strong enough back when we pulled Cassandra off of that ship. It most likely carried hundreds of them south along the coast, and some got tangled up in the marshes along the Intracoastal Waterway. If they didn't get eaten by the bottom feeders, they eventually got washed ashore."

"Makes sense, but that sure is a lot of them," I said.

"It makes me wonder if they haven't found a way to get through Georgetown."

I was never too sure how Hampton really felt about coming back to Mud Island and being this close to where he had grown up, but I always expected that sooner or later he would want to know. His suggestion about getting a buoy from Georgetown may have just been a clue that he at least wanted to see it for himself.

My thoughts were interrupted when Molly said there was something on the camera facing the main beach area that we should see. We all gathered around the monitors where Molly shifted the picture to the main screen.

The camera was aimed slightly to the northeast, and there were two ships moving slowly toward the south. The one in front was flying a United States Navy flag and appeared to be either a destroyer or a cruiser. I would have needed a desk reference to be sure which it might be. The second ship was a huge submarine that was traveling on the surface.

In my video game days, I had played one that included ballistic missile submarines, and I was sure I was watching one of them cruise by.

While we were watching them silently brush past the coast of South Carolina, we all saw the activity on the deck of the surface ship, and it didn't take a rocket scientist to know what they were about to do.

The bursts of machine gun fire from the deck of the destroyer were not totally unexpected, but the devastation was. A weird shaped structure on the deck of the destroyer had rotated left and right for only a few seconds, and every infected dead on the beach was down. Some were still moving, but they had mostly been sawed in half or outright shredded by the bullets.

Another camera angle that showed the tree line of Mud Island also showed that trees had been cut down by the same bullets. It was like a hurricane had passed over the area.

"What was that?" I asked no one in particular.

Jean said, "That ship is like one of the ships that warned us away from the Atlantic Spirit before it was sank."

Tom and Hampton were searching through reference books that had been stocked in the shelter, and Bus was busy doing the same through data drives connected to the computer.

Hampton found it first.

"It appears they just used their missile defense system to obliterate the infected that were walking around on the beach."

Hampton laid an open book out in front of us and put his finger on the place in the text with a picture next to it.

"If it was painted blue and white, I would think it was a big R2-D2," I said.

The thing was actually more rounded and smooth than the famous Star Wars robot, but from a distance they weren't all that different.

"That's the nickname they use for it," said Hampton, "but it's actually a Phalanx CIWS, which stands for Close In Weapons System. It's the last line of defense for a ship to shoot down an incoming missile."

"It seems like they found another use for it," said Tom. "I'm glad we weren't out there when they opened fire."

"What now?" said Cassandra. "We're still going out, aren't we?"

"Now we have a better reason to go out," I answered. "We still have to watch for infected that might try to bite our ankles, but that's a lot more manageable than going out while they're able to walk. Besides, we only need to wait about thirty minutes for the crabs to do their thing."

Everyone glanced back at the screens to see what I had pointed at. The ships had already left the range of vision covered by our cameras, but the main attraction was the swarm of blue crabs that had emerged from the surf. Judging by the thousands of scurrying crustaceans, there wouldn't be much left on the beach in a few minutes. They climbed over each other as if they were one shifting, undulating blanket as they covered the remains of the infected that had been cut to pieces by the odd shaped gun on the destroyer.

"That bothers me," said Hampton. "The crabs could have come out of the water after the infected before they were minced by the bullets. Why didn't they?"

"They were probably already on their way," said Bus, "but they've evolved. It could be their instincts have evolved, too. It's easier for them to feed on the infected that are not able to walk."

"Molly, is the beach clear around the southern exit, and did the gun do anything up at the front door?"

Molly switched to those views, and my questions were answered. The southern tip of the island was covered by the blue blanket of crabs. The front door was clear of infected dead that were in one piece, but trees above the entrance had been shredded, and several had fallen from on top of the overhang above the door. I had to laugh at that.

"Those trees have fallen across the opening in a way that conceals the main entrance even better than before," I said.

Jean tried to see through the trees and asked, "Will we be able to go out through them?"

"They don't bite, so we can clear them enough to get through and leave the rest as camouflage over the entrance," said Tom. "When Kathy and the Chief get back, we can tell them we made some improvements while they were gone."

Cassandra asked, "Why didn't we try to establish radio contact with those ships? They could be searching for survivors."

We all regarded each other in silence for a few moments before answering.

"We have to consider the possibility that the Navy has operational orders of their own," I said.

"What does that mean?" she asked.

"Let me explain," said Hampton.

"According to Captain Miller, the Navy was under orders that caused the task force where he was located to be wiped out. After he and his squad left, who knows what became of the remnants of that force, but one thing was for certain. They weren't happy about him pulling out his troops."

"So the military might see them as deserters," said Cassandra.

We all nodded, and Hampton continued.

"In case you're wondering, the Navy was bringing the infected back to their ships to study. They thought they could keep it contained while they tried to find a cure. As you well know, a ship at sea is hardly the place to play around with this virus, or whatever it is."

"Does the military know about the virus getting into the food chain?" she asked.

Bus answered, "It wouldn't surprise me one bit if they know by now. Every navy in the world must have learned it the hard way. Those that were lucky learned it from other ships at sea."

"You mean like mine," said Cassandra. "When it became obvious that the crew of the Mercy ship had become poisoned by the food, they had the sense to begin broadcasting a distress call that warned everyone about the food."

"Where do you suppose they were going?" asked Jean.

Tom said, "I think I can give some suggestions about that, but it would make just as much sense for them to be going north."

"What do you mean by that?" I asked.

"Well, they're either on a mission, or they're going south to any of the many ports that need to be guarded from foreign invaders. That Russian corvette that parked behind Mud Island just wanted a place to hide, but the last thing we need is a foreign navy parking in Charleston, Savannah, Jacksonville, or Kings Bay. Those two ships won't be the last ones to go by. As the US Navy regroups, they're going to spread out up and down the coast. Norfolk, New York, and Boston also need to be protected."

Colleen had been listening quietly as everyone else shared their thoughts about the two ships, and Hampton noticed she had a distant frown on her face.

"A penny for your thoughts?"

She didn't answer right away and seemed to be a million miles away. Colleen was startled when she realized everyone was waiting for her to answer.

"Oh, I'm sorry. I was in a world of my own," she said.

"We saw that. Care to let us know what's going on inside that beautiful head of yours?"

Hampton had been captivated by Colleen's Irish nose and freckles since the moment he met her. He hadn't even known a woman with strawberry blonde hair and green eyes before Colleen, and if the world was a normal place, he would want to visit Ireland.

"I was wondering something," she said. "Didn't anyone tell the military about the shelters? I mean, what if those two ships are searching the coast for this one. Someone important was supposed to come to this shelter but never made it. Who was that person, and why hasn't anyone come here to see if they made it to the shelter?"

"We've actually had that discussion with Bus," I said. "When my uncle died and left me the shelter in his will, he didn't tell me anything about the shelters being built as a means to keep the country's command and control functions intact."

Bus cleared his throat to get our attention, and then he dropped a small bombshell on all of us.

"By now all of you have noticed that the Mud Island shelter is the smallest of the shelters you've seen. That's because Uncle Titus wasn't going to be required to share it with some unknown dignitary the way the rest of us were supposed to."

"What are you saying, Bus?" I was as surprised by the news as everyone else, but I didn't connect enough dots to know why he was telling us this piece of news now.

Bus smiled as he answered, "Mud Island wasn't on the list that was given to the military. As a matter of fact, the only shelters on the list given to the military were the shelters that were to receive people in the line of succession to the Presidency."

"So they know about Fort Sumter?" asked Jean.

"Most likely, but there are two things we will never know when we see US Navy warships go by. We won't know if they were considered as needing to know the shelter locations, and we won't know if they are acting under presidential authority or on their own."

It was a sobering thought to consider they might have somehow become rogue, but the conditions of the world could have caused anything to happen.

"If they do know about a shelter," I said, "it doesn't necessarily mean they know how to get inside, does it?"

Bus smiled as he shook his head back and forth.

******

For a second time we gathered at the main entrance to the shelter. The cameras showed that there was nothing moving outside the entrance. On the beach and on the southern tip of Mud Island the blue crabs were still feeding on the bodies of the infected that were scattered in the sand.

We made the trip from the door to our boat dock as quickly as we could, and as expected, we ran into several stray infected dead that had wandered far enough from the beach before the arrival of the US Navy. Our training was obvious as we removed threats faster every time we found another.

We piled into the boat as we cast off the mooring lines, and Bus expertly started the engines and pulled away from the dock seemingly at the same time.

The group was in agreement that we needed to see what was happening along the coast. There were more infected dead than usual, and they couldn't all be coming from the sunken Mercy ship. While we were at it, it wouldn't hurt to see if we can tow a buoy back from Georgetown to here, and we can place it over the wreckage of the ship.

It didn't take long for us to exit from behind Mud Island at the southern tip, but we slowed our progress just enough to be sure the two Navy ships had not decided to stay in the area.

Everyone was concentrating on the shoreline, watching for the infected. The story was the same everywhere. The infected were drawn from the trees by the sound of our twin engines, and we watched as they walked into the water as easily as if it had been a paved road. The blue crabs would undoubtedly be harvesting the dead for weeks.

There was no need to talk, and we were all too fascinated by the large numbers of the infected. The only time anyone said anything at length was when Hampton speculated that it was like a rebound. So many thousands of the infected had moved toward Georgetown only to find they couldn't go further than the river. Some still tried to walk out onto the mud flats and were inevitably stuck when the mud sucked on their legs, but plenty of them just turned around and began walking back the way they had come.

Highway 17 to Georgetown was once again a parade of the infected, but they had become so spread out along the banks of the river at Georgetown that thousands had left the road and begun going north through the trees along the Intracoastal Waterway. Thousands more had turned west, only to find themselves hemmed in by the river as it meandered north toward Myrtle Beach. Some tried to cross the river on that side, some bounced back and joined the unholy parade on Highway 17, and some crossed the highway walking straight toward the coast.

Whichever way they chose to go, everyone was getting their fair share, and there was no reason to expect that the migration wouldn't repeat itself as the infected dead met with obstacles toward the north that would turn them around and send them back to Mud Island.

Hampton tapped Bus on the shoulder and pointed at something in the distance. Then he pointed further out toward the ocean.

I followed the direction he had pointed first and saw a lighthouse. Hampton turned to the rest of us to explain as we felt Bus turning the boat to go further out to sea.

"That's the North Island Lighthouse. When you can see it from the ocean, it means you're approaching Winyah Bay where the Great Pee Dee and Waccamaw Rivers meet. You need to watch out for the jetty that extends from the tip of land south of the lighthouse."

Bus steered them far enough out to sea to go around the jetty and then head back toward the mouth of the bay. As we approached the stretch of beach where the jetty touched land, we were amazed by the number of infected that were walking out of the trees. The only explanation had to be that they walked into the rivers and were carried by the current, eventually washing ashore on the narrow strip of land near the lighthouse.

Hampton said, "Those infected will never come north again. This spit of land is totally surrounded by water, and they're going to be a food source for blue crabs for the next ten years or so."

The thought that there was a nature preserve that was fully stocked with the infected was not particularly reassuring, but at least they couldn't get out without becoming fish food.

We couldn't hear them over the sound of our engines as we went by, but if Bus had cut the engine power, it was obvious that we would. They crowded out onto the shoreline and walked senselessly into the deeper water, disappearing as they tried to reach for us.

Jean checked in with Molly to give her a progress report, and Molly said she had received a message from the Army at Fort Sumter. She referred to them as "our friends in the hotel" just in case the Navy heard the broadcast.

They all wondered what it meant when Molly told them the Army said the Chief was going to go into professional landscaping when this was all over. There was something about a weed-whacker, but we all knew the Chief well enough to know it had to be one of his crazy stunts. If the Navy was listening, they undoubtedly thought it was some kind of code.

Jean asked Molly to relay that there were more tourists out celebrating the good beach weather than usual. She figured the Navy wouldn't have a hard time figuring out that one for themselves, but there was no sense in giving away their position by saying it openly.

Bus had cut their forward speed down to a slow pace as they entered Winyah Bay. There were shoals and debris in the water that could sink a power boat that was carrying seven heavily armed adults. Their weapons and ammunition weighed considerably more than fishing gear, so they were drafting deeper than normal.

Georgetown came up on the port side, and Colleen instinctively laid one hand on Hampton's left shoulder. He appreciated the gesture and brought his right hand up to cover hers, but he didn't take his eyes off of the town.

There was nothing moving in the ruins that lined the river near the base of the bridge they had partially collapsed, but what disturbed us all the most was the ropes that hung from the remains of the bridge. A row of struggling but obviously dead corpses hung from the ropes, the nooses tied tightly around the necks. One rope was empty, and they could only assume that the head had detached from the body. The combination of decay and struggling had eventually separated the head from the heavier part below the noose.

"Guys," said Jean, "how long would it take for the infected to wiggle around until that happens?"

Being a doctor, Bus was the best qualified person in the boat to give an opinion.

"Not too long," said Bus. "Weather conditions could speed up or slow down the process some, but I would have to say a week at the longest."

"You're saying those are recent?" asked Tom.

Bus nodded and cut the engine at the same time. He let the current grab the bow and turn them around to face back the way they had come. Everyone felt the danger at the same time, and I felt the hair on the back of my neck bristle.

Everyone in the boat followed Tom's lead and got lower while aiming outward toward the ruined building.

"Anyone able to get binoculars on those signs up on the bridge above the bodies?" asked Jean.

"I'm checking them out right now," said Cassandra. "They say something about being infected and keeping it secret. One says for strangers to keep going or die."

Bus restarted the engines and hit the throttle at the same time. Shots rang out that were just loud enough to be heard above the roar of the engines, but Bus had timed their escape perfectly.

Bullets peppered the water where they had been, sending up small plumes of water.

Hampton gazed longingly at the town where he had grown up, but it also appeared that something had been resolved. He had expressed guilt over the way he had left Georgetown, and he even speculated that he might have made a difference if he had stayed to help his neighbors.

Now he could see for himself that his hometown had fallen along with all of the other towns and cities. Worse, it had fallen from within because people tried to hide their bitten family members until it was too late.

"What about the buoy?" Cassandra yelled over the sound of the engines.

Hampton moved closer to her so he wouldn't have to shout.

"Did you see those whitecaps on the surface about a hundred yards from shore at the tip of the land? It was near where the jetty touches shore?"

Cassandra had spent enough time on the Mercy ship to be aware of changes in the water color. When whitecaps appeared on the surface of water that someone might expect to be deep, it meant someone was going to run into a reef or a shoal.

"I saw it, but I didn't see any buoys that warned of a fishing bank."

Hampton smiled at her because he was pleased that she was so smart about the sea. It could help keep them alive.

"Did you notice there were two on the other side by the shoals? One of them broke loose from its mooring line and drifted over there from the fishing banks. We can retrieve it and take it back to Mud Island."

******

There are beaches that are real tourist traps, and there are beaches that are just traps. The beach on the other side of Winyah Bay was nothing but a couple of miles of beach that ran along a useless strip of land. Water-locked on all sides, it couldn't be developed, and the curve of the landscape caused the rivers to dump fine silt along the bottom.

The fine silt had created an attractive beach, but the infected dead that were carried out to sea on the current were also being stranded on the uninhabited beach. Some were stuck in the muddy bottom, but some found their way ashore.

Mother Norton Shoal extended unseen into the bay, and one of the two buoys was intended to warn boaters that the bottom tended to rise up rather quickly. Hampton didn't warn Bus soon enough.

Bus had been listening to what Hampton was saying about the buoys and had steered straight toward the closer of the two. When the boat drove into shallow water, the luckiest members of our group were the ones who were standing. They were the ones who were thrown over the front of the boat without hitting the windshield.

Bus had taken the worst hit because he had gone straight into the steering wheel. He was unconscious from what I could see, and the blood in my eyes made me wish my head didn't hurt so much. I'm not sure what I hit, but it was something hard.

I searched around for Jean and didn't see her in the boat. Cassandra was up on the bow and unsuccessfully trying to push herself to her feet. One of her arms wasn't cooperating. Tom and Hampton were getting untangled from the back of the seats where they had literally slammed into each other. Both were getting up, but they were clearly stunned.

Colleen was also missing from the boat, and I could see the panic in Hampton's eyes. I must have had the same expression on my face, and I began wildly spinning around in all directions trying to find Jean.

A shot rang out from the bow. Cassandra was up on one knee and carefully aiming her M4 toward the beach. One glance in that direction was all I needed. Someone had rung the dinner bell.

I climbed past the slumped body of our doctor thinking that someone should help him, but I had to find Jean. I went over the center console where the windshield used to be and stopped next to Cassandra. I could see Jean's body in the dark water about twenty feet in front of the boat. She was on her back, face up, and with her arms spread wide like she was trying to make a snow angel, but she wasn't moving. A few feet to her right was Colleen.

Both of them were in water no more than an inch or two deep, but when a boat throws its passengers, it's anything but graceful. It's more like being inside a clothes dryer set on a high speed tumble.

As I jumped from the bow, Hampton reached my side and made the jump with me. The sand had been solid enough to stop the boat, but it sucked at our feet and slowed our progress as we fought desperately to reach the women.

More shots came from the bow as Cassandra realized she would be the only one covering us. Tom was easing Bus away from the seats and the steering column and trying to stop the flow of blood from a nasty cut on his forehead. He was breathing, but he was going to be in a world of hurt when he woke up.

I made it to Jean and saw that she was conscious but not really aware of anything. She was so short that I was able to scoop her up and start back for the boat in one motion. My skin crawled when I saw the blue crabs that had already converged where she landed.

"Hampton, watch out for the crabs. They're everywhere," I shouted.

Hampton didn't hesitate when he got to Colleen. He didn't waste any time getting her out of the water away from the bottom feeders that had smelled fresh meat.

On the beach the number of infected had grown, and they were coming from every direction. The trees must have been full of them because there were too many to shoot.

After Cassandra helped me to lift Jean into the boat, we both helped Hampton with Colleen. We laid them next to Bus and covered them with blankets to keep them warm.

"We have to get Bus back to the shelter as quickly as possible," said Tom. "At the very least he has several broken ribs. We won't know about internal injuries until we get him stabilized. If we're lucky, he'll wake up and be able to tell us what to do. How're the women?"

"I think they just got banged up," I said, "but they're in no shape to help fight that horde coming onto the beach."

We all turned in that direction and saw just how bad it was.

"Come on," said Tom. "We need to get off of this sand. They're going to be able to walk right up to us."

"I think there's a hole in the bow," said Cassandra.

"More good news," said Hampton. "Let me check the hull."

Cassandra stayed with Bus, Jean, and Colleen while the rest of us went over the bow for a second time.

"The tide's coming in," said Hampton. "At least we have that on our side. With just a little more water under us, you two should be able to lift the bow just high enough for me to see if we're taking on any water."

I don't think Tom and I got the boat more than an inch or two off of the sand, but it was enough for Hampton to see a nasty dent in the keel. He said it would need to be repaired, but he thought it was solid enough to get us across to the lighthouse.

"Why would we go to the lighthouse?" Tom and I asked at the same time.

Hampton shook his head and said, "The boat went far enough into the sand to drag the motors. I'm going to bet one or both have a broken propellor. If only one is broken, it's a fair guess that it won't start."

The three of us froze only long enough for it to sink in that we were hearing moans behind us. We pushed with everything we had, but the boat seemed to slide much more slowly than we needed. Cassandra was back on the bow and picking off the infected that had come the closest.

If the tide had been going out instead of coming in, we wouldn't have gotten the boat free in time. As it slipped away from the beach, we scrambled onto the bow and reached for the paddles. The bottom still seemed to be too close as we pushed away, and the infected dead in the lead began reaching for the railing around the bow.

Once again Cassandra demonstrated her skills. Instead of wasting bullets, she was swinging her machete, and the dead were losing fingers. We slid backwards from their grasping hands, and the infected began falling forward on their faces.

As we coasted on the surface of the water, infected dead that had been in the second row of the advancing horde began stepping on the bodies that had fallen in their path. For a moment they had an effective bridge and gained on us again. Suddenly, the bottom dropped away, and they were falling into water that was over their heads.

Hampton was by far the most skilled boat mechanic we had, so he climbed over the stern onto a step between the engines to see how bad it was. It was bad.

"Both propellors are bent too much to use, and the repairs would be a waste of time. It would be far easier to just get a new boat."

"That's the long-term fix," said Tom. "What's the short-term goal?"

I said, "We need to find a safe place to spend the night. I don't think we should move Bus around too much until we know how bad it is."

"The radio's busted," said Cassandra. She held up the microphone and clicked it a few times for effect.

Jean was sitting up in the bottom of the boat, and Colleen was trying to do the same.

Hampton handed his paddle to Tom and said, "We need to make it to that lighthouse, but we need to be really quiet about it."

We tied our lines to a small dock near the lighthouse just as dusk settled over the bay, and we had a choice. We could either try to reach the lighthouse in the cover of darkness, or we could wait in the boat until dawn. Bus was only breathing in shallow, raspy breaths, and we didn't know if we could wait that long.

10 WAITING ROOM SURVIVAL

Painting the big plate glass windows had been hard, but it didn't need to be pretty. It only needed to block out their light. He studied his handiwork and it occurred to him that he had come a long way. They had all come a long way.

It had taken several days of hunger and fear before they had been able to face reality and venture a second time from the plane. Eventually, it sank in that they had to try.

Garrett Carson had tried to stop thinking of himself as a pilot. He didn't like to think about how he had been called upon to carry the President of the United States to a place of safety, and he especially didn't want to let himself think about how POTUS had left him and his flight crew to die.

Thinking about it wouldn't change the fact they had their fifteen minutes of fame as Executive One, and then they had what seemed like a lifetime of exile to this waiting room, and eventually to the concourse where they had been forced to make a home.

He tried even harder not to think about his wife and three children in Arlington, Virginia. At fifty years of age, he had always been healthy because he liked to work out on layovers. It made him fit the part of an airline pilot, and more importantly, the man in charge. He had been one of the youngest pilots in the commercial airline business when he had started, so he had been looking forward to retiring to a quiet piece of property in the country.

The kids were all in high school and ready to get out on their own. His daughters were both thinking of college, but his son had his eyes on the military. He was the youngest, so he had time to decide, but he knew he wanted to be in the cockpit of a fighter plane.

Trying not to think about the decisions his kids were making only caused him to think of them more, and thinking of them more made him think about getting out of John Glenn International Airport. That made him think even more about how POTUS had gotten him stranded there in the first place. It was a never ending vicious circle.

Garrett's thoughts were interrupted by the return of the first group of scavengers. They had agreed to meet in the waiting room at the concourse exit that led back to their home base in the 737. The plane was comfortable enough for seven people, and the door was strong enough to guarantee no surprises in the middle of the night. Besides, he doubted he could convince any of the others to sleep in the airport.

A pair of men's shoes dangled through an opening in the ceiling, and Garrett recognized the feet from spending so many months together. He had a funny revelation about the shoes. He wasn't entirely sure what day it was, but he knew the shoes belonged to Mike Wood, the male flight attendant.

Mike dropped onto the cushions that had been placed below the hole and reached back up to take some kind of duffel bag from another flight attendant, Susan Morris. If all had gone well, Anne Hill, the senior flight attendant would be up in the ceiling right behind Susan. As soon as Susan handed the duffel bag to Mike, he reached up to half-catch her as she dropped through the hole. Garrett was relieved to see Anne's feet come through next.

None of them spoke as Garrett pointed toward the exit to the corridor that said Gate Four above it. They knew from experience that speaking out loud in the waiting room caused the dead on the other side of the chained doors to become agitated. They all agreed that everyone would remain silent until they were on the other side of the exit.

How long the dead would remain on the other side of the chained doors had become nothing more than speculation. Every time one of the flight crew members checked to see if they were gone, the doors would start shaking from the impact of several bodies against it.

The last reports the crew had received before losing all radio contact with the outside world had simply referred to the dead as being infected. It took the seven of them only a short while to figure out that being bitten meant you were infected and going to die, and after you died you were going to get back up and bite living people. There had been some nonsense on the radio about it being a virus that could think, but the small group of survivors couldn't have cared less. They just wanted to know when someone would be coming to their rescue.

Garrett nodded to Susan and Anne as they followed Mike through Gate Four. He would wait for the second group to return and then go with them to the plane to see if they had any luck finding supplies.

A rope ladder hung down through a second hole in the ceiling where an air conditioning return had been. They had quietly worked at the grate covering the opening and then managed to open a hole big enough to climb through.

They didn't risk trying to crawl through the ductwork because the thin aluminum would have made far too much noise. Besides, Addison was the only crew member small enough to fit inside comfortably, and she wasn't about to squeeze into the dark tunnel.

The ductwork did give them a huge advantage, though. Where the ductwork went was like a map. They could follow its branches and mark it with arrows and directions. Where trunks of ductwork went to new rooms, they wrote in big red letters, 'DEAD BELOW' when there were infected. Green arrows pointing downward meant the room was safe.

Garrett saw the rope ladder twitch and then a pair of legs. His navigator, co-pilot, and last flight attendant came down the rope ladder. Each of them wore a backpack, and judging by the bulging pockets on each one, they had managed to find an untapped source of supplies. They were all smiling, so it must have been good news.

He walked over and helped Addison get out of her backpack as soon as she had her feet on the floor. She opened her mouth to say something, but all three men put a finger over their mouths at the same time. She was excited and mouthed the words that she was sorry.

They headed for Gate Four, and as soon as they passed through into the corridor where they couldn't be heard, Addison blurted out what she had been holding in.

"I couldn't believe it."

It came out almost as a squeal.

"Please tell me you found a Star Trek transporter," said Garrett. "One that can put us anywhere else."

Terrance, the former navigator said, "Where would you like for me to beam you, boss? You know there's no place safer than this."

Terrance had started calling Garrett 'boss' after they determined they weren't going anywhere soon. Garrett had told him it made him a little uncomfortable, and that if he called him 'boss' again, he'd start calling him Terry. Terrance preferred to go by 'Sim' which was short for Simmons, his last name.

"Anywhere would be better than here, Terry."

He managed to put just the smallest amount of sarcasm in his tone so he could make it sound like he had just slipped.

"Sorry, Sim, you know what I mean."

"What did you find, Addison?"

"It was like someone gave me the keys to a mall," she beamed.

Addison still wore her blond hair in a ponytail, but it had gotten so much longer that it swayed with every move.

Garrett couldn't believe it, but he found himself trying to gauge how much time had passed since the first day in the airport by remembering how long Addison's hair had been at the time. She was still good for the morale of the crew because she was as bouncy as her hair.

"It was the mall," said the remaining member of the group.

Jon King had been a co-pilot flying with Garrett for about eight years. He was fifteen years younger than Garrett, but he had always been jealous of Garrett's hair. Jon had lost enough of his hair that he had started shaving his head, and he wasn't happy about the way it was growing back on the sides. Addison had volunteered to wax it for him, but he wasn't sure about the idea.

"You guys finally found a way into the mall? Did you get into the Starbucks?"

One of the perks of the airport was the local shopping. It wasn't a full-sized mall, but it had enough to keep them alive much longer.

"We brought back a whole backpack full of coffee," said Jon. "You weren't the only one dying for a fresh cup of coffee, and if this winter gets as bad as the last one, we're going to need it."

"The others came back just a few minutes ahead of you. I didn't ask them if they had any success this time, but judging by the expressions on their faces, I think they may have found a way into the security office."

"You think they had guns in there?" asked Sim.

"They didn't have any rifles, but I would bet they gave more consideration to handguns than to rifles. We can always go back for rifles, but they had a heavy duffel bag when they came through the hole."

The group walked as they talked, but Addison sprinted ahead to give the others the good news. It was safe for her to be alone in this part of the concourse.

Their concourse had four more retractable passenger gates extending out from it, and each of them had a plane at the other end. One of the first things the crew of Executive One had done was to ensure those planes were all closed. Unless the infected became smart enough to move the big latches on the inside of the planes, the doors would remain sealed forever. It wasn't something that could be done by accident.

From their plane they had watched faces press against the glass leaving smears of blood and saliva on the windows until they were no longer visible. Whatever was left on the windows dried until the glass was opaque with a brown film. Gradually, the faces weren't pressed against the windows as the infected in the planes could no longer see anything of interest to them through the film. Without light inside the planes, the survivors on Executive One could only imagine what kind of hell existed inside the other planes.

Despite the fact that nothing was interested in them at the moment, they had drawn the shades down on all of their own windows. During the daylight hours they were able to open one or two windows, but they avoided moving around where something walking outside would see the subtle change inside.

******

After that first time when they had gone into the terminal, they had returned to the plane for the night. The devastation of the 737 that crashed into downtown Columbus was indescribable. They watched the smoke and flames from a distance, and being experts they knew that the explosion had been more than just jet fuel.

Despondent and totally clueless about what they were going to do, they had returned to familiar territory and sealed themselves inside. Anne, Susan, Mike, and Addison went down the rows pulling the shades closed on the windows. Garrett, Jon, and Sim went into the flight deck and powered down anything that gave off light with the exception of the radio.

No one really felt like eating, but the light meal of sandwiches and iced tea turned out to be comforting. Sim had gotten hooked on sweetened iced tea while visiting Charleston, South Carolina, and he always asked the flight attendants to have some ready for him. Being well liked by the people who flew with him, it was a common beverage on his flights, and he'd gotten pilots and co-pilots hooked, too.

While they took turns on the radio trying to make contact with other survivors, the seven crew members found themselves sitting around the walls of the flight deck talking about what had happened. One thing they all had in common was the short-lived elation of being the official aircraft for the President.

As it turned out, only Garrett and Jon knew they were designated as Executive One, and Sim didn't know it until he heard them use the designation on the radio. The flight crew had wondered if they were Air Force One, but they weren't disappointed that they had written a page into the history books and were given another name.

They weren't disappointed until they were left behind by the people they had saved. Each of the seven took a turn at expressing their feelings, and there was one thing they found to be totally frustrating. They didn't even know where the people on Air Force One went. All they knew was that the plane had tucked its nose inside the big hangar. They speculated that maybe Air Force One was still populated, but they had seen the combat vehicles that had directed them toward the open hangar, and they doubted the military had left POTUS in his plane. They also didn't think the flight crew of Air Force One would have simply ignored their repeated radio calls.

When the Strykers came out and tried to clear the infected dead from around their wheels, they thought at first that they were leaving with the military. Then they watched as the military was unable to reduce the numbers of the dead that were walking around the runways, and when they gave up, they only felt hopeless.

Jon held up one hand to signal that he had something on the radio. He took off his headset and switched to a speaker so everyone could hear. It was a recorded broadcast, and it did very little to lift their spirits.

The male voice was giving updates from around the country, and although there wasn't much that they hadn't already heard, there was nothing said that gave them the slightest hope. They were all holding onto slim hopes to hear something about their home cities so they could believe their loved ones were safe, but one by one they heard the opposite.

Most of them lived in the eastern part of Virginia, but all of them had relatives across the country. Anne was originally from Oregon, and Sim was from Georgia. The voice said that Portland, home to over three million people was being completely evacuated. Atlanta had almost six million people, and according to the voice, it was already evacuated as much as it could be. The voice didn't explain what that meant for the people who weren't evacuated.

"Where would everyone evacuate to if everywhere was being evacuated?" asked Addison.

She didn't realize how rhetorically she had phrased the question, and she thought someone might actually answer. She turned from one face to the next in the dim light, but no one said anything.

They listened to the radio and talked late into the night, but in the early hours of the morning Garrett suggested that everyone should get some sleep. He told them that he would take the first watch and gave time assignments to the rest of the crew. Everyone got settled in, and despite the tragedies of the day, fatigue took its toll.

Garrett sat quietly at the radio and listened to several broadcasts. Most were recorded and being broadcast on a loop, but he got a few shortwave operators and was even able to talk with one for a few minutes.

The man on the radio told him through the static that he was somewhere in Maine, and that he wouldn't last long where he was. The man told Garrett that he thought he had planned for the apocalypse, but he didn't plan for this one.

Garrett asked him if that's what this was, the apocalypse. The man had laughed at the question and only said Garrett could make up his own mind.

That was the first night, and the crew of Executive One met on the flight deck every night for three days to listen for new information on the radio. When even the loops stopped broadcasting, they started settling in for the night without much discussion at all.

They snapped out of their daze at the end of the first week when Sim said something to Jon and Mike that made complete sense. He said it was a miracle that they were alive. It was so obvious that they were all sitting around licking their wounds when there were so many people who didn't have that luxury.

"Sim is right," said Mike. "All we have to do is check through the window across the runway. That 737 full of passengers must have found food and water somewhere to have made it this long."

As if on cue, they saw the door was opening again. They weren't the only ones who noticed. Every infected dead at the airport seemed to notice, and those that could move began stumbling toward the plane.

Someone dropped from the plane and tried to run through the least populated area, but he didn't make it too far before he seemed to just disappear. He was probably weak from hunger and dehydration and had very little awareness of what was happening to him. A second passenger, possibly thinking the first jumper had distracted enough of the infected, tried to hang from the open door before dropping to the ground. The passenger didn't even get to run because the infected were holding onto his legs before he let go of the door.

The crew of Executive One watched in stunned horror as passenger after passenger tried to jump from the plane and run. If the plane was at capacity, there were around two hundred people inside, and it must have been near capacity judging by the sudden flow of jumpers.

They didn't think that it could get more awful, but it did. The escape slide inflated from the bottom of the door and shot outward from the plane. Because the front wheel strut had collapsed, the nose of the plane was lower than it should have been, and it would have been easier to walk down the slide standing up than it was to slide down it.

The first passenger tried to slide and came to a stop only halfway to the bottom. There was a pileup of passengers as people kept coming through the door, and people began falling off the slide into the waiting arms of the infected.

"There's only one thing that could be making everyone jump from the plane like that," said Garrett. "Someone on board had the infection and just died."

When they pulled themselves away from the windows, they saw their situation in a new light. Sim was right. They were alive, and not everyone could make that claim.

"We have to pull ourselves together," said Garrett. "We've been crying about POTUS and the military leaving us out here to die. Who's to say they're doing any better? If we're going to live through this, we're the ones who have to make it happen."

"Good speech," said Mike. "What have you got in mind?"

Anne stepped forward and asked, "Are we going to leave here?"

Garrett shook his head from side to side.

"And go where? I think the only way we're going to stay alive is to dig in. Everyone else tried to escape to somewhere else. When you think about it, while we were coming here, people were escaping from here. Nowhere is safe, so the only way to stay alive is to stay put."

"Where do we start?" asked Susan.

"We start by making our immediate area safe, and then we'll expand outward. Our supplies can't last forever, so we have to find other sources. We'll forage during the day, and we'll seal ourselves into the plane at night. That way we'll get a good night sleep and be ready to work again the next day."

"I think we're all in agreement with you," said Jon. "As the pilot of this flight, you're still in charge as far as I'm concerned."

******

That discussion had been over a year ago, and Garrett thought it was closer to eighteen months instead of twelve. Now he found himself inspecting the precious packages of coffee that had been brought back by Addison. Anne was already heating up the water as Garrett held his nose over an open bag and savored the aroma of the fresh, bold roast coffee.

He lifted his face from the bag and smiled at the rest of them. He hadn't been aware that they were all watching him expectantly.

"What?" asked Garrett.

"Nothing," said Jon, "but Addison did the same thing when we found the coffee, and we agreed to let you open the next one. It's my turn after that."

"What happened to ladies first?" asked Anne with a mock scowl on her face. "Have we become uncivilized?"

Mike said, "A lady did go first, but to answer your question, just take Garrett, Jon, Sim, and me, for example. Our grooming is getting more uncivilized every day, and I'll bet you ladies are wishing you could shave your legs at least once."

Susan popped Mike on the back of the head, but he still laughed. Out off reflex everyone put a finger to their mouths and made a shhhh sound to remind them to keep the noise down.

One of the worst scares they had gotten was when they realized their walking in the retractable passageway could be heard below them. Infected dead were gathering there and hanging around for hours until the crew figured out that they were making too much noise. Even Addison running ahead of them to the plane had been different. Instead of running as if she was 'pounding the pavement' she ran as quietly as she could.

Over the months they had established routines and took nothing for granted. They always sealed themselves in the plane at night, just as they had decided at the beginning, but there were some drawbacks. The air in the plane had become a bit stale, and the chemicals in the sanitation tank had overwhelmed them by leaking into the plane through the toilets. The smells outside the plane weren't much better, but at least the air moved, so they posted a guard at the entrance to the gateway and left the plane open on the door during the daytime.

It didn't take long for them to inspect the other planes to be sure their doors were sealed tight, but they carried every piece of furniture that could be moved from the concourse and blocked the other retractable gateways as well as they could. If something got out of the planes they could meet the threat head on and keep it contained.

Mike was the one who discovered what they already suspected to be true about the best way to kill the infected. He had been using a pair of binoculars to scan the airport and spotted a man who wasn't walking like he was infected. The man was carrying something that was shaped like a spear, and he had a variety of weapons on a belt that had most likely come from a hardware store. A hammer and a crowbar weren't typical weapons.

The man was pretty far away, and walking parallel to the terminal. Garrett joined Mike at the window, and they watched the man approach a group of infected as if it was an every day thing to him. He used his spear on one, reaching it out toward the face of the nearest infected and then impaling the creature straight through the face.

Before the first one even reached the ground, the man had pulled the crowbar and hammer free from his belt. He went from one to the other, permanently dropping six more of them.

"You notice how he's doing nothing but headshots?" asked Mike.

"Couldn't help but notice. You suppose that's the only way to kill them?"

"While you and Jon were busy driving the plane around, I had a chance to watch what was going on outside. I saw plenty of them get shot and get back up again, but the ones that took a bullet to the head stayed down."

In the evenings before they turned in, they always sat around in a cramped circle and discussed the day. Any ideas, plans, fears, or other emotions were talked out. That way they stayed close, and they stayed sane.

In one of the first evening meetings they talked about what Mike and Jon had seen. Susan's first reaction was wanting to know why they hadn't gotten the man's attention. Maybe he could have rescued them.

Garrett had to remind her they had also agreed they weren't going to count on being rescued. They were going to rely on their own will to live. If the man had been standing right next to the airplane, maybe they would have called out to him, but they couldn't have even been sure he wasn't a risk.

"What if he had already been bitten?" said Anne. "What if he was crazy and tried to kill us? You need to stop thinking that a knight in shining white armor is going to ride in and save us, Susan."

Susan had been the last one to mentally accept their situation. She had become quiet and moody. She hadn't told them her age, but everyone could guess she was in her thirties. She had left behind a husband and a three-year-old boy who was at a day care center when she had gotten onto the 737 at Dulles International Airport. She was surprised when the plane took off without passengers and made a quick trip to Andrews Air Force Base. None of the flight crew knew they were part of a contingency plan to get the President out of the area if he couldn't board Air Force One. At least two other planes had been redirected to Andrews, but they had drawn the short straw by arriving first.

They had all lost someone, so they were dependent upon each other to hold themselves together. Garrett and Jon both expected

Addison to cave in first, but it had been Susan. Her moody behavior deteriorated into long crying fits, and they had to waste some of their manpower on keeping her under watch. They were sure she would get like the people on the other 737 and simply try to get out of the terminal and run all the way home.

Her sullen behavior came to an abrupt end when Addison cut her hand on a piece of metal furniture they had dismantled in the concourse. The wound needed a few stitches, and the motherly instinct Susan felt toward her lost child was redirected to Addison. She surprised everyone when she stepped in and took over, cleaning and stitching the cut with expertise. When Garrett designated her as the doctor for their group, Susan immediately set up a first aid center in the plane and did an inventory of their medical supplies. She showed up at the evening meeting as if she had never missed one.

Garrett studied her neat appearance, her brushed back brown hair and noticed for the first time that she was the living definition of a suburban soccer mom. Even though her son was only a toddler, she had already bought him his first soccer ball. Susan had a future, and she was just starting to live it when the infection took everything away from her. No wonder she had been the last to accept their circumstances.

The next day they had all gone out to the main concourse with specific goals in mind. They needed to find a way to move throughout the terminal and to locate supplies. The more they brought back, the longer they would survive.

Sim suggested that they go through the ceilings, which was immediately denounced by the others as a bad idea because airports were made with security in mind. At least that was what they thought until Sim reminded them there was no power to the terminal, and there had been so many major renovations and expansions to the airport that they were bound to find ways to get through the places where the expansions were connected.

Sim was right. Getting into the ceiling was just a couple of hours of manual labor, and they quickly learned the air conditioning ducts were like a road map. Being a navigator, he was also the one who came up with the idea to mark the ductwork with arrows, directions, and warnings.

The part that bothered them the most was knowing what was on the other side of each door to the waiting area. There were also big plate glass windows that made them feel exposed. Garrett suggested that they should keep an eye out for paint in the maintenance areas, and maybe they could feel more secure after they painted the glass. He didn't know it would take almost a year and a half to complete that little chore.

At first they went as one group, and not everyone went. Garrett, Jon, and Sim told Mike to keep an eye on things while they foraged. They spent most of the day tunneling through firewalls into different sections of the main terminal building, and at first they didn't really find anything to bring back other than a few personal hygiene items.

At the evening meeting, Anne had led the women in a rebellion, giving the cockpit crew an earful. She told them they would have rather faced the infected if the men had come back with a tub for the women to wash their clothes in.

From that day on they had gone out in groups, often rotating the members so everyone got to work together. Their goal had become a food court in the middle of a mall that had been renovated into the terminal during the last expansion. They knew most of the food would be spoiled, but the canned and packaged food could be rationed for a couple of years.

They had finally reached the Starbucks in the food court and Addison had gone straight for the coffee storeroom.

The coffee had been the icing on the cake, but over the last eighteen or so months they had other milestones. When Jon had returned with the news that he had found the Security office, and there were likely to be guns, Garrett felt like they were actually going to live through this ordeal. Of course, there was some bad news. The office was occupied by an unknown number of the infected.

Garrett and Anne climbed into the ceiling and made the long trip to the Security office with Jon. They each carried a piece of long metal pipe with sharpened points on the end. Most of the way they had to walk stooped over with their feet placed carefully on supports no more than two inches wide. It was tough on their backs and on the muscles in their legs, but they had long since given up on complaining.

When they reached places where they could walk upright, they took a few minutes to stretch out the aches that came from going so far bent over at the waist.

"This is the worst part up here," said Jon.

They could see where Jon had widened a hole above an aluminum duct that went through a wall and then downward at a forty-five degree angle.

"I went around the ductwork on the side like we always do, but I noticed the duct took a dive so I made the hole on top. It's hard to go down it without making noise."

"Is it occupied in the room below it?" asked Anne.

"Yeah, it got kind of noisy in there when I slid down to the next level. I pulled a light fixture out of the ceiling to see how many of those infected I woke up and had one staring straight up at me."

Garrett asked, "How many do you figure?"

"No way to tell. It wasn't a security officer, so my guess is that security was trying to protect some people by bringing them into their office."

"You said it was right under the hole?" asked Anne. "Was it close enough for you to stick him? Did you give away your position to the others?"

Jon couldn't make eye contact with them at first, and both Anne and Garrett wondered what she had said that made Jon act like he had done something wrong.

"I sort of reacted since he was so close to the hole, and I was practically on top of him."

"What does that mean?" asked Anne.

Garrett suddenly understood, and he had to suppress a laugh. He managed to keep himself quiet, but he couldn't hide the big smile even in the gloomy light of the ceiling.

Anne didn't get it yet and swiveled her head from Garrett to Jon and back again for a straight answer.

"I sort of yelled," said Jon.

Garrett interpreted for Anne.

"He means he screamed like a little girl. Yes, he gave away his position when he peed in his pants."

Jon started to say something, but Anne stopped him.

"You did what any of us would have done. The screaming part I mean, not the peeing part."

Garrett tried not to laugh but failed miserably. When it came out, it was the release he had needed for a long time. Needless to say, they could hear the responding moans up ahead. There was no reason to stay quiet anymore, so they followed Jon as he climbed on top of the ductwork and slid feet first through the hole.

Garrett watched Anne as she went through and thought about how far she had come in such a short amount of time. She had always been dependable as a member of his flight crew, but it had become more than that. She had adapted to her new role as a member of a team in which one person was no more dependent on someone else, nor was any one person more capable than another. On the plane, Garrett and Jon were the only ones who could fly the thing, so their jobs had been more important. Now that it was survival, Garrett was still in charge, but everyone had to pull their weight.

Garrett also saw that Anne had become more agile in her new role. Either that or she was just letting other skills show more. He wasn't sure of her age, but he was guessing she was a little over fifty years old. Of course if she ever asked him to guess out loud, he would say forty-nine. When he thought about it a moment longer, he settled on answering forty-six. It would be safer.

When he went through the hole the aluminum ductwork made enough racket to wake the dead, and it certainly did. He didn't know how many were in the Security office below his feet, but he hoped the ceiling was stronger than it felt under him.

When he slid down the sloping ductwork he was surprised to find they were no longer in a dark space above a ceiling. The section they were over was one of the renovations that had been done in the last few years, and they were under some sort of glass enclosure. He could tilt his head upward and see the sky over him, but there was a brick wall around the entire area that kept the general public from being able to see the ductwork and air conditioning units that were scattered around the enclosure. Glass walls rose above the brick until they met with a glass roof. Modern architecture had to hide the ugly machinery somehow.

Jon and Anne were already standing on either side of a hole that was only about six inches wide, and there were snarling faces a couple of feet below it.

"You just pulled up a light fixture and found this?" asked Garrett.

Jon nodded as if to say he didn't believe it either. The contractors must have cut some corners when they upgraded the terminal.

Garrett peered down through the hole in time to see the infected dead get jostled out of the way by another infected. A third, fourth, and fifth infected all pushed the others trying to get a bite from the living meat standing above them.

"You were right about the pipes," said Garrett. "Try not to get the tips stuck too deep in a skull, and try not to let any of them get too good of a grip, either."

Jon put one foot on either side of the hole, took aim, and let the heavy pipe go like a spear. He immediately jerked it back up and took aim at a second infected. After spearing a few more he started having trouble hitting his targets because of the pile of bodies around the area under the hole.

"This is like ice fishing," he said. "We need to find a new hole."

When they were finally done and didn't hear snarling under them, they had pulled up four light fixtures. There were at least thirty bodies under them, and they hoped there was no way for more infected to get into the area below.

Garrett found the air conditioning return and practically destroyed it to get it out of the way. He stuck his whole upper body down through the opening and turned in every direction to make sure it was safe.

Satisfied that they had disposed of every infected in Security, he swung his feet around and dropped through the hole. Anne and Jon were right behind him. They spread out to check the bodies of the infected to be sure they were no longer a threat, and then began searching for things they needed.

They found more than they could carry, but it wasn't going anywhere, and they could come back for the rest. They loaded up the handguns first. Whoever was in charge of arming the security force had a thing for the Beretta APX, but they weren't going to complain. They were semiautomatic and each held a fifteen round magazine of nine millimeter shells. There was also enough ammunition in the storeroom for a war.

They pushed bags of guns and ammunition up through the hole, and then they worked the rest of the day to get it back to the plane. It took two more trips to get everything hauled from one place to the other, but when they were done they felt like they were ready to take on the world.

11 LIGHTHOUSE

The tarmac where planes were usually lined up at the Charleston Air Force Base was like a war zone. Hundreds of bodies covered the pavement, mostly in pieces. The same couldn't be said for the far end of the runway.

From the rooftops of the buildings around the three US Navy VH-92A's, the Chief and Kathy were watching the advancing horde of the infected. Now that they had reached the wide open fields around that end of the airport, their numbers could be more fully appreciated.

When they had crossed the highway in front of the leading edge of the horde, they had no idea that they were about to be pursued by thousands of the infected.

"What do you think?" asked the Chief. "Should I gas up the weed-whacker?"

Kathy lowered her binoculars and glared at the Chief. When no answer was heard, he lowered his and saw the way she was frowning at him.

"What?"

"You know what," she answered. "Just because it worked this time doesn't mean it will work again. You mowed down a couple hundred of infected. There are thousands in that horde. All it would take is one time going too deep into the crowd with your rotors for you to lose control. You said it yourself, the blades could go too low and hit the pavement, or the impacts could drive you over at an angle."

"But it worked."

The Chief sounded like a little kid who wanted to go on the ride at the circus just one more time.

"Don't even think about it," said Kathy. "I'll tell Captain Miller and ask his men to restrain you."

"You'll tell me what?"

Captain Miller had come up behind them just in time to hear his own name.

"He wants to do it again with that big horde."

Kathy gestured toward the wall of ragged creatures that were slowly covering the airport runways and encroaching onto the military base.

Jim Miller had learned to enjoy these humorous moments with the Chief. Tension was high every day, so he welcomed the Chief's smile. It made his men relax, too.

He leaned over the edge of the building and caught the attention of one of his snipers.

"If you see this man climbing into the pilot seat of a helicopter without hearing from me first, shoot him."

"Sir?"

The young man with the sniper rifle rotated his head back and forth between his commanding officer and the Chief, unsure if the

Captain was kidding. The Chief was smiling, but the Captain wasn't.

Captain Miller saw the confusion and said, "I didn't say to kill him. Just shoot him in the leg."

For a fraction of a second, the soldier appeared to be relieved to have gotten clarification, but then the confused face came back.

"Your men aren't trained to kid around," said the Chief. "Maybe you need to tell him."

"Chief, if you try that again, I'll shoot you myself. If helicopters were meant for mowing down people, they'd have sharp blades. Do you seriously not know that?"

The Captain's choice of words only served to make the Chief smile grow even wider, and Kathy had to turn away to keep from laughing.

"How long before your men will be able to spin up these birds?" asked the Chief.

"Any minute now. As a matter of fact, I think they're going to roll the first one out to have room for the rotors to turn."

They watched as the efficient soldiers hooked a small towing cart to the front of the first helicopter and began rotating it away from the place where it had been hidden under a tarp.

The blades were fully extended and locked into place, so wing-walkers positioned themselves to the left and right of the craft as the soldier towing it turned onto the paved surface leading to the gate. It appeared that the gate was wide enough for the blades to clear both sides, but they wanted to be sure. The wing-walkers were good at their jobs as they rotated the blades just slightly to clear the gate.

As soon as the first helicopter was clear, the second one was in motion. The soldiers were well aware of the progress the horde was making across the runways, and they wanted to be in the air with plenty of time to spare.

The third helicopter was being rotated, and the Chief had to comment to Captain Miller about the proficiency his men showed.

"Jim, I've read the Secretary of Defense's joint statement to all branches of the military about towing aircraft. Some of it is pretty good reading, but your men move helicopters like they wrote the manual."

"Thank you, I'll pass that along to them. After what they saw you do today, I'm pretty sure they think you wrote the manual. They'll appreciate the compliment."

The Chief waited for a minute, and then he cleared his throat.

"I have another favor to ask. Do you mind my asking if you could have one of your men fly that nice executive Sikorsky back for me? It makes more sense for me to fly that thing up north than the seaplane."

Kathy's head jerked around, and this time it was her turn to grin.

"I wouldn't mind riding in the back of that thing on a trip."

Captain Miller said it made sense to him, and then he twirled one finger over his head. On that signal, the VH-92A's all turned their rotors. He walked toward the ladder that would take them to the ground, and told the Chief they needed to grab one of the copilots before they took off.

All three of the Navy helicopters were rapidly reaching their operating temperatures, and Captain Miller put together a crew for the executive bird. They had cleaned the rotors and refueled it, so it was ready to leave with the rest of them.

As they climbed on board, they surveyed the advancing horde one last time. The four sets of rotors were making an incredible amount of noise, so they couldn't hear the sound of the horde. One thing was certain, and that was the horde could hear them, and they had increased their pace across the runways.

The Chief asked the pilot of the Sikorsky to let the others know they should exit to the north and then circle back to the south to get to the Cormorant and the seaplane. It was better to keep the horde moving away from the river, and if they flew directly over them on the way back, the horde would just turn around and follow them.

The first VH92A lifted into the air, rotated to face the opposite direction, and then started forward. The second waited until the first was well away, and then it did the same.

Kathy watched the helicopters fly ahead of them from the comfort of the leather seats in the Sikorsky, and she couldn't help wondering what a survivor on the ground would think if they saw a convoy of four helicopters pass overhead. She felt a moment of sadness for the unknown souls who saw them come toward them, only to disappear in the distance. Maybe it would give someone hope, or maybe it would make them feel hopeless.

They were banking in a row far too soon for Kathy. She felt like riding in comfort just a little bit longer.

The first three helicopters only paused above the Cormorant on the Ashley River long enough to lower their additional personnel and gear to the deck, and then they sped off downriver in the direction of Fort Sumter. At the speed they were going, they would be landing in just a few minutes.

When the Sikorsky was in position over the Coast Guard ship, the pilot gave Kathy and the Chief a thumbs up, and they lowered themselves down. As it pulled away, they jumped into an inflatable rigid hull boat and crossed over to the de Havilland Beaver. It wasn't as comfortable inside the cockpit, but Kathy felt the comfort of the familiar surroundings.

"Where we heading, Chief? Are we spending the night at Fort Sumter or heading home?"

"We need to check in with Mud Island to be sure all is well, then I think it would be safer to spend one night at Fort Sumter. With four helicopters added to the inventory, the Captain will need to keep control of the surface. He can post a watch on the Cormorant and stand guard over the Beaver. Besides, I don't really like night landings with hostile natives everywhere."

"Fort Sumter it is," said Kathy. "We can check in with their radio better. They have much better range than we do."

The Chief rotated the noisy but dependable Beaver to face downriver and brought the plane to full power. The Cormorant was already turning behind them, and he knew everyone was eager to get back to the safety of their shelter.

The Beaver needed a long stretch of river to take off, so it seemed like they were hardly in the air for three minutes before they could see Fort Sumter in the distance. The helicopters were in a neat row across the largest grassy area inside the fort, and they could see several soldiers waiting on the dock for them.

******

"Machetes, everyone," said Tom.

He and Cassandra were already at the end of the dock meeting a small group of infected head on. There was just enough light for us to be able to see the lighthouse up ahead and the gravel path that led to it. The trees weren't too thick, so we could tell if there were infected dead coming our way even in the fading light.

Hampton and I had put together a stretcher using the long poles we had used for depth soundings and to push the boat away from docks. They weren't standard equipment on power boats, but they were useful on ours.

We always had at least one tarp stashed under a seat, so putting together a stretcher wasn't a problem. Our problem was going to be carrying Bus to the lighthouse while fighting off the infected. We could already hear their moans, but we didn't have much choice.

Tom came back to the boat and traded places with me. I wasn't offended by the obvious insinuation that he was stronger and faster than me. Bus had a much better chance to make it to the lighthouse with Tom and Hampton doing the heavy lifting.

Colleen and Jean were still nursing bruises and cuts, but neither of them wanted any special attention. The desperation we all felt was the same. We were about to do a hundred yard dash through the middle of a dimly lit grove of trees, surrounded by an unknown number of the infected.

"Everybody ready?" asked Hampton.

He was on the leading end of the stretcher. He and Tom both lifted as he asked the question.

Cassandra went up ahead and to his right while Colleen took up a position ahead and to the left. Jean and I covered Tom on the left and right. I leaned forward around Tom to where Jean stood with her machete. She gave me a half smile, but I could tell she was scared. We all were.

There were plenty of times when we had our backs against a wall, but we never got over being scared.

"Don't stop, change course, or try to run back to the boat once we get going," said Hampton. "Let's go."

The first infected to step out onto the path ahead of us was so far away that we forgot there would be more before we reached it. As soon as it saw us running straight at it, it moved our way. Less than half way to it, the path suddenly filled with them.

Hampton almost forgot his own advice as the overwhelming urge to change direction caused him to veer slightly to the right. Instinct made him do it, but discipline forced him to straighten out their forward charge again. The discipline saved him.

Cassandra glanced back quickly to be sure everyone was still with her, and that she wasn't charging into the mob of infected all by herself. She saw Hampton swerve slightly and swung her head back around to the right just in time to see that Hampton was only inches from the waiting arms and teeth of two infected.

She hadn't survived on the Mercy ship for as long as she did by being afraid to use unconventional methods. Her machete would have saved Hampton from one of the clutching pair of hands, but not the other. She lowered her right shoulder like a football player and drove it up under the outstretched arm of the infected. It connected squarely with a soft, decayed ribcage, and the infected was launched sideways into a row of them that had suddenly appeared from the trees.

On the back right side, Jean swung high at the nearest head, but her machete found nothing but air because they had all fallen like dominos. She was surprised by the disappearance of her target, but she was ready to deliver a vicious backhand on her next target because her long swinging forehand had set it up so well. She caught one just as it stepped forward, and half of the head disintegrated under her swing.

Tom felt helpless as he watched the events unfold around him. Instead of carrying a stretcher, he wanted to be swinging deadly blows at the infected. Still, he was impressed by the women in our group. He didn't know how they did it, but they seemed to be able to anticipate the places where the next infected would appear.

Colleen had a difficult moment when three stepped onto the path. The Chief had described a similar situation when he had faced three in a grocery store, and I knew her only chance with this group would be to control the one leading the pack.

In what appeared to be one single motion, Colleen slid her machete into her belt and used both hands to reach for the first of the infected, grab its forearms, and spin it around toward the other two. She pushed it right between the shoulder blades, and it disappeared back into the trees on top of the second one. Before it was even out of the way, the machete had reappeared in her hand, and her backswing caught the third one just above the jawline.

Jean and I both had our hands full at the same time, and I desperately wanted to help her, but I couldn't leave the left flank undefended. We both kept running and swinging, and I didn't even notice when we reached the lighthouse.

Cassandra took the lead and went straight through the lighthouse door. Finding it unlocked was such a small blessing after everything else we had been through.

"Clear," she yelled from inside.

Colleen dropped back to join me and Jean as we made room for Hampton and Tom to go through the door to safety. There were two steps up to the door, and Tom stumbled when he hit them, but our forward momentum caused everyone to all land inside.

No one had to tell the rest of us to get inside, and we kicked the heavy wooden door shut behind us. It was totally dark for a moment until Cassandra's flashlight clicked on. She had one hand over the bright end of it so she could limit drawing attention to the light, but it was enough for us to see that we had not found ourselves in bad company.

The room was a stucco side-building attached to the lighthouse, and it was little more than a mud room. A set of steps in one corner led to a second wooden door that was closed. Hopefully, the first floor of the lighthouse would also be as hospitable as the mud room.

"Anybody scratched or bitten?" asked Hampton.

We all started feeling along our own arms and legs to see if there were any injuries, and we had done pretty good considering we had just run a gauntlet.

"It's hard to tell what's new and what's old," said Jean. "I got so many cuts and scrapes from flying onto the beach that I can't tell."

I knew she would need to be checked by someone other than me. We had made it a rule. When we inspected for bites, it had to be done by someone other than a spouse, relative, boyfriend, or girlfriend. Cassandra and Colleen both took Jean off to one corner where they took turns checking each other.

"I have to admit," said Hampton, "you guys can be really bad when you have to be. There can't be many people left alive who could have made that run and come out in one piece."

Tom said, "You should have seen it from my end. It's a sick feeling to be the caboose on a train that can't stop. You ladies up front were scaring me half to death."

Jean added as the ladies finished their injury inspections, "I have a feeling we're all going to be even more scared when we're able to see outside from up above. If there were that many infected between us and the lighthouse, how many are on this strip of land?"

It was a sobering thought, but it reminded us all that we weren't done yet. We needed to get into the main part of the lighthouse to see if there was a functioning radio, and to be able to assess our situation. A view from above might be useless until dawn, but we also needed to find out if the rest of the lighthouse was safe.

Jean checked Bus to be sure he was still with us, and she reported his condition hadn't changed. A lump had appeared on one side of his head, and that at least explained why he was still unconscious.

"He must've turned away at the last second before we hit," she said. "He has some big bruises on his ribcage, too. I'll stay here with him while you guys go check things out. We wouldn't want him to wake up while we're gone."

Jean got comfortable next to Bus, and I gave her a hug.

"Are you sure?"

"I could use the rest, anyway. Getting thrown from the boat was like getting shot out of a cannon. I feel like everything hurts."

We made sure the door was going to stay shut and then added a large storage locker just to be sure. We dragged it over to the door after inspecting its contents and finding nothing really useful. There were some metal pipe fittings that were made out of heavy brass, but unless we could drop them on the heads of the infected, the best thing we could use them for was to leave them in the locker against the door.

We all listened at the door for a moment, and it sounded like the steps outside were overflowing with the infected.

Hampton listened at the door to the next room for a long time and then gently turned the handle. It was also unlocked, but when he pushed on the door, it didn't budge.

"Give me a hand, Tom. I think someone barricaded the door on the other side just like we did."

It was hard for them to get enough leverage, but the door very slowly moved inward. A gap appeared along the left side, and Tom held his flashlight up to the dark line and shone the light into the room. He was just saying he couldn't see anything when purple fingers grabbed the flashlight.

There must not have been air moving on the other side of the door because the smell didn't reach us in time for anyone to warn Tom. When it poured through the gap, everyone gagged, and Hampton pulled the door shut.

"What in hell died in there?" asked Hampton through gasps. "I didn't think there was anything left in the world that could stink worse than what we've already smelled, but that's something new."

"I have to agree," said Cassandra. "When I had to climb down into the ship and go past crew's berthing, I thought I would never get that smell off of me, but whatever it is that died on the other side of that door, it must have been special."

"It's probably just because there's no ventilation," I said, "but we still have to go through there."

"I have an idea," said Jean. "Did I see some old newspapers and stuff in there with those brass couplings?"

Cassandra was the nearest to the storage locker, so she checked inside.

"Yeah, there's a stack of them. Why?"

Jean walked over and picked up some paper and a piece of brass about the size of a baseball and immediately began pushing the paper into the coupling.

"I don't have a clue what this piece of pipe was used for before, but today it's going to be an air freshener. I don't know about the rest of you, but I prefer the smell of burning paper over the smell of......well, whatever that is in there."

Colleen said, "Aren't you afraid it will set the lighthouse on fire?"

Hampton said, "The fire should stay inside the pipe and burn out before it could set fire to anything."

Jean got three of the pipes ready and got close to the door.

"Ed, you can light these for me one at a time as I hold them out to you. Tom, you can push the door just far enough for me to push these through. Hampton, the infected will go after a burning pipe, so you can shoot them when they get in view from the door. With any luck, we can clear the room from here."

Jean paused for a moment as if she was waiting for something. We were all in position and ready to do our part as soon as she gave the word.

"Come on, guys. Isn't anyone going to say that was a good pun or something? You know, like clear the room and clear the air?"

"I knew it," said Tom. "She's been spending too much time around the Chief."

Something groaned on the other side of the door, and Jean said, "At least someone got it."

She held out one of the pipes, and I lit one end. She held it until it was getting enough air flowing through it to keep burning then nodded at Tom. He pushed the door open just far enough, and

Jean shoved it through the opening hard enough to make it roll across the dark room on the other side.

The infected on the other side of the door followed the rolling pipe. Small embers were trailing behind it, but they were burning out as expected.

Nothing tried to fill the gap in the door as the burning pipe rolled to the far side of the room, so Jean held the second one out to me. She was right. The smell of burning paper was better.

She shoved the second one through, and as the infected turned and came back to it, Hampton took his shot. The bullet knocked the infected clear out of our field of vision, and we didn't have much choice but to keep going.

This time Tom pushed harder on the door as I lit the pipe, and Jean was able to throw it to a different spot because of the increasing gap between the door and the frame. Nothing went after it, so Tom and Hampton both pushed against the door together. Something heavy slid out of the way.

Jean dropped back behind Hampton and Tom as we all clicked on our flashlights. Tom retrieved his from the floor nearby, and we went in with our weapons ready.

"Just as we expected," said Tom. "No open windows, and there's another door up there."

A staircase went up one floor and came to an abrupt end at another door. I think all of us studied the door with the same feeling, and our shoulders slumped. It was pretty good odds that the infected we had just killed had been trapped in this level of the lighthouse by someone who had retreated to the level above.

"How many times are we going to have to go through this?" asked Colleen.

"I'll get some more pipes and paper," said Jean.

Despite the possibilities, Hampton was smiling.

"Jean, hold off on the pipe bombs until we check. It could be that the next door was locked, so our friend in here was just stuck."

"He's an optimist," said Colleen.

Despite the fact that none of us believed we were going to be that lucky, we went up the stairs in a group. The wooden stairs creaked enough to wake the dead, but no noise came from the other side of the door. Also, despite Hampton's rationale for why the infected was stuck on this floor, the door was unlocked. Nothing stopped it from opening, but the room also wasn't dark. There were windows on all four sides of the circular walls, and just enough light was coming in from the outside to allow them to see that the room was safe.

A spiral staircase dominated the center of the room, and it went to a trapdoor that stood open. It was at least a reasonable assumption that there were no infected above or they would have rolled down that spiral staircase a long time ago.

There were tables around the walls with equipment of all types. Judging by the assortment of materials, someone had tried to make this place their last refuge. There were boxes of canned food and jugs of water. Batteries, flashlights, propane canisters, a portable cook stove, and best of all, a shortwave radio set.

Tom and Hampton went back downstairs for Bus while the rest of us got busy trying to piece together what we could from the survival gear. There was no power to the cable that ran along one wall to the bench where the radio sat, so there had to be a generator on the grounds near the lighthouse. That wouldn't do us much good unless it was inside a walled area.

"Maybe we can spot the generator from above," I suggested.

I cautiously made my way up the spiral staircase. It was metal, and despite my theory that there were no infected dead on the highest level, I walked as quietly up the stairs as I could.

When I reached the trapdoor, I barely poked my head above the floor above and turned in a circle. From what I could see, the huge light was undamaged, and there were no broken windows.

I climbed up the rest of the way, and first I circled the entire floor searching as best as I could, trying to spot the power source for the lighthouse. The sun had completely set, though, and I couldn't make out anything except the water in the bay. I couldn't even spot the dock where we had left our boat. There was a catwalk surrounding the top of the lighthouse, but I had no urge to test its state of repair by walking out onto it through a small glass door.

I turned to the immense glass and shiny metal device in the center of the room that could only be the light itself. I had never seen one up close before, and I didn't have a clue how it worked, but I imagined anyone standing in front of it when it was turned on was either going to go blind or catch fire.

I don't know what made me do it, but I reached out with both hands and grabbed the light by something that was shaped like handles and turned it. I was totally surprised when it rotated smoothly and silently.

I stuck my head down through the open hatch and called to the others to come up and see the light.

There was less standing room in the top of the lighthouse once we were all up there, but for the moment at least, we were all like a bunch of kids. None of us had ever been in a lighthouse before, and everyone was blown away by how easily the light rotated, and just for the hell of it, we made it spin pretty fast.

"If we could get it to light up, we could at least signal the Chief when he starts searching for us," said Colleen.

"If it lights up," said Tom, "it's going to signal more than the Chief."

I let out a sigh and said, "When Jean was trapped on that Russian ship, all she needed was a little flashlight."

It was totally quiet in the lantern room, as Hampton had called it. He and Cassandra both knew something about lighthouses and at least knew the correct terminology.

It was quiet because they were all staring at me. I was as clueless, as I tended to be sometimes before I realized I was the center of attention.

"When she used the flashlight to signal Mud Island, was anyone watching for her signal?" Hampton asked.

I thought a second and said, "No one would have thought to be watching for a signal if they weren't hoping to see one, and if the Chief starts searching for us, he's most likely going to fly right by here. We just have to be ready with our flashlights."

"There's one option," said Hampton. "The second option is this monster sized lantern. If the Chief searches for us, his first chance to see us is going to be in daylight tomorrow. If we spin this lantern when the sun isn't too high, it should reflect like crazy in all directions, and even if it isn't reflecting much light, the movement of it should be enough to catch the eye of the Chief or Kathy."

We agreed to set up watches in case the Chief flew by at night, and we opened the door to the catwalk so we could hear the sound of the Beaver as it approached. A bonus to that thinking was the fresh air that came through the door and then traveled downward to air out the floor below.

Bus was in bad condition when I checked on him the next time. I not only wanted to see my friend survive, I also wanted to avoid the unpleasant consequences his death would cause. As we settled in for the night, I wanted nothing more than to hear the person on watch yell that the Chief was flying by.

We moved Bus into the room where the lone infected had been stranded, and it was a good thing we did because the door to the mudroom didn't hold. Actually, it wasn't just the door, it was the wall that held the door. The lighthouse was old, and the base walls were thick and strong all the way to the ground, but the mudroom had been added to the outside of the lighthouse.

There was constant pressure being put on the door for hours, and eventually the whole thing collapsed. When it did, we all got ready to go as high as we could because it sounded like hundreds of infected were pushing on the next door. We even considered the possibility that they would be able to push the lighthouse over.

******

The welcoming committee at Fort Sumter wasn't what the Chief and Kathy expected. Captain Miller was waiting out on the dock with an armed squad in case the Chief wanted to start searching for his missing people immediately.

The only non-military people out on the dock were Olivia, Chase, Whitney, and Sam. Under normal circumstances, they would have been all smiles when Kathy and the Chief saw them, but bad news couldn't be delivered with a smile.

Olivia and Chase were an African American couple, rescued from the surface of Fort Sumter by their Mud Island friends when they first took control of the shelter. The surface part of the fort was little more than a savage camp where a sadistic band of survivors was holding people in cages. That's where they were when the Mud Island group showed up.

The other two, Whitney and Sam were hardly more than kids, and they had survived inside the Cormorant at the Coast Guard station for months. They were rescued by Kathy and the Chief when they liberated the Cormorant and put it to good use.

The four friends exchanged hugs and kisses with Kathy and the Chief and broke the news to them about the rest of their friends being missing.

The Chief had listened to the news with a grim face and then gone into the shelter to talk with Molly. She was crying and afraid, but Kathy was able to get her to pull herself together. She told her that everyone was going to need for her to be strong, and that she needed to show she could be strong if she wanted to go outside with them.

Through a series of hiccups and sniffles, Molly described her last contact with her father and the rest of the group. Jean was an aunt to her, and Bus was like her grandfather. They were all family to her, and the radio had gone quiet. She told Kathy that the last time she heard from them, they were entering the bay that went to Georgetown.

"They weren't having any problems up until that time?" asked Kathy.

"No, they were trying to find a buoy they could tow out to the reef where Cassandra's ship sank, and Hampton said there were plenty where he used to live."

"Then there was no more contact?"

"No, Ma'am."

Molly sounded like she was going to cry again, so Kathy distracted her from the topic of the missing friends.

"What are the conditions on Mud Island? Do the camera views show it's safe to come home?"

"There were a lot of the infected out there yesterday. They were everywhere, but a couple of ships went by, and one of them shot some kind of machine gun at them that killed them all."

The Chief was paying close attention, and being a former Navy SEAL, he was keenly interested in the appearance of the ships.

He leaned in toward the microphone and said, "Molly, did your dad or anybody say what kind of ships they were?"

"One of them was a submarine," said Molly. "It was following the ship that shot at the infected. I heard everyone talking about it being a destroyer or a cruiser."

"Were they flying flags, Molly?"

"The ship in front had an American flag on it. The submarine wasn't flying a flag, but it was a really big submarine."

Kathy turned to the Chief.

"What do you make of that?"

"Sounds to me like one of our big ballistic missile subs. It was probably a Trident from Kings Bay, Georgia. I'm glad at least one of them survived. It would make a foreign power think twice about trying to invade while this infection runs its course."

"Should we try to make contact?"

"I'd leave that totally up to Jim Miller. As far as I'm concerned, he's the closest thing to a government representative. Martial law was declared one day into this mess, so he's in charge."

"Okay, Molly, listen to me," said Kathy. "It's getting dark outside, too dark to see. We could go right by them, and even if we do find them, we wouldn't be able to tell what else is out there. You know how tough they are, so you also know they can take care of themselves. What I want you to do is not broadcast from the radio for the rest of the night. You can listen for them, but there could be someone else listening, so don't broadcast unless you hear from us or them. We'll start searching at sunrise."

"Yes, Ma'am."

"That's not all. I want you to watch the cameras and try to keep track of the infected, and I want you to keep an eye out for those ships. Don't broadcast if you see them. Just note the time and give three clicks on the microphone. Wait one minute and give three more clicks. You got it?"

"Okay, Aunt Kathy. I've got it. Over and out."

Kathy signed off and turned toward the Chief.

"What was that all about?" he asked. "Why do you want her counting the infected?"

"I just wanted her to stay busy until she gets sleepy, so I figured she could count sheep. She'll probably fall asleep before she gets to twenty. It's pretty dark out there, and watching those things stumble around through infrared can get boring."

The Chief eyed Kathy and said, "You know, dads are famous for making things up when their kids ask questions they can't answer. I have a feeling your dad did that to you."

"Hey, that's not nice. My dad always answered my questions," said Kathy indignantly.

"That's exactly what I'm talking about."

The Chief walked away fast enough to keep Kathy from answering, and after a minute or two she had a strange feeling that she understood what he meant. All she could do was grin, because in a weird sort of way she felt like it was a compliment.

******

It was an easy decision to use a helicopter for the search because they could get in closer if they were in a tight spot. Captain Miller wanted to send one of the military helicopters along because of the armament, but the Chief convinced him the search area only required one helicopter at the start. Besides, they were completely fueled for the trip north, and he didn't want to stop at the airport to refuel if he didn't have to. He doubted that would be a hospitable place to stop for gas, and they would need to map out locations for the special hybrid fuel used by the VH-92A's.

The sun was just making an appearance above the horizon, but the executive helicopter was already warmed up. Captain Miller leaned closer to the Chief's ear and said something Kathy couldn't hear, but she thought the Chief turned a little red in the cheeks.

Kathy put on a headset and got his attention.

"What did Jim want?"

"Nothing," he said. "He just said he would appreciate it if I would take off straight up instead of the way I did the first time."

"Oh, you mean that thing you did when you went left, then right, then turned around in a circle before you went straight up? I thought you meant to do that."

"I did mean to do that. You always circle to make sure you're clear on all sides."

Kathy thought about it then asked, "Was that a dad answer?"

The Chief lifted the helicopter straight up, then tilted it forward and headed out toward the sea.

Kathy was laughing despite the fact that she felt like her stomach fell on the floor.

They were flying straight at the sun until the Chief passed the end of the jetties, and he made a hard turn to the left. As the crow flies, it was less than sixty miles from Fort Sumter to Georgetown. The Sikorsky S-76D could travel three times that distance in one hour, so the Chief pushed it up to its maximum speed for just a few minutes.

A few miles down the coast from the entrance to the bay that led to Georgetown, he brought the helicopter down to treetop level but stayed out over the water.

He hovered above the jetty with the bird facing inland, and Kathy began scanning the area with her binoculars. She was watching the water, but when she scanned to the right, there was a lighthouse in her field of vision.

"This has to be the shortest search and rescue mission in history," she said.

She pointed at the white lighthouse that stood out brightly with the sun reflecting off of it from the east. Kathy and the Chief had both silently hoped their friends had made it to the lighthouse. As often as they had passed the entrance to the bay, they were well aware of its location, and they knew their friends would have tried to get to the lighthouse if they were stranded in the area.

"The search part of it, yes, but the rescue part might have to be by air. Check out the ground around the lighthouse."

Kathy surveyed the area and let out a low whistle. It seemed like a horde had marched out onto the spit of land surrounding the lighthouse and they were all wondering where the people went.

"I wonder if they knew what was outside when they went into the lighthouse. That crowd is as big as an outdoor rock concert down there."

The Chief pointed toward the small dock where they had left the boat and the path that ran from the dock to the lighthouse.

"They left a trail of bodies, so I'm sure they weren't stopping there because they wanted to. Does the windshield on the boat appear to be half gone to you?"

"Sure does. Something went wrong, and the lighthouse was their only choice."

******

We were expecting to hear the Beaver approaching, and we were going to scramble to the lantern room to start spinning the huge lamp. The sun was at just the right angle to the lighthouse for us to put on a show, but something was different. Jean was on watch and started yelling for us to get up there with her.

The de Havilland Beaver was noisy, but in a really deep throated roar. The sound we heard was powerful, but it was a higher pitch. It was kind of like the difference between a Mustang GT with chrome pipes and one of those cars in the Grand Prix.

Everyone was falling all over each other to get up the stairs, but we eventually all crowded into the lantern room and got ready to spin the light. Jean pointed out toward the jetty, and we all stopped moving. There was a blue and white helicopter flying straight at us at low speed.

Even before it was close enough for us to see who was in the cockpit we knew it would be Kathy and the Chief, and they deserved a welcoming celebration.

It didn't take more than a couple of words, and everyone got the idea. We started rotating the light, and as it spun smoothly around, the mirrors inside caught the sunlight and reflected it toward them.

Although it was something we did because we were overjoyed to see them, it also told them we didn't have a working radio.

Colleen disappeared into the room below and came back with a notebook she had found in a desk drawer. It seems like I can never find a Sharpie when I need one, but Colleen magically produced one and wrote in big letters, "DOC INJURED. STRETCHER."

The Chief maneuvered the helicopter as close as he could to the lighthouse and Kathy held up a sign written on the back of a page she had ripped from a manual. It said, "STAY PUT."

When we gave a thumbs up in their direction, the helicopter banked away sharply and headed south. We all smiled at each other as silence settled over us. We were ready to celebrate, but our friend Bus was still unconscious, and we were all getting worried.

It felt like time was dragging by when we saw the dots appear in the distance. As they grew, the sound of their engines reached us. We had expected the Chief to come back with a helicopter, but we didn't expect this. Two big helicopters were flying straight at us.

The helicopter in the lead hovered in close, and we saw the big US NAVY letters on the side. The side door slid open as the craft hovered in above the lighthouse, and one of Captain Miller's men slid down a rope onto the catwalk.

It turned out to be one of the women in Captain Miller's squad, and she yelled over the buffeting wind of the rotors that she was a medic. She wanted to see Bus before they tried to lift him out.

A second medic slid into view with a stretcher being lowered on a separate line. As soon as he was on the catwalk he grabbed the stretcher and guided it through the door. They were the picture of efficiency as they went down the stairs from the lantern room.

The first helicopter backed away to a safe distance as the second moved in closer. A soldier landed on the catwalk with a second harness line, and before Jean could object, he strapped her in and signaled to raise her up.

One by one we were all lifted from the lighthouse. We all wanted to see them take Bus out first, but the medics insisted that they were stabilizing him and for us to go. As the last of us was pulled inside, the helicopter banked away from the lighthouse so the first one could move in closer for the medics and Bus.

12 GUNTERSVILLE

Bus had a serious concussion, and there was no doubt about whether or not he would be making the trip to Columbus with us. X-rays revealed three broken ribs where he hit the steering wheel in the boat, so he was going to be hurting for a long time.

The medic explained that the concussion was bad, but she didn't think it was life threatening, and she said she expected him to regain consciousness at any time. Thanks to some really fine and well equipped medical bays in the shelters, the medics promised to have Bus back on his feet before we got back from our trip to Ohio.

The helicopters had carried us back to Fort Sumter, and even though we had planned to take all of the medics with us, one would have to stay to take care of Bus. Doctors were scarce in the new world, and we wanted ours to recover.

We had all been impressed by the helicopters, and everyone sat down to make some solid plans about our trip. Any pretense about the Army being in Fort Sumter had been totally abandoned, so we decided to leave the Beaver parked next to the Cormorant. Captain Miller had about one hundred soldiers under his command, so he would be leaving behind more than enough fire power to defend the fort.

If there was someone watching from the Yorktown, the flurry of activity at Fort Sumter had to cause them great concern. That is, if they were hostiles. If they were friendly survivors, it was in their best interests to make their intentions known. Especially since there were now four helicopters, a seaplane, and a Coast Guard vessel at the fort.

We also decided to grant Molly her wish by letting her stay at Fort Sumter while we were gone. Of course, she would have to take care of little Josh for us, but that wasn't going to be a problem for her. There were plenty of troops who couldn't wait to see a real baby in the shelter.

Molly didn't know it, but Captain Miller had already informed his troops that they were to each consider themselves to be her mother and father, and as such, they would be responsible for her every move. Molly was going to have plenty of chaperones, and Sam would be more likely to be kissed by the Chief than he would by Tom's little girl. Not to mention Olivia and Chase. They had lived with Sam at the fort long enough to know he was head over heels in love with Molly, and raging teenage hormones were going to be under constant supervision.

As a strategic precaution we decided to have a small squad of four soldiers stay inside Mud Island. They were given strict orders not to open the door after they were sealed inside, no matter what was happening outside. Their mission was strictly to be nothing more than an observation post, and they would otherwise remain undetected. They would stand six hours of watch and report anything unusual to Fort Sumter. What they did with the rest of their time was their business, but they were told to remember who they were.

Now that we had transportation, we could plan the trip more easily. Until we had helicopters, it didn't make much sense to waste time on the logistics, so we were almost starting from scratch. The Chief had been making detailed plans all along, but as usual, he was being forced to revise those plans.

Bus had gone over locations for fuel with the Chief in the past, and it appeared we were going to be able to choose alternate refueling sites if things weren't quite safe at the main sites.

Just after noon on the day we were lifted from the lighthouse, the Chief spread maps out across the dining room table and traced our route with his finger.

To make the trip easier, his plan was to take us around the mountains instead of over them. West Virginia weather could be pretty hostile when it got cold, and we could avoid the higher elevations by going northwest first.

For those of us who had been there, we recognized our first stop at Guntersville, Alabama. We could refuel there and then fly north to Ohio without having to burn as much fuel as we would by going over the mountains.

"Are we going to go by the Guntersville shelter while we're in the area," I asked.

The Chief nodded.

"The same strategy applies to that shelter as Mud Island. We're going to leave behind a small contingent of soldiers to man it as a listening post. It'll be nice to have eyes and ears in five shelters. That reminds me, someone be sure to check in on our friends at Lake Norman. Let them know that we'll be leaving for Ohio tomorrow since we have transportation."

The Chief didn't direct his instructions at anyone in particular, but we all knew that he was just as likely to be in the control room when the Lake Norman shelter was contacted. We could also see that he thought about Iris Mason from time to time, and he was anticipating the day when people could come and go from the North Carolina shelter.

The excitement of the evening was somewhat tempered by the fact that Bus had been injured, but the mood lightened considerably when one of the medics came in with the word that Bus was conscious.

The medic said he could have a visitor but only one. Then she had to get out of the way as the room cleared in the direction of the medical bay. There wasn't a single one of us that would be left out.

We found Bus propped up on a bed in the room that passed as a medical ward. There were eight beds, and he was in the corner bed farthest from the door. A curtain had been drawn around him for privacy, but that didn't slow down the gang of friends as we burst into the room. Everyone squeezed into the corner with him despite the somewhat amazed pleas of the medic. She finally gave up and sat down on one of the other beds to just watch.

It was Bus who held up a hand and got everyone to be quiet for just a moment. He motioned for Jean to come a little closer to his ear, most likely because she was the shortest person in the room and already closest to him. He whispered something, and Jean understood what she had to do.

She said to all of us in a low voice, "Bus said he has the world's worst headache, and he needs everyone to whisper."

Everyone frowned at each other as if someone else was being too loud, and Jean held a finger to her mouth.

"Everyone line up." Jean took over for the medic. "You get ten seconds to hug Bus and tell him you're glad he's okay, then get out."

We all did as we were told, but it was clear that Bus wanted the Chief and Tom to stay when everyone else was gone. The two of them were huddled over him when the rest of us moved into the hall to wait.

The Chief and Tom came out a few minutes later and explained that Bus was disappointed about not making the trip, but he felt better when they told him they would be leaving a few soldiers in the Guntersville shelter. He had remembered a few personal items that he hoped we would bring back for him, so he gave them a list.

Tom said Bus had wanted to sleep then, but his parting words to them were how much it meant to him that they all came by.

The mood did get better once we knew he was going to be okay. Everyone was more motivated than before, so we all began packing for the trip. Our best guess about the weather in Ohio was that there would be plenty of snow and freezing temperatures at night, so everyone packed cold weather gear.

How long we would stay in Columbus depended upon a lot of things. Our main goal was to find the Presidential shelter, and our secondary goal was to kill as many of the infected as possible.

We were already pretty good at our secondary goal, but we were hoping that the cold weather would have an effect on the infected dead. If they could freeze, we wanted to find out what it did to them the next day. If it made them slower, we could hunt for them during the daylight hours as well as the hours between sundown and sunrise.

The Chief and Captain Miller had spent long hours discussing how we would hunt for the infected. We didn't need the supplies that were left behind in the houses and other buildings, so we decided we would only hunt for the infected that were out in the open. If we made good enough progress outside, then we could begin clearing inside the buildings.

As for the Columbus shelter, it was our hope that we would find the President had made it to safety. If he had, then there would be the beginning of a government in place, and that would be the first step toward recovery from this disaster.

When the hour was getting late I finished packing my gear and went in search of the rest of the group. Jean had finished faster than me and had gone in search of the soldiers who would be the primary caregivers for our son. They would be bringing Josh back with them in the morning when they dropped off the soldiers who were going to stay at Mud Island.

It was a bit strange knowing someone would be living there without any of our Mud Island family, but the soldiers were constantly reminding us that we had saved them more than once. We knew they would take good care of our home for us while we were gone.

I finally found someone who said they knew where my friends had gone. Apparently, they were making a rare visit to the surface of Fort Sumter to enjoy the cool night time air. January on Fort Sumter would mean no mosquitoes. I decided to join them for one of those rare times when we would be able to just enjoy each other's company.

I found them sitting along the wall of the fort facing the harbor. It was as cool as I had expected, which was a good sign for us. If it was freezing in South Carolina, it would be nasty cold in Columbus, Ohio.

To get to the spot where they were sitting, I had to walk up a narrow set of stone stairs and walk the length of the wall that ran parallel to the dock, and I remembered how we had fought off an army of the infected from that same wall. I was close to breathing my last breath when the Chief had appeared out of nowhere and snatched up an infected dead that was just about to sink its teeth into me. I shivered, but it wasn't from the cold.

"Hey, everyone. Am I missing the party?"

They all gave good natured hellos, but of course the Chief had to throw in a comment or two about them not being able to hide well enough.

"I thought you said he never comes up here," he said under his breath to Jean. Of course it was just loud enough for me to hear.

"Honestly, Chief. He's never thought to check up here when I've needed some time for myself," she answered.

I sat down on the wall next to Jean and gave her a kiss on the cheek.

"Anything happening over there?"

I gestured toward the Yorktown over at Patriots Point, but everyone knew I was speaking in general terms about everywhere but Fort Sumter. That included Patriots Point, the big Arthur Ravenel Bridge, and of course the city of Charleston.

"All quiet over by the Yorktown," said Tom, "but we saw lights in the city."

I immediately spun my head to the left as if I would see something over there. It was pitch black and gloomy. The quiet that came from the city was unnerving.

Jean pointed toward the left of the city and said, "It was almost as if someone was walking in White Point Garden with a lantern."

"It disappeared about ten minutes ago," said Cassandra.

We all sat without speaking for a few minutes, and although we were enjoying the solitude, it was likely that each of us was having similar thoughts. The city of Charleston used to be so beautiful at night. The lights along White Point Garden were usually from the streetlights and slow moving traffic, but the park had been there for hundreds of years and had seen everything from the hanging of pirates, Civil War, hurricanes, and now the infected dead wandering along its sidewalks.

"Do you think it was someone?" I asked to no one in particular.

"It had to be someone," said Jean. "We all saw it."

The Chief was usually the one to jump on an opportunity to tease me, and I half expected him to say something about an infected dead carrying a flashlight, but he was uncharacteristically quiet.

"Chief? No comment?" I asked.

The Chief leaned back on his hands and let out a sigh, but his eyes remained fixed on the dark city.

"We're going to have to deal with someone over there sooner or later," he said in a serious voice. "Whoever that was, if they can walk around over there at night, they must have been able to take control of the city without us even knowing it. I can't help but wonder what they think of us, and I hope whatever it is they have planned for us can wait until we get back from Ohio."

******

We had many mornings like this one. Every time we decided we were going to go off and do something crazy, it began this way. Breakfast that was more like a Sunday morning get together of a big family. We had plenty of food, plenty of laughter, and some interesting topics of discussion. One thing that was being avoided was discussion about failure. We had come to believe that we would succeed. Oddly enough, though, the Chief's comment the night before about the inevitable contact with whoever was carrying that lantern seemed to have me unnerved.

The world was still a big place, but there were less living people. The problem was that the living people could now be sorted into a handful of categories. There were those who had plenty and were willing to share. That category described us, and before they were forced to hole up in the Lake Norman shelter, it also described Iris Mason and her band of survivors. There were close to one hundred of them, but they were stuck underground for the time being. When the day finally came that they would be able to leave their shelter, they would be a powerful ally.

The next category of people were those who took from others and had no rule of law. I guess those people have always existed, but in this new world there were fewer people who could stand up against them. So far, we had run into far too many of those types of people, and so far we had managed to reduce their numbers. Over this breakfast, my mind was drifting back to what the Chief had said, and I was wondering which category described the unknown person with the lantern.

I caught just a piece of a conversation that seemed to be gaining interest, or at least a fair number of opinions. Someone had asked the question, "Do you think this disease will ever be cured?"

Opinions ranged from the absolute positive to the absolute negative, but no one differed in their opinion about what would happen if it was cured. Everyone agreed that there was already too much damage done, and that civilization had been set back a long way.

"Cassandra, how close would you say those scientist friends of yours were to finding a cure before they became infected?" asked Kathy.

Cassandra didn't have the right words for what she had seen. It had been so hard to watch them all die as they worked on the cure. She opened her mouth to speak, but then she stopped and started over again.

After a few tries, she said, "They thought they were close, but something tells me it was wishful thinking. They always felt like they had the answer, and they were always scribbling out these weird formulas, but then they would argue, change the formula, and then erase the whole thing. I think they died with wishful thinking but were no closer to a cure than they had been at the start."

That was the only time I had ever seen our big breakfast before a mission become so quiet.

"So, you're saying there's no hope?" asked Olivia.

"I didn't say that. I said the doctors on my ship didn't find the cure. All they really proved was you can get the virus by eating some infected species in the food chain. I suspect it has to be a species that eats the infected as a main source of food in order to increase the content of the disease in their own bodies."

"Makes sense," said the Chief. "That could also mean that people who eat the infected wouldn't necessarily be able to infect other people until after they die."

Colleen put her elbows on the table in front of her and buried her face in her hands. She let out a low groan that caught Hampton's worried attention.

"Are you okay?"

"It's what the Chief just said. It hurts my head just trying to keep up with the way he thinks sometimes."

There seemed to always be that moment when the tension in the group was released by one comment, and Colleen had found it this time. Everyone laughed until they cried, and of course the Chief was trying to innocently explain what he had said. It fell on deaf ears, though, because everyone wanted to move on from a topic we didn't really want to think about until it actually happened.

A few people, myself included, began clearing away their breakfast dishes, and it was like the signal had been given. It was time to go again.

We began gathering our gear at the shaft that led to the surface, and Captain Miller's men took over hauling it up and loading the helicopters. One helicopter pulled away from Fort Sumter to carry the four lucky soldiers to Mud Island and to bring back Molly and Josh. It amazed me to think of how far we had come that we were able to make the transfer of people in such a short time. Compared to our first trip away from Mud Island, it was no more difficult than going to the corner grocery store.

The trip to Ohio was another matter. It was a long trip that was at the outer edge of the range of the Navy VH-92A's which could travel just over five hundred miles without refueling. On a positive note, they could make the trip in less than three hours if they had to. The executive helicopter was just a bit slower than the big Navy birds, but it could still make the trip in about the same amount of time. The plan was to let the Chief set the cruising speed for the group.

We estimated the trip to Guntersville to be no more than four hours including the brief layover to refuel, and then another three hours to fly to Columbus. With any luck, we would be somewhere in the area of the shelter by three o'clock in the afternoon.

By the time we had all of our gear loaded in the helicopters, the Mud Island flight was landing at Fort Sumter. We had each taken a few minutes to drop in on Bus. He needed a lot of reassurance that we would be okay, but he understood why we had to go.

It was also going to be a short but sweet reunion with Molly and Josh. Jean was ready to make the sprint to the big helicopter before its wheels touched the ground, and Tom was right by her side. The Chief had to get in between them and the landing pad and put his toughest expression on his face. He didn't need to say a word, and he would have tackled them if necessary. After what he had done at the Air Force Base, he didn't want to see one more head removed by a helicopter rotor unless it was from an infected dead.

When it was safe to approach, he simply nodded his head at them and they bolted past him.

Molly was towing a suitcase on wheels behind her just as if she was making a trip to visit relatives. Someone had shown considerable concern and placed a big set of soundproof headphones over her ears. She was a lot taller to me, probably because I hadn't seen her away from Mud Island that I could recall.

I saw one of the soldiers hold out a squirming bundle to Jean, and she smothered poor Josh with kisses. The headphones were big on Molly, but they were just plain ridiculous on Josh. Jean hugged him as she walked in my direction.

I didn't think I would ever get used to being a father, and the way I saw it, that was more fun than being used to it. I wanted each time I saw Josh to feel like the miracle he was. He was born at a time when so many people had lost their loved ones, and I wanted to soak in every detail about him with complete disbelief for as long as I could.

Jean handed him to me, and I was rewarded with a smile that rivaled any I had seen on the face of his namesake, Chief Joshua Barnes. He was just over six months old, and he was growing too fast. Jean didn't realize how much I had missed him when we were forced to spend the night in the lighthouse, and neither one of us had let on to the other how afraid we were that he would lose one of us that night.

I got my chance to hold Josh for a few minutes, and then Jean ran away with him to show him off to Olivia and Whitney. Poor Chase didn't know what to do with a baby, so he just kind of hung back and watched, probably wondering if that was in his future.

The helicopters increased power as they were brought up to their optimum flight temperatures. Unlike at the Air Force Base, we had the luxury of time to treat them properly as we prepared to leave.

I saw Tom and Kathy talking with Molly, and Molly wiped the back of one arm across her eyes. Tom was doing his best to reassure her, but this would be the longest trip so far, and we had no idea what we would find in Columbus.

Captain Miller came up to where I was standing and gave me a good slap on the back. Even though I was ready for it, he was a strong man, and I wound up taking a couple of steps forward.

"Status lights for the active shelters still shows green for Columbus," he shouted over the sound of the helicopters.

"That's good," I yelled back. "At least we know someone made it there safely."

Tom had let Molly loose, and she was in a big neck hug with Kathy. Tom, in the meantime, had found Sam and was having a little talk with him. Sam didn't seem like he was afraid, but he was standing at attention like one of Captain Miller's soldiers.

"Tom's explaining life to Sam," I shouted.

"I have a feeling Sam understands life and death better than most people right at this moment," laughed Captain Miller.

If I recalled correctly, Sam was two, almost three years older than Molly, so Tom was willing to put up with a crush, but that was all. For Sam's sake, as well as Molly's, I hoped their time together was memorable, but not too memorable.

All too soon the signals were given for everyone to climb aboard their assigned helicopters, and I had to give Josh a quick hug then help Jean to break away from him. The surprise on her face when we climbed into the spacious cabin of the executive Sikorsky S-76D helped get her past the sadness of leaving again.

There were wide, brown leather seats for everyone and a table that came down across the center of the cabin. The refrigerator had been stocked and our extra gear was tucked away but not where we couldn't get to our weapons fast. Since Kathy was up front with the Chief, we had an extra seat that allowed us to spread out even more.

When the door slid shut, we were amazed by how quiet it got. Apparently the designers of the Sikorsky took comfort seriously. The Chief turned around and told everyone not to worry about the noise. The rotors tilted forward in flight to reduce it even further.

The Chief was getting a little better from practice, and his lift off from Fort Sumter was slow and easy. I didn't have a good view straight down at the fort, but as the helicopter rotated to point west, I saw the big Navy helicopters hovering in formation. The Chief talked into his microphone, and I heard him telling the other pilots that he was ready to proceed to the first destination. The helicopter tilted forward, and we left Charleston behind.

Kathy turned around and motioned for everyone to put in the earphones that she was passing out. She pointed at digital ports located near each seat, and we all plugged them in. Her voice came through clearly.

"As you can guess, these are miniature headsets. There's a small microphone located on your cords. Find it and give it a little squeeze when you talk. Everyone please give me a sound check."

We each tested our microphones so Kathy could tell we were all receiving her.

"Okay, everyone. We should reach Guntersville in about three hours, and the plan is to land on the golf course. We'll move in one at a time to refuel, but for those of you who were with us on the first trip, you'll recall that the fuel pump is located on the dock. We don't know who, if anyone, has been on those docks since we were there before, but we should anticipate that someone has been at least trying to get to the fuel. If the infected are still climbing out of the lake through the boathouse, they're bound to get excited when they hear four helicopters landing on their lawn. We'll be landing in formation with the Navy helicopters surrounding us. They will deploy shooters as soon as we touch down. Does anyone have any questions?"

I raised my hand and then squeezed the microphone.

"I don't have a question, but I want to remind everyone of something else. The grass will be much taller on the golf course, and the infected may be unable to leave without falling in the water. Some will stray inland and fall down in the grass. Don't let anyone get bitten on the ankles."

The Chief's voice came over the radio. He thanked me for the suggestion and then made a radio call to the other three helicopters. If it was as peaceful as it had been when we saw the country club for the first time, no one would expect it to be as dangerous as we knew it could be.

Tom keyed his microphone and asked, "How are we going to get into the shelter? I'm sure everyone can see that the helicopters can't land close enough to Green Cavern, and there's no way someone could risk swimming to the entrance."

Green Cavern was the main entrance to the shelter. A lake went right up to the cave, and there wasn't a piece of ground big enough for a helicopter to land. The shelter entrance was an elevator that was lowered from the ceiling of the cavern. When it was recessed into its original location, you couldn't even tell it was there.

"Couldn't we use one of the escape hatches to get inside?" asked Jean.

The Chief shook his head from side to side.

"We could lower people to one of the hatches, but we would be advertising its location too well. We want to get Captain Miller's people inside quickly without drawing too much attention to the shelter."

"So, what's the plan?" Tom asked for a second time.

"We have two options," said the Chief. "We can use one of the seaplanes or one of the boats from the country club. I know we failed at our last attempt to get another seaplane from there, but we have more firepower this time."

After discussing our plans a bit more, we settled in for the trip. At times it seemed like it was taking forever to get there, but when I checked my watch, I was really surprised to see how fast time went by.

We were passing Atlanta at high speed, but there was plenty of time to use binoculars to study the city. It would be an understatement to say that we were surprised by what we saw. The tallest buildings in Atlanta were still safe from being completely swallowed by green, but even the lower temperatures of winter hadn't completely turned the invading plant life brown. It was just too thick along the streets. Where it had turned brown, we could see that it had completely blanketed the cars and lower buildings. Roads were hidden, as well as bridges and overpasses.

"It must be ten to twenty degrees warmer down there than usual," said Tom. "The kudzu growing wild must've swallowed everything last summer."

"What's kudzu?" asked Colleen.

It seemed like everyone in our helicopter knew what kudzu was except Colleen because we all started to tell her at the same time. We all stopped when we realized everyone was talking.

Colleen held up both hands and said, "I get it. I'm not from the south, but I heard enough in all that to know kudzu is a pain in the butt vine that grows like mad and is hard to get rid of."

"Before the infection," added Tom, "Atlanta had a crew of about twenty-five people whose only job was to go around Atlanta cutting down the kudzu."

As we left Atlanta behind us, the foothills got higher, and before we knew it, we were entering the valley between the mountains that surrounded Guntersville, Alabama.

We used the same route as the first time, and the convoy of helicopters flew across the quiet town at high speed. If there was anyone on the ground as we approached, they didn't reveal their presence.

We saw that the main street leading through town in the direction of the country club had been barricaded at some point in time. Whether the reason was to keep something in or keep something out, there was no sign of the people who put it there. Buildings inside the barricades were also boarded up, and more had been burned to the ground.

The most striking difference about the town of Guntersville was how green it had become. Lawns weren't just overgrown, they had also become homes to a variety of shrubs and vines. When the yards had become choked and unable to contain the vegetation, it had climbed the buildings. Some buildings had completely disappeared beneath the greenery.

There was also a noticeable difference in the water. It had risen considerably, and in some places it had crested roads and streets among the houses. The only explanation was that the Tennessee Valley Authority was no longer in a position to regulate water levels at the dams. If the water came through the dams, towns like Guntersville might be completely submerged in a year or two.

We were over water a few moments later and moving straight for the country club.

"Okay," said the Chief. "Heads up everyone. Be alert for anything unusual. If you think something feels wrong, say so."

If anyone was watching, it had to be an impressive sight to see four helicopters arriving in the valley. It was almost noon, and the sky was a startling blue, unlike our first visit when it seemed like all it did was rain.

The country club had been a magnificent structure at the upper end of the small peninsula that jutted out into one of the large lakes. The last time we had seen it, it was mostly intact with the exception of the big plate glass windows facing the golf course to the south.

It had aged a hundred years already. Without the insulated windows to keep the elements out, the building had suffered greatly. We figured in a year or two it would collapse under the rot caused by the rain and the cold temperatures.

The grass on the golf course had grown tall, but it was as green as ever. If anyone cared, the grounds keepers could cut it and have people on the tees within a couple of hours. Of course they would still be forced to deal with thousands of tiny pine trees that had also managed to sprout on the fairways and the greens.

In the distance we could see the brick wall that had surrounded the exclusive country club, and it had disappeared under vines that totally concealed the red of the bricks beneath it.

We sat down facing the small dock near the maintenance building where we had found the infected waiting for the chance to walk out of the lake. The lead helicopter was the closest to the maintenance building, and we saw Captain Miller's men fan out to the left and right as they jumped to the ground.

Once they were clear of the rotors, they began moving forward and targeting something inside the building. It was only a few seconds before the first of the infected began wandering out into the open from the darkness of the building.

When the soldiers opened fire, they moved forward fast and reached the big door that had caught us by surprise on our first visit to the country club.

The last time we had seen it, we were caught off guard when it had opened too easily. Counterweights had made it go up too fast for us to stop it, and we found ourselves facing off with several guard dogs that were ready to find something to kill. This time Army M4's beat back the threat from inside, and then the soldiers pulled the door permanently closed.

The Chief was talking to someone in the lead VH-92A and then relayed to us that the infected were still using the boat ramp to get back onto the golf course. He said the building was full of them.

It was when the Chief was facing us that he saw movement beyond the helicopter that had landed on the right flank. There was a lot of activity in the trees that divided the fairways on the golf course. He immediately radioed to the others that the threat was at three o'clock from their position.

Apparently the infected had wandered off in that direction instead of just walking back into the water by the boat dock. At least one hundred of them were walking slowly toward the newcomers that had landed on their piece of property.

Captain Miller's voice came over the radio, and he asked if anyone had any guesses about why they were moving so slowly.

Kathy answered that the temperature had been in the twenties the night before if it had been anywhere near the average for this time of year, and maybe they were slowed down by the freezing cold.

"That would be good news considering where we're going," he answered. "What's the temperature in Columbus today?"

Kathy flipped through some notes and answered, "Twenty-two with a high of about thirty-six. They should be having a really hard time getting started without their morning coffee."

Captain Miller's voice came over the radio, and despite the Chief's tendency to call the shots, he had to remember that there were three helicopters full of the Captain's men on this trip, and he was their commanding officer.

His orders to all pilots was to rotate landing and refueling, then move off to a safe distance and land but keep the engines hot. The VH-92A that was transporting the new residents of the Guntersville shelter was instructed to refuel while standing guard over them as they checked out the boats and seaplanes that were still tied up at the dock.

One by one the helicopters moved into position for refueling while keeping a close eye on the slowly advancing horde. There was no real reason to waste ammunition firing at them because they were so slow it would take them a week to cross the golf course. We were glad to see that we had been correct in our assumption that they could freeze.

The two float planes that had the big TWA on each wing refused to start. There had been more planes when we were in Guntersville the last time, and it was no surprise to see some were gone.

The soldiers moved to the boats that were tied up alongside the float planes and had better luck. Since it would take longer for them to reach Green Cavern by boat, they were ordered to proceed to the shelter while we refueled.

The Chief took his turn at the fuel pumps and didn't waste any time. The trip to Columbus was going as planned, and we were on schedule.

The last of the Navy helicopters was refueling when we got a radio report from the soldiers who had left by boat. They were under attack and needed support.

The fishing boats that were chasing the four soldiers must not have seen the helicopters over at the country club, or they would have thought twice about what they were trying to do. The VH-92A's weren't combat helicopters, but they were loaded with combat veterans.

It didn't take long for us to catch up with the boats, and we could tell Captain Miller had developed a real sense of humor. He didn't need to kill anyone today, and there was always a chance that the men in the boats were just trying to survive. They weren't firing at the soldiers even though we could see they were armed.

Instead of just closing in on the two fishing boats and provoking them to shoot at the helicopters, Captain Miller had his formation drop down to only a few feet above the water and ease up slowly behind them. When they heard the thumping of the rotors behind them and saw what was there, they couldn't break off their pursuit fast enough. Both boats turned so sharply that they almost capsized.

The order was given not to waste fuel by following the boats. Our goal was Columbus, Ohio, and all we needed to do here was to see the soldiers safely inside the shelter. To save even more fuel, we all flew to the nearest highway and followed it to a large parking area where we could all land together.

Highway 67 was close enough to Green Cavern for us to respond again if the men needed help, so we kept the engines hot and waited.

When the idea of returning to Green Cavern first came up, Bus was so happy to know his shelter would be occupied again that he couldn't wait to pass along his secret about how to lower the ceiling elevator that would carry the soldiers up to the hidden entrance. There was a remote hidden in the cave entrance that had to be activated by a code. He gave them the location of the remote and the code, and if the infected weren't in the way, they would have no problem getting inside.

The last time we had come to Green Cavern, there was a unique hazard we were hoping had run its course. Bodies were falling over the cliff from above.

Just like Mud Island and Lake Norman, every shelter had something outside that appeared to be a place of refuge for survivors. That way, the survivors wouldn't investigate any further. The mountain that hid the shelter inside Green Cavern had a small town built on top of it, and the town had been populated by survivors when the infection spread. The problem was that someone made a hole in the wall that surrounded the town, and the infected were thrown through the hole. Eventually, there were too many infected outside the walls, and they began falling into the lake right in front of the entrance to Green Cavern.

Getting in or out of the Cavern meant dodging falling bodies, not an easy thing to do in a boat or seaplane. The soldiers were told to approach carefully, and hopefully the body storm had abated over time.

They were also warned that the infected that landed close enough to shore could walk up the gentle slope of the bank at the cavern entrance, and some could be either in the water or already inside the cavern.

We listened to their radio reports as they approached, and there were no bodies dropping from above. There also didn't appear to be any inside the cavern. That meant they were either in the water or had wandered too far into the cavern.

Since our maps and reference information showed there were one hundred and eight square miles of lakes, time had allowed the infected to become spread out as they filled the lake. That was almost as big as Atlanta, so they had plenty of room to spread out. None of us would recommend swimming there, but it was becoming less likely that you could run into the infected in the water.

The soldiers found the remote and had lowered the ceiling elevator. We waited until we got a radio transmission that they were safely inside, and then the signal was given to begin our trip to Columbus.

13 COLUMBUS COLD

Staying warm was possible during their first winter in John Glenn International Airport, but that didn't make the crew of Executive One feel lucky. Before the infection some people who lived in Columbus would talk about anything except winter. That was an off-limits subject. There were colder places in the world, but that didn't make them feel better, either.

When the temperature started getting down below freezing, they added layers of clothing. They all knew their feet needed to be kept warm, but they almost learned the hard way that your feet will sweat and get cold, so they had to change their socks more often. Fortunately, there were plenty of socks and pantyhose in airport luggage. The men balked at first, but the women convinced them to try the pantyhose, and they finally gave in.

When it got even colder, which was hard for them to believe, they used some of their precious battery power in their plane to run the microwave.

Mike liked to camp during his off time between flights, and he had learned some crazy survival techniques. There was an Asian restaurant in the terminal, so they weren't surprised when they found a tremendous supply of rice. Susan had joked about them not going hungry, but Mike was the one who told them it would help them stay warm in the winter. He searched the terminal and found enough fleece to sew together a pile of small bags filled with rice. He warmed the bags in the microwave and then shoved them into the bottoms of the sleeping bags they had made from coats and blankets. Surprisingly, the rice bags stayed warm most of the night, and so did they.

On sunny days, the large windows of the terminal would heat small sections for the survivors, but the ceilings were so high that the heat was quickly lost. They were forced to put doors over their access points in the ceilings because of the updrafts they created. In the end, they stayed covered at night and moved around during the day to stay warm.

The security office was a treasure trove of useful equipment, and when they found binoculars they didn't seem half as important as the guns, flashlights, or foul weather gear. They were added to the inventory the crew had compiled.

When Sim remembered the binoculars, he knew how much he needed them. He also had to get as high as he could to be able to see in all directions. He had navigated planes for so long that it was only natural for him to map the ceilings of the terminal, but when he finished that chore, he wanted to start learning more about the area around the airport.

When he talked it over with Jon, the copilot wasn't too sure it was going to make a difference if they learned the terrain or not. He pointed out to Sim that there were just as many of the infected out there now as there had been when they first landed.

Sim wasn't sold on the idea that there were more infected, but he was sold on the idea of knowing which way they should go if they ever tried to leave the airport.

The open area over the security office gave him what he needed. He went there because he knew he could at least see the runways without the infected seeing him. Once he had managed to scale the low wall that kept the unsightly air conditioning and heating units hidden, he was able to begin circling the terminal, and he was surprised to find maintenance doors that gave him access to other parts of the roof even higher than before.

Sim spent weeks during the warmer weather circling the top of the airport and making notes on a stack of maps. When the weather got colder, he was so busy mapping that he didn't realize it at first, but the infected were moving slower. Not only that, there weren't as many as before.

When he told the rest of the crew about what he had seen, there had been several days of debates about making a break for it when the weather got really cold. He was convinced that they could find a place that was much more secure than the airport, and that their supplies couldn't last forever.

When they put it to a vote, they were tied at three votes for and three votes against leaving, but Anne hadn't voted yet. In a lot of ways, she was even more experienced than the pilot, and at the age of fifty she was so used to people asking for her opinion that she seldom ever offered it unless she was asked.

This was one of those times. She listened to the debates without saying anything, weighing one side then the other. It made sense that the airport was limited to whatever they could find, but it also made sense when Jon, their copilot, said there were a lot of people out there who would love to have a place like the airport to hole up.

When Susan voted that they should leave the airport, Anne knew it was only because Susan wanted to try to reach home where she would be safe with her husband and three-year-old son. Anne doubted Susan would ever see home again, and neither would she, for that matter.

Addison also sided with Sim, but Anne noticed how the young flight attendant seemed to hang on to every word that Sim said, and she especially liked calling him by his nickname. Anne didn't believe the attraction was enough reason to give up the safety of the airport terminal, but she tried not to let that be her deciding factor.

The pilot and copilot were sticking together, and Sim tried to make an issue of that, saying it was only because they had flown together so many times, but even Susan and Addison didn't agree with his reasoning.

Sim was ready to leave the airport on his own when Garrett asked Anne what she thought.

"How long have we been here?" asked Anne.

"Several months," answered Sim a bit more harshly than he intended.

"I'm sorry, Anne. This place is getting to me, and it's getting colder every day."

"That was my reason for asking, Sim. Ever been through an Ohio winter before? There are lots of places that get colder, but it always feels colder here."

"What are you getting at, Anne?" asked Mike.

The lone male flight attendant had sided with the pilot and copilot and been accused of siding with the men, but the expressions on the faces of the entire crew had been enough for Sim to apologize immediately.

"I think we wouldn't last a day out there because we wouldn't be just trying to keep from being bitten. We would be freezing to the bone at the same time. It's kind of hard to stop and build a campfire when Jack Frost is nipping at your nose and dead people are nipping at everything else."

The rest of the crew was totally quiet. Most of them were inspecting their fingernails or some spot on a piece of clothing, but it was Sim who broke the silence.

"Jack Frost?"

He didn't think he would ever quit laughing, and everyone was wiping tears away from their cheeks by the time they got done.

"Where did you come up with that, Anne? I have to admit, the visual even had me changing my mind. Too cold to go. I get it."

The decision was made that they would stay, but once it got warmer they would talk about it again. They also agreed it would give them time to be rescued, and it would give them time to figure out where they should go if they weren't rescued. They also would have a chance to find out if those creatures could freeze to death, and if they did, they could consider whether or not they should go further north to the Great Lakes.

As the seasons changed, the crew of Executive One became more and more like family and neighbors, and just like any family or neighbor, there were disagreements and changes in the relationships.

Garrett Carson had been a pilot for too long to be anything except the father figure he had always been toward his crews. No matter how long the flight or how many times he flew with the same people, he felt a sense of responsibility that kept him from feeling attractions. Addison Yancy had become his daughter. When she started thinking too much about her parents or the young boyfriend she had left behind, Garrett's broad shoulders were where she would turn.

Eventually she and Mike Wood began spending more time together, and the prospect of romance was enough to keep both of them going.

Anne Hill had maintained the composure for the group on more than one occasion. Sim had accepted the agreement to wait through the winter before trying to venture out from the airport, but he was like a caged animal at times. He didn't mean to take his frustrations out on everyone else, but sometimes his temper just boiled over. Anne couldn't help but notice she had far more gray hair than the day when they had taken off from Andrews Air Force Base with the President of the United States on board. It seemed like yesterday at times, and it was also such a distant memory that sometimes she felt like it didn't happen.

One night when they were all bundled up and huddled together inside a makeshift shelter they had built in the corner of one of the restaurants, Sim confessed to them that he had decided to leave without any of them knowing it.

They were all surprised, especially since they could still see the infected wandering around outside. There weren't as many, and they were moving slower because it was so cold, but there were still far too many to get far without being seen by them.

Jon King and Susan Morris were close to each other in age, so it wasn't really a surprise to anyone that their common losses and grief had made them close to each other. When Sim made his confession, Jon and Susan were together under a blanket sharing their body warmth.

"Why would you do that?" asked Jon. "You know what it's like out there. If the infected don't get you, the cold will."

"I'm the odd man out," said Sim. "I'm not saying you guys wouldn't be glad to get back to your families, but at least you have each other."

"You have all of us, too, Sim. You know that," said Garrett.

"You know what I mean, boss. It's not the same thing."

All of them called Garrett "boss" when they wanted to make a point about who was in charge. Even now, Sim didn't say it in a derogatory way. It was more of a sad sounding term of respect.

No one could really find a way to make it sound like Sim was wrong. Each of them searched in vain to come up with a way to say that he had as much to live for as they did, but no matter how they said it, Sim said it had nothing to do with living. It had everything to do with how they lived.

The subject dropped, but during the night when Sim said he had to go to the bathroom, he didn't come back. After it became a prolonged trip from the warmth of the shelter, the rest of the crew split up into pairs and began the search. It didn't take long for them to know Sim must have gone up through one of the ceilings, and wherever he was trying to go in the middle of a cold, snowy night, he had too much of a head start for them to find him.

Over precious cups of coffee from their dwindling supplies, the remainder of the crew spent the rest of the night talking about Terrance Simmons and hoping he found a way to be safe.

******

Sim felt colder than he had ever been in his life, but he thought all he had to do was make it one day at a time. He knew he wanted

240

to head south even though the warmer climate meant more chance of meeting with the infected, but he didn't think there was a reason to stay where it got so cold that they could hear your teeth chattering.

He had followed his usual path through the ceilings until he reached the spot where he had put together a small stash of supplies. He felt guilty about taking them from his friends, but he told himself he wasn't taking more than his share. As a matter of fact, he could take less because he could find more supplies on the road.

Sim gathered together his traveling gear and climbed out onto the broad, flat roof of the main terminal. His goal was an access ladder he had found that was originally sealed off by a steel gate and a lock. He had removed the lock well in advance and even made one exploratory trip down the ladder. In daylight he had found that it came down behind a row of luggage trams that had been parked in a way that was to his advantage. If he found there were too many infected nearby, he could climb over the trams faster than they could.

Snow was swirling around him as he started down the ladder, and he almost slipped on the icy metal rungs several times. He felt lucky that they had found cold weather gear in abundance when they searched maintenance areas, and the gloves were keeping his fingers from freezing. He still couldn't believe people actually chose to live in such a cold place.

A few feet from the bottom of the ladder Sim stopped and listened for the low moaning sound those monsters made. He used to think they only made that sound when they were after people, but he had heard them from the safety of the roof many times before the cold weather came, and he knew they just made the sound because that was something they did.

They also stood still for long periods of time for no particular reason, and that's what scared him even more than the moaning and groaning. At least then he knew where they were.

Satisfied that there wasn't anything to hear, Sim went down another rung. He tried to adjust his eyes to the darkness and the swirling snow, but all he could see was big, dark shapes. He couldn't tell if there was anything else.

Two more rungs down, and his feet would be at the end of the ladder. That would put him just within reach of anything standing in the dark that he couldn't see. He listened again and decided that this wouldn't be the last chance he would have to take. He extended his left leg downward and reached for the ground with his toes. He was committed now, and if something was there, he wouldn't be able to get away from it. He braced himself for the bite he imagined would hurt worse than the cold, and slowly got both feet onto the ground. He kept his hands above his head on the ladder and listened, but the pounding of his heart would have drowned out almost everything else.

It was too dark for him to see the infected that were standing nearby, but it wasn't too dark for him to see his own breath. He let it out in one big burst, not realizing that he had been holding it in. It sounded like a gust of wind, and there had been plenty of such gusts every cold night, but at the end of his exhale, he heard a groan, and he only needed to say one word.

"No."

That brought out a chorus of groans from all around him, and they were close.

The ladder wasn't an option, and Sim knew it. His legs would have been ripped to shreds before he could pull them to safety. He felt something tugging at him from behind, but he saw movement out of the corner of his right eye at the same time, so he spun in that direction first.

He would never know how that single move had saved him from an infected dead that had grabbed his backpack. As he spun to his right to face the infected he had seen, the infected behind him had been unable to let go of the straps, so it had spun along with him until it hit hard against the metal ladder. The impact would have knocked a living person unconscious, but the emaciated head of the infected dead cracked like an egg. In the darkness Sim felt as if his backpack was lighter.

Sim fell forward with all of his weight onto the infected that he had turned to face. They both went down hard onto the nearest luggage tram, and the infected stopped moving. Its head had hit the tram just right.

Sim lifted his head from where he was laying on top of the grisly mess that used to be a person. All he could see was the dark shapes of the trams and the long ago unclaimed luggage that was piled with snow. He would have given anything to use his flashlight just for a moment, but he forced himself to stay calm and wait.

There was a plane sitting on the tarmac not far away, and it seemed to blend in with the snow and the darkness at the same time, but all Sim could do was focus on the extended wheel struts. His eyes kept trying to tell him that there were people or infected dead standing still next to the wheels.

After several moments of doubt and wondering if he could make it back up the ladder, Sim crawled off of the body and stayed on the ground. He was thinking how crazy he had been to try this at night. At least in daylight he would have been able to start covering some ground. He didn't know how much time had passed already, but he didn't consider this to be progress,

He came to a gap between the trams and saw he had just enough light to be able to tell there was nothing moving in his path, so he eased himself forward and began a halfhearted jog away from the terminal. For the first time in months he felt alive.

That feeling lasted about a minute. Out in the open with no real cover he saw his mistake. Thousands of people had died at the airport, and even though many of them had wandered away from the airport to other places, the infected dead had emerged from the neighborhoods around the airport in even greater numbers. They had been drawn to the flames, the frantic activity of that terrible day, and the screams of the dying. More and more infected had been in the area or were on their way.

Sim had seen them from the top of the terminal, but he had not seen them travel in hordes as if they were going somewhere special. He didn't know that so many had come from the highways and the runways into the wind shelter of the airport buildings, and he knew that he should have checked one more time before sneaking away from his friends.

The infected horde had stopped moving, and where they stopped, the cold, the wind, and the snow had piled up against them in drifts. Some remained standing, but hundreds of them gave in to the elements and sat down. There they had been buried in a motionless state until they heard the collective excitement of the infected nearest to them. One by one they were stirred into motion and shook off the snow.

The lower limbs of the infected that had remained still for too long didn't want to cooperate. Those infected crawled or stumbled even slower than usual, but there were so many. Sim turned in a circle, and in the darkness he could see movement close by on all sides.

He didn't run because being free made him feel alive. This time he ran to stay alive, and he ran as hard as he could on the slippery ground. He knew he was passing hundreds of the infected that were reaching for him, and he no longer had a clear path in a straight line. He began weaving past the mounds of snow that dotted the ground.

He didn't know if he was on asphalt or grass when his lungs started to hurt, but he also didn't think there was anywhere he could go that was safe. He felt tired, and he felt his will fade.

The dark building loomed above him, and the tail of a large plane was extended out into the open above his head. Sim stumbled blindly between the huge wheels of the plane and climbed the front wheel strut without really thinking about it, but in the back of his mind there was a memory about what might be at the top of the wheel.

******

Sim thought he had been cold before, but he decided he didn't know the meaning of the word before spending the night in the wheel well of Air Force One.

He remembered climbing up into the well, and he remembered that there was a whole gang of the infected following him. After that, he was so tired and cold that he just wanted to sleep. When he woke up he was a bit surprised to be alive because he thought falling asleep was what everyone did when they froze to death.

Sim moved his right leg, and the pain was almost enough to make him scream. The same thing happened when he grabbed at it and his left leg moved. He bit his tongue, gritted his teeth, and squeezed his eyes shut as hard as he could. When he opened his eyes, he was staring downward into the faces of several infected dead.

Even though he hadn't screamed, his movement had been enough to draw their attention. They started groaning and reaching upward, and the crowd grew.

Sim inspected the inside of the wheel well and tried to remember why he had climbed up there in the first place. He studied the seam of shiny aluminum above him and remembered that the Boeing 747 had a hatch in the cockpit that would allow the crew to lower the nose landing gear manually with a hand lever of some kind. The problem was, it wasn't likely to be unlocked. After all, this had been the President's plane.

He laughed softly to himself when the thought crossed his mind that maybe all he had to do was knock. Then he slowly moved over inside the well until the hungry faces below couldn't see him anymore.

At sunrise of the following day, the crew of Executive One decided they should at least try to trace Sim's steps in case he was in trouble and still nearby. They had been surviving together in the terminal for a long time, and family didn't just let family die.

They knew his most likely escape route would be the roof, and he wasn't the only one who had found the ladder. As a matter of fact, Garrett knew of at least four more just like it. They carried weapons with them they had gotten from the security arms locker, but they were for defensive purposes only because there was nothing suitable for distances beyond a few yards. Besides, they didn't plan to leave the safety of the roof unless they had to.

The snow had stopped falling, but it had snowed enough through the night to cover Sim's tracks, so they decided to go straight for the ladders. It didn't take long for them to get a good idea where Sim had gone even without footprints.

All six of them sat down on the roof when they reached the ladder facing across the airport toward the big hangar where Air Force One was parked. It was like another big crowd at an air show. Air Force One was in town, and everyone showed up to see it. For over one hundred yards in every direction, the infected were pushing their way in under the tail of the big 747.

"I guess I don't have to ask if anyone else thinks Sim went in there," said Garrett.

Addison cried quietly, and Mike put his arm around her shoulders. She just leaned her face into him and sobbed.

Anne said, "Do you think we could draw them all away from there with gunfire? I mean, what's the worst that could happen? All they would do is come over here. They can't get in."

They had spent so long trying to remain undetected by the dead that the idea of drawing their attention was unthinkable. They were sure about the concourses being totally closed off, and even if they weren't, they doubted the dead could navigate the airport to find them just because they were attracted to this single spot. Anne could see that she had them interested by the way they reacted, but they still weren't convinced.

"We know something's making the infected go into that hangar," said Susan. "How do we know it's because Sim went in there?"

"I hate to say it," said Jon, "but Susan has a point. What if it's not Sim?"

"What if it is?"

Addison's voice sounded weak, and no one expected her to be the one to make a strong stand either way, but she had felt sorry for Sim when he told them he felt like the odd man out. She saw how alone he felt even though he had the rest of the crew.

"I think we have to know," she added. "If we don't find out for sure, we'll always wonder if we left him to die."

"How should we do this?" asked Jon. "Whatever has them interested in the hangar has got to be something they won't forget easily."

"Gradually," said Garrett. "We'll start by just firing a couple of shots downward at the nearest ones. There's no sense in wasting bullets by shooting them into the air. The infected close to us will move this way, and the others will follow."

"Allow me," said Mike.

Mike got up from Addison's side and walked over to the ladder. All he saw at the bottom were two infected dead mostly covered with snow, but he could see the skull was smashed on one of them.

"Sim probably took care of that pair already. I'll have to take a longer shot at something farther from the terminal."

Mike targeted the infected farther away, but Anne stopped him.

"Hang on for just a second, Mike. You don't need to take a longer shot."

Anne cupped her hands around her mouth and screamed as loud as she could.

It wasn't the beginning of an exodus, but heads turned in their direction. Even the infected that hadn't been able to do more than crawl toward Sim crawled toward the source of the scream.

The mass of infected continued to try to squeeze into the hangar, but hundreds began coming toward the terminal. Mike took careful aim and shot the first one to arrive in the forehead as soon as it turned its face up at him.

As the infected fell to the ground, hundreds more stopped where they were and started searching. Some of them saw the living people waving their arms on top of the building, but the ones that didn't see the crew yet still followed the horde.

Mike fired a second shot, and a tidal wave of the infected began moving faster. On the third shot some of the infected inside the hangar walked back out into the daylight. The fourth shot was all it took.

"What have we done?" asked Jon.

To the crew of Executive One, the horde was big enough to collapse the building as they began crowding around below. The infected in back were so frantic to reach the living people that they were crushing the first arrivals against the wall.

"Someone get a set of binoculars aimed at the hangar," said Garrett. "If Sim comes out we need to really rile up our fans."

******

Sim thought he imagined how quiet it had become below him. He didn't hear the scream that got the change started, and he didn't hear the first three gunshots. He thought he heard the fourth one.

He didn't want to get them worked up again, so he very slowly leaned to one side until he could just barely see the area around the wheel. There were still infected dead going by, but they were walking away. Then he was sure he heard gunshots.

His legs were cramped and numb from the cold, but he felt his heart pound with excitement when he figured out that the infected were being drawn out of the hangar.

He knew he couldn't move too soon, so he tried to stay patient. When he finally lowered his head down to check his surroundings, the last of the infected had walked into daylight by the tail. He rotated his head and let his eyes adjust to the dark in the back of the hangar, and there were no stragglers. It was time to start moving.

It hurt when his feet landed on the wheel, but it was only his circulation coming back. Sim quietly stepped to the floor of the hangar and ran toward the wall on the left side of the plane. The whole time he kept his eyes on the backs of the infected walking away from the hangar door.

When he got to the wall he immediately started along it to the corner closest to where the big plane's tail was lit by the sunlight. By the time he made it to that corner, he was sure he would be in the clear outside, so he stuck his head around the corner. The biggest horde of infected he could imagine was literally ramming itself against the airport terminal. On the roof his friends were shooting down at them.

He knew he only had a few moments, and he couldn't go toward the south, but Sim felt alive again. He didn't know if they would see him, but he waved in the direction of his friends. He was rewarded by the sight of them frantically jumping up and down and waving back. Then they all aimed their guns at the crowd and poured it on. He went in the only direction he could, and he could see the skyscrapers of downtown Columbus in the distance.

From the top of the airport terminal, Anne screamed again when she saw Sim come out of the hangar, and the six friends began shooting and yelling. The horde went into such a frenzy that they felt the building shake under their feet and it seemed to ram against the wall.

A nearby jet airplane rocked back and forth, and it gradually rotated as bodies were unable to go around the nose gear. They wouldn't have believed it if they hadn't seen it with their own eyes, but the plane was soon pointed directly at them and rolled toward the terminal.

"The brakes are on, and they're still able to move it," said Garrett. "Let's get inside, everybody. This party should go on for a few hours, and Sim got away. Anyone see where he went?"

"I was able to see him until he reached that row of buildings over there," Anne said.

She pointed in the direction of a row of administration buildings that belonged to companies that did business with the airlines.

"Well, I'd rather know he's alive and trying to make it out there than to wonder if he even made it out of the airport," said Mike.

"What now?" asked Addison.

"Business as usual, I think," said Garrett. "We decided to stay this winter, and then we'll talk about next winter before it gets too cold."

There were general nods of agreement and the group made their way back to the relative warmth inside the terminal. Even though it was cold everywhere, without the wind and drifting snow, it wasn't long before the trip through the ceilings made them sweat.

"When we get back, everyone needs to change clothes and get warm fast," said Susan.

The shelter they had made in the back corner of the restaurant was a welcome sight. The security cage was down, and it would stop a small horde if the infected ever managed to find a way into the huge terminal, so it gave them some measure of safety, and they were able to sleep without posting a watch. In hindsight, they wondered if that had given Sim too much opportunity to leave. Then again, if he wanted to leave that badly, they weren't sure they would have tried to stop him.

The crew had gathered together every cardboard box they could find and with a little ingenuity they had created layers of insulation over a lattice of storage shelves from the restaurant supply rooms. It was tall enough for them to stand upright, and roomy enough for them to spread out, but they didn't make it so big that they lost body heat.

The restaurant was conveniently located next door to one of the largest gift shops. Every airport in the country had at least one shop that specialized in clothing advertising the local sports teams, so the first stop was for fresh, dry clothes. Thanks to the Ohio State University, they were all layered in red and white Buckeye sweatshirts and winter caps. Each of them had new bleacher blankets under their arms, and under normal circumstances, they would easily pass for a group of fans on their way to a tailgating party.

"I'll start breakfast," said Addison. "Believe it or not that expensive place that advertised authentic food from twelve different countries had a large supply of canned goods. There were also plenty of sacks of flour and sugar."

Despite the loss of a crew member, the rest of the group had good appetites, and they decided to make pancakes. Seeing Sim get away actually made them feel a bit upbeat, and breakfast was more of a sendoff for him than a normal meal.

They sat in a circle passing the sticky maple syrup bottle around and dug in while the pancakes were still warm.

"Should we consider the possibility that Sim might try to come back?" asked Susan. "He might not have a choice. If he does, we should put some alternatives in place for him to use to reach the roof."

"He has the other ladders," said Mike.

Garrett said, "They're locked, and if we unlock them, he won't know they are. I suppose we could put up a big sign, or something."

"Yeah, and advertise our position to other survivors who might not be as friendly as we are," said Jon.

They all went quiet as the thought just hung in the air. So far, there hadn't been attempts by survivors to use the airport terminal as a safe haven.

They had suspected for a long time that there were people living in some of the other buildings, but after the first few weeks, the only signs of movement were the infected as they wandered aimlessly from one place to another. Many of the planes were occupied, but as the supplies ran out and people tried to escape their little prisons, the dead intercepted them. The population of the infected dead grew, and if anyone else tried to get into the airport, the crew was not aware of them.

"If Sim tries to come back," Mike began, "I think it's only logical that he would try to reach the ladder he left unlocked. Maybe we could paint a message on the side of the buildings that faces the way we saw him leave. We have plenty of paint."

Addison was a little confused.

"Mike, how would we paint a message on the side of the building?"

"The same way they paint ships in the Navy. Lower someone on a swing and lower the paint bucket separately by another rope," said Mike.

The general consensus was that it could be done despite the fact that everyone thought the idea of hanging over the side of the building was insane.

"To answer Jon's question about giving away our location," said Garrett, "we could try to write something cryptic that only Sim would understand, or we could just go ahead and do it. Either way, if I was a survivor out there in the cold and I saw a welcome sign, I would be grateful."

"So you're saying it's worth the chance," said Susan. "For the record, I agree."

After breakfast they put together everything they would need to get the job done. Paint, brush, ropes, and a harness were packed in supply bags. They decided the whole group would go in case they needed to take turns painting, but they wanted enough strength holding the ropes. They also wanted binoculars watching for problems they wouldn't otherwise see.

For all of her early timid behavior, Addison surprised everyone by volunteering to do the painting.

Mike stepped up immediately to protest, but Addison stopped him with one hand in the air, palm aimed at his face.

"It makes the most sense, Mike. I'm the lightest one of all of us, and three men aren't going to let go of a rope that has a pretty blonde hanging from the other end."

No one needed to say more, so that was settled. They also decided the message should be to the point, and Addison tucked a piece of paper in a shirt pocket with the message written on it. She knew herself well enough to know that her nerves would be frayed by the time she got done, and the note would help her remember what to write.

Within the hour they were climbing for the roof for a second time. When they emerged into the open they found that snow clouds had covered the sky, and they were really going to be blanketed that night.

They got right to work and found places to anchor the ropes. If the three men did let go, Addison was still going to be supported well above the ground.

As soon as they gathered at the side of the building, a crowd formed below. All it took was one infected to see them, and the groaning started drawing more in their direction.

"Let's get this over with," said Addison.

Anne took the first watch on the area around the airport while Susan handled the rope that was tied to the bucket of paint.

Addison got down on her knees with her feet facing the ledge and backed up slowly. Once she was completely supported by the rope, she sat back comfortably in the harness and was able to begin using her feet for balance. She reached for the bucket and dipped her brush into the paint.

Oblivious to the big drops and splashes of paint that she didn't get on the wall, she worked quickly on the message. Below her there were dozens and then hundreds of hands reaching up at her as she moved from the left to the right.

She only looked down again when she had finished the job, and she was surprised by the size of the crowd. Some of them had painted faces, but the crowd was so large that the painted faces were being crushed against the wall the way they had been when Sim had escaped the hangar.

Addison used her feet to push herself out from the wall as if she was in a standing position and inspected her work.

SIM, ALL LADDERS ARE UNLOCKED. EXECUTIVE ONE

It was messy, but it was clear enough to read. She was proud of the finishing touch they had agreed to when Garrett suggested they should put their temporary call sign on the message. After all, the President was responsible for them being stuck in the airport in the first place.

******

Sim didn't return. As the winter wore on, the snow became deeper and deeper until trams, luggage trains, and the infected dead themselves disappeared under a white blanket. Snow removal equipment that would normally be clearing the runways and taxiways remained parked in their buildings.

After they found the body of a man at the top of a ladder, they began posting watches on the roof of the terminal at the highest points that weren't buried in snow.

The man had been bitten several times, but what had killed him was the single shot to the side of his head. There was a gun frozen to one hand. It wasn't hard for them to guess what had happened, but the smart decision of one man didn't mean everyone would be as smart.

Until the snow began to melt, the days were quiet. The white blanket showed no new signs of movement for months, and the crew of Executive One reached a decision. As much as they hated the cold, if they wanted to live, they would have to go north. They didn't know if the freezing cold temperatures killed the infected, but they could see for themselves that the infected could be frozen solid.

As the snow melted, they could see the heads appear. It was a really strange sight as they surveyed the tarmac between the buildings and the grounded planes. Dots of dark colors rose above the white blanket, and gradually the faces.

They remained still as the snow melted to their necks, but as the sun warmed their heads, they rotated. They turned left and right as they searched for living flesh, but their bodies remained frozen beneath them.

Jon, Mike, and Garrett stood at the top of the ladder Sim had used when he left. They were watching the heads moving in the deep snow, and Jon had commented that it would be a good time for them to go down and thin the infected population a bit.

As the others pointed out to him, they would be walking on the backs, shoulders, and heads of the ones they couldn't see yet.

"I know," said Jon. "It was just wishful thinking. It makes me think of that game where you try to use a big mallet to hit a mole when it sticks its head out of the ground."

"Wack-a-mole?" asked Garrett.

"That's the one. I picture myself pushing something like a big mower around on the surface of the snow just mowing over all of those heads," said Jon.

"If it was only that easy," said Mike. "I think we could nail a bunch of them after they freeze, but it's already too late this year. It already feels like we've been here for a few years. Would one of you please remind me when it began snowing this year?"

They gave it some thought, and Jon said, "I think it was around the third of January, but I don't think they seriously froze for a couple of weeks after that. Why?"

Mike said, "We should be ready to move around then next year. We can travel north toward Minnesota until we get to a place where we can survive better than them. Then every winter we can go out and hunt for them while they're popsicles."

"Why Minnesota?" asked Jon.

"That's easy," said Garrett. "We can't reach Barrow, Alaska, so we need to go to International Falls, Minnesota."

"It gets cold there?"

Mike and Garrett couldn't believe Jon had never heard of the coldest town in the United States.

"They stay below freezing almost nine months out of the year," said Mike.

"Well, if we can make it here until then, count me in," said Mike.

That evening the men told the three women what they had discussed. The resignation on Susan's face was obvious. It meant she had to give up any idea of ever seeing her family again. She had been gradually letting the fact sink in, but going north would make it final.

In the end, it was agreed to by all. They would go to Minnesota as soon as it froze in Ohio. The further they would go, the colder it would get, and if they were right about the infected dead freezing, they could destroy them as they traveled.

14 FIGHTING BACK

They might have felt differently if they had a clue they would need to survive another year in the airport, but eventually the late night campfire discussions got around to delivering some payback. They felt like getting even with the mindless creatures that were trying to end their lives.

The flight crew of Executive One had survived most of their first winter in John Glenn International Airport. Sim was gone, but the rest of them were determined to stay together.

When they talked about how Sim had slipped away, they had mixed feelings about him. They hoped he had survived, but they felt abandoned by him, too. The rest of the crew made a solemn promise to each other to stay together no matter how long it took for them to either be rescued or find a better place.

It was Jon's crazy idea to try to eliminate some of the infected, and it was just in time. The temperature was still below freezing, but toward the middle of the day it was getting warmer. The ice melted and refroze until there were large patches of ice with body parts sticking out of them.

They had seen a pack of wild dogs, maybe wolves or coyotes, crossing a field at the perimeter of the airport. Whatever they were, they took advantage of the abundance of meat that wasn't trying to get away from them. They showed up in the morning, fed, and then disappeared again until the next morning.

The crew of Executive One was up on the roof watching for activity, human or otherwise, and the dogs had just appeared for their morning meal.

Jon said, "Maybe they have the right idea. What's to stop us from disposing of a few of them while it's still cold?"

"It's dangerous down there," said Susan.

"It's dangerous everywhere," Jon snapped back just a little more forcefully than he intended. "I'm talking about being careful and not overdoing it."

Garrett said, "I like the idea, but I think we can take it a step further."

He had the attention of the others, half with interest and half with concern. They all felt like fighting back, but they had become accustomed to the idea of going north next winter, not doing something so soon.

He spoke as if he couldn't believe what he was suggesting himself, and he grinned just a bit. At another place and time someone might think he was kidding.

"We have all that jet fuel sitting down there in trucks. We could put that to better use."

Jon said, "Boss, we don't want to blow the place to pieces."

Garrett chuckled and said, "I was thinking of something a little more controlled. What if we just got some fuel into smaller containers and went around pouring it on their heads? Then we could set their heads on fire."

261

All six of them surveyed the frozen sheets of ice that still covered the airport. There were very large places that were completely white and dipped downward toward the middle. They knew those were places that were too deep to go near. It would be easy to fall into those drifts and disappear from view.

The other places that were higher, the runways, taxiways, docking areas, maintenance areas, and parking lots near buildings were all peppered with parts of the frozen infected sticking out of the ice.

"Aren't we too late?" asked Anne. "I mean, isn't it a bit dangerous now because it's getting warmer? Sorry Jon, I don't want to upset you, but if we were going to kill them, we should have started a long time ago."

"I think I see what he's getting at," said Mike. "If we go down there and try to kill them, it will take time, but if we just go down there and put a little fuel on each one, we could cover a lot of ground in a hurry. Then we would just have to light them."

Garrett added, "We have lots of buckets and lots of cups. What if we just go down and pour a cup of fuel on as many as we can. I'm not talking about trying to do too much, and if we're careful and don't spill any on the ground between them we won't start a wildfire that will spread to the airport or the fuel trucks. We can also just get the ones with their heads poking out of the ice since burning them won't kill the ones that are buried."

A couple of hours later, they were standing at the top of a ladder.

"I don't believe we're doing this," said Susan.

"You can stay here with Addison and keep watch if you like," said Jon.

Susan gave him a withering stare but went down the ladder anyway.

They decided to use a ladder on the opposite side of the building from the one they had originally drawn the infected dead toward on the day Sim made his escape. The bodies were piled so deep around that ladder that many of the infected were already totally dead, but some weren't, so they wouldn't know exactly where it was safe to step.

There was also no direct sunlight on the area at the bottom of the second ladder, and there was a beautiful sheet of ice where they wouldn't run into anything that was likely to bite them.

Garrett tied a couple of ropes to the bottom rung of the ladder and explained that the ice would be too slippery to walk on, so if they had to reach a ladder in a hurry, they should grab a rope and pull themselves to the ladder.

The nearest fuel truck wasn't far away, and Mike had already filled six buckets. They had considered cups and even paint brushes as the method of distribution, but they were worried about exposure to the fuel. It was toxic to breathe, and if it got on their skin or their clothes, they could be severely burned.

In the end, it was the expensive restaurant that offered the best tools. Long handled soup ladles were sticking out of each bucket. They would allow for safety, and as Mike suggested, maximum and accurate distribution.

It seemed as if the sun was reflecting off of everything, and even though it was still freezing, the sky had never appeared so blue. They wove a path through the body parts that were exposed above the ice and worked their way almost to the hangar where Air Force One served as a daily reminder of how they had come to be abandoned in John Glenn International Airport.

They stayed away from the uncertain shaped drifts that could either be vehicles or solid fixtures they shouldn't burn. Some of them were also groups of the infected that had been so close to each other that they had remained frozen together all winter.

"Is this far enough?" asked Anne.

Garrett studied their progress and saw that it appeared they could each wet down a large number of heads where they were.

"Yes, this is a good place to start. Remember, it won't take much, so use about a half ladle for each head."

To the casual observer, they would have been a strange sight. They resembled farmers going through a white field of crops, each one tending to some unusual plants.

It wasn't hard work, but it was nerve wracking. As the fuel was poured across each icy head, ice melted away, and more than one of the infected twitched. If they had started this project a week or two later, it would have been too late.

Their buckets went empty at about the same time, and they each returned for refills. When they returned to where they had left off, there was some satisfaction in seeing how many of the frozen infected had wet heads.

Within no time they had each been able to douse about fifty or sixty heads each, and they stood in a small circle at the bottom of the ladder.

"Okay, now comes the fun part," said Garrett.

They unpacked a bag of flares, and Jon passed them out.

"Let's see who has a good arm," he said when he was done.

Jon lit his first flare and lobbed it almost all the way to the back row of heads. The flare bounced neatly off the top of one head and hit another. From there it rolled and bounced to a stop in the snow.

Anne gave Jon a scowl normally reserved for juvenile delinquents, and Jon got the message. If the best he could do was light two heads with one flare, they would be at it all day, and they would need a few hundred flares.

They all made their way back out to the last row of heads and began systematically lighting them with their flares. As they did, they worked their rows so they would be back at the ladder before the last ones were lit.

It was a spectacular sight, and Addison was waving for them to get back up the ladder. At first they thought it was because she wanted them to see what the view was like from above, but then they noticed her movements were just a bit more frantic than normal.

They used the ropes to pull themselves across the slippery ice to the ladder and started climbing. Anne and Susan went up first with Jon, Garrett, and Mike trailing behind.

When they reached the roof, Addison was pointing excitedly beyond the cloud of smoke that was coming from the hundreds of burning heads.

Even though Addison was trying to get their attention, they couldn't tear their eyes from what they had done. Across the white, shining surface of snow and ice, flames shot up from row after row of burning heads that were moving forward, backward, and side to side. The infected were still trapped in the ice, but their burning heads flailed wildly. The smoke came together above them and rose into one massive column.

Addison started screaming, and the others finally understood that she was pointing at something beyond the smoke and fire.

When they saw what she was pointing at, they were glad to be back on the roof of the terminal.

The horde of infected moving their way was beyond anything they had seen so far. The crowd they had drawn to the side of the building on the night when Sim had escaped from the hangar was a handful of stragglers compared to what was moving their way now. They stretched from the horizon on the right to where the buildings blocked their view on the left.

Jon said, "I think this is one of those times when you just have to say it seemed like a good idea at the time."

"But where are they all coming from if these are all frozen around here?" asked Garrett.

"The city," said Anne. "We waited too long, but this is something we need to remember when we head north to Minnesota. If they get caught out in the open when it freezes, they'll stay frozen, but if they get inside a building before they freeze, they may stay mobile all winter."

"I guess we learned something even if it didn't work out the way we planned," said Garrett. "We destroyed several hundred of them even if it attracted more to the area."

The horde had reached the other side of the column of smoke and was disappearing behind it when Anne realized they had made another mistake. It wasn't too late to fix this one, though.

Anne began dragging at the rest of them and screaming to get down.

"They can't see us up here yet. They're being drawn to the fire and smoke."

Everyone dropped flat to the roof and then eased forward toward the edge of the building. It was too fascinating not to watch.

The column of smoke was gray and black, and the jet fuel gave it a greasy, oily appearance. At the base of the smoke, heads were snapping back and forth so hard they could have broken off at the neck. Beyond the smoke they could see patches of the horde, and it was so immense that it was approaching from the sides.

Within minutes there were bodies stumbling around in the smoke, falling over on the burning heads and catching their own ragged clothing on fire. Then the smell blew over the top of the terminal.

It smelled like someone was roasting fatty, greasy pork. Gagging was unavoidable, and they all started pulling scarfs over their faces. Their eyes were watering, but they couldn't take their eyes away from the spectacle.

Throughout the smoke there were flare-ups as new bodies caught fire. There would be a bright flash of yellow and orange, and then the smoke would close in to hide the rest of the scene. A short distance away there would be another burst of color, and it would happen again. Sometimes there were several new fires at the same time, and it was just like the 4th of July with fireworks when the audience just had to make exclamations out loud to show its appreciation.

"I keep expecting a finale," whispered Jon.

"I have an idea," said Garrett as he crawled backward from the edge. "Jon just said what we're all thinking. We need to see this from another angle so we can get an idea about how long it will go on."

Garrett got close to the center of the roof and ran back toward the main terminal. He kept going until he was able to cross over onto a wing that was roughly ninety degrees to the position of the rest of the group. When he was sure he could see the other side of the column of smoke, he got low to the roof again and crawled forward.

Anne reached for her radio when Garrett keyed his microphone. The batteries would need to be charged again, but as long as the plane had enough power left, they would have the radios as one of the luxuries.

"How bad is it, Garrett?"

The answer came across in a low voice with some static, but there was no mistaking his excitement.

"Thousands. There must be thousands of them. There might have been a horde moving on the interstate when we lit the fire."

"We couldn't have known," she answered.

"I'm not saying we shouldn't have done it. We couldn't see the interstate from here, anyway. As a matter of fact, it's going to improve the neighborhood. They aren't close enough to the terminal for the fire to spread to us or any of the fuel trucks, and we're thinning their population a bit."

"This should burn for a couple days?"

"That's my guess," said Garrett. "Let's post watches until we know for certain that the fire won't get out of hand. It wouldn't be my first choice, but if it spreads to the terminal we might be forced to evacuate. I'll stay here for two hours. You guys decide who can stay on your spot. The rest of you can get inside and get warm."

Mike took the first watch as the others tore themselves away from the show. Even as they climbed back through the maintenance door, they had to take in the spectacle of the pillar of smoke that seemed like it was miles high.

******

Even though he couldn't see the airport from his hiding place, Sim could tell the tower of dark smoke was coming from that direction. Whatever was fueling that fire, he was sure it was a really large supply. Judging by the color of the smoke, Sim guessed jet fuel and anything that was dry enough to burn. He wished he had some way to know for sure, and hoped it wasn't the main terminal itself.

Sim's current residence was a hotel balcony. It was cold, but with any luck the next balcony would have an unlocked sliding glass door and the room wouldn't be occupied.

He was tired of climbing, but the small gathering of interested parties hanging around on the ground below had given him no choice. He peered over the edge, and he could see that they were still there. The infected didn't move on until they had something more interesting to pursue, and they hadn't seen the column of smoke yet.

Sim silently hoped there would be at least one explosion that would draw them away, but whatever was burning, it wasn't making the right amount of noise to help him. He stood up, rubbed some feeling back into his legs, and got ready to throw his makeshift grappling hook up to the next balcony railing.

As soon as he leaned outward, the infected below started making their usual racket, and even though he couldn't hear the dead occupants of the room next to him, he imagined they were doing the same. They had their faces and hands pressed against the thick glass door as if they could bite him at any moment.

He played out some line to start the heavy hook swinging, and then let the arc of the rope go upward when there was enough momentum. He saw the motorcycle handlebars disappear over the railing, and he felt a sense of satisfaction when he saw one end come back through the railing and neatly protrude out above his head.

Now all he had to do was throw some rope over the handle and pull it down. The best part was that it was easy to pull it tight across the rails once he got the second rope onto it, and he could climb again.

Sim had gotten the idea when he was trying to figure out how to get into the hotel. He found a motorcycle in the parking lot across the street, and he had been disappointed that the saddlebags on the bike only held a tool kit and a bag of weed.

He had thought, "Great, I can get stoned and fix the motorcycle."

Then he remembered a guy he knew who got high before trying to fix his car. For some reason he thought he needed to completely remove the hood to work on the engine. Sim studied the handlebars.

Removal of the handlebars on most bikes is complicated, but these had been customized by the previous owner, and Sim was a good mechanic. He had them off the bike in no time, and getting the rope was easy. It was strung all around the parking lot.

There were infected nearby, but something had gotten their attention down the street, and he was taking advantage of it. He already had the hotel he wanted to scale picked out, and it was his first choice because he had found himself close to downtown Columbus. The tall buildings were keeping him from getting his bearings, and he couldn't climb the office buildings.

Sim had never been to Columbus before, and he found himself wishing he had seen it before all of the streets became littered with bodies and derelict vehicles. Garbage was everywhere, and even though the streets were beautifully made of brick in many places, the dark stains told a story about what it must have been like when the infection began to spread.

The groaning below brought Sim back around to the present, and he saw that his crowd of admirers had gotten larger. He pulled in the slack on the rope and climbed, hoping this was the last time.

Of course there was always the chance that a door from a balcony would be unlocked but also open. The prone bodies that were broken and piled along the street were a testament to the number of people who had jumped, were pushed, or had just plain fallen from above. For a moment he wondered if any of them had been people who were trying to climb upward instead of down.

As soon as he cleared the railing he crab-walked to the wall by the door and got out of view from the inside of the room. No faces were pressed against the glass. As a matter of fact, there were no rust red smears on the glass like the other rooms.

There was a big stain on the railing of the balcony that faced the street. He had noticed the stains on other railings and seen that they were probably caused by falling bodies bouncing on the railings as they went by.

Sim cautiously reached across to the handle of the sliding glass door and pulled gently. He didn't want to open it all the way for lots of reasons, but mostly because he was tired of surprises. More than once he thought it was literally possible to jump out of his own skin.

The door moved silently about an inch, and he held his breath. A glance over one shoulder confirmed he had climbed to the fifth floor, and he was praying that he wouldn't have to climb to the sixth. This was the first unlocked door, but the fact that it was closed made him feel like he hadn't gotten lucky yet.

He pulled a little harder, and the door opened a few inches. It was quiet inside the room, and more importantly, there was no smell. Sim stepped hopefully across the door and peered through the opening. The beds were made. There could have been any number of reasons why the beds were made, but the most likely explanation was that the room had been unoccupied.

He sampled the air first. It was stale. The doors had been closed for months, and the air conditioning had died with the power, but he didn't smell any decay from human remains.

The room was gloomy, and there were plenty of shadows in the corners for his imagination to play with. His imagination was working overtime on one particular shadow in a corner that he was sure had moved.

He stared at it for several moments and held his breath, waiting for the movement to come again. It couldn't be an infected because they weren't shy about announcing that they had spotted you. If it was a live person, there was a good reason why they had survived so long, meaning they were almost as dangerous to him.

Sim's eyes adjusted to the gloom, and as they did, the shadow took shape. He wasn't completely sure what it was, but someone had taken the time to lean something into the corner. It needed to be investigated, but for now he judged it to be safe.

He took his eyes away from the shadow and surveyed the rest of the room. It was a suite, and he couldn't see all of it from the balcony. Staying low he crawled into the room onto the deep pile of carpet. The balcony was attached to the bedroom, so he was safely out of view behind the first neatly made bed. He reached back behind him and gently closed the sliding glass door.

There was a room without a door that Sim guessed would be the bathroom, and he could see from his hiding place that the other door went into a sitting area. The door was open, and the room beyond felt empty.

The last thing he wanted to do was use a gun inside the room and give away his position. He might as well hang a sign on the doorknob that said there was free meat inside the room.

Sim slipped his long blade from the sheath that was attached to his belt and stood to his full height. He gave the shadow in the corner one final glance and walked quietly toward the open door.

As soon as he stepped through the door, his shoulders dropped a couple of inches, and he felt the tension fall away for the first time since the night he decided to leave on his own. In hindsight it had been a bad decision because he hadn't been able to go south. Everywhere he went, it seemed like the infected dead decided which direction he should go. Instead of south, they had made him go west into the city, the last place he wanted to be.

The sitting area was in front of a big, plate glass window with the curtains drawn. Off to the right was a full kitchen and a hallway that led to the door of the suite. Even in the gloom he could make out the signs on the back of the door. One of them would tell him the hotel rules and check out time. The other would tell him which way to the emergency exits. He got a quick mental image of the guests who had stopped in front of that sign for just a moment.

Sim decided he needed some light, and five floors up seemed safe enough for open curtains. Before sliding them open he peeked around the corner to study the parking garage across the street. The movement of the curtains could draw the attention of the infected, but that wouldn't be as bad as drawing the attention of someone who had a rifle and tended to take things from other survivors rather than to share.

It was quiet across the street, so he slid the curtains open slowly and brightened up the room. The kitchen was spotless and unused. Sim wasn't sure what he would find in the refrigerator, but he walked straight to it.

The air that drifted out of the tightly closed appliance wasn't as bad as he expected. There were no perishables he could see, but the doors and shelves were stocked with bottled water, a variety of sodas, and beer.

His hand shot out and wrapped around the neck of the first bottle of beer before he had a chance to even think about it, and he laughed quietly as his conscience reminded him it wasn't free.

"I know," he said in a low voice. "Put it on my bill."

The minibar was built into a wall to the right of the kitchen, and he hardly thought about it as he opened it and retrieved a small bottle of bourbon. He started checking the cabinets as he unscrewed the cap from the bottle and drank it in one shot. By the time he had chased it with warm beer he had found the snacks. It wasn't the most nutritional meal, but it was mentally satisfying.

He stopped in the middle of opening a bag of chips and listened as something went by his door in the hall. He stood still and held his breath. Both of his elbows were extended out to the left and right while both hands gripped the top of the bag of chips. The sound outside the door gradually faded away, and Sim knew that it was more likely to stop at another door than his. Some of his new neighbors were having no respect for the other guests. They were moaning and groaning, bumping into things, and knocking them over. They would keep the infected in the hallway busy for years.

Before opening the chips he stepped back into the kitchen so the sound wouldn't carry into the hall. He retrieved a second bottle of beer and a shot of bourbon and went back into the bedroom. A quick check of the bathroom revealed that he had been safe when he made the decision to bypass it before. It was obvious that no one had been using the room and the little bars of soap still sat neatly next to the bottles of shampoo and conditioner.

Back in the bedroom again, Sim found himself facing the corner that held the shadow that had fueled his imagination. It seemed like something out of place that was just left leaning there.

Whatever it was, it was made of cloth and was wrapped around two poles of equal length. He lifted it easily from the corner and laid it across the first bed. Just as he rolled it out, his foot caught against something under the bed, and he instinctively jumped backward.

There was a suitcase under the bed and several small cardboard boxes. A quick check under both beds showed him he was still safe, but he was apparently wrong about the room not being occupied. The guests just hadn't been in the room at the time the world went to hell.

Sim went back to the thing on the bed and found that it was a long and high banner between the two poles. It was a map of Columbus, but something about the streets was different. They didn't seem to have nearly as many intersections as he had already seen. There was a big caption along the top of the banner that said, "Visit the Lost Tunnels Under Columbus."

Sim studied the streets on the map and knew what the map was really for, but when he thought about going down into those tunnels, he couldn't imagine why it would be a good idea.

******

Two days later the refrigerator was empty, and Sim had enjoyed the solid sleep. Fatigue, bourbon, and beer were the combination that made him worry less about whether or not the hotel room door was enough security. His half alert mind told him it had been enough before the infection, and people knew how to break down doors back then.

The neighbors were still being inconsiderate, and the hallway wandering dead bounced against his door from time to time, but Sim just needed to shut down for a couple of days. He decided he would figure out what to do after that.

When it became obvious that his break was coming to an end, he started listing his options. Down from the balcony was possible because his fan club in the street had moved on to bigger and better things. There never was an explosion where the smoke climbed into the sky in the direction of the airport, but bigger and better than nothing could have been something as small as a piece of paper blowing by.

Sim didn't see the point to climbing back down, though. Eventually, he would have to climb back up again unless he had somewhere to go once he was on the ground.

His second option was up. He could climb more balconies to check the rooms above him, but he couldn't come up with a good reason to do so. The only thing he could think of was more refrigerators and stocked mini bars. That choice would be no more than a mental escape from reality.

The only thing he could think of that had a possible positive outcome was to take control of the hallway outside of his room. Then he would have access to the stairs at either end, and he would be able to go up or down. He would at least have a choice between the two, but Sim couldn't think of a reason for going in either direction at the moment.

If his third option was to stay, Sim knew he would need more than what the room had to offer. It was that thought that made him remember the suitcase under the bed. He rolled over and dropped his feet to the floor. When he pulled out the suitcase, he doubted it would be a survivalist's bug-out-bag, but it had to at least satisfy his curiosity.

There was a second suitcase next to the first, and he tossed them both onto the bed before opening one. They were both locked, but a screwdriver was all he needed to pop the first one open. Sim rifled through clothing that was suitable for someone younger than him and much smaller.

The second suitcase was more interesting, but any hope of a magic survival kit being inside quickly faded. Flyers and magazines that went with the banner were the only contents. Maybe it was boredom, or maybe it was because Sim was feeling no sense of urgency, but he picked up one of the magazines and leaned back against a pillow.

According to the magazine, people were always finding reasons to dig more tunnels under Columbus. Drainage projects were begun and then abandoned. Underground pedestrian crossings were dug, opened, closed, and then buried. Someone started construction on a subway system but didn't finish. The builders went bankrupt, and it became nothing more than a dangerous temptation to thrill seekers and kids with skateboards.

Legends were repeated often enough to become fact, and over the years, an unknown number of people had disappeared while exploring the tunnels. That was likely to be partially fact, because some of the tunnels had vertical shafts that were uncharted. One had been discovered that dropped straight down for almost two hundred feet.

The magazine conveniently omitted whether or not bodies were found at the bottom of that shaft, but it wasn't the only one, and it had to be at least partially true. Danger signs and no trespassing signs weren't enough to keep people out, so the city eventually had the defunct subway project permanently sealed.

Then came the big headline. The not so secret tunnel system under the Ohio State University campus was a way to gain access to several tunnel projects that had been closed over the years.

Despite an initial feeling of being underwhelmed, Sim found himself to be engrossed by the articles in the magazine. Some of it was true, some of it wasn't, but most of it was intriguing. One of the articles talked about a group of OSU students who had become lost in the tunnels and were never rescued.

The real truth was that the tunnels held all of the steam pipes for heating, wiring for electricity and internet, and various pipes for plumbing. There was no mystery to the fact that buildings had to get power and water from point A to point B, and under the buildings was a convenient way to do it.

Despite the obvious hype that was added to the articles, Sim enjoyed the speculation, and there was something about hidden tunnels that seemed to nag at him.

He flipped to the next page and read an article that had some old photographs of Columbus that were dated as having been made around 1876. There was a picture of a train station and another of a wagon going into the mouth of a large tunnel. The caption said it was for pedestrian and wagon traffic under the railroad tracks.

The article didn't say too much about tourists being able to visit the tunnel. It just described that it was built quickly by the federal government, and it was eventually closed due to lack of use. It seems that the drainage, ventilation, and lighting were so poor that wagons and pedestrians preferred to take their chances crossing the tracks in front of the trains up above. The tunnel was closed and forgotten, but an unknown source for the article claimed there was more to the tunnel than the city had been aware. The source claimed there was some sort of Presidential survival shelter hidden in the tunnel by the Ulysses S. Grant administration.

Sim scanned the article to see if it said how big the tunnel was, and when he saw it was over six hundred feet long, he thought that was a pretty big tunnel and an even bigger coincidence.

He sat the magazine down and thought about the night he had spent inside the wheel well of Air Force One. All night he had wondered if there was a zombie president wandering around in the plane above him, and if there wasn't, where would he be. By morning, the quiet above the wheel well made him more sure that he had spent the night under an empty airplane.

When Sim thought about that day when Executive One sat in line at the tail of Air Force One, all of the cockpit crew had felt that there was something going on inside the hangar in front of them that included getting the President to safety. It was logical to assume that there had been a plan in place before they had arrived, and a tunnel wasn't such a far fetched idea. The entrance was probably not far from where Sim had been hiding, but it had been dark inside the hangar, and it didn't really occur to him that he should be searching for a hidden tunnel entrance.

Sim had learned a trick years ago that had paid off as a navigator. He found that closing his eyes had enabled him to visualize maps and charts, and it also gave him better recall. He closed his eyes as he leaned backward on the bed into a comfortable pillow. He let his mind go back to that night.

Although he had climbed the wheel in a hurry and had his eyes focused on where he was going, he had surveyed his surroundings. The big blue and white plane, the symbols of America, the absence of a passenger bridge, and there was something else. He couldn't put his finger on it, but something had been different about the floor.

It was like having someone's name on the tip of his tongue. He knew if he tried to hard, it would escape him like a waking dream. Sim moved his memories forward to the next day and visualized his climb down from the wheel well. He had climbed down facing the tail because he wanted to watch the last of the infected stumble out of the hangar door into the light. Then he had crossed under the plane to his right to go to the wall that was straight across from the passenger door on the left side of the plane.

There it was again. That memory that was just beyond recall. He had approached the nose gear from the same general direction, so he was just seeing something vague in his mind from the other side.

Then he remembered. Just like the tip of the tongue phenomenon, he was remembering the first letter of the word he was trying to recall, and the word popped out.

"It was the floor," he said to the quiet hotel room.

There were bodies everywhere in the hangar. The floor was littered with the remains of the infected that had been killed by the military that had obviously been waiting for the plane to taxi inside, but there was something odd, something different about the bodies in the area directly below the passenger door on that side of Air Force One.

Sim had only paused for a second and surveyed the scene before he weaved a path between the infected that were no longer a danger to anyone, and he remembered that he wasn't afraid that he would be bitten by any of them. He wasn't afraid because he didn't see any heads. Every body around an area of about one to two hundred square feet had been decapitated, and there were two more things. They were all facing inward toward the center of that area, and they were all around the perimeter.

His eyes opened as a thud hit the outside of his room a little louder than usual, and Sim jumped from the bed and ran to the door. He saw through the peephole that two of the infected had collided with each other, and now both were trying to get up from the floor. One was leaning hard against his door, and he mentally saw his opportunity to eliminate one by opening the door. It would fall inside head first, and he would only need to slam the heavy door again. The force would most likely sever the head at the neck.

Sim was smart enough to understand that his mind was still trying to fill in the blanks about the hangar, and it had given him the final piece of the puzzle.

"Was there a big door in the floor of the hangar that had been slammed shut on the heads of the infected dead that surrounded it?" he thought.

His own words told him something still didn't fit. The puzzle piece might be the right one, but he still needed to put it in the puzzle in the right direction.

Sim stepped back from his hotel room door and pictured it closing on the neck of the infected leaning against it. It would only happen along the left side of the door. It wouldn't happen at the top, the bottom, or on the right side of the door for obvious reasons. He pictured a door being closed on the floor of the hangar, and he saw that it would crush or remove the heads of the infected along three sides, and they would all be facing inward, but along the fourth edge, there would be no decapitated bodies.

In his mind's eye he saw it again. There were bodies on four sides, and there was only one way that could happen. The floor had been lowered into place.

Sim backed away from his hotel room door and tried to digest what he was thinking.

"What kind of door could lower itself into the floor, and how heavy would it have to be to remove the heads of the infected along every edge of its perimeter?"

By the time he sat down on the end of a bed, he could see it happening. There was one clue he had ignored, and it showed him how to fit the last piece into the puzzle. Some of the bodies were missing more than a head. Some, as a matter of fact, many of the bodies were missing their upper torsos and were even missing everything from the waist up.

The only thing that heavy had to have been something big enough to carry passengers from Air Force One all the way from the door of the plane and through the floor of the hangar…an elevator.

Sim didn't notice his own mouth was hanging open as he pictured the elevator being raised and lowered repeatedly while he and his fellow crew members had sat waiting patiently behind Air Force One. He pictured the infected dead walking into the elevator shaft while it was open, and he pictured the elevator seamlessly fitting back into the floor onto the extended arms and bodies of the infected that tried to squeeze into the shaft at the last moment.

The infected that only lost an outstretched arm would have shrugged it off and continued their search for living victims.

"Rub a little dirt on it and walk it off."

Sim laughed as he said it, remembering his Little League coaches trying to keep kids from crying when they got a little scrape.

"So, an elevator had come out of the floor, risen to the door of Air Force One, then lowered itself back into the floor, but where did it take the President and everyone else to?"

Sim frowned at the banner and the contents of the suitcase spread out across the bed, and he knew where they had gone.

"Tunnels," he said, "but tunnels to where? President Grant's secret shelter?"

He knew he shouldn't be laughing out loud, but he couldn't help himself, and there were more thuds against his hotel room door. A series of groans told him there were at least two visitors, and he finally forced himself to be quiet again.

15 NORTH TO COLUMBUS

Wheels up from Guntersville, Alabama to begin the second leg of our mission had to be an impressive sight to the survivors we had briefly encountered. They still didn't trust us enough to approach us even though they could tell there were United States Army troops in our company, but they were at least bold enough to come out and watch us leave.

All four helicopters lifted off one after the other from the highway where they warmed their engines, and as they lifted they also began banking away to the right. Maybe the local survivors would investigate Green Cavern again. If they did, they wouldn't have any better luck than they had on previous attempts.

The secrets of Green Cavern had always been a topic of discussion in local bars, restaurants, schools, and among neighbors. People who knew Dr. Bus had tried for years to get him to admit that he had done something to the mountain, but all he would say was that he loved to go there for privacy. It was his own special getaway just like the cabins built by other rich people around the lakes.

After today, anyone who was still around from the pre-infection days would know there was more to it than a cabin in the woods. They would know it was much bigger, and they would search for it. The soldiers left behind were ordered to remain quiet unless the shelter was breached, and the likelihood of such an event was slim.

On the off chance they had been observed accessing the hidden controls to the ceiling elevator, the power supply to the controls had been removed. If the controls were found, they wouldn't respond even if a substitute power supply was installed.

The weak points of the shelter were the elevator itself and the blast screens that could open and close giving the occupants of the shelter a panoramic view of the lakes. The ceiling of Green Cavern was too high for anyone to reach the elevator door that blended seamlessly into the ceiling of the cavern, but the blast screens could be seen from the mountain across the valley if someone just happened to be watching when they opened or closed. For that reason, the soldiers were ordered to keep them closed at all times.

As the helicopters faded in the distance, the boats of the local survivors closed in on Green Cavern to begin the search. Unfortunately for them, there had been others drawn to the activity where the water of the lake lapped against the entrance to the cavern. Heads began appearing above the surface of the water as the infected dragged their water-logged bodies out of the lake.

The survivors had seen the infected make such an appearance wherever the banks sloped enough to allow them to leave their domain below the surface. Just as the infected on land weren't aware of their surroundings unless prey was moving nearby, the infected under water simply stayed where they were until something gave them a reason to go somewhere else. The activity at the entrance to Green Cavern was just such a reason.

The search for the elevator controls was short lived because of the number of heads rising above the surface. The survivors didn't waste their ammunition because there were so many infected. They quickly agreed among themselves that they would be able to return on another day after the infected had moved on.

Hands reached for the railings of the four boats as they pushed away from the cavern, and dull thumps sounded from each hull as they bumped their way through the heads.

One of the boats started its outboard engine too soon, and the propellor was immediately wrapped in body parts and shredded clothing. Someone yelled at them to stop trying to increase power and to put the engine in reverse for a few seconds.

The boat lurched backward as the propellor spun freely in the opposite direction and it was the quick thinking of the survivors in a second boat that saved their lives.

Using the poles they had all begun carrying as a means of pushing away the infected, they shoved themselves over to their friends until the two boats were against each other. With greater stability they were able to keep the boats from rocking with the weight of the infected that had gained handholds along the rails. A few hard pushes from the men and women on both boats was enough to start them forward against the growing number of infected emerging from the water.

The occupants of the four boats felt the spray of water being carried on the increasing wind before they heard the thumping sound of rotors behind them. Then they heard the rapid fire from the soldiers hanging from the doors with their weapons on automatic.

The natural instincts of the people in the boats made them duck as low as they could until it became apparent that the infected were being efficiently eliminated. The firing reached a peak and then gradually decreased until there was no more movement in the water.

The helicopter slowly backed away from the cavern, but the voice of Captain Miller boomed through a loudspeaker.

"Occupy the fenced village above this mountain. Fortify it against the dead and welcome all survivors. We will return and discuss further government assistance if you have established a community that abides by laws. Is this acceptable to you?"

Unknown to our convoy at the time, the men and women in the boats had been a group of survivors that had clung to their humanity. They had met their share of people who only took from others, killing anyone who got in their way. They already knew about the village on the mountain, and they knew it would be hard to supply, but with the help of the US Army, they were grateful for the chance.

Captain Miller and the crew of his helicopter understood the answer as one by one the people in the boats stood and delivered salutes in their direction. Unknown to the people, their measure of respect had earned them points toward living somewhere even better than the top of the mountain.

The helicopter backed away and then rose out of sight while the survivors in the boats began moving away toward safety.

Captain Miller caught up with us near the border of Alabama and Tennessee and radioed information about the way it had gone down at the entrance to the cavern.

Before he had decided to turn back as we flew north, he had radioed the Chief and broached the subject of how to treat survivors. He told us it wasn't enough to assume everyone was bad, and the way the boat had abandoned its pursuit without gunfire had made him think we should give people a chance.

We had quickly agreed that if he made contact and they weren't aggressive, we could give them a little test. See if they were a supportive community for a week or so in the village, and if they were, we would consider putting them inside the shelter.

Captain Miller was encouraged by their reaction to his intervention at Green Cavern, and he expressed his belief that we would find a civilized community when we returned. We could only wait and see. If they turned out to be good people, then they deserved the chance to rebuild in a safe place.

"Smoke to the west," said Kathy through the headsets.

We all faced toward west and saw a huge pillar of black smoke rising to an elevation well above our own.

"Anyone know what that could be over there?" I asked.

Jean answered, "Memphis is my guess."

"I agree," said the Chief. "More specifically, I would guess that it's the oil refinery."

"I thought all of our refineries were on the Gulf coast," I said.

"That one's on the Mississippi River," added the Chief. "Think about it. We have pipelines that carry raw and refined products, but a refinery on the Mississippi can supply cheaper fuel to the states upriver."

There wasn't one of us who didn't think the Chief knew everything, so I couldn't help asking him.

"How do you think the fire started?"

"Take your pick of a hundred different ways," he answered. "The most likely reason for a fire would be the same reason why the Oconee Nuclear Plant had an explosion. So many things in industrial plants involve regulating pressure. I don't know how oil is refined, but wherever you find heat and liquids that move through pipes, you'll also find pressure. Without people to monitor those pressures, there will be explosions and fires."

Hampton leaned forward and added, "Lightning strikes, survivors with good intentions."

"Survivors with bad intentions," Colleen chimed in.

"I saw a runaway barge hit a refinery in Houston once," said Cassandra. "Things got ugly in a hurry."

"The possibility of a runaway barge on the Mississippi wouldn't be so far fetched anymore," said the Chief. "One day people just quit showing up for work, and the loaded barge that was supposed to be moved that day just wasn't moored well enough for a long stay. Storms and wind break it free of its moorings, and the next thing you know, it's picking up speed downriver. It doesn't stop until it slams into the refinery."

We all sat quietly as the plume of black smoke disappeared behind us. First, Atlanta was almost unrecognizable because of the uncontrolled growth of vegetation, and then Memphis was burning because there wasn't anyone to put out a fire at a refinery. It was sinking in that surviving the infection wasn't just about not getting bitten anymore. It was also about the damage to our country's infrastructure.

"What next, Chief?"

I said the question into the microphone, and I was more or less just thinking out loud, but it couldn't just be about refineries, barges, and plants.

"Water would be my guess," said the Chief. "Everywhere that either supplies water to a dry place, or gets water from somewhere else is going to be effected sooner or later. Chicago for instance. It gets water from the Great Lakes, but it has to control how much water comes in. Without people to open and close dams, pressure is going to build up somewhere. Dams will eventually fail, and cities are going to flood. There are other cities that will see the same thing. Imagine New Orleans, Venice, and even Washington DC. We've built a lot of cities on top of marshes and swamps. Even Charleston filled in swamps to build more houses."

Jean leaned forward and tapped the Chief on the shoulder.

"Is it just me, or does it seem like there are more alligators in the marshes and swamps surrounding Mud Island than there were before?"

"I almost shot one a few days ago," said Hampton. "Then I remembered they eat the infected more efficiently than the blue crabs."

The Chief chuckled a bit and then said, "I can imagine there are environments too hostile for the infected to survive. If we want to just get away from them, all we have to do is go where it's either too hot or too cold for them, or we could go where there are more natural predators."

"There's an attractive thought," said Kathy. "Hot or cold doesn't sound so bad when you consider the predators that eat the infected would also sink their teeth into the uninfected."

"Where are we talking about?" asked Tom.

"We could move to the Everglades," said Cassandra. "Alligators and Burmese pythons would keep the infected under control."

It didn't take a vote. The way everyone stared at Cassandra was enough to get her to say she was just kidding, and she told us she didn't want to live anywhere that sold hunting licenses for pythons.

"Sooner or later, fuel is going to become an issue," said Kathy. "It's all fine for us to be hitting Columbus just in case the President has established some command and control from his shelter, but we may be forced to consider the long haul and move to a safer place. We should do it while we have the fuel and supplies."

None of us wanted to move away from Mud Island, but Kathy had a point. When we did the math, there were a lot of infected to destroy before we would be able to sleep at night. If Cassandra had been right, the numbers calculated by the doctors on her ship were so high that we could destroy the infected every day for the rest of our lives and still not run out of them. Maybe it was going to come down to just trying to survive.

We all went back to our own private thoughts for a second time. The comfortable ride in the executive helicopter made it possible to relax, and I found myself thinking about where we could go if we left Mud Island.

It seemed sort of ironic when it occurred to me that my uncle Titus could have picked anywhere in the country to build his shelter, and we were picking apart his survival plans as if he had been wrong. He had apparently given a lot of thought to his location, and he had been right about choosing Mud Island in many ways, but if his old group was having a meeting today, the topic would be why they hadn't considered a zombie apocalypse.

My eyes focused on Jean, and I caught her watching me. I realized I was frowning, and she wasn't the only one who had noticed.

"Busted," said Jean. "Care to fill us in on what has you acting like someone licked all the red off your candy?"

There wasn't any sense in hiding it, but I had to get the Chief on board with a little terminology discussion first.

"I was thinking about the end of the world club that Bus and my uncle belonged to. I wish Bus was here so we could ask him if anyone ever brought up the possibility of a zombie apocalypse."

The Chief visibly shifted in his seat like he wanted to be able to reach me. We had been down this road before, and I stopped him before he got started. We had been friends long enough for him to value my survival skills and quick thinking, even though I did appear to be slow to catch on from time to time.

"Hang on a second, Chief. Hear me out. If the survivors club decided to spend some time talking about what was going to happen, and they probably did, would they have discussed the possibility of reanimated corpses running around trying to eat living people, and what would they have called those corpses?"

No one answered for the Chief, and I thought he was going to disagree at first, but he finally gave in.

"Most people wouldn't know why they're not zombies," he admitted. "Most people would only care that the things are acting like zombies."

I know I smiled with satisfaction to finally hear the Chief concede the point, but I didn't feel like rubbing it in.

Tom asked, "So, when they talked about making the shelters and they included the military, they must have had a list of possible reasons to build the shelters, right?"

"That's what I was thinking about," I answered. "The list probably had a nuclear attack as the number one item, and a zombie outbreak as the last item."

"Why the last item?" asked Colleen.

"That's not a bad question," I said, "but I can come up with a list of things that would be a lot more likely than zombies."

The conversation was something we had touched on from time to time, and it was more of a way to make time pass than a way to plan for the future, but seeing the refinery burning had made the future come to us.

We had to face the fact that the infected had started this new world, but it wasn't over yet. Whether it was a burning refinery, an attack by a foreign enemy, a nuclear plant melting down, a flood, an earthquake, alligators, pythons, or man-eating kudzu, we were going to see new obstacles in our path every day. Even the food supply was tainted because seafood had been taken off the menu.

"I didn't mean to depress everyone," I said, "but when Kathy brought up the fact that fuel will become an issue, I started thinking about what's going to happen next. We haven't had to face other doomsday scenarios, but the longer this one goes on, the more damage it will do. We have enough supplies to last for our entire lives, but what will we leave behind?"

The conversation hadn't gone quite the way any of us had planned, and the weight of the topic once again drove the group to silence.

******

Sim decided that his attempt to go home on his own had been a big mistake, but it hadn't been a waste of time. He knew how the President had escaped from Air Force One, and he could put that information to use. All he had to do was live long enough to get back to his friends at the airport. Maybe then they could figure out how to get into that elevator. They might have to wait until next winter, but that would give them time to plan their attempt. They could also start trying to access the elevator when the infected were mostly frozen instead of thawing out.

That reminded him of something. It was still cold, and the infected were still mostly frozen, but warmer days were about to begin, and that meant there would be more of them to avoid.

It wasn't as easy as just going back the way he had come, though. There were new obstacles along the way. Pipes had frozen and burst as the cold winter weather seeped into normally heated buildings. Streets flooded until ice formed where the pipes broke, leaving vast lakes of ice under bridges and overpasses on the interstates surrounding Columbus. Once it would thaw, flooding would replace the ice.

In normal winters, cars and trucks would drive along salted roads, but now the roads disappeared under snow drifts. Places Sim had crossed getting to downtown Columbus might not be passable anymore, and there were more infected dead in the city where the cold hadn't been able to get to them. No matter what he decided to do, the infected had steered him away from his original goal. They might do the same thing to him as he tried to go back to the airport.

"Well, I can't phone it in to the airport," he said in a low voice.

Sim was standing on the balcony with his back pressed against the sliding glass door. It was dark enough for him to go undetected if he didn't make too much noise or move too quickly. The concrete floor of the balcony was also covered with ice, and he wondered if he could even make it back to the airport in this weather.

It was bitter cold because the wind whistled across frozen streets and buildings. The only reason he was outside was because he knew he would appreciate his warm room even more when he went back in. The snow had started again, and Sim was actually encouraged when he saw it. Even though he had grown up in the south, he believed it when people told him it could get too cold to snow.

Sim eased the door open just far enough to squeeze back inside, and he wondered again if there was a warmer room in the building. Over the last couple of days he noticed there was less noise in the hallway, and he wondered if the cold had overcome the infected that wandered back and forth.

Earlier thoughts about overcoming the infected outside his door had one major flaw, and Sim had to remind himself to stop thinking like things were normal anywhere. There was less light in the hallway than in his room. He discovered that little problem when he tried to watch one of them go by. He saw a shape, but he couldn't make out enough detail to tell if it was a new one or the same one that had gone by earlier.

Nonetheless, Sim's options were all bad. He could climb down and try to forage on his way back to the airport, or he could try to reach the hotel kitchen by using the stairs. The canned foods would still be good, and he could get enough supplies to last until he made it back to his friends.

There was one other thing the hotel would have that Sim wanted, and he felt like crying when he thought about it. Restaurants had cases full of Sterno, and one small can could burn for two hours. That meant heat and coffee. He would settle for tea, but the thought of a hot cup of coffee was almost enough to make him charge out into the hallway.

Sim made his decision on the spot. He had been putting it off and putting it off until he couldn't stand himself anymore. He was out of food and drinks, and judging by the trickle he was getting from the spigots in the suite, water was about to be a thing of the past.

He found a couple of decent kitchen knives in a drawer, but what he really wanted was a baseball bat. Then he remembered the banner and the poles at the ends.

Sim had learned that the best way to deal with the infected was to outrun them, but when that wasn't an option, a ball bat or a pipe was the best weapon because they didn't make as much noise as a gun. A pole was almost as good because you could use them to hold an infected away at a distance or push them over while you ran by. In a narrow hallway, he could have the advantage.

Fifteen minutes of listening at the door of the suite seemed like hours. He sat huddled against the door with a pile of blankets covering him, trying to get warm while he waited. He didn't know if it would be warmer or colder in the hallway, but his reasoning told him it would be freezing on either side of the door.

If it was freezing in the hallway, the infected would be standing still. He could listen all night, and there wouldn't be a sound that gave away their position because the infected would be too cold to move.

Sim was surprised to find he had his hand on the doorknob and was turning it very slowly. Judging by the fact that the metal felt warm under his hand, he must have been doing it for longer than he had known. The knob reached the end of its turn, and there was the tiniest of clicks as the latch mechanism was totally freed from the doorjamb. He leaned his weight into the door in case something in the hallway heard that barely audible sound. If something crashed into the door on the other side, he would just let go of the knob, and the door would be locked again.

His hand was sweating, and even though the knob wasn't slipping in his grip, it felt like it was. There was no groan from the other side of the door and no crashing disappointment, so Sim forced himself to relax just a bit. He leaned his weight away from the door and slowly created a gap by letting the door come with him.

A small window at the end of the hallway was letting some light land on the walls in one direction, but even more light was coming from the left side out of his field of vision. To see down the hallway to his left, he would be forced to open the door further and take a peek around the corner.

He let his eyes adjust to the light down the side where he could already see, and there was a heap of shadow in the left corner below the small window. It was shaped like a pile of clothes, and Sim thought back to his first night in the hotel. He had stared at the poles and the banner in the corner wondering if it was a really tall person for the longest time. Of course his imagination had been working overtime as he tried to find a safe place to rest for a few days.

Sim told himself to expect this shadow to be an infected dead because he knew there was at least one in the hallway. He was at least ten rooms down the hall from the dark heap, and he knew he could get back inside the door if it came for him, so he slowly turned and extended his head through the door only about two inches above the carpet.

At first Sim thought his eyes were playing tricks on him because he didn't think he was in the last room on the hallway. There was something blocking his field of vision that was so close Sim thought it was a wall. Then he smelled it.

Sim felt his stomach heave a bit, and he fought to keep control. The infected dead had slumped against the wall next to his door. A few inches closer, and it would have been leaning against his door. That click in the lock was nothing compared to an infected falling into the room on top of him.

Sim eased himself back into the room, but he carefully placed a foot in the door as he raised himself to a standing position.

He leaned out past the frozen body only inches from his left foot and studied the hallway. He could see the extra light was coming from an alcove a few rooms away. A small sign with an arrow on it said there was an ice machine around the corner, and judging by the light streaming into the hall, a bigger window.

Letting his eyes focus on the shadows further down the hall, he could see nothing that resembled another heap against a wall or door, so it was time to move.

Sim brought the kitchen knife around gripping it with the blade pointing inward. He was vaguely surprised at how noiselessly it penetrated the side of the head and sank all the way in until his fist was against the infected's temple. He pulled it back out and returned his attention down the hall in time to see the heap of clothes by the window pushing itself stiffly from the floor. It was slow and almost painful to watch.

Sim propped his door open with one of his poles and walked calmly toward the second infected. He held the second pole out in front of himself like a jousting lance and steadily raised the end until it pointed directly at the forehead of the infected. He expected a collision but only got a slight jolt. The skull of the infected seemed to just collapse away.

He had to put his foot on the infected to pull out the pole, and he wiped it clean against the body. The smell in the hallway was getting to him, so he decided he would need to keep going. He retrieved his second pole and a small backpack of useful belongings from his room and went to the stairs. One quick peek was all he needed to know it wasn't going to be easy. The stairwells were so dark they might as well have been filled with black ink.

Sim mentally kicked himself for not planning what to do in the stairwells, and he came to the conclusion that he hadn't gotten that desperate yet. Now that he was faced with the problem, and now that he was desperate, the answer didn't seem so impossible.

When he thought about whether or not there would be any infected dead in the stairwell, he reasoned that they would all be at the bottom, especially after so many months had gone by. After all, there wasn't anything to keep them from falling down the stairs, and the more decrepit they got, the harder it would be to go up the stairs. His only concern besides darkness was how many would be at the bottom.

Sim dragged the body of the infected dead over to the door. He stopped for a moment and tore one of his room towels into a long strip then tied it around his face. Then he used a second strip to tie the body's hands and feet together.

"Can't expect you to roll with your arms and legs flailing all around, and man is this is gonna stink," he said out loud.

The dry, weather worn clothes of the infected burned easily, but Sim held the matches to several places before he was sure the fire wouldn't go out too soon. He pushed open the door to the stairwell and gave the body a shove that was hard enough to get it down to the next landing.

Sim followed closely behind and only needed to glance upward once to know he was not being attacked from the floor above. As soon as he arrived on the landing, he grabbed the body and gave it a second shove toward the landing outside the door of the fourth floor. The flames burned just high enough to light the stairwell, and that was fine with Sim. It would be much harder to do if the infected turned into a flaming inferno.

Sim couldn't believe how well it was working, and he didn't try to be too cautious. He was already making enough noise to draw out any infected that might have been in the stairwell.

"Whoa," he yelled as he followed the burning body. "I guess this isn't what you had in mind when you learned about stop, drop, and roll. I know that's got to hurt."

The rolling body went much faster than he expected, and when the body hit the door to the ground floor, Sim was happy to find that there was another set of stairs that went down to the garage level. Groaning came from that level. Sim gave the burning body one last shove, and it rolled nicely into the middle of a pile of infected that reached up hopefully toward Sim. He only watched for a moment as they all ignited and burned. Then he ducked quickly into the first floor of the hotel and began working his way toward the kitchen.

The lobby of the hotel wasn't far away, and Sim spotted a restaurant across from the customer service desk. The tall buildings surrounding the hotel cast shadows that made the lobby appear to be in permanent evening hours, but the atrium skylight over the lobby let enough light in for Sim to be able to tell shadows from the infected. There were unmoving bodies in various states of decay spread around the entire first floor.

He changed directions so many times crossing the lobby that he felt like a football player running with the ball. He had to avoid stepping on the bodies because he didn't want to fall, but he also had to watch for any infected that might try to grab him as he went by.

The last days of civilization had been bad for Sim and his friends, but he considered himself to be fortunate when he compared everything he had seen to the lobby he had just crossed. Judging from the number of dead bodies, the infected must have swarmed the hotel from all directions. He wondered for a moment why more people hadn't gotten out of the building, but he saw the answer to that question when he spotted the main entrance.

Revolving doors were hard for some living people to navigate on a good day. With people trying to get inside while others were trying to get out, the door had become jammed in both directions. An infected that was nearly frozen still occupied one of the sections, and it made a feeble attempt to make the door turn when it saw Sim.

Tables and chairs were upended and scattered around the restaurant. Besides the wrecked furniture and bodies, there was evidence that some of the customers had been armed. Bullet holes were everywhere. Some of the tablecloths were heavily burned where candles had been upended. Sim could only imagine the mayhem that must have broken out in the hotel. He thought he remembered something about Ohio having some liberal gun laws. When he thought about it, if he had been eating in this restaurant, he would have been happy if the diners sitting next to him were armed on that particular day.

The kitchen had typical swinging doors, and the gloom of the lobby was cut in half once he entered the kitchen. Sim knew that he wasn't going to be able to collect supplies in the storage areas because they would only be darker. He didn't waste time trying to decide what to do and immediately went back to the dining area for candles.

Within a few minutes he had enough candles lit to be able to move about freely. He even found an employee area and retrieved a couple of backpacks from lockers. There was a coat that was several sizes too big for him, so it was perfect to wear over his own coat. Since the weather had been nice back when the infection started, he was surprised to find a coat, but he wasn't going to complain.

He loaded the backpacks with everything that could be useful. The sterno was in boxes stacked on storage shelves, and he used one entire backpack for them. There was a box of long candle lighters, and there were also matchbooks and boxes of matches. He found freezer bags and bagged a large supply of the matches to keep them dry.

There was a treasure trove of canned foods, but most of them were cans too large to mess with. In the end, he settled for things he might usually ignore because they fit in the backpack.

Sim studied one can for a few minutes, unsure of its value to him. On a whim he opened the can and got a sleeve of crackers out of a box. He spooned a bit of the dark contents onto a cracker and popped it in his mouth. It was curiously odd tasting, but its salty flavor was satisfying. Maybe it was because he had never eaten caviar, and it was a very expensive brand.

"Well, it took an apocalypse and the end of the world for it to happen, but I finally ate something I couldn't afford," he said out loud. He felt like washing it down with some beer, but for some strange reason he had to have some more.

"I always heard it was an acquired taste, and I acquired it in a hurry."

Sim didn't want his load to be too heavy, but he couldn't resist stuffing a few more of the cans of caviar into the backpacks. He was thinking about the reaction of his friends at the airport when they would see what he had returned with.

There were too few items in the restaurant storeroom that were useful for backpacking through a zombie infested city, and Sim started trying to think where he could find something that didn't need to be cooked. The sterno wasn't going to go to waste on hot food. It would be used for heat and hot water.

He didn't expect to find anything like instant coffee or tea, but he was pleasantly surprised to find both. The supply closet where the hotel kept the little packs of sugar and the single-cup coffee packs had just what he needed. There was even a couple of random boxes he didn't expect but were quite valuable. One was a box of beef sticks and one was a box of beef jerky. Both were obviously intended for vending machines but had found their way into the kitchen storage area.

He fit everything into the backpack until it was hard to close and then scanned around for anything he may have forgotten.

Weapons were easy to find in the kitchen. He settled on a meat cleaver, a long knife, and a knife sharpener on a handle. It was a traditional serrated style that was heavy and could be used like a short baton.

Once he was satisfied with his scavenging, Sim cautiously approached the revolving front door. It was time to brave the cold, and he had enough daylight ahead of him to make it a good distance. All he needed was a little luck.

Sim squeezed into the revolving door on the side opposite the one infected dead that was still trying to move. Sim didn't want to turn the door far enough to free the infected from his prison. After all, there could be another survivor around, and Sim wanted to leave the kitchen for the next lucky person.

As soon as he was free of the revolving door, the cold air slapped him in the face. The hotel entrance was in the middle of several high rise buildings and the street out front was like a sheet of ice, descending down a steep hill.

He mentally pictured how easy it would be to slide from the front door all the way to the bottom of the hill, but there was one thing he had learned about random survival thoughts. As soon as he had one, he tended to follow up with what could possibly go wrong. He pictured himself sliding at high speed with the cold wind whistling by, and when he would glance back over his shoulders there were several dozen of the infected dead sliding on their rear ends right behind him. Worse, they were gaining on him.

Sim decided he would stick to stealthy progress instead of rapid progress. He had pictured the cold wind accurately, and two steps out onto the icy sidewalk were enough for him to know that if he slipped, he would slide a long way. He pulled his collar tight around his neck and tugged a wool ski cap from a pocket. It was worse than he remembered.

It was uncomfortable walking with his feet spread so far apart, but he eventually felt like he could do it without falling down. Crossing the street made him feel naked and exposed, but he would need to cross plenty more streets before he got back to the airport.

Sim decided time was too important. When he was just trying to get away, time didn't matter as much. He knew he was going to be on the road for years if he lived that long. Now that he was going back, time mattered more for several reasons. One of them was that the cold weather would be ending soon, and the warmer it got, the more infected he would have to face. Another reason seemed silly when he thought about it, but knowing he was so close to the airport was like being able to see the finish line. He would hate to die so close to being safe with his friends again.

As he crossed the once beautiful brick streets, he could see an overpass in the distance. His navigator's memory told him he had reached the interchanges on the interstate that went right by the airport. I-670 would take him to I-270, and if I-270 was clear, he could make it most of the way back by nightfall, and he could go the rest of the way in the morning. The problem was the interstates.

Once you were on an interstate, it was hard to get back off again. They rose above the streets of neighborhoods, and when the infection spread, thousands of people died on the interstates. Sim was afraid to find out if the interstates were still that bad, but he had already experienced the nightmares of neighborhood streets. He didn't want to repeat the experience of ducking from house to house, being driven away from where he wanted to go, and only being alive because he could climb fences, and they couldn't. In the end, he decided he would try the interstates, and if he had to jump from an overpass it was better than spending two weeks climbing fences.

It took longer to get from the Arena District onto the mess where I-71 merged with I-670, but once he was up on the raised concrete highway he felt a little better. At least he could see more than a block at a time, and he wasn't tripped over the orange and white construction barrels every few feet.

He could also see that the snow drifts in the neighborhoods below were so deep that he could have walked straight into parked cars without knowing they were there. He could also have walked straight into the waiting arms of the infected that had been frozen outside.

The interstates weren't spared the snowdrifts, and they were as choked with cars, trucks, and buses as the streets below, but at least the infected dead up on the interstate were still frozen solid. Maybe it was because of the cold air under the highway. Whatever the reason, Sim started moving as quickly as he could.

He made good time, and even he was surprised by how determined he had become since the year before. Everything around him was covered with snow, and the light reflected into his eyes, making him squint as he ran.

To take his mind off the cold and the difficulty of running in the snow drifts, he thought about what it would be like back at the airport, and he thought about what he had survived just trying to leave. This was not a world that welcomed lone survivors. The only way to make it was in a group. Of course he was feeling a little proud of himself for thinking of a way to see in that dark stairwell. For a fleeting moment he imagined an old friend telling him that one day he would set fire to a zombie and roll it down five flights of stairs. It hurt to laugh and run at the same time, but he couldn't help himself.

That night Sim holed up in a musician's tour bus. On the side of the bus was the name of some country group he had never heard of, but the bus was such a perfect place to stay that he swore he would start listening to country music if he survived long enough.

The doors had all been locked, so Sim had gotten inside by prying open a small window. He was convinced it would be full of infected dead just waiting for someone to open a door, but it was empty. Whoever had abandoned the bus on the first day of the infection hadn't realized how safe they would have been to just stay where they were until they could escape.

After searching with cautious amazement, Sim sat down on a brushed leather sofa and let himself sink into the luxury around him. He didn't know which surprised him more, an extremely safe tour bus or the fact that he was crying.

When he was finally able to regain control, Sim made sure all of the windows were well covered with the heavy curtains and then opened the hatch that served as a sky light in the ceiling. He propped his elbows on the frame around the opening and aimed his binoculars at the airport.

Smoke was still rising from the end of the concourse at the end of the terminal, but he couldn't make out the details of what had been burned. The terminal didn't appear to have burned and neither had the planes. He wasn't sure, but it had to be an infected that was walking into the center of the area that was still burning, and it wasn't long before the glowing cinders of the dying fire caused that infected to flare up like a match.

"Well, if the infected are burning, there won't be as many for me to outrun when I get down there."

Sim lowered the hatch most of the way closed as he climbed down into the comfort of the tour bus. He needed to vent the fumes from his sterno, and that meant losing heat, but he would have more than enough to keep him alive.

He set up the little cans and lit a few of them, then he used one of his precious bottles of water to make some coffee. While it was getting hot, he warmed his hands, but he also checked the cabinets. There was a whole case of bottled water, and someone had really liked Johnny Walker Red.

After the sun went down Sim had shaded the light from his sterno cans and climbed up to see if anything new was happening at the airport. The fire was getting smaller, and he thought he saw a flashlight on the roof of the terminal.

He was sure he would make it home to his friends. That was his final thought as he drifted off to sleep in a warm bed, compliments of someone he wished he had listened to before the infection.

16 THE LONGEST YEAR

When they decided to burn the frozen infected, they went from elation to worry. Then they went from worry to fear, and then all the way back to elation again. They couldn't get over how well the infected had burned, and then with the arrival of the horde from the interstate they had worried about how many of them were catching fire and then wandering away in different directions.

Flaming infected dead were drawn toward other flaming bodies, and some walking unnaturally long distances before their bodies gave into the inevitable damage that caused them to fall over.

They saw more and more of them get together into smaller, burning, wandering groups, and it seemed like sooner of later one of those groups would find its way to the underbelly of a fuel truck or airplane. There was no way to tell how much heat it would take to light off a chain reaction of fires and explosions, but they were sure it would happen.

When Jon made his last inspection rounds for the night, he took a chance and turned on his flashlight because he wanted to see if any of the infected had managed to douse their own flames in the snowdrifts along the buildings. He knew there was a chance of being seen, but he didn't believe there could be anyone left alive who would be watching.

It crossed his mind that Sim was out there, but he firmly believed Sim was at least making his way through West Virginia by now. If anyone else was out there, Jon had a little faith that they would appreciate a warm place to be.

When he was done circling the roof of the terminal, he was satisfied that they hadn't made a bad situation worse and headed for the access door to the roof.

A scraping noise carried across the otherwise quiet night, and Jon instinctively lowered himself to the graveled roof. It was almost totally dark already, and Jon put his back to the area where some small fires still burned. He wanted to be facing away from the light to allow his eyes to adjust, and he knew that he would be silhouetted against the only light in the area. As quietly as he could, he lowered himself into a prone shooter's position.

As his eyes got used to the dark, he scanned from left to right and back again. As he watched he listened, and he heard something on the ladder. He held his breath. He knew that anyone who came over the edge of the roof on the ladder would immediately be facing the light behind where he was stretched out, and that was a big advantage for Jon unless the person saw his irregular form first.

Jon was sure he could see a shadow grow in between the bars of the ladder, and it seemed to stop as if it was in a crouch. The quiet was complete, but Jon saw the shadow slowly rotate. He had the advantage, so he had to use it. If it was a person, they would still have their hands on the ladder.

"Stay completely still until I say you can move."

Jon was surprised by how calm his own voice sounded.

The shadow jerked just enough to mean the person was startled, but Jon had expected it, so he kept his finger off of the trigger. The dark shape moved from side to side which was also expected. Whoever it was, they would try to see where the voice had come from.

Jon eased his finger onto the trigger and said, "That's enough of trying to figure out where I am. I said to stay completely still until I say you can move."

From somewhere behind the shadow and probably a few rungs down the ladder, Jon heard someone else.

"What's the hold up?"

The shadow made a shhh sound but stayed still.

Jon said, "If you have a flashlight, shine it in your own face. If I see it point my way, I'll pull the trigger of the gun I have aimed at your chest."

Jon knew if the shadow on the ladder had a flashlight in his eyes for even a split second, he would have an even bigger advantage, but if he had the same done to him, he would have to fight at least two people. He couldn't take that chance, so he put a little more pressure on the trigger.

By this time, his eyes had adjusted well enough for him to make out the details of the person between the bars of the ladder, but more importantly, he could see his hands. There was something shaped like a flashlight, and the stranger had to hook one arm around the bar of the ladder to be able to hold onto whatever it was in his hand, but something was wrong. Jon wasn't sure what it was when he pulled the trigger, but his gut reaction probably saved his life.

Two taser darts on wires harmlessly hit the wet roof to his left, but his shot didn't miss. The dark shadow flew several feet away from the wall before descending to the ground. Jon stayed where he was and waited for the second shadow to appear, more quickly than the first.

Whoever this guy was, he was under the impression that being mad counted for more than a bullet. He came over the edge ready to fight.

Jon shouted, "One warning is all you get."

The man charged Jon, but he wasn't fast enough. Jon shot him twice before he fell back over the edge.

He waited several minutes to be sure there was no one else, then he crawled over to the edge by the ladder. All he could see below was the big dark shadows cast by the building.

Jon was breathing heavy and was scared. It didn't feel good to kill the men, but he was satisfied that he had given them a chance. He would never know if they were good or bad people, but he didn't think good people would try to tase you first and talk later.

When he got back inside and told the others what had happened, Garrett insisted that they should go up and search the area just to be sure it was safe. After an hour they decided they could go back inside, but they posted a watch inside the roof access door. Until they knew for sure that the fires hadn't drawn more survivors to the airport, they decided they would post the watch every night.

******

Garrett told Susan she could stand watch from inside the access door to the roof, but she preferred to sit outside on watch for as long as she could. Every sound of expanding or contracting metal, every creak that was no more than an echo back to her own position from some movement she made, and every breeze that squeezed through a small gap somewhere made her feel like she wasn't alone.

At least when she was out on the roof she could put her back up against something and focus on what was in front of her. If something came up behind her, it wouldn't see her until it stepped into her side view.

The infected didn't sneak up on you, but the uncertainty of the night before had left them all on edge. Jon was second guessing everything while Garrett was trying to reassure him that he had no choice. If the unknown men had been friendly, the first one wouldn't have tried to use a taser, and the second one wouldn't have tried to charge him. They would have tried to talk with him.

Jon had rationalized the situation to the point that he was sure he could have told the man not to try what he was about to do. Time moved differently in memories, and Jon questioned whether or not he had pulled the trigger too quickly.

No one blamed him, especially when he had shown them the taser. Garrett studied the spot where Jon had been, and it occurred to him just how lucky Jon was. In the darkness, Jon had put his body directly across a big puddle of ice water. His heart rate was probably going up like a sky rocket along with his adrenaline, but he told Garrett he was surprised how calm his voice had sounded. With his blood pounding in his ears, the taser might have been enough to kill him. There was always that risk.

Susan told herself that she would have to be as strong as Jon had been, even if it meant second guessing herself later. It may have been two men with families who were waiting for them to come back, or it could have been two men who would have cut their throats. They would probably never know, but if the man had listened to Jon, he would most likely still be alive right now.

A breeze swirled around the corner of the HVAC unit she was hiding behind, and the last bit of sunlight was disappearing beyond the horizon. She didn't know if she hated the midnight watch more than sundown. She would be sleepier at midnight, but the temperature always seemed to drop like a rock as the light disappeared.

Susan decided it was time to walk the perimeter of the rooftop. It would get her blood circulating a bit, and she would get to see if there was anything going on near all of the ladders. Something told her that someone on the ground would wait for sundown before letting themselves be exposed on a ladder.

The first ladder she checked was the one where the two men had tried to climb up behind Jon, and Susan just took a quick glance over the edge before pulling her head back.

A confused expression crossed her face as she tried to match what she saw with what she remembered from the last time she had seen it. Shadows were everywhere, and if you stared at one long enough it would move. Sometimes a shadow would appear to be moving when you didn't stare at it. This was one of those times.

Susan stood at the top of the ladder wondering if she should risk a glance again or if she should do as Jon had done. When she had heard his story, she remembered how impressed she had been when he said he just slowly lowered himself to the gravel roof and waited. Jon had heard a sound, and he could have waited where he was forever if nothing had been there, but he had been right.

She decided to take a page from Jon's book and backed away from the ladder. She lowered herself to the roof and aimed her Beretta at the spot between the two handrails of the ladder.

Susan willed herself to stay calm, and she heard Jon's voice talking about how he put his finger on the outside of the trigger guard until he was sure someone was there. She did the same, and just as she made the move, she felt herself involuntarily suck in her breath and then hold it.

A curved mound of shadow appeared very slowly at the edge of the roof between the bars. Susan realized she was feeling everything Jon had. She could feel her heart pounding, and hear it in her ears.

The shadow grew larger as someone rose up another step on the ladder. Susan could make out the arms, and the hands were both holding the rails. That meant whoever it was couldn't let go quickly.

"I would say freeze, but it's too damned cold out here already, so I'm just going to say don't make any sudden moves."

Susan couldn't have been more pleased with the way she sounded. She delivered her warning without even mentioning her gun, but she sounded so calm and sure of herself that the person on the ladder could only believe she meant business.

The shadow did what it was told to do, and it seemed to shift its weight slowly to one hip so it could lean up against the hand-railing on one side. The left hand came up palm first to show it was empty while the right hand stayed on the railing.

"I have one hand on a trigger, and the other hand has a flashlight. I'm going to shine it in your face, so don't fall off the ladder."

Susan hoped her expression of concern would buy a bit of goodwill from the person on the ladder.

She clicked the switch on and the beam blinded the man.

He said, "You've always been considerate, Susan. That's why everyone likes you so much."

She was so surprised to see Sim's smile that she kept the light on his face longer than she needed to. She pulled her hand away from the trigger of the gun as if it had suddenly become hot to the touch, and if Sim hadn't taken the chance to step further onto the roof, her diving bear hug would probably have carried both of them over the side.

Susan was laughing and crying at the same time, and Sim was trying to figure out what she was saying in between sobs and laughs. There was something about not getting shot, but there was also something about last night.

"Wait a minute. Wait, Susan, wait."

He was having a hard time getting her to stop long enough to make sense, so he had gotten a good hold on her arms and held his face down closer to hers.

"Are you saying someone was shot? Is everyone okay?"

He had heard it last night. Feeling like he was more comfortable than anyone had a right to be, he had heard three gunshots. They didn't sound too close, and he wasn't so sure he wanted to stick his head up through the skylight to see where they had come from. For one thing, he would lose some of his heat, and for another, he could give away his position.

The shots had been closely spaced, and then it had become quiet again. It wasn't the first time he had heard gunshots in the city, and he didn't think for a minute he and the crew of Executive

One had been the only survivors. He just doubted there was such a thing as a survivor who wouldn't shoot you for your boots.

Susan managed to choke out that everyone was fine, and Sim was able to gradually piece together that Jon had shot two men on the same ladder last night. When Sim understood that part, he knew that he had been in Susan's crosshairs. That's why she was crying so much.

In a very gentle voice he said, "It's okay now. You didn't shoot me. I know you could have, but you didn't."

Sim had debated long and hard with himself about how he was going to approach the airport terminal, especially after hearing the gunshots the night before. It could have been that someone was shooting at his friends, and there was nothing to stop either side from shooting at him.

He finally decided that he couldn't approach the terminal exposed. He spent the day getting closer to the airport and studying the terrain for signs of other people. He didn't see any living people, and most of the infected were still frozen, but he saw something beyond comprehension where the fire had been burning. From what he could tell, someone had set fire to the infected, but the fire didn't burn out. That could only mean one thing. Some kind of fuel had been used as an accelerant.

Sim thought it was possible that there had been a fuel spill, and someone lit the spill, but if that was true, it would have burned more violently and even spread to the buildings. In an odd sort of way, this was like it had been a calculated or controlled burn. If he didn't know better, he would think Jon had something to do with it.

It seemed like most of the infected in the area had been drawn into the fire. He saw plenty that were frozen in place, and they would be a problem when the weather got warm again, but he was able to move quickly and give them a lot of room.

When the ladder was in sight, Sim patrolled the area until sunset, then he eased closer. He never saw Susan take up her position on the roof, and he had to give her a lot of credit for that. He knew there were people in the building, and she still managed to get the drop on him. After what he had seen out there on his own, he was glad to see his friends had become so aware of the dangers they were facing.

Speaking of which, Sim was suddenly more afraid of what he had left behind. If Jon had shot two people the night before, there could be more of them, and standing at the top of the ladder would make them an easy target.

He took Susan by the arm and led her toward cover. The way he was shying away from the darkness was all she needed to keep her from resisting.

"How long have you been on watch tonight?" he asked.

"Since four o'clock. I'm on until eight," she said.

"Well, I'm not going to drop in on the others after last night. If they see me coming by myself, they could think I'm just someone who made it past you. I'll stay up here with you, and we can go in together when your relief comes out. Who's up after you?"

"Mike, and he was begging Garrett to let Addison stand watch with him, not because he was trying for some alone time. All of us are scared and don't want to be out here by ourselves. There are four ladders to the roof. What if those two guys had chosen a different ladder to climb?"

"Jon would have heard them and been waiting at that ladder," said Sim. He said it as if it was a fact. "Jon's taking the threat seriously, and because he did, he put an end to it, at least for the time being."

They settled in behind an HVAC unit with Sim sitting along one side and Susan around the corner ninety degrees from him. That way they could keep watch and whisper to each other.

"It's so good to see you again, Sim. Was it bad out there?"

"Yes, it was stupid for me to think I could make it back home on my own. No one's going anywhere by themselves if they want to survive."

"What was it like?"

Sim didn't know where to begin. There was so much between the airport and Columbus.

"I spent one night inside a dumpster. There was a raccoon in there with me that kept attracting the attention of the infected. Every time it was quiet enough for me to climb out, he would start making a racket."

"How did you get out?"

"Well, remember I'm from the South, so getting the drop on a raccoon isn't something new to me."

Susan's face appeared around the corner of the HVAC unit to see if he was smiling as he described it. He did smile when he saw her skeptical expression.

"I'm not lying to you. I chucked the raccoon out, and while the infected chased after it I got away."

Before she could ask him what happened next he went on.

"I found a tunnel, and I thought I could use it to cover some ground without freezing to death, but let me tell you, that was a bad idea. I got lost, couldn't see most of the time, and I didn't know if I would ever find my way out of there again."

Sim was thinking back, but he was also thinking ahead to what they were going to do if there really was an elevator next to Air Force One.

"After I got out of the tunnel, I kept trying to go south, but I kept running into hordes of those infected. I had to run from them and try to flank them at the same time, but every time I thought I was ahead of them, there were more. They kept me moving west, right into downtown Columbus."

"You didn't see any other living people?"

Sim just shook his head, not even thinking about whether or not Susan could see him do it. The devastation and the loss of life had been so complete. It was a miracle that they were still alive.

"I slept in a lot of cars, but it was funny how they still found you. You could be on the floor buried under blankets, and the car would start rocking. You knew what you were going to find when you lifted your head. You just didn't know how you were going to get out of the car without a scratch."

Before Susan could ask another question, he said, "I gotta know what happened over there before I tell you anything else. When I saw that big open area and all of those blackened heads it reminded me of my aunt's Thanksgiving ham. What the hell happened over there?"

Susan was thoroughly confused.

"What in the world did your aunt do to her Thanksgiving ham?"

Both of them had to put their hands over their mouths and muffle the laughing until they could stop.

"We need to do better on watch," said Sim. "Let's make a pass around to the other ladders, then I'll tell you about the ham."

Fifteen minutes later they settled back in next to the HVAC unit again, but they rotated to the other sides. They resumed whispering but kept their eyes and ears on the areas where the ladders reached the roof.

"About that ham," said Sim. "My aunt would use a whole can of cloves on the outside of her ham. You know, she'd stick them in the ham in a pattern until the ham was covered with these little black things poking out everywhere. That's what all those heads were like. It was like someone went around and poked big black cloves in the ice, then they set fire to them."

Susan thought a minute. They actually did have an appearance like someone had put them there, but it only seemed like that because they only burned the ones they could reach. They tossed ladles of fuel on their heads, but sometimes they couldn't get close enough to torch them.

"I guess it smelled a little worse than ham and cloves," said Susan. "Jon got this idea that we could control the fire if we only put fuel on the infected. What we didn't count on was a big horde strolling in from the interstate and catching fire along with the heads."

"That interstate?"

Sim pointed toward the place where he had spent the night.

"Yeah. The interstate must've been loaded with them until we set the others on fire. Then they just seemed to keep coming."

"That explains why I didn't see many up there. So, you guys did that. You may have thinned out the neighborhood enough for us to get away."

"Get away? Are you going back out and trying again?"

"No, we all are. Not until next winter, but I think I know a way out. I'll tell you all about it when we get back inside with the others."

Sim checked his watch.

"It's almost time for Mike to be taking over the watch. Keep an eye out for him. We don't want him to get too excited when he sees two people up here."

Mike appeared from the access door right on schedule, and Susan was waiting for him at the door. They exchanged a few words, and Mike started excitedly trying to see into the darkness on the roof. Sim stood up and walked over to him, and they exchanged big hugs.

Sim took a moment to reassure Mike that he was okay and said he had a little present for him. He fished around in his bag and produced a can of caviar, a can opener, some crackers, and a small spoon. He promised he would save some Johnny Walker Red for him and told him he needed to get Susan inside.

Mike felt like it was just what he needed to help him make it through four cold hours on the roof.

Sim felt like he was back in familiar territory when he ducked in through the door. Even though it was still cold in the ceiling of the terminal, it was much warmer than it was outside.

Susan led the way, and eventually they reached the spot where the mark on the ductwork indicated they were near their main shelter. Sim saw the word written on the aluminum and realized, it had been their shelter for a long time, but they needed to make it their home for a while longer. He didn't think he would find it too difficult to convince the others once he told them what he suspected.

Garrett told them all to keep an eye on the ceilings, and not just where they had put holes they used to get around. He told them to watch for bulges where it had been flat before, and to watch for wet spots in case water started getting in. Water could mean they were walking on a soft part of the roof. Bulges could mean someone else was walking around in the ceiling.

Garrett was facing in the direction of the hole in the main terminal when he saw Susan's feet dangling through. They had a rope tied to a rafter, and they had become quite good at climbing up and sliding down.

Susan slid down, and Garrett glanced away just as Sim came through the hole. Addison was just coming out of the tunnel that led to the passenger bridge still attached to their plane, and she saw Sim follow Susan. Her shriek scared the hell out of Garrett, and he pulled his Beretta.

By the time Garrett got in position with his gun, he couldn't quite understand what he was seeing. Addison was hugging someone taller than her and her feet were swinging in the air. Then Sim turned his way and a broad smile spread across Sim's face.

"Hey, Garrett. I'll settle for getting chewed out if you're still mad at me for leaving."

Garrett let out a sigh of relief as Anne and Jon both came out of the shelter to see what was going on.

Susan got Addison to stop squealing by pointing at the chained doors at the far end of the terminal. From time to time they still heard the unmistakable sounds made by the infected coming from that hallway, and they hadn't decided whether to eliminate them or leave them there as a buffer against people.

Sim and Garrett walked toward each other, and even though Sim wouldn't have blamed Garrett for being upset with him, he saw that Garrett was as relieved to see Sim as the others were. Garrett probably hugged him harder than Susan or Addison.

"Let's get you two warmed up," said Anne. "I just made some fresh coffee."

They led Sim to the restaurant they had modified as if he didn't know the way, but he had to admit, they had really improved it since he had left.

They had lowered the chain cage gate across the front of the store half way. If they had to pull it down in a hurry, they would only need to pull it six more feet. They had also built barricades along the entrance until the only way in was through a space no bigger than a normal door. If anyone or any thing got into the hallway outside the restaurant, they would have to face whatever was waiting for them in a smaller entrance.

Sim pushed a curtain away with one hand and ducked inside. Directly in front of him was a row of sharpened steel posts all aimed waist high and secured by some heavy furniture.

"I can see you guys hired a decorator while I was gone," said Sim. "I like what you've done with the place."

Anne went past Sim into the main living area and poured him some coffee. Sim gratefully accepted the cup, and moved toward a place to sit.

"Here, I'll trade you this for the coffee."

He handed Anne his overstuffed backpacks as he sat down. Anne's curiosity got the best of her, and she started digging through the contents. The sterno cans were a nice surprise, but they still had a pretty good supply because there were several restaurants in the concourse.

The cans of caviar made her laugh, and she started passing out crackers and plates to everyone.

"I don't think we need to ration this," she said to no one in particular. "Besides, we're celebrating."

"What about Mike?" asked Addison.

"I promised we'd save him some caviar, but Sim gave him some to snack on while he's on watch," said Susan.

"Yeah, that's gonna happen," said Jon as he dug into a can.

They laughed, but they set aside another can for him. Next out of the backpacks was a bottle of Johnny Walker Red, and everyone grabbed for the plastic cups. A little shot would go a long way to lift their spirits even though they were already picked up by the surprise return of Sim.

"What are these?" asked Anne.

She held up some single sheets of advertising that was printed on fliers like the junk mail everyone used to sort out and throw away without a second glance.

"I found those when I stayed in a hotel in downtown Columbus. I thought you guys might be interested in them."

"You stayed in a hotel?" asked Garrett. "How in the world did you get reservations?"

Jon said, "I'm going to put my money on Sim having a story about how he got a room."

"Let's just say, I didn't check in by conventional means, and the practice I got climbing ropes in this place came in handy. Room service wasn't so hot, I had noisy neighbors, but that place really believed in stocking their minibars."

Sim spent about an hour describing what life was like outside the airport terminal. Susan pushed him into telling them about the raccoon, and they all had a good time hearing about it.

The conversation got much more somber in tone as Sim described the close calls and the long cold nights when he had to settle for sleeping in cars or under cardboard boxes.

One of his best nights had been when he came to a train that was sitting on some tracks he needed to cross. Sim had climbed to the top of one of the cars with the idea that he could simply use it to survey his surroundings, but he found something even better. One of the cars was stacked with SUV's, and Sim was able to get some sleep inside one of them without the usual wake-up call from the infected.

That night it had snowed like he had never seen before, and Sim couldn't imagine being colder, but at least he was out of the wind. On a whim he reached up and pressed a button that said IGNITION, and he was surprised when the engine started. He was worried about the noise of the engine, but the heater felt too good for him to turn it off. He lowered a window a few inches to vent the fumes and turned the heater up as high as it could go.

Just before sunrise Sim felt a chill. He wasn't surprised that the gas had run out. He was just grateful for the few hours of warmth the SUV had given him. The problem was the crowd that had gathered around the train on both sides.

It was still too dark to really see how bad things were, but judging by the moaning, it was really bad. Sim turned off the indoor light switch and opened the door just far enough to stick his head outside. From what he could tell, the infected were getting buried in the snow drifts on both sides of the railroad tracks, but on the side where the wind was pushing the snow straight at the train, the infected were disappearing several yards away.

Sim planned to go that way, so he was very interested in why they were disappearing over their heads so soon. He kept watching as the sun peeked over the horizon, and it seemed like the infected were still disappearing. Then he saw why. The train was sitting at the top of a hill.

He climbed further forward, and he saw there were no infected at all. He thought he was the luckiest man in the world when he figured out that the train wasn't sitting on a hill. It was an overpass above an interstate.

Sim carefully climbed out of the SUV and began working his way forward. The climbing was easy, but the cold wind made his eyes water. As the sun came up, he saw that some of the infected were trying to follow him, but they were falling over the edge of the embankment and rolling away into drifts that were at least twenty feet deep.

The flight crew of Executive One sipped at their drinks and listened quietly as Sim described his attempt to go home. Any of them could have said, "I told you so," but the truth was they had each hoped he would make it. They may have been safe and warm, but a close friend was risking his life.

After his night on the train Sim was closer to the tall buildings of the city, but he kept trying to go south. He spent days trying to keep from being pushed into the city, but everywhere he went he ran into barriers. More and more of the infected were frozen solid, but it seemed like whole gangs of them found ways to accidentally stay warm. Sim had crawled through the window of a house only to jump from another window on the second floor of the same house. He had been chased up the stairs by at least a dozen of the infected that had been warm enough not to freeze. When he landed outside in the snowbank at the side of the house, the street was full of them, and it just happened to be the direction he needed to go.

Eventually Sim got around to telling them about the hotel. The infected had won the battle when it came to preventing him from going south, but if they hadn't, he wouldn't have been able to get some rest, warm his bones, and recharge his batteries for the trip back to the airport.

He explained how he got into the hotel using the handlebars from a motorcycle, and it was obvious that everyone was cheered up just a bit by his ingenuity. Picturing him throwing the handlebars combined with the Johnny Walker Red made it funnier than it had been at the time.

When Sim finally got around to telling them about his discovery in the hotel room and his theory about the elevator under Air Force One, his friends sat in stunned silence. Cups weren't moving, and no one spoke.

He told them that he remembered the odd pattern of body parts on the floor of the hangar, but he didn't connect the dots until he read the literature in the suitcases. It made sense that a city with a hidden tunnel already in place would be perfect for a shelter.

Garrett asked, "Are you trying to tell us the President has been under that hangar this entire time?"

Sim shook his head.

"No, I'm just saying that's where he went underground. Remember, the military was waiting in there with armored vehicles. They had the plane taxi partially into the hangar, and then they fought off the infected while the plane unloaded."

"But what's this thing about the bodies being cut in half?" asked Anne.

"They had this thing planned ahead of time, and they spared no expense. They knew which airport to land at, and they even suggested that we should go check out Rickenbacker. I think they were trying to get rid of us. The military led them into the hangar, and an elevator came out of the floor. When it was in the air, the infected fell into the elevator shaft, but when it came back down, it caught the ones that were extended over the edge. Whatever got caught was cut off."

"You saw some that were cut in half?" asked Garrett.

"All around it, on all four sides, and even though I didn't make anything of it at the time, there were some that were mashed in half instead of clean cuts."

Sim made a motion with his hands like he was trying to recreate the effect, but it was Anne who came up with the best way to visualize it.

"It would be something like this," she said, as she held a beer bottle above a rubber Ohio State coozie.

She lowered the bottle slowly into place, but she kept one finger extended over the opening. Since it was rubber, the bottle stretched the coozie and squeezed her finger against the side of the beer bottle.

"Right," said Sim excitedly, "but since the elevator is heavy and the floor is hard, the downward force would probably smash the bodies into the gap before the inevitable happened."

They all exchanged nods with each other as if they were confirming what they were each thinking. There were silent nods of agreement that Sim had stumbled upon how the President had made it to safety.

"How many bodies would you guess you saw?" asked Garrett.

"Hard to tell," said Sim. "When I climbed up into the wheel well, my only thought was getting into a safe place. When it became obvious that I had made a mistake, my goal changed to just staying out of sight. Those things were everywhere around the wheels. I couldn't even take a chance that they would see me up there."

Jon said, "Regardless of how many there were, it's the only way to explain why they were cut in half at the waist, why the upper halves of the bodies were gone, why they were all spread out around a perimeter, and why they were oriented as if they were facing the center of that perimeter."

"So, what are we going to do about it?" asked Susan.

Sometimes the youngest member of any group doesn't get the respect they deserve because the others feel like they have to protect the kids. It's natural for older people to be paternal toward the young, but sometimes the young come up with the simplest, most logical approaches to problems.

Addison said, "Every elevator has an up button. We just have to figure out where it is."

If Addison had suddenly materialized where she was sitting, it couldn't have surprised everyone more.

The debate started after everyone got over the surprising answer. Jon said he would have used a remote to operate the elevator. Garrett disagreed because the planners wouldn't have wanted to rely on the survival of the remote operator, and they couldn't give everyone remote control because that wouldn't ensure the safety of the President.

Jon argued that the President could be the remote operator, but no one agreed the planners would leave the President's safety in his own hands.

"I think it had to be the pilot," said Garrett. "He has to get the plane to the elevator to start with."

"No," said Susan. "I don't think the pilot even knew he was supposed to stick the nose of Air Force One into the hangar, and remember, they scramble more than one plane during an emergency, and they drafted us to be Executive One. What would have happened if they weren't able to switch back to the President's plane?"

They eventually abandoned the idea of the remote control and started hammering on ideas about where to put the physical button. Anne suggested that they had some of the same problems with a physical button and a remote control. Who would be in charge of pressing it? Who would know where it was? What if they couldn't get to the button in a time of crisis?

Sim snapped his fingers, and everyone glued their eyes to him hopefully.

"Oh, man. It's so obvious I can't believe it."

"Enlighten us," laughed Garrett.

"How many planes are standing by in the event of a national crisis?" asked Sim.

One at a time, they all shrugged. They answered more or less at the same time that there were several planes, and they were at more than one airport.

Sim was ready to give more examples of backup plans, but everyone else saw where he was going immediately.

Anne said, "There could be an up button and there could be a remote control, but at least two people would have known where either was located."

"Right," said Garrett, "and my guess would have been the Secret Service detail and the cockpit crew. Probably a sealed package with a cross check of code cards."

The military and federal agencies had all kinds of validation procedures that had to be verified by more than one person. They would both break the seals on their packages and read their codes. If the codes were given correctly, the people would do their jobs.

"No, they weren't both on Air Force One with each other. It had to be someone on the plane and someone on the ground," said Jon.

"Someone in the control tower?" asked Addison.

"I would have the pilot talking with someone in a safer place than the control tower," said Garrett. "If it was a terrorist attack, the control tower would be one of the first places they would hit with a rocket launcher. Besides, the same people aren't in the tower all the time."

As he said it, Garrett knew he had hit on something. The Secret Service detail had primary people under their protection, and the detail members would all know the plan. They would have the pilot talk with someone to get them to open the elevator, and the most likely person had to be someone who had the same vested interest as the Secret Service.

"TSA," said Garrett. "It makes sense. The Secret Service knows there's a shelter for the President in the event of a national crisis, and they don't want just anybody knowing where it is, so they put a TSA crew in the airport that coordinates in advance with the Secret Service."

Sim said, "Are you trying to tell us the elevator power is located in the airport security office?"

When they had gotten into the security office the first time, they were mainly interested in the weapons, the key cabinet, and the electrical circuit breakers. It was no surprise when the power went out in the airport, but the power to the elevator had to be on a backup system. Since then they had made several trips back to security for medical supplies and maps of the airport.

"Now we're getting somewhere," said Jon.

Before he could ask where they were, Anne was dragging a long box out of a supply closet. Maps of John Glenn International Airport were divided into electrical, plumbing, and dimensional.

"Which maps do you want?" she asked.

Sim, Garrett, and Jon all said, "Electrical."

Jon added, "One of the electrical drawings has to show a power switch and a line that goes from security all the way to the hangar, and on the other side of the switch will be the symbol for a power supply."

Three hours later Jon grumbled because he needed to relieve Mike on watch before they found it.

As he bundled up and got his gun, he asked them to do him a favor and let him know if they found it.

Mike showed up a bit later and told the others Jon had brought him up to speed. They had the maps spread out on tables and counters, and he joined in on the search.

"What if it's a remote control?" asked Anne. "There might be a switch with a power supply, but there wouldn't be a power line that goes to the hangar."

"That would be a long way for a remote to send a signal," said Sim.

"Could they have just left the line off of the drawings?" asked Mike.

"No," said Sim. "The airport repair crews would need to know where the line is so they wouldn't cut it by accident if they have to dig or bust up pavement."

Addison was busy working on something, and he saw that she was using a plastic menu as a straight edge to draw a line on a map. Her blonde hair was hanging down over it as she concentrated. When she was done she saw Sim was watching her.

"We don't need to prove the power line is there, so I figured it wouldn't hurt to add it to the map. When I got to the building I drew it to the same place where other lines come in. Is that okay?"

"Better than okay, Addison. That's how they most likely installed it."

Sim reached for her drawing and said, "Wait a minute. They could have left it off the maps as long as they required approval by TSA and airport security before doing maintenance."

"So, we're back where we started," said Garrett. "Well, we have some time on our hands. Might as well keep searching."

17 ANSWERS

They had been so sure of themselves when Sim had arrived back at the airport. It seemed so logical that he was right about the elevator, and they felt like their deductive reasoning was sound when it came to the location of the controls for the elevator.

Days went by with everyone pouring over the maps, trying to discover a hidden clue or some kind of code. They even talked about invisible ink and whether or not there was some big conspiracy like the movie National Treasure.

Garrett felt like he was going crazy when he started experimenting with different colored lights and glasses as he returned to the drawings more times than he could count. Now he knew why everyone thought Nicholas Cage was crazy when he was carrying on about rubbing vinegar on the Declaration of Independence. Garrett wasn't sure if it was vinegar because he only saw the movie once, but the problem was that he was wondering if this hadn't all been blown out of proportion.

They had eventually carried tools to the security office and began tearing out the walls one at a time. Garrett told them all that he wouldn't have to believe what was on the drawings if he could see the wires with his own two eyes.

After a week of ripping holes in sheetrock, the security office was like a big room that was never finished. They were stepping through walls as shortcuts to where they had left off the day before, but no one was finding any wiring that went anywhere other than an outlet or a light switch.

Sim started standing watch when it was his turn, and he found himself so fixated on the hangar that he would forget to walk the perimeter of the roof. He studied the big building with the tail of Air Force One poking out in their general direction, and he used his binoculars to study every detail so many times that he thought he could take the building apart and rebuild it.

They weren't exactly sure of the date, but the snow was melting away, and the infected were wandering around again. They were slower and less coordinated than they had been before, and there were definitely fewer. There were no groups out on the runways, and it seemed that there were more unmoving bodies than moving.

The wide expanse where the survivors had set fire to the exposed heads of the infected resembled a Halloween display. Dead bodies with charred, blackened heads were spaced in that odd pattern that could pass for Sim's aunt's ham, and he couldn't shake the thought. Without the snow covering the bodies he could still see the pattern.

Garrett walked up beside Sim and waited for him to lower the binoculars before speaking.

"Anything new?"

"Naw, snow's melting, and I haven't seen anything wander into or out of the hangar since I came on watch. Any idea what the date is?"

"I lost track," said Garrett. "When does it usually stop snowing in this part of the country?"

"April, I think, but I wouldn't know firsthand. We should get together and decide what day everyone wants it to be and then start keeping track again. When it starts snowing next winter we could call it the middle of November. Maybe we could do Thanksgiving a week or so after the first snow. We could do up a ham the way my aunt used to."

Garrett wondered if he should bother to ask Sim where he planned to find a ham, or cloves for that matter, but he decided to just let it go.

"What happens if we don't find the controls to that elevator by then?" asked Sim. "Are we going to keep searching for it or head for International Falls like we talked about?"

"We have plenty of time to decide, Sim. Don't get too dejected just yet. I know how much you want to get into that elevator and find out where the President went."

They stood without speaking for a few minutes, but Garrett was grinning. Sim finally noticed and grinned back, but he waited for Garrett to tell him what was so funny.

"Have you thought about what you're going to say to the President when we find out where he went to?" asked Garrett.

"I don't think anyone's going to let me wring his neck, but I would like to tell him I won't be voting for him next time, and by the way, thanks for shutting the door on us once you were safe."

"Well, that's keeping it polite, but we should have plenty of time to think about that, too."

Jon's head appeared from the door they used to get on the roof, and he had an expression on his face that made him seem younger.

"Don't tell me," said Garrett. "You found it."

"We think so, but we're not sure."

"Take Sim with you, Jon. He deserves to see it."

Sim was all smiles as he followed Jon through the door and then through the ceiling. They still used the shortcuts they had learned above the hallways, and they still hadn't figured out how to clear the infected out of a couple of places, so they hopped over ductwork and made it to the security hallway as fast as possible.

"Who found it?" asked Sim.

"The women," said Jon.

"All three of them?"

Sim was trying to picture all three of the women saying, "I found it. Here it is."

"You'll see in a minute," Jon laughed.

They dropped down through the ceiling into the security offices, and Sim tried to spot the women. He heard their voices coming down the hall from the holding cells, so he went in that direction. He found them sitting in one of the cells waiting for him. All three of them pointed at the panel of light switches in the hallway outside the three cells.

Sim followed their fingers to where they were pointing, and all he saw was a light switch panel that they had checked plenty of times before. They saw his confused expression, but they weren't going to make it too easy for him. When he interpreted their expressions as playful, he turned back to the switches and studied it.

A long time ago he had decided that it had to be something that was right in front of their eyes. Something so obvious that they were going right past it.

Sim frowned at the open panel and saw three rows of wires running along the exposed frame. They came out of the floor, attached to the bottom screw and top screws on the switches, and then traveled upward to the lights in the hallway.

He didn't want to give up, and he was just about to ask them what was different about this particular panel when he saw it.

"Why are there three switches on this panel when there are only two lights in this hallway?" he asked no one in particular.

Sim reached out to flip the three switches upward, but Jon reached out and stopped him.

"You don't want to do that. If there's power to one of these switches, and the elevator rises out of the floor in the hangar, we want to be there for it."

They had become accustomed to the lack of power in the terminal. In the first few weeks they instinctively reached for wall switches to turn on the lights, but after the first time they went down this hallway, there had never been a reason for any of them to go there again. Three empty jail cells with nothing useful inside them wasn't worth their time. By the time they checked this hallway again, they had stopped automatically flipping light switches up.

All three of the switches were in the down position, and Sim still didn't get it.

"Why do you guys think one of these switches would operate the elevator?"

"We have a theory," said Anne. "We can only test part of it, but Jon was only kidding about the elevator rising out of the floor. We think the switch actually just sends power to the elevator. Once it was powered, someone was able to raise the elevator from somewhere else."

"Okay," said Sim, "that's reasonable."

When he thought about it, the theory was huge. As a failsafe against someone randomly opening the elevator, they would have wanted someone to press the up button while within visible proximity, and to keep someone from breaching it, the elevator controls had to be powered from security. The "on" button would also have been somewhere secure where it couldn't be pressed by just anyone.

"What makes you think it's this panel?" he asked the ladies.

Addison got up and carried a lamp over to the panel. She had cut off the plug and spread the bare wires apart. She let the lamp dangle toward the floor and held it up by the wires.

"My daddy taught me this," she said as she held the wires of the lamp up to a wire that ran to the switch on the right.

Nothing happened, so she moved to the switch in the center. Nothing happened there, either. Addison carefully touched a bare spot on the third switch with one wire from the lamp while she touched the other wire to a ground wire of the first switch.

The lightbulb in the lamp came on. The third wire had power to it.

Sim stared into the tiny hole in the frame of the wall where the wire came through along with the others.

"That means there's an independent power supply below this room somewhere," said Sim.

"I don't know about you," said Anne, "but I don't really feel like beating a hole in the floor."

"I agree," said Garrett. "Besides, all we're going to find is a low voltage power supply that powers a switch somewhere in the hangar. I'm more inclined to find that switch, but getting into that hangar won't be too easy now that the snow has melted."

"You mean we're just going to hang out here until next winter?" asked Susan. "You guys are all I have left, but I'm going crazy by then. Get me a shopping cart and just let me wander around the terminal."

"It should be cold enough in November, but we won't be just sitting around until then," said Garrett. "We're going to make two sets of plans. One will be how we can get that elevator to come up, but the other will be how to travel across hostile country to Minnesota. We can't just stroll out the door and go north."

Sim added, "Just working on the best bug-out bags is going to be a job. Six months will go by fast enough."

******

Sim had been right. Time went by fast as they got back into their routines. The snow melted, and they watched as some of the infected struggled to their feet after they thawed out. The survivors all reported the same as they returned from their watches on the roof.

One night there was a heavy rain followed by a late freeze, and the infected suffered a setback in their thawing process. It gave the survivors a chance to get out and make a mad dash for the hangar one last time. A quick examination of the bodies inside the hangar was reassuring to all of them that there was something to the rectangle that fit seamlessly into the floor, but the hangar didn't give up any secrets about how to get the elevator to come up.

If nothing else, the lack of information about the elevator door was the encouragement they needed to prepare better for a long trip to Minnesota, and if by some miracle they figured out the puzzle of the elevator before leaving the safety of the terminal, they could always take their bug-out bags with them.

After the last thaw, they settled into a routine. Watches were far less boring than they had been in the previous year, and they all found themselves looking forward to their shifts. At least they did until the rain started.

It wasn't unusual to see explosions in the distance. At first they were assumed to be signs of life, but then they more correctly decided they were signs of human neglect. Natural gas pilot lights were burning everywhere, and with no one around to smell the leaks and no one around to fix them, the explosions were inevitable. Entire neighborhoods were burning down, and all they could do was watch.

When the rains started the fires didn't burn as long, but it seemed like there were always pillars of black smoke rising from somewhere no matter which direction they faced.

It wasn't easy to stay dry on top of the terminal, so they decided to build small shelters at key locations where they could stand watch without getting soaked. Instead of patrolling in the rain, they strung wires across the roof. The small construction jobs helped to pass a few more days, and they at least felt a sense of purpose. It was sitting around doing nothing that would make time slow down.

They never saw other people in the area, but Susan had a keen eye and began making a chart of the bodies after she noticed bodies she hadn't seen before. When she told Garrett what she saw, he decided to schedule two people on watch for extra coverage, but they relaxed again after seeing nothing unusual after a few days. Still, the possibility of other survivors being in the airport gave them a break in their daily routines that served to make time go by faster.

A new problem arrived with the warm weather, and it gave them more to worry about than other people.

Susan was updating her body chart, and some were missing. When she used binoculars to get a better view of the tarmac between the terminal and the big hangar, she thought one of the bodies was moving even though its head had been burned until there was nothing left. Then she saw the rat sitting on its shoulder.

Susan scanned each body one at a time and saw rats were on them all, and as she watched, more were joining the feast.

It was one of the few times that Susan had felt complete disgust since the nightmare had begun. There were plenty of times when she had felt fear and revulsion, but seeing the rats hungrily feeding on the bodies of the infected was beyond her ability to keep her cool.

"Garrett, I need you on the roof, now."

The power in the plane was still enough to keep the security radios charged, and Susan's voice carried well enough for Garrett to tell she was just barely holding it together.

"On my way."

Garrett didn't hesitate on his way to the roof, but he waved at Jon, Mike, and Sim as he dashed for the nearest rope that would take him into the ceiling. They saw his urgency and grabbed weapons as they joined in behind him.

When they arrived in force, Susan felt better even though they would need flame throwers to stop the number of rats on the tarmac. She couldn't estimate the number of rats below them, but she was glad she saw them in daylight and not at night.

"Does anyone know if rats will go after living people?" asked Mike.

"My guess is only when they run out of dead things and rotting food," said Sim. "Which leads me to a really logical question. The infected are already dead, and they're rotting even as they walk around, so are the rats eating them?"

"There's the answer to your question," said Garrett.

He pointed at a group of infected that was walking along the side of a fuel truck between the terminal and the hangar. Each of the infected had easily reached down and scooped up a rat because there were so many. As soon as they had one squirming in their hands, they were forcing them into their mouths, but from what they could tell, the rats were doing their fair share of biting as they died.

Even as far away as the roof, they were able to hear the shrieking of the rats that were being eaten. Over the squealing of thousands of rats that were feeding on bodies, the shrieking seemed to excite the mass of gray scavengers. Many of them broke away from the unmoving bodies of the infected and began attacking the infected that were wading into the swarms as if it was ankle deep water.

The rats climbed the standing infected even as the infected continued to try to eat them. It was a losing battle for anything on two legs.

"If we were down there in the middle of that," said Jon, "we wouldn't last seconds because we can feel pain. The infected are still feeding even as they go down."

"Will they come for us after the bodies of the infected are all gone?" asked Susan.

"Rats will turn on each other when the competition for food gets too hard," said Sim. "I would expect them to take advantage of the opportunity to come after us. We may be forced to move back to the plane."

"For how long?" Susan asked with obvious shock.

"I know it started feeling claustrophobic in there after a while," said Garrett, "but Sim's right. We wouldn't last ten minutes if those things find a way in, but I have an idea. Let's get inside. You too, Susan. We might not need a watch for a while."

On the way back to their shelter in the restaurant they collected the rest of the group, and Garrett explained what he was thinking.

"The rats are multiplying too fast and there's no one around to stop them. Two rats can lead to a population of fifteen thousand in one year. That's if nothing gets in their way. I don't know how many rats were here before this all started, but I think it was more than two."

Sim did some quick math and said, "If there were twenty, and each pair of ten grew to a population of fifteen thousand, that would be one hundred and fifty-thousand rats. Guys, we're talking about millions of rats. How're we going to keep millions of rats from getting in?"

"That's why we're moving to the plane, Sim. Rats are omnivores. They'll eat anything. They'll eat the coating off of wires if there's no food around, but since there's no nutritional value in wires, the population will start self-correcting when they run out of food in a large enough supply. We just have to wait them out."

When they got back to their shelter, half of them grabbed their bug-out bags and ran for the passenger bridge still attached to their plane. The rest of them began moving everything edible into the big walk-in freezer. They had emptied it and cleaned it months ago because they knew what it would smell like if they left it stocked.

Once every box or bag that held food was stashed safely inside the freezer, they began carrying food as fast as they could to the plane. Garrett gave orders as they moved as quickly as possible, and he explained that they would take it all if they had enough time, but if the rats got inside, the nearest person should be sure the freezer is shut.

They moved a remarkable amount of food before Addison spotted the first rat. Anne heard her yell and closed the freezer door. They all began a final dash carrying one last box. Together as a group they ran down the concourse and through the boarding bridge. As the last one boarded, Anne locked the door, just as she had done for a countless number of flights. The flight crew of Executive One was back where they had started.

Inside the terminal the rats had found a hallway jammed full of the infected. From there they had moved throughout the building, finding the smallest of cracks to exploit until the inside of the terminal was as covered as the tarmac outside.

They could smell the food that had been inside the shelter, and they searched around the freezer door in vain. They also began following the scent of the boxes that had been moved to the plane. Frenzied rats bit each other, and the smell of blood from those with wounds caused others to attack them. The population was self-correcting already.

Inside the safety of Executive One, a few of the crew were curious enough to watch through the small window on the center of the door, but not for long. It would have been a terrible way to die for any of them if they had been caught in the passenger bridge. The carpeted tunnel was about as wide as the lane on a road, but the floor was totally blanketed by the gray and brown swarm that scurried down the hallway.

Sim said with a slight shiver, "I am one lucky fool."

"Why's that?" asked Garrett.

"While I was out there freezing my rear end off, those things were breeding. If I was still out there when they started swarming out to find food, I would have been on their menu."

There were nods of agreement all around as they settled in for the siege.

******

November seemed to take longer to arrive once the survivors were confined to a smaller area, but as the time passed the view outside of the plane went through drastic changes. The hungry rats were like efficient eating machines that removed every scrap except bones.

The first day had been like listening to a storm approach as rats jumped against the door trying to find the food that had been in the tunnel. There was the smell of the humans who had become a food source, as well.

Above the plane, the rats were dropping from the roof of the terminal onto all of the passenger bridges. The sound of the running and bouncing rodents echoed inside the bridges like rolling thunder. All the crew could do was get comfortable and wait.

No one spoke as the attack went on for hours. Garrett sat in the familiar and reassuring surroundings of the flight deck. He had made sure the windows were all locked into place, but the furry bodies with black eyes were hanging onto the windows until they were pushed off by larger rats. He kept checking the locks and watching for cracks to appear every time a bigger, heavier rat would land.

Most of the crew just burrowed down into piles of blankets and tried to block out the noise with earphones or plugs. Sleep eluded all of them for the first few hours, but when enough time passed, they all began drifting off.

Jon joined Garrett in the flight deck, but neither man spoke. The infection had been bad, and surviving in an airport terminal was a ridiculous way to stay alive, but this was adding insult to injury.

The runways, taxiways, and grassy areas were all blanketed, and they rippled with movement going out in all directions. It was more like a choppy sea than waves rolling toward the shore.

The remaining hours of the first day passed by, and when nightfall arrived, even the pilot and copilot became tired enough to sleep. Throughout the night they were awakened when they heard the noise levels increase, but gradually they tuned out the squeals and the thumps. They all fell into a fitful sleep that left them feeling drained.

The smell of coffee was enough to wake everyone up, and Anne stepped into the flight deck with two cups. There was a faint murmuring inside the plane as opinions were exchanged about whether or not the siege had subsided at all. The sun was still below the horizon, and the frenzy outside could only be judged by what they could see and hear in the passenger bridge. No one felt like the rats could hear them inside the plane, but they agreed they didn't want to find out the hard way.

Anne quietly moved down the aisle passing out the steaming coffee, and Mike asked her if she thought the rats could smell the coffee outside the door.

She leaned closer to him and whispered that she had run a line of duct tape around the seams of the door, but she doubted it was needed in the first place. He was grateful for the extra effort and was glad that she had done it just in case.

The next three days were almost the same as the first day, but there were patches of tarmac and grass appearing slowly. The rats appeared to be turning on each other more and more as the other food sources dwindled. That included the infected dead.

When it came down to the lesser of evils, getting bitten and dying from the infection or getting eaten by rats were both a bad way to go, but the infected didn't attack each other. They did nothing to cause their numbers to decrease. The rats, however, were eating each other.

At the end of the first week after the rats arrived, they were all gathered into the area of a couple of rows of seats to have a meeting about their current situation. It wasn't uncomfortable because Mike and Jon had removed several rows of seats a long time ago when they thought they would be staying inside the plane. The extra seats were stacked to allow some privacy in other parts of the plane, and the open space was great for group meetings.

Garrett started by asking each person how he or she was holding up, and did they feel like they were overwhelmed. It was his way of getting everyone to face the gravity of the situation.

One by one the crew members all confirmed that they were still in one piece. Susan admitted that she thought her breaking point was far less than what she had already exceeded. When she did that, they all nodded in agreement.

None of them ever expected they could have survived what they had seen, and it wasn't over yet. As a matter of fact, that was one of the reasons for the meeting. They needed to talk about what they thought was going to happen next.

Garrett put the question out there, and everyone got the same disbelieving expressions on their faces.

"Wait a minute," said Addison, "I never dreamed we would ever see zombies running around biting people. I saw plenty of them in movies and on TV just like everyone else, but I didn't think it would really happen. Then came the rats, but if you had asked me what I thought would happen next before the rats appeared, I would have thought you were nuts."

"Do you think I'm nuts by asking now?"

Addison was thinking it over and wasn't quite sure, but Garrett held her gaze with a straight face.

"No, but that doesn't mean you aren't nuts," she said.

That could have come across totally wrong, but when you got right down to it, that's what Garrett was asking them to do. They were either going to go nuts, or they were going to figure out what could happen next and try to be prepared for it.

Garrett smiled at Addison. He was genuinely impressed by how well she had held up under the pressure. She might be the youngest member of the crew, but she was being as solid as a rock.

"You're asking what we think will happen next," said Sim, "but why didn't any of us see it coming? I mean the rats. Why didn't we think of that?"

"Good question," said Garrett. "We're all educated. We're all smart people. Why didn't one of us think of the consequences of this infection? What if we hadn't realized what was about to happen when we first saw the rats?"

"We'd be having this discussion inside the walk-in freezer," said Jon.

"Exactly," said Garrett. "If I haven't said it yet, you guys deserve a medal for the way you got everything to the plane in time."

"Speaking of which," said Anne, "our inventory is good to last until November if we ration."

"What about water?" asked Garrett.

Mike said, "When we took out some of the seats, Jon and I talked about what else we needed to do, and we figured the hardest thing to do was keep us supplied with water. So, we ran water hoses to two places."

"Two? Is that why Anne always has fresh coffee that tastes good?"

Garrett earned a smile from Anne and gave one to the two men for thinking of their water supply.

"We probably told you about it, Boss, but you can't keep track of everything," said Jon.

Garrett had a new appreciation for his flight crew. They could stay alive inside the plane for months while all around them sat planes full of people that had died in the first few days of the infection. If any of those people had survived longer, he doubted any would have survived the rats.

"So, who wants to tell me what's going to happen next?"

"We can tell there will be fires," said Sim. "Plenty of those burning out there right now."

"Okay," said Garrett. "What can we do if the terminal catches fire? Can we detach from the passenger bridge without letting the rats in?"

"If we have to," said Jon, "but I don't think it will come to that. The most we could expect if the passenger bridge burned would be some scorching around the door."

"Okay, so if our next problem isn't fire, what will it be? Locusts?"

Anne answered for the group, "I think the plagues are in the Bible but not so much about zombies."

"Rats again," said Sim.

Everyone turned in his direction, and they wore the same expression of disbelief.

Mike said, "They're reducing their own population, Sim. Give them a few weeks, and the only rats we'll see are the ones hiding in the dark corners. It won't be any worse than it was before."

"No, I think Sim's right," said Susan, "but he doesn't mean there will be swarms again. The food supply wouldn't support that. What he's talking about is a new breed of rats, more aggressive and possibly more dangerous."

"Thanks, Susan. That's exactly what I meant with one more totally psycho twist."

Everyone waited for Sim to go on, but he gave them a moment to let it sink in. He could see the dawn of understanding on their faces, and with understanding came the fear mixed with revulsion.

Sim went on, "The rats ate all of the infected that we disposed of by burning their heads, then they attacked the infected that were still on their feet. I don't know which is worse, slow moving zombies or fast moving rats that have been eating infected meat."

"Do you think they'll attack living people like us once their numbers are back down?" asked Addison.

"Rats didn't generally attack people before the infection because the food supply was large enough to support their population," said Sim. "People were the biggest enemy to rats, and after the first few days of the infection reduced the number of people who controlled rats, there was enough rotten food to support a larger population of rats. Now that they've eaten the available food, including themselves, their next logical food source will be survivors. The only places where people will be safe are places that have other predators that will eat the rats."

Jon shook his head and added, "And whatever eats the rats will eventually turn to attacking people."

Sim said, "I was thinking along the lines of things that were already dangerous to people. Something like alligators. An island on the coast would be the safest place, but cities will be the worst place to be."

"We're a long way from the coast," said Garrett. "Are we still in agreement that a cold climate is our best bet?"

There were general nods of agreement, but Garrett could tell everyone was still trying to wrap their minds around rats that were infected because they had eaten the infected dead.

"I hate to admit it," said Sim, "but I didn't think of it myself until I started considering rats as a food source."

If they weren't shocked before, they were now. Sim held up his hands in mock self-defense.

"Hey, I was only trying to think about what we would do for food if we don't find caches of canned food. Then it occurred to me that the rats that ate the infected dead may be able to pass the infection on to humans by biting them."

Jon ran his hand over his bald head and felt a little old for a man of thirty-five. He wondered if everyone would still be together when they got to International Falls, Minnesota. It was only about a thousand miles from Columbus, Ohio.

******

The months passed, and November promised to be everything that they hoped it would be. There were signs of snow by the middle of October, and the first white flakes began to fall as soon as the month ended.

The water supply had kept the survivors of Executive One from going crazy. Aside from water for cooking and drinking, they were at least able to keep hygiene from becoming a major problem. They would all kill for a long, hot shower, but being able to shave and wash their hair made them stay civilized. Susan had even shaved Jon's head for him a few times, and everyone pretended not to notice they were closer to each other than before.

The same could be said for Mike and Addison. They were a natural fit due to their ages, and they had plenty of similar interests. Despite their youth, they were also as discreet as possible given the close quarters.

Anne and Garrett were the oldest members of the crew and by no means unattractive to each other or the others, but they couldn't let go of their seniority and professional relationships. They maintained an air of that professionalism for the sake of the others, especially Sim. As the only African American male on the crew he had also felt the difference to some extent, but he had to admit, he did think of all of them as his family.

Anne, Jon, and Sim passed much of their time planning for the day when they would be leaving the plane. They covered every aspect of an overland trip north to the border of Canada and Minnesota, and they were somewhat afraid they couldn't cover one thousand miles before the weather became warm again, but then it dawned on them that the winter weather would last longer the further they traveled. All they had to do was keep moving and stay away from whatever came next after infection and rats.

On the topic of what came next, the trio played cards on the floor of the galley and chatted every night. It was as if that time of the evening was reserved for recreation and discussing hypothetical situations.

Sim didn't have to work very hard to convince them that the rats would become aggressive and seek out new prey because they had seen it for themselves. The runways, taxiways, and grass were all clear of rats and bodies, so the rats were either dying off or searching somewhere for another food source. They saw what desperation the rats were being driven to when they saw larger animals run across the airport with rats clinging to them.

A bear had come into full view with a dozen rats biting it, and the enraged animal was removing them one at a time. It had apparently gotten close enough to the terminal for them to attack as a group but had run far enough to get away from their hiding place. Smaller animals wouldn't do as well.

After the bear had removed the rats, crushing them in its powerful jaws, it had sat and licked its wounds before moving on. It would undoubtedly learn to stay away from buildings.

The scenario was repeated with smaller, faster animals, but it hadn't worked out as well for them. Coyotes had become more common in the wide open fields as the grass had grown, but speed didn't help them once they were caught by the rats. Sometimes they would all disappear into the tall grass, and a few hours later the rats would emerge and scurry off to their dark hiding places.

The next danger after the rats was unanimously accepted as being other survivors who hadn't done as well as the flight crew. They had to consider anyone they met as being a threat until they had a reason to believe otherwise. That also meant being sure that anyone they met wasn't already infected.

When the suggestion was made by Garrett that the other survivors may pose a threat to them because they were a superior force, they decided they wouldn't let anyone get close enough to them to use their superiority. They were going to make it to International Falls by being stealthy.

Sooner or later, the hangar had come up during every card game, and they agreed that no idea was too outrageous to consider. They ruled out crazy suggestions, but they talked about them first.

Sim was the one who had originally noticed the floor of the hangar and the way body parts were distributed around the square seam in the otherwise perfect floor, and he constantly felt like it was right before his eyes. He felt like it was so obvious that anyone could see it.

During a card game at the beginning of October, Anne pointed out that they were running out of time to solve the riddle of the hangar and whatever that thing was in the floor. She had just made the comment when Sim got a strange, far off look on his face.

"I think I've got it," he said. "Or maybe I've got part of it."

"Does it have something to do with not having much time left?" asked Anne.

"Not really, but it's the way you said it that made me think of how quickly everything happened that day. When that Army vehicle got out in front of Air Force One and led it into the hangar, the pilot was directed to that exact spot so the elevator, if that's what it is, would line up with the door of the plane."

Garrett said, "X marks the spot?"

"Yeah, the front wheels must have been positioned exactly where they needed to be. Then the elevator was raised. If the distance had been too far, they would have needed to jump from the plane to the elevator, and I can't see the President being told to make that jump."

"So, how did they know where to stop?" asked Anne.

Garrett was scratching his head and staring into space as if he was thinking of something and could see it at the same time.

"Remember when you were a kid, and you had to park the family car in the garage the first time?" he asked.

Anne and Sim both smiled and talked at the same time. They laughed, and Sim said, "Ladies first."

"My dad hung a tennis ball on a string, and when I was far enough inside, the ball would barely touch the windshield, and I would stop."

Sim added, "At least that was the theory. My brother would try to hit the tennis ball hard enough to bounce it into the wall and then try to stop in time."

"How'd that work out for him?" asked Garrett.

"Exactly how you would expect," said Sim. "My dad didn't speak for a whole week."

"Well, maybe we should just look for a tennis ball on a string," said Garrett.

18 COLUMBUS STREETS

Arriving at night wasn't part of the plan, but it was becoming obvious we wouldn't make it before the sun went down. Plumes of smoke rose from so many locations that we had to change course several times. Detours around billowing clouds of smoke was better than flying through them and then learning they were chemical fires. Smoke from chemical fires was not only toxic to the passengers, it could put a helicopter out of commission.

We were forced to land in an open field in the middle of Tennessee when Captain Miller's chopper sounded a warning that the engine was being starved of fuel. That particular problem didn't surprise the pilots who had already expressed concerns about using fuel that had been sitting still inside storage tanks for over a year.

One of the helicopters sat down next to Captain Miller's to keep an eye on their surroundings while the crew went to work on the problem. Cleaning out a series of filters would make it good as new, but it would take more time than they liked. While they worked, the Chief circled along with the third Navy helicopter to survey the damage in the area and clear the area of threats.

When they were sure the area was reasonably safe, they both landed with the others, and everyone took the opportunity to stretch their legs. It wasn't uncomfortable riding in the helicopters. As a matter of fact it was better than riding in a car or a commercial airliner, but we were all eager to reach Columbus and begin our double mission of finding the President's shelter and eliminating some of the infected.

The Chief and Kathy crossed the grassy field to meet with Captain Miller while the rest of the group broke out their gear and set up a mess tent. We figured we might as well have some hot food for lunch if we had to be on the ground.

"Anything in the area?" Captain Miller asked the Chief as they approached.

"A small town a mile or so up the road. We didn't see any activity around the buildings."

"Funny thing," said Kathy, "but we're seeing less infected than I thought we would. Where are they? Did they all migrate to the coast?"

"I noticed that, too," said Captain Miller. "I also noticed farm animals are almost nonexistent. The few I've seen had been killed in the fields and stripped to the bones."

"The temperature is dropping fast as we go north," said Kathy. She had pulled on a foul weather coat as she got out of the helicopter. "Are those snow clouds up ahead?"

"There's so much smoke that I can't tell for sure," said the Chief, "but I think so."

We finished our hot meal and stowed the gear then sat and waited impatiently as the mechanics did their job. When the rotors slowly started to turn, no one had to be told to warm up the other choppers.

Checking the time, we all agreed we wouldn't arrive until after dark, and our best bet would be to find a parking garage with enough room on top for all of the helicopters to land. We would sleep inside the aircraft and assess the situation when the sun came up.

The helicopters lifted off and fell into formation, hopefully to reach Columbus without further delays.

It seemed like only a few minutes had gone by when the sun began to set, and the Chief had to slow his forward speed in order to avoid the smoke from more fires.

Jean yelled a playful, "Are we there yet?"

Everyone enjoyed the reminder of what road trips had been like before the infection, but the closer we got to Columbus the more serious everyone seemed to be. Going into a big city was going to open the door to new questions about the survival of civilization, and our survival on the coast was a different world from the tall buildings we were about to see. The suburbs were also different. They surrounded the city in all directions, unlike the coast where suburbs were prevented from expanding by natural barriers such as the ocean and the marshes.

"Not long now," answered the Chief. He spoke into his radio and then pointed out the front windshield.

"If there was power to the city we would be able to see the tallest buildings by now. We're only about thirty minutes out."

Kathy turned around and motioned for Tom to turn off the cabin lights, and we all started trying to catch a glimpse of anything out the windows.

The Chief and Captain Miller agreed that they needed the strobe lights on to prevent the chance of them colliding with each other, but cabin lights would present a tempting target for anyone with a good hunting rifle.

There were a few small fires burning in the city, mostly on the outskirts of downtown, but the smoke was drifting between the tall buildings making it more difficult to make the approach. Other than the fires, the city was dark and dead.

I was working on a serious case of eye strain trying to see anything at all. I thought I saw lights moving on the roof of a two story building, but by the time I focused my attention on the spot, I wasn't sure what I had seen.

"Did anyone else see lights on a roof a minute ago?"

I figured someone else would have yelled if they had seen them, but I had to be sure.

"Yes, but I think it may be the strobe lights reflecting back from patches of snow that have already accumulated in drifts," said Colleen.

I watched the rooftops as we sped past and saw our reflection from ice on the top of a building. First there was a white light, followed closely by a red. The Chief began banking a little to pass between two tall buildings that rose up higher than the helicopters, and the ride got a little bumpy from the wind currents bouncing back from the buildings.

Our forward speed slowed to a crawl as the Chief began scouting for a place to land. He was on his radio again, and I heard him say we needed the headlights. A moment later the darkness below and ahead of us was illuminated, and we could see the devastation that could follow years without people.

Entire blocks of buildings were charred from fires that had burned unchecked by man. Vehicles of all kinds were everywhere in the streets, and the downdraft from the rotors made the snow swirl and dance over everything. Mixed with the snow was a storm of debris and litter. Anything that wasn't frozen in place was flying around below us.

We were over something that had probably been a busy plaza. It was surrounded by buildings, but the bare trees were in neat rows as if it had been a park during better days. Restaurants surrounded the plaza with plenty of outdoor seating.

"If there weren't so many cars in the streets we could sit down here," said Kathy.

"I'm going to check out the parking garages," said the Chief as he gained altitude and steered between buildings.

Behind us was a trail of swirling snow as the three Navy helicopters followed slowly. For at least a minute, the entire plaza was bathed in light, and something was conspicuous in its absence. There were no infected dead, and there were no bodies, no human remains anywhere.

The parking garage we found just past the plaza had been full when the infection started because it was still full after all this time. The wreckage of cars blocking both lanes were testimony to the chaos as people tried to do the impossible by escaping in a car. They must have begun wrecking as soon as they began trying to evacuate.

A second garage was better, and there was room to land two of the helicopters. I heard the Chief telling Captain Miller we could split up if necessary. Captain Miller agreed but suggested that we should try to locate the next garage together. If only two could land on the next one, at least we would know where the other helicopters had landed.

The third garage had landing space for three helicopters, but instead of letting one land somewhere alone, Captain Miller had his and one other land together, and then the last Navy helicopter followed us back to the other garage.

Both landed with extreme caution and rotated to illuminate the area first. When the wheels were on a solid surface, the team in the Navy aircraft fanned out and established a perimeter. We were pretty good at protecting ourselves, but watching the soldiers do their jobs was reassuring.

"Where are the infected?" asked Tom.

"I was about to ask the same thing," said Hampton.

Cassandra had joined the soldiers as soon as our doors had opened. She felt much more at home being on the move and putting her training to use.

"Good question," said the Chief, "and where are the remains?"

The Chief fixed his gaze on the area bathed in light from the helicopters and thought about his night in Charleston when his plane had been shot down over the harbor. There were infected dead stumbling around everywhere as he and Allison tried to survive long enough to find a boat and head for Fort Sumter.

"Anybody see any rats?" he asked suddenly.

"Rats?" said Jean and Colleen together as if they had rehearsed it.

"Yes, rats. When I was stranded in Charleston with Allison, there were rats out in broad daylight going after the food that was rotting everywhere. I imagine when the food and garbage was all gone, they started cleaning up all the bodies. How long it took before there were more rats than food depended on how many rats there were to start with."

"I don't see any rats," I said, "but I don't see any bodies either. There's no garbage that appears to be edible."

"The rats have already cleaned everything up," said the Chief. "Let the soldiers know we'll be sleeping in the helicopters tonight."

We signaled the soldiers and told them to get everyone back in the helicopters for the night, but keep the external lights on.

Cassandra climbed back into her seat and asked, "What's up?"

Kathy leaned around from her seat in front and asked her, "Did the Mercy ship get overrun by rats after everyone else was dead?"

Cassandra was shaking her head before Kathy even finished her question.

"The whole crew was eating the rats before they had a chance to breed. The living members of the crew were having trouble getting to food supplies, and the infected were eating anything they could catch."

It was obvious that the infected would win in a closed environment, but in an open environment where the rats could flee from the infected, they could eat, breed, and bide their time. When there were finally enough of them, they would go after the infected and the bodies in the streets.

I could see where the Chief was going with his questions, and I breathed a sigh of relief.

"You're saying that the rats have already had their day, aren't you, Chief?"

"That's the good news, Ed."

"Do I want to know the bad news?" I asked.

"It's nothing you haven't heard before," said Jean. "Remember what happened when the blue crabs started eating the infected. Then when they were done cleaning up the moat, they started getting aggressive and attacking anything."

Hampton said, "Judging by how clean these streets are of bodies and edible garbage, the rats have exhausted their food supply and would attack people if given the chance."

"That's why we're sleeping inside tonight. Everyone get some sleep," said the Chief. "We'll start searching for the entrance to the shelter at sunrise."

******

Sunrise was gray and white. The sky seemed closer because the sun wasn't visible, and the snow was swirling around the two helicopters. The Chief and the pilot of the Navy helicopter had both switched off their lights as soon as sunlight started to filter through the clouds. Everyone was warm enough, but they knew that would change soon.

"There's a coffee maker behind this panel," I said.

There was a chorus of groans mixed with a demand to quit talking and start making coffee. It was a one cup machine, but it was spitting them out fast. Jean found cream and sugar and passed it around.

"This isn't fair to the crews of the other choppers," said Tom. "I mean, how can we even tell them about this?"

The Chief sipped at his and said, "They're soldiers. They would want some, but if they couldn't get any, they wouldn't want us to deny ourselves of the pleasure."

As he took another sip he peered over the cup at the military helicopter that was facing us a short distance away. The pilot was holding up his middle finger, but he was smiling.

"See what I mean?" said the Chief. "We're still number one to him."

Jean rummaged around in the supplies and came up with lids that fit the disposable cups. With a little help, we put together a care package for the other crew. Colleen had the seat closest to the door, so she ran the coffee over to them. The pilot gave the Chief two thumbs up.

When she got back she said she had the impression that it was colder than normal outside, even for the month of November.

"Another side effect of people being gone?" she asked.

"No heat coming from any of the buildings in the city would be my guess," said Jean. "No matter how well insulated the buildings are, they had to be losing a little heat to the outside. All of them combined would have made thermal drafts through the streets."

"That's some sharp thinking," said the Chief. "That's what I like about this group. You guys are smart."

"Saw it on the news," said Jean. "Satellites doing thermal scans of the planet, and heat blooms over cities."

The Chief interrupted the conversation by keying his radio and talking with Captain Miller. He had received a call saying they were ready to either warm up the engines or disembark at their current location. The Chief told him to stand by for an update on their location relevant to their destination.

"Jim, I have you on GPS as being closer to us than I had expected. A sign up here says we're on the top of the Hickory Garage, and you guys are in the center of the top floor of the Marconi Cinema Garage. You're only about a block away."

"Close enough for someone to run us over some of that coffee?"

"I'll have to get back to you on that."

Kathy was tracing her finger along lines on a map and said, "We're only a block west of High Street. Any idea where we need to go?"

The Chief leaned over and started tracing along a line that was drawn on the map in red ink. He stared at it for a few minutes and then asked Kathy if there was a scale of the map. She found one at the bottom in the corner, and the Chief folded the map up to the red line.

"Does that seem to be about six hundred feet to you?"

Kathy glanced from the scale to the line and agreed. The red line had to be the tunnel. One end of the line stopped at a spot close to the intersection of North Front Street, and the other end stopped directly under an overpass on North High Street. Railroad tracks disappeared under the overpass.

"The entrance to the shelter has to be under here."

The Chief put his finger directly on top of the overpass.

"There's a small, egg shaped park right before the overpass," said Kathy. "Do you think we could land there?"

"I don't think we can get all four birds in there. I didn't really get a good view of it when we landed, but it seemed like that whole area was congested. We passed right between that really tall building and that hotel by the overpass, and I was busy with the wind bouncing back at us."

I was listening close enough to remember what I had seen in that area, so I volunteered what I saw.

"I don't know if it helps much, but I think I remember the spot you guys are talking about. I think someone dropped a bomb in there."

"What makes you say that?" asked the Chief.

"I saw a wrecked train right here where the tracks go under Nationwide Blvd."

I reached up and held my finger to the spot.

"I guess we're on foot from here," said the Chief. "I'll call it in to Jim. Am I reading this map right? The tracks go under this building."

"If it's all the same to you Chief, I don't think we need to take that shortcut to get there."

The idea of using a tunnel to get where we were going wasn't too inviting after what we had discussed the night before. A good place to find rats would be in a tunnel.

"I agree," said the Chief. "Let's call it in and suggest a rendezvous point where Marconi Blvd. curves by the tracks."

While the Chief called it in to Captain Miller we began unloading our gear. It was bitter cold, and the snow was already piling up. Colleen stepped on a patch of ice and slipped. She landed on her rear end and slid about twenty feet on the down ramp before she could stop herself. The only thing hurt was her pride, but she taught everyone a valuable lesson about how tricky this little walk was going to be.

"The worst part will be walking on this concrete," said the Chief. "After we get down on the streets it will be more of the same, so we'll stick to grassy areas wherever we can."

"That's reassuring," said Colleen.

Her face was so red that she must have felt warmer than the rest of us.

Cassandra went over to the other helicopter to fill them in on the plan. When they saw us unloading, they had done the same on the assumption that we would be walking from the top of the garage to our destination.

The stairwells didn't offer enough light for anyone to be interested in saving time or getting in out of the cold. We decided to walk down the center of the garage.

We formed up single file with Cassandra in the lead. She had convinced the Chief that her military training had prepared her for this type situation. When the Chief said his military training had exceeded hers, she countered with the fact that she was younger than him.

Those of us who knew the Chief knew that he had given in because he was glad to let Cassandra step up, rather than because he was older. She had been itching for the chance to contribute to the group since the day we pulled her off of the Mercy ship, and the Chief was happy to accommodate her.

We descended from the bleak light on the roof into the shadows of the garage. The snow couldn't reach the center of the building, but unfortunately it could reach the corkscrew driveway that ran close to the sides of the garage. The wind blew the snow in our faces most of the way.

Two floors down there was a massive snarl of cars where someone had gotten into a bigger rush than everyone else. From the way the cars were sandwiched in the middle, it wasn't hard to picture the events. As the infected worked their way from floor to floor, more people began abandoning their cars. Those who didn't try to run tried to drive through.

There were no bodies around, but the building would only be free of vehicles when they were totally rusted away by the weather. The rats must have worked hard to clean the building so well.

We had to climb over the wreckage carefully. Cassandra told us that the Mercy ship had reached a point where broken metal was as dangerous as getting bitten. A cut on a piece of scrap metal was a source of infection long before the infection that turned people into flesh eating zombies, and in the long run it could be just as deadly.

Climbing over the jagged metal in the tangle of vehicles was like trying to climb over barbed wire because everywhere we put our feet was also slippery.

I kept expecting to see an infected dead inside the cars, but even the cars that were closed shut were empty of bodies. A quick glance inside those cars was enough to make me worry more about the rats.

It was amazing how a rat could get through a small hole, and when enough hungry rats were chewing on the same spot under a car, they would make their own hole eventually.

"How many rats do you suppose were here?" I asked.

Cassandra glanced back toward me and said, "Judging by the smell of ammonia, I would say about a million."

I couldn't tell for sure if she was kidding, but she waited for me to catch up with her before she moved forward again.

"This happened months ago, Ed. When the weather was warmer and there were bodies everywhere besides the ones that were still walking around. In a city this size, there are lots of places where they could have been breeding since the first days of the infection. When they came out, they came out by the hundreds of thousands, and they went for what was easy to get first. Then they went after everything that tried to get away. That would have included the living and the infected. It's just a good thing we didn't come here in the summer."

"Where do you suppose they are now?"

"Can you guess?"

"Well, I would say that a million rats would need a lot of food, and when they ran out of food, they moved on, but that wouldn't be the best way for them to survive."

Cassandra was surprised by my answer, but I had been hanging around the Chief longer than her, and some of him had rubbed off on me.

"It's not like all of the rats were right here in this one spot. They were spread out across the city and all of the surrounding areas. There may have been a concentration of them here, but since rats will eat absolutely anything, there were a lot of grocery stores in the suburbs for them to empty out. When the concentration of them spread outward, they found everything already picked clean by their cousins. Eventually, the only thing left for them to eat was each other."

"I agree, but what bothers me is that we can still smell the ammonia from their urine months later and after big weather changes. It must have been one crawling mass of rats."

Cassandra shook her head like she was trying to get rid of the image.

Behind us the rest of the group was cautiously picking its way through the cars that all tried to exit together. We were down to the second level, and I went over to the edge of the garage to see if I could locate our rendezvous point. I could see the tracks, and it felt weird to know that we were so close to another shelter. The soldiers from the other two helicopters were emerging from the first floor of the Marconi garage. They had made better time than we did, but we would have less distance to go from our exit.

On the first floor of the garage we were surprised to see a group of infected dead standing ankle deep in a snow drift. They were doing what the infected tended to do when they had no prey to attack, and the cold weather was also slowing them down, but they were instantly agitated by the sight of living flesh.

There were a dozen of them, and they started moving toward us. Their movements were stiff from the cold, but there was no hesitation. On a signal from Cassandra, everyone drew out their machete, and we spread out in a half circle as they approached. It was less of a battle and more of a minor skirmish as we went first toward their legs and then for the head blows.

When it was all over, we didn't form up immediately into single file again. Something was wrong. There shouldn't have been that many of the infected in this area if the cold had done as we had expected, and there was also the clean up job done by the rats. These infected were either recently deceased, or recently exposed from a place where they had been trapped.

The Chief and the pilot of the other helicopter were checking the bodies and confirmed what we were thinking. The clothing wasn't as degraded as it should have been, and five of the infected were wearing similar neckties. Even more surprising was that they were wearing shoulder holsters.

When we gathered around to see what the Chief thought about the similarities, he held out a wallet that folded open to show a badge and an identification card. It said the man had been Winston Griswald of the United States Secret Service.

The Chief said in a low voice, "There may be more around, so let's keep the noise to a minimum. His weapon is a SIG Sauer P229. Holds a big .357 round. All of them were armed, but all of them had their weapons holstered. They either didn't know the threat, or they died some way other than being bitten."

"They must have come from the shelter," I said. "The question would be why."

The Army pilot said, "I served in a detail that helped prepare a city for a Presidential visit. Prior to the President's arrival the area was flooded with Secret Service personnel. These people may have had nothing to do with the shelter."

"Let's all hope so," I said.

We had enough weapons, but shoulder holstered SIG Sauers were a bonus we couldn't leave behind. The Chief collected the ID wallets from the agents. He explained that someday we might be able to show that they had died doing what they were sworn to do.

Our rendezvous point was to our left on the other side of a low wall, so we took a shortcut and just jumped over the wall into the gray morning. The sky was so dark with low clouds that it was more like evening than morning.

The Captain's group had already reached the curve on Marconi Blvd, and had set up a perimeter. We only had to cross a double set of railroad tracks to reach them.

It was an odd sight when we scanned left and right as we were crossing the tracks. The tracks to our left were clear, but to the right the tracks entered a tunnel that passed under the parking garage that had been too full for us to land. The huge locomotive that had been pulling a freight train behind it was blocking the tunnel, but it wasn't sitting on the tracks. It was lying on its left side.

We all stopped to stare at it, undoubtedly all wondering how a locomotive could wind up lying on its side in a location where it could not have been traveling at a high rate of speed.

I turned toward the Chief, and his reaction was a shrug of the shoulders.

"If you're going to ask me how that happened, don't bother. I can't imagine."

Captain Miller crossed the street from the other garage and stared at the locomotive with his mouth hanging open.

"Ever seen anything like that before?" asked the Chief.

"I saw a bomb do that once in Iraq, or rather a surface to air missile. It hit one of the last trailing cars just right, and it caused the whole train to fall over on its side," said the Captain.

"Don't ask me how I know this," I said, "but that thing probably weighs two hundred tons."

"Any of your video games have trains in them?" asked the Chief.

Before I could answer the Chief just held up one hand and said, "Never mind. I would have guessed around that, too. I don't know if it will matter or not, but judging from the size of that thing, it must have been pulling about seventy-five cars. That means the caboose on this thing is somewhere past where we're going. We'll find out what happened in a few minutes."

We all fell in as one long patrol with Captain Miller's men taking point. Everyone had strict instructions to hold their fire unless it was absolutely necessary, but half of the group had their rifles out instead of machetes. I can't say that I blamed them because walking down Marconi Blvd. to the intersection with Nationwide Blvd. was like walking through a snowy canyon. The street would have been in the shadows on a sunny day, but it felt like a death trap with the wind blowing the snow into our faces.

At the last building before the intersection we got our first glimpse inside a building that must have been rat proof. The lobby was separated from the outside by two sets of swinging doors, and every square inch of the glass walls of the lobby had a face pressed against it. Judging by the lack of coats on these infected, they had either been inside already or gone inside for safety when the weather was warmer, but they never got to leave.

There wasn't much that needed to be done about that group of infected, Our plan was to eliminate as many infected as possible, but only the easy ones. If we wanted to try to destroy all of them, we would have to let them out first. That wasn't our preference.

Nationwide Blvd. was nice and wide, and visibility got better. As soon as the lead man reached the intersection, he raised one hand and gave the signal to stop. He also went down to one knee to indicate he had acquired a target.

The second man behind him got a report from the man on point, and then he came back down the line to let everyone know what had caused them to stop. With the clear visibility ahead, the man reported there were multiple infected dead between us and our objective which was only three blocks away.

"The rats didn't do a thorough job,"said Kathy.

Tom and Hampton had both grown up learning how to hunt from their fathers, and although neither had any formal military training, they were applying the same principles to this approach as they would hunting. Hampton heard what Kathy said as he eased up on the rest of the group.

"The rats had their breeding and feeding cycles, but now they're in decline, especially because of the freezing cold temperatures. The infected dead that survived the feeding cycle are coming back out into the open."

"I don't buy it," said Kathy. "You're making it sound like they know it's safe to come out now."

"I see what you mean, but that means there's a new supply of them coming from somewhere. It would have to be somewhere the rats couldn't reach before."

Kathy furrowed her brow for a moment. Something wasn't quite right about what Tom said.

"If the rats couldn't get to them, how are they getting out of wherever it was they were before? Something must have changed nearby that let them come out of wherever they were trapped. How many are there?" she said in a low voice to the soldier on point.

He leaned forward and remained motionless for a long time. When he slowly pulled himself back from the corner, he shook his head and shrugged his shoulders.

Captain Miller came up behind Kathy and said, "He isn't even giving you a guess. Count on that meaning too many for us to cross the intersection without being seen. "

He went up to the corner and saw the situation for himself then came back to where the Chief and I had moved up next to Kathy.

"There are several dozen, but they're spread out. I think we can take them all with machetes by going down the street in two squads. Each squad will be followed by two soldiers with their M4's ready if the lead soldiers are overwhelmed. If they have to open fire, the people in front should fall back on my command."

The plan of attack was passed down the line, and everyone shouldered their rifles except the last four. With almost two dozen machetes backed by rifle power it was manageable as long as the new infected dead weren't coming out in larger numbers.

Colleen nudged Hampton and whispered something to him. Hampton turned and did the same in the direction of the Chief.

"Colleen wants to know if that coliseum up ahead could be the source of the new infected dead. If so, that building can hold thousands of people," said the Chief.

Captain Miller studied the large arena on the other side of Nationwide Blvd. and then shook his head.

"I hear you people. This city went down just like every other city. People didn't know which way to go, and maybe someone even tried to set up a shelter in that arena when the hospitals overflowed. But we can't worry about every building between here and the shelter. If we get overwhelmed, our escape route has to be to the right at the nearest intersection, and then we'll rally at the first pair of helicopters. As for the arena being a threat, the rats would have found a thousand ways to get inside a building that big. Now, let's move out."

We formed up into two squads, and on the Captain's order we went around the corner directly at the infected that were wandering around through a maze of vehicles that had been abandoned over a year ago. The first of them were only a few yards away.

As a group we had learned that attacking the dead one on one was less effective than attacking in pairs. One person would take off a leg, and the next would go for the head blow that would destroy whatever it was they had that passed as a brain. As the first pair of soldiers engaged an infected, the next two would pass them and engage the next infected. If it went well, the first pair of soldiers would be passing the second pair before they completed their kill.

It didn't always go exactly as planned, though. Sometimes a machete got stuck, so a pair of soldiers would be delayed from moving forward. That was when the third group would step forward and join the fight.

We probably made it to the eighth or ninth infected before the third pair had to move up, but the tangle of vehicles was making it harder to work in pairs than it would have been on an open road. A scream was all we needed to know that someone had their pattern of attack broken.

We had to hold the line the best we could on our side, but we could see that the pair of soldiers to our right had tried to take out too many infected at one time, and someone had fallen between the cars.

I heard someone behind us yell, "Down in front," and I didn't know or even care if they just meant that the leading soldiers on the right should drop. I didn't want to be between the infected and someone with an M4.

The four soldiers in the rear targeted the infected and laid down a withering barrage. Once we had given away our position to every infected dead in the downtown area it didn't make any sense to stay quiet.

The soldiers advanced as they fired, and as they went by, we sheathed our machetes and pulled our M4's from our backs. Once we joined in, we were targeting the infected over two blocks away.

A big clearing came up on our left after we crossed Front Street, and I realized we had picked up speed as we fired. Getting to our goal fast was important now that we had made so much noise, but as cold as it was, we were facing far more of the infected than we had anticipated. We planned on being able to eliminate frozen bodies, but these things were almost fresh compared to what we had seen in South Carolina or Alabama.

The clearing turned out to be the same clearing I had spotted from the air and thought it could be a good place to land, but from the sky I hadn't been able to see all of the debris on the ground. What should have been a flat park was instead a mass of twisted metal scraps with sharp, blackened edges.

There were two things that became apparent at almost the same moment to most of us. There were still a few sporadic shots being fired, but most of us were stunned by what we saw once we had a clear view across the park.

North High Street had been the hub of Columbus railroad traffic since the early nineteenth century, but that part of Columbus had disappeared under towering buildings and sprawling hotels. The tracks were still there, running below North High Street, and the trains still carried freight through the heart of the city, but something in the recent history of the place caused a drastic change.

The first thing we saw was the massive black crater that appeared to be exactly on the spot where North High Street crossed over the railroad tracks. The cause of the crater was obviously related to the large wing with an engine still attached to it. The second thing we saw was the source for all of the infected that had not been exposed to the elements.

The tail of the airplane had sheared the facade from the front of a large hotel sitting next to the place where the plane had crashed. Several of the lower floors were exposed, and even as we watched, more infected were dropping from openings in the walls. It didn't matter to us how they had survived the feeding cycle of the rats. It only mattered that we had to survive with so many infected in the area. Our guess was that the front of the hotel had waited until now to fall off.

The Chief caught up with Captain Miller and pulled him to one side.

"Jim, we have a problem. By the map that Bus prepared for me, I would guess that 737 went nose first right into the spot where the shelter is located. Must have been one hell of an explosion."

Captain Miller nodded.

"Remember that locomotive on its side? This is the other end of it, and whatever it was that blew up, it was powerful enough to twist the whole train until it flipped over."

The Chief mentally calculated the distance the explosion had thrown the tail of the airplane and how it had sheared off the front of the hotel, and all he could imagine was that the train had been carrying something beyond the definition of hazardous.

"Well, this does present a bit of a problem for us," said the Chief.

"Just one problem?"

"I imagine more than one, but the biggest problem on my mind at the moment is that Bus told me the nearest emergency entrance for this shelter is under the big hotel sitting on the right side of the tracks. I think he must have meant that one."

Both men stared at the hotel and the steady stream of infected that were falling out of blast holes from the lower floors like sacks of flour.

"You mean we have to go in there?" asked Captain Miller.

19 BELOW COLUMBUS STREETS

Seeing the helicopters pass overhead was a sign that made them optimistic and wary at the same time. They had lost their trust in organized government when they were abandoned, essentially exiled to the airport terminal. They had made life better for themselves all on their own. Government did it to them, but they had taken matters into their own hands to make it better.

Still, they were drawn to what they had seen. Four helicopters traveling together spoke volumes about someone. Whatever the organization was that orchestrated the survival of the people in those helicopters, it had to be powerful, and the crew of Executive One knew they needed to find them.

The rats were gone. They didn't know why they were gone or where, but if they were correct in their thinking, the only danger from the rats was that they could carry the infection that led to death. Otherwise, they would behave as most rats do and avoid humans unless they invaded their space, which was exactly what they were about to do.

No one could sleep, so everyone spent the night getting their bug-out bags packed for a second time. All available rations they could carry were packed for the trip. Their hope was to never return to John Glenn International Airport. They were either going to find the President or the people in the helicopters, or they were going to move on to International Falls, Minnesota. Of course there was the less cheerful possibility of giving up the safest place they could have hoped for when so many had died on the runways.

After the bags were packed, the crew of Executive One finished dressing in layers that included duct tape around arms and legs as insulation against the cold and rat bites. They even joked a bit about being more afraid of rats than the infected dead, but the joking didn't last long. The rats may have diminished the population of the infected, but they knew it would be dangerous to take for granted the possibility that they wouldn't see any on their journey away from safety.

Just to be sure everyone understood what they were doing, Garrett had asked the group if anyone had any reservations. Some of them, especially Anne and Addison, felt that they should just stay above ground and head north on the long trip to Minnesota. Everyone understood, but they were outnumbered when it was put to a vote. Sim reassured them that the one thousand mile trip would be hard for them all, and the trip down through the floor of the hangar would be much shorter. When Anne argued that the rats would be down there, the others convinced her that the President's security staff would have ensured against such a mundane problem as rats. The passage to where ever it went was probably air tight against such things as rats.

At sunrise they were climbing down the ladder to a tarmac that was covered in white. There were no blemishes in the snow, and Sim was quick to point it out to Anne and Addison. The rats had done them a favor, and now the rats were gone.

They could only tell it was sunrise by virtue of the fact that it wasn't as dark outside as it had been. As they went by the security office, Jon went inside and made sure the third switch was in the up position. Hopefully, it meant there was power to the door in the hangar. They had moved to the roof, closing doors behind them one last time. Then they had sat cold and quiet on the roof and waited.

The walk to the hangar had their hearts pounding. Other than the day they had run around lighting heads on fire, they had spent most of the last two years in the airport.

It was so cold that they could see and hear themselves breathing. Garrett couldn't resist.

"Did anybody else see that Tom Hanks movie where he was from a foreign country, so he had to stay in the airport until some bureaucratic red tape was straightened out? I think he had to live in the airport for several…weeks."

He hooked everyone with the long pause between the last two words, and they all visibly relaxed a bit as they choked back the laughing. Rather than winding them up tighter, they just became more alert when he told everyone to keep their eyes open. The big tail of Air Force One was reaching out above them, and they were just about to walk into the gloom of the hangar.

Sim moved faster and got up to the front of the group. After all this time, he had to take a few minutes to see the place where he had spent the night. He reached the big rear landing gear with hardly a glance to his left or right, but this time there was nothing inside that he would have seen. He increased his speed and practically jumped onto the nose gear. He climbed up into the wheel well and clicked on his flashlight. He just wanted to be sure that he hadn't missed something on that night.

The seams around the door that would have allowed him to reach the cockpit were sealed tight. Being afraid hadn't made him miss anything. He dropped back onto the wheel and joined his friends who were standing in a circle around a section of the hangar floor.

Mike and Jon were busy tossing ropes over the wing and securing them to the wheel under the wing. Mike made rope climbing seem easy in the airport, so he was the logical choice to climb to the top of the plane and walk up to the cockpit. There was just enough light for them to see the cord that hung from the roof of the hangar down to the windshield over the pilot's seat.

He yelled down, "I found the tennis ball hanging from the garage ceiling. It must have come down when we turned on the light switch back in the security office."

When Mike climbed out to the cord, he reached out to inspect it. There was a row of labeled buttons on a black, flat panel.

"No wonder it was hard to see in the dark," he said out loud.

He pulled a pad out of his pocket, drew a picture of the panel, and tossed it down to the others. Anne picked it up and handed it to Garrett.

They were gathered around Garrett when Jon sensed more than heard something behind them. He spun around and found himself face to face with the destroyed features of an infected dead.

The smell of the thing was overpowering, and Jon had a brief thought that it had to be his imagination or he would have smelled it coming.

Jon fell over backwards and landed hard, but just as he was ready for the infected to fall on top of him, the foul smelling creature changed direction.

From the left knee down, its leg had collapsed toward the right leg at an unnatural angle. Susan was slightly behind it with her arm raised to come back in the other direction. When it came down, the hammer in her hand hit the side of the thing's head and sank in over an inch.

Garrett didn't have to say much, but he said it anyway.

"Let's not make that mistake again. I'll help Mike get this thing open. Everyone else face outward and keep your flashlights on."

When the lights clicked on, their beams reached far enough for them to see that the rest of the hangar was empty, but their nerves were already so jangled that they left the lights on.

Garrett studied the pad that Mike had tossed down. He saw that Mike had numbered the labels, so he stood in a flashlight beam and held up one finger. He saw Mike lift up the panel and press a button.

There was only a faint vibration under his feet, but Garrett felt it. Judging by the reactions of the others, they were all feeling movement around their feet, too. They moved outward away from the edges of the rectangle on the floor.

It wasn't obvious until they swung their flashlights down toward the seams. The floor appeared to be growing at first, but it was just an illusion. It was, however, rising upward.

On an impulse, Garrett stepped over to the side of the rectangle that faced Air Force One. It was nothing more than a big black box in the dim light of the hangar, but anyone would recognize an elevator door when they saw one.

It came to a stop at floor level, and Garrett saw there was a large lever type handle on the door rather than an up or down button beside it. He reached out and pushed the lever to the left, and the door opened. He couldn't have been more surprised when a light came on inside.

He held the door open with his left hand out of habit, but he wasn't about to let that door close. He stuck his head inside and saw there were buttons that matched the dark panel Mike had reached above the cockpit. He motioned for Mike to come down from his perch on the plane. He didn't have to clarify his message because Mike was running along the fuselage of the plane so fast that Garrett was afraid he would fall and break his neck.

Everyone else only needed the smile on Garrett's face to know it was time to find out what was at the bottom of the rabbit hole. They all hurried around and went inside. When Mike swung down from the wing and ran for the door, they teased him about taking so long, and said they were full.

Once they were all inside and ready, Garrett shut the door and pressed a button that said they were going down to a subway.

******

It didn't take long to decide to leave the helicopter pilots behind. Whatever happened inside that hotel, they couldn't afford to lose their pilots. The six men were reluctant to go back to the helicopters, but Captain Miller felt like it was a better choice. That still left a sizable force of soldiers plus our group. We had left Charleston with thirty-six soldiers, not counting the Captain or the pilots. We didn't want to leave Fort Sumter undermanned if they were attacked while we were gone. Four had stayed behind at Guntersville, but seeing thirty-two soldiers covering our civilian group, we felt like we would be able to handle whatever we were walking into.

The hotel entrance was a mangled wreck where there was evidence of the massive explosion, so we began circling around it to the side entrance that faced a tall skyscraper across Nationwide Blvd. It would be locked, but it wouldn't be a problem.

The Mud Island group was mixed in with the trained military, and I had the feeling that they had been given orders to keep us alive. We had gained a lot of experience since the first days of the infection, but so had they. That experience added to their military training made me glad they were on our side.

We hugged the front of the huge hotel all the way to the corner and then waited up against the wall while a small group rounded the corner to make short work of the door. When they signaled that we were in, we moved quickly to the corner in single file. The cold wind was like a slap across the face when we stepped around the corner toward the door, but it could have been worse. At least a soldier was holding open the door to block some of the wind.

To get everyone inside fast, we formed two columns on the left and right sides of the hall. I was back toward the middle, so I saw the soldiers switching from M4's to handguns. Our group chose machetes for close combat. As far as I could tell, there were about twenty of us on each side of a long hallway, so we were strung out with a few handicap accessible rooms along each side. The doors were all shut, so they were being bypassed in favor of a bigger prize.

The Chief was at the front of our column across from Captain Miller, and he whispered in a low voice that we had to find the basement. Elevators weren't an option, so we needed to find the stairs that went down to a sub level. Word was passed down the line for someone to check the emergency exit stairs that were located near the door we had entered, and a small group of soldiers quietly disappeared through the door.

They returned in five minutes with the message that they had checked upward five floors, and it was all clear. When they went down to a sub level they found at least a dozen of the infected packed into the narrow landing in front of a door that had a small red and white sign on it indicating it was for staff only.

The Chief motioned for Cassandra, Hampton, and Colleen to go to the lower floor to assess the situation. Besides Kathy, they were the most proficient in close quarters with machetes.

Even though they were only told to assess the situation, they saw that their advantage of being on higher steps gave them the reach they needed to be able to do more than assess.

"We've got this," said Cassandra.

She stepped a little closer to the crowd squeezed together on the small landing and swung downward at an infected that was reaching for her. Her swing removed its arm and caused it to fall forward on the stairs at the same time, exposing it to her second strike on the top of its head.

Hampton and Colleen moved downward with Cassandra. They were too close together on the stairs to swing across, so they used the same tactic as Cassandra. Overhand swings straight down to remove arms and follow-up blows to the heads.

It was easy at first, but as the steps became choked with the bodies of the infected, they had to wait for the next ones to climb upward first.

Hampton was grateful for the thick layer of duct tape he had wrapped around his legs when he felt the sharp pain from the pressure of a bite. Despite being dead, the infected seemed to have retained the strength in their jaws to at least inflict pain, even if their teeth didn't penetrate the skin. The culprit that had gotten him was one of the dead he thought he had eliminated, so he started making sure it wouldn't happen again.

They had to step on the backs of the infected to reach the last of them, but there were no more close calls. Colleen checked the bite carefully to be sure it didn't break through the tape and was satisfied that he was okay.

They helped each other move the bodies from the stairs and from the landing in front of the service door, then Cassandra eased the door open just enough to see through. It was just another dark hallway with the exception that the doors closest to them had the red and white signs on them to identify specific services.

"Let's check in," said Hampton. "We need a lot of light down here."

Fifteen minutes later our squad of soldiers and civilians were ready to move into the sub level. The Chief had explained to Captain Miller that the emergency exit wasn't supposed to be something that could be accessed by everyone on the hotel staff, so it would probably be locked. As a matter of fact, it had to be hidden well enough for hotel management to not even know about it.

"The survival group that built these shelters were eccentric, so we need to find a sign that seems out of place. Once we find the room, the door itself will be hidden. Bus said I would know the door when I saw it. He said it was supposed to have something to do with Uncle Titus."

The squad moved into the dark hallway and took up positions along the walls. The soldiers had night vision gear, but the Chief had suggested they stick to flashlights. The Mud Island group wouldn't be able to do anything but follow the soldiers in the pitch black hall, and the clue might not be obvious in the green glow of the night vision gear.

It turned out to be a good thing because they might have missed their first clue. Every small rectangular sign on every door was red with white letters embossed into them except one. It was white with red letters that said Reserve Under Structure Housing.

"What in the world is that supposed to be?" asked Captain Miller.

"Nothing anyone would think is their responsibility," I said, "but the first letter of each word spells my uncle's last name."

The Captain gave a nod to the soldier on point, and he tested the handle. The door was locked, but it was the same style lock as all of the doors.

The Chief was right on it, and he passed word down the line to Tom who was at the back of the squad. Tom ducked back into the stairwell with Hampton. Jean and Colleen held flashlights on the bodies while Tom and Hampton went through the pockets of the ones who were dressed like hotel employees. It was only a minute or two before they found master keys and passed them up to the front of the line.

The Chief slid one into the lock, and they were rewarded by the click as the door unlocked.

Inside was an unremarkable room with several large pieces of machinery that were designed for no purpose other than to confuse anyone who didn't know what the room really was. The machinery had meters attached that measured everything from PSI to humidity. The important thing was that each machine had the word RUSH stenciled on it.

In the darkness we fanned out to find the door, and the Chief reminded us to count on Titus Rush and his sense of humor.

"I found it," said Captain Miller only a minute later.

He pointed at a half door on the end of the machinery. It was round, just like the escape hatches inside Mud Island.

"How do you know it's an emergency exit that comes up from the shelter?" I asked as I walked over to his side.

Stenciled on the door was EXIT ONLY, but there was no visible handle.

"I don't see a keypad for entering the combination," said Jean. "There must be some other way of opening this door."

Everyone spread out again, but this time we were searching for the combination dial like we had seen at the other shelters.

"Everyone keep in mind what we were saying earlier about Titus Rush having a sense of humor," said the Chief. "It can't be as easy as finding the door."

Colleen said, "This reminds me of one of those places where you go with a group of family members or friends. They put you all together in one room, lock the doors, and you're supposed to use clues hidden in the room to find a way to get out."

"Sounds like a good way for families and friends to get mad at each other," said Kathy. "Put a bunch of cops in a room with clues hanging on the cork boards, and watch how fast an argument starts. Someone makes a suggestion, someone calls them stupid, and the next thing you know everyone is bringing up family trees."

"So you're saying if I make a stupid suggestion about where the combination lock is then someone will get personal?" asked Colleen.

"Not me," said Kathy, "but toss in something to increase the pressure a bit, and people could get testy with each other."

"As I recall, there was a time limit, and you had to pay to do it, so people wouldn't be happy if they paid to be in there, and then someone made a stupid suggestion."

"I don't understand something," I said. "What if someone figured out the clues immediately? Wouldn't people feel like they didn't get their money's worth?"

"Maybe," said Captain Miller, "but this is one puzzle I'd like to solve fast rather than slow."

Cassandra was standing in front of the machinery with RUSH stenciled on it.

"Anyone notice these big things are white with red letters on them? Just like the sign on the door."

"Here's where the family gets into a fight," said Tom.

Cassandra didn't take the bait and ran her hands over the sides of the big metal wall of the machinery.

"This thing has gauges, but what does it do? Chief, how many sets of numbers are in your combination?"

The Chief could hear it in her voice. She was onto something, and we all moved over to where she was touching the meters.

"Check this out," she said. "One gauge says Pounds per Square Inch, but the next gauge says Decibels, and the next one says Temperature. One has nothing to do with the other two."

The Chief was shining his light into the first gauge, and he could read the numbers going around in a circle. He reached up and pulled the top cover right off of the gauge and turned the needle easily with his finger to three, the first number in the combination. He put the lid back on the gauge just like the cap on a medicine bottle.

Cassandra already had the second lid off of the gauge that said decibels.

"How did you know it was three?" asked Cassandra.

"I have a cheat-sheet from Bus, but if you were following the clues, the band named RUSH had a hit in 1981. The album reached number three on the charts, and judging by the scale on the gauge your decibel range should be set to forty-four. A song on the album named Tom Sawyer reached number forty-four on the singles chart."

"Wait a minute," said Jean. "You have to be a trivia expert to figure this out?"

"It's not supposed to be easy," said the Chief, "but think about the year. Titus Rush and his prepper friends started these shelters in 1969. It took them over ten years to build them, so the combinations were probably one of the last details. The clue is written right there on the wall in front of you. RUSH. The band must have been big with them since they had his name."

"I think he might have known them personally," I said.

That got a slight chuckle out of everyone, but Captain Miller pointed out politely that they were in a dark room and his men were stretched out in a dark hallway.

"Okay, the first gauge had numbers one through ten, so I set it on three. The second gauge has numbers one through fifty, so I set it on forty-four. The temperature gauge goes how high?

"All the way to two-thousand," said Cassandra. "She stuck a finger inside and turned the needle until it reached 1981."

As she put the cap back on the gauge, we all saw the needles spinning at the same time, and to our left there was the unmistakeable sound of moving machinery. Somewhere gears were turning, being driven by an unseen power supply.

Light appeared at the small seam of the hatch. Gradually the light got brighter as the door opened.

We were understandably delighted, but at the same time I could literally feel the fear in the room. The door was open, and the lights were on, but the smell that drifted out through that bright circle was a mixture of rot and decayed flesh.

******

There was no turning back. The railroad tracks were buried under tons of debris, much of which made the cause of the explosion unknown because it was so massive. Whatever blew up, it was enough to hide the main entrance to the Columbus shelter. Then when the large section of the hotel fell off, it freed the infected that were trapped inside. The rats probably got some of them, but too many had been imprisoned in their rooms.

On the inside of the sub-level of a hotel that was still crawling with the infected, they didn't have the luxury of finding another entrance. The remaining choice was to go forward into an emergency exit that smelled like it hadn't saved any lives.

Captain Miller talked with his men, and they agreed it should be one of his sergeants who went down first. One in particular, Sergeant Marino, enjoyed SCUBA diving into underwater caverns. He was the least claustrophobic person in the world according to his friends, and he was a quick thinker. If there was trouble at the bottom of the narrow escape tunnel, he would take care of it.

Marino's name fit him well. He had curly black hair and olive colored Italian features. He flashed a smile at the worried faces surrounding the hatch as he lowered himself through feet first.

"Don't worry about me, folks. This is what I came along for. I'm ready to mix it up with some bad guys. Besides, right now the only thing I see wrong with this place is the smell."

Marino slid forward into the shaft that was forty to fifty feet long, and a safety line played out behind him. There were small handholds that descended in a neat row, and he was able to move downward quickly. He was wearing his communications headset and checked in to be sure there was a strong signal.

He said his feet had reached the standing area at the bottom where he could straddle the access hatch, but there would be no need to enter a code on the combination keypad because the door was open.

That was not a good sign. Someone must have tried to use the escape hatch but didn't make it. Marino reported that the hatch was hanging into the room below, and it was covered with dark streaks. He also said the smell was much worse.

"Lowering a lantern," said Marino.

The interior of the tunnel had been well lit by the shelter's power source, and that was at least a minor blessing. It meant the destruction above had buried the location of the main entrance, but it didn't necessarily mean there were no survivors. The smell, however, was putting a dent in our hopes.

We all saw the light become brighter as Marino turned it on, but then it dimmed as he lowered it into the darkness below.

It was like fishing. The groans came for the bait, and Marino said he was having trouble hanging onto the light. He reported that he had attached the lanyard to his belt to keep from losing it, but now he was trying desperately to release it.

"Captain, I don't see the lantern. It's being pulled back around the corner, and I can't get it unhooked from my belt."

Marino sounded like he was being as brave as he could, but there was an edge to his voice. No one wanted to be pulled down a dark hole when there was no doubt what was in there.

"Can you release your belt, Marino?"

"Yessir, but my safety line is attached to the back of it."

"Do it, Sergeant. That's an order."

In the panic that was happening at the bottom of the shaft, the training that had made Marino a good soldier kicked in at the sound of his Commanding Officer giving an order. He reached down and squeezed the catches that would release the belt. It immediately popped apart and pulled tight from the bottom of the shaft all the way to the top. It took two soldiers to hang onto the line.

A second safety line was dropped into the tunnel for Marino, and we started talking about a plan for getting people into the room below.

Like the Mud Island shelter, the hatch was either high on a wall or it had to be accessed by climbing a ladder on the wall. It was obvious that there were infected in the room that couldn't reach Marino because they couldn't climb, but that also meant he couldn't reach them.

We thought about dropping a flare into his field of vision so he could shoot the infected, but we didn't know what was below that might burn. In the end, we decided on another lantern with a shorter lanyard attached to the handhold. That way the infected would be within Marino's kill zone.

The plan worked as hoped. As soon as the light was lowered into the room, a group of six infected went for it. Marino put in some earplugs and used his Glock to start eliminating them.

As soon as Marino opened fire, more of the infected came into view. He was surprised at first because he thought they had all arrived for the lights, but the sound of his gun had brought more into the room. That could only mean one thing. The room below wasn't sealed off from the rest of the shelter.

From the safety of his vantage point above the infected, Marino shot so many of the infected that we had to lower more ammunition to him. Eventually, there was a long pause, and he reported that it was all over for the moment.

We considered the possibility that more infected might be working their way toward the sounds of the shots, but the Captain told us they were trained to move in once they established a breach.

Marino was joined by three more soldiers at the bottom of the tunnel, and as they dropped into the room below, more of them jumped feet first into the shaft.

Once the room below was under control, Marino reported the room was much larger than expected. It appeared to be some sort of common area, like a cafeteria. That was why the first light had moved so far from his field of vision. The room was open to hallways in several locations, and there were tables and chairs scattered everywhere.

"Sounds like the crew dining area on the Mercy Ship," said Cassandra, "but the tables were latched in place when we got rough weather. There's most likely a kitchen somewhere nearby, so tell them to watch out for swinging doors that can be pushed open easily."

The word was relayed to the squad below, and they said they would locate the door to the kitchen. A few minutes later they had placed a sentry across from the door to intercept any uninvited guests. The same was done at all of the open corridors, and ceiling lights were gradually illuminated as the soldiers found the reset buttons on the emergency lighting.

The infected were checked to see if there were any still moving, and the all clear signal was sent up to the rest of the group. Everyone gratefully slid into the shaft. The Chief came in last and pulled the hatch shut behind him, but just before he did, he received a radio report from the pilots confirming that they had returned to the helicopters without incident. The pilot who had climbed aboard the private Sikorsky couldn't resist thanking the Chief for the coffee.

When the Chief reached the bottom of the shaft he had to drop to the floor about six or seven feet below. He suggested to Captain Miller that they should place a heavy piece of furniture below the hatch. If they had to make a rapid departure, it would be nice to reach the hatch a little easier.

There were soldiers at every corridor and the kitchen door, and the Mud Island survivors were spread out with them. No one was going to venture into a dark room on their own. The emergency lighting was doing a good job illuminating the dining hall, but the light didn't penetrate too far into the darkness.

Captain Miller came up beside the Chief and quietly whispered, "We don't know what we're up against beyond this room, Chief. I'm going to have everyone build up barricades with all these tables. We can block all of the corridors except one. After we explore it we can do a second one."

"Sounds like a plan. Has anyone checked the infected for ID?"

"Yeah, almost every one of them was Secret Service."

The Chief was hesitant to ask, but it needed to be out in the open.

"Were any of the ones without Secret Service credentials familiar faces?"

"The President wasn't with them, if that's what you mean."

"Well, hopefully we'll find him in one of the other rooms or levels. If this was his shelter, you know it has to be big."

It only took a few minutes to create tangles of furniture blocking the four corridors and the swinging kitchen doors. A fifth corridor only got a partial barricade, and a squad of men was assembled to begin searching and activating emergency lights. Furniture was placed over most of the opening after they passed through, and guards took up their positions.

The Mud Island group was ready to go into the halls with them, but they were also ready to defer to the training of their uniformed friends. There was a reason why they were the best in the world, and they had survived this long because they really were that good.

******

The elevator dropped slowly, lurched several times causing everyone to get nervous, but eventually came to a stop. There was no ding from a bell that signaled the end of the ride.

The lights were still on, and the former flight crew of Executive One was doing what they wanted to do, but a small part of them was screaming not to open the door. Garrett's hand rested on the lever that would slide it open, and he felt the perspiration practically running down from his fingers to his wrist.

He made eye contact with each of his former flight crew and received a nod of agreement. It felt like the lever would slide from his hand, but he gripped it tighter and pulled the door open.

There was light coming from somewhere, but not as much as they would have liked. The door was wide enough for them to all get off together, so they moved forward slowly as if they were one person.

They found themselves facing a landing that ended at a wall, but one glance to their right showed them there was a lot more to this rabbit hole than a landing and a wall. It was like any train station they had ever seen, except it was smaller. There was plenty of seating along a wall that was level with their landing, but then there were rows of steps that descended toward another landing down below. That landing ended at a subway train that was parked with its doors open and dark.

The light was coming from a couple of small fixtures that were recessed in the ceiling above the train, and it appeared there were more of them in the distance down a tunnel that was obviously the way the train would travel.

"At least we won't have to walk down that tunnel in total darkness," said Anne.

As if on cue, one of the light fixtures flickered but stayed on.

"That must be some kind of good power source for those lights to be on this long," said Jon. "Too bad the train doesn't work."

"I'm not sure I would want to use that train," said Sim. "Those streaks on the glass are familiar."

They stayed together, but they spread out just a bit. There were obvious signs that things didn't go so well in this underground railroad.

"I wonder if they got the President to safety before it went wrong down here," said Addison. "There aren't any bodies. You think there were rats?"

"If I built an underground subway for the President, it would be rat proof," said Garrett. "I don't think they had a zombie apocalypse in mind when they built this place, but whatever they thought would happen, they would have sealed it tight against bugs and rats."

"So, you think the people who came down here either made it to safety, or they got infected and walked off?" asked Addison.

"I'll bet they didn't check people for bites, and someone infected got down here with them," said Susan.

"What makes you think that?" asked Mike.

"I think she's right," said Garrett. "We got the Presidential party out of DC, but Air Force One was packed with reporters and staffers. If they didn't understand what they were up against, they might not have been checking for bites. In an enclosed place like this, it would only have taken one infected to get it started."

The small train station was the perfect place to run into an infected dead that was hanging out in the shadows. The lights didn't reach every corner, and the inside of the subway train was totally dark.

"We've come this far," said Garrett. "We might as well go where everyone else did."

Garrett walked past the train and dropped over the edge of the landing onto the tracks. The others didn't move immediately and stood frozen as if uncertain about what to do.

Garrett walked toward the tunnel, keeping his eyes fixed on the darkness ahead of him, but he said in a loud enough voice, "Of course you could always go back to the airport."

That was enough to get all of them moving, and one by one they walked over to the edge of the landing and jumped off.

They walked for several hours, stopping only twice to rest and eat some of their rations. During the first stop they speculated about what there might be up ahead. There had been general agreement all along that the President had a bunker somewhere, and this was a likely place. The speculation ended when Addison asked if anyone thought they would let them in.

Now they walked in silence, and when they stopped for their second break, everyone just sat and quietly ate their rations. Speculation only led to one thing. The President and his staff had abandoned them before, and they would probably do it again.

The light was just a little brighter ahead, and they all noticed it at the same time. They didn't know how many miles they had walked, but if they had to guess, they were somewhere under the city of Columbus by now. They couldn't help but hope this was the end of the line.

The tunnel curved slightly to the right, and when it straightened out again, there was a platform similar to the first one. The tracks ended, but a new set of tracks went into another tunnel. It was obvious that this was just a way station, and a second train had been used to go from here to the next stop.

Whatever this was, it had a little more light than the tunnel, and everyone was glad to climb up onto the platform just to be out of the darkness.

This way station left little doubt about the outcome of at least some of the passengers. The smears of blood across the platform were far too obvious. It appeared almost as if someone was dragged from where the first train would have stopped all the way to where the next train would have been parked.

"I think we all know what's up ahead," said Garrett. "If anyone wants to go back, you can. At least you know it's safe all of the way back to the airport."

Everyone was resigned to their fate, so no one voted to go back. They suspected something bad had happened up ahead, but it was also the way to the place where the President had been taken to safety.

One by one they got up and started down the last tunnel and began walking toward the main entrance of the Columbus, Ohio Presidential shelter.

20 POTUS

There didn't feel like much reason to expect anyone to be alive in the Presidential shelter, but according to Bus, it was the biggest one of them all. It spread out under the city of Columbus and was virtually a suburb of the city above. Some of the people who worked in the shelter were even regular citizens of the many suburbs that surrounded the city.

Galloway, Dublin, Bexley, and Grove City all had neighborhoods that secretly supported the shelter, and so did most of the other suburbs. It was even a private joke within the nation's capitol, among the few people who knew of the shelters, that the people living in the Columbus area kept secrets better than the CIA. No one ever leaked the existence of the shelter.

There was, however, a mad rush to reach the shelter as the infection spread across the country. The people who had been so discreet for so long found themselves unable to open the access points they had used for years. Doors in remote places that hid security checkpoints wouldn't open. Elevators that had previously descended to unmarked basements and sub-levels using special keys no longer went anywhere but up.

What the surface-citizens, as they were called by the full-time staff of the shelter, didn't know was that they were trusted with the secret, but not with access if the shelter was ever needed. The government planners knew that every surface-citizen would show up with their families, friends, neighbors, and even strangers who they wanted to save. The sad reality was that they weren't wrong.

On the day the infection first hit the airwaves, people who worked in the shelter but lived above ground began sharing what they knew about the shelter. It would be safe, it had plenty of room for everyone. There was so much food that they could stay in there forever. Those things made believers out of anyone who had seen a television broadcast.

Parents packed bags with everything from family photo albums to souvenirs bought during family vacations. They loaded their Sport Utility Vehicles with clothes for a long trip. They squeezed in the children and the family pets and headed for the mystery shelter their neighbor suddenly revealed to them, and along the way they stopped at a mother's house, a brother's house, a boyfriend or girlfriend's house and told them about the shelter, too.

The planners knew it would happen, so precisely one minute after the coded message went out that POTUS was in danger, all entrances to the shelter except the main entrance were sealed from the inside. A communications technician toggled a switch that sent out a signal that the Columbus shelter was online. Emergency escape mechanisms were remotely locked, and exit codes were activated. Since surface-citizens were never shown the main entrance or the escape hatches, there was no concern that they would be breached.

At over fifty locations around Columbus, parking lots near secret entrances filled quickly. As workers tried to flee the city, they were blocked by desperate people trying to reach the hidden entrances. What they found were doors that no longer unlocked using the special keys their neighbors or relatives claimed were their keys to safety. Thousands of people carrying their possessions and holding their children watched expectantly as key after key failed to open doors to the supposed super-shelter.

When the crowds became mobs, the doors were attacked with crowbars and hammers. When the doors fell away, there was nothing on the other side except shiny, stainless steel walls that had no seams at the tops, bottoms, or sides. They were doors to nowhere.

When no way could be found to open the steel walls, some people rammed them with cars, and some tried to shoot them down. All of the attempts failed, and there was nothing left to do but to try to escape.

Some of the first to die were not the people who were bitten. Those would come later by the thousands, but the few who died at the very beginning were the surface-citizens who had lied for no apparent reason about a shelter that could save them all. As the infected began stumbling into the streets where thousands of people from neighboring suburbs had been lured by false hope, the crowds were already turning on each other so much that they weren't even aware the infected dead were among them. The people who worked in downtown Columbus were caught in between.

******

The first squad of soldiers to enter a dimly lit corridor was surprised by the contrasting surroundings. Dim overhead lights allowed them to enter rooms quickly and then move on. Some rooms were well furnished offices that were ready for their occupants to begin work. Others were ravaged by bloody attacks of the infected on fellow workers, and some of the workers were still falling over wastepaper cans, bodies, and other debris to reach the soldiers. In those rooms the smells were nauseating.

If not for the fact that POTUS was possibly in the shelter, they would be able to just mark the rooms as hostile and move on to the next. Unfortunately, they had to eliminate the infected and examine all of the dead in the rooms to see if POTUS was among them.

The squad was told to extend the clear zone outward for thirty minutes and then return to the dining hall. Barricades of heavy furniture were then carried to the new limits of the clear zone where guards would be stationed while a new group began moving forward.

Two hours later the corridor where they had begun searching produced few meaningful results. They learned that the infected had been trapped in rooms, and only a few had been found in the corridor. An internal email that someone had printed for others to see had proclaimed a national emergency and announced the lockdown of the entire shelter. All workers were to remain inside their spaces, and prepare for the arrival of the President.

The corridor ended at an elevator that wouldn't open, and all efforts to pry the doors apart failed. A barricade was erected outside the elevator, and soldiers were left to guard it.

The second corridor provided an even more useful document than the email about the emergency. Actually, it was more than a document. It was a binder about four inches thick that had a directory of the levels and the rooms in the entire shelter. The most exciting column next to each room was the internal telephone number.

Captain Miller and the Chief were sitting at a table going over the individual pages to find anything that would tell them how to navigate the shelter. So far there was nothing about the operation of the elevators or where to find stairwells. The assumption was that the President would be in a part of the shelter separate from the staff, and the binder was not about to tell the holder how to find the President.

"How many rooms are there?" asked the Chief.

"If the numbers are right, about two-thousand."

The Chief had a hard time holding back his surprise.

"That's about three times the size of the hotel above us."

"Then we need to get started with the calls. The squad that cleared the first hallway said there were dial tones in the offices. We can put them to work dialing numbers while second squad clears the next corridor. Who knows, there could be people surviving on other levels."

"I can vouch for that theory, Captain."

Cassandra Gibbs had walked up to the table with her M-4 and a machete. She was obviously getting restless.

"When I was hiding on the parking level of the Mercy ship, I listened in on an interior communications radio as the decks were overrun one at a time. Some of the crew tried to hole up in cabins, but if the dead didn't get to them other survivors tried to. There could be people holed up all over this place."

"I'll take that as firsthand intelligence, Ms. Gibbs."

"Any chance I can go with your squads, Captain? I'm ex-military, and I know my way around my M-4. I'm just getting more and more restless."

Captain Miller nodded his agreement. He had seen all of the Mud Island people in action, and he knew we could handle ourselves when there was trouble. Cassandra could be lethal when she had to be.

"See Sgt. Marino and tell him I said to assign you to a squad, and don't let him put you in first squad. They're going to be busy making phone calls, and I don't think that's what you had in mind."

Cassandra snapped to attention then pivoted in place as she left. Captain Miller smiled at the Chief. Old habits were hard to break, and the military had plenty of old habits.

The first squad went back to the offices that appeared relatively untouched. They each got comfortable and started calling phone numbers on their lists. They had been ordered to let each number ring at least ten times in case someone was trying to get to a phone before it stopped ringing. There were some unexpected results.

Of the six soldiers dialing numbers, two of them got answers by the fifth ring, but not the answers they had expected. The phones were knocked from their cradles, and groaning could be heard through the headsets.

Captain Miller immediately sent a runner after the second squad to have them hold their positions while he had the rooms in the second corridor called. Six rooms had the same results, so they knew which rooms were hostile before the doors were opened. First squad was told to update third squad before they began their search of the next corridor.

It was a long day of calling, updating, and searching, but by the end of the day every corridor on the level had been searched. The infected had all been eliminated, and the President was not among them. There were several bodies with Secret Service credentials in their pockets, and the others had a variety of badges that identified them as analysts, clerical, communications, and other personnel.

Once the corridors were secured, the kitchen was opened. Cassandra felt like she was going back in time when she stepped through the swinging doors and saw a huge aluminum door that had to be a loading or delivery bay. She didn't have to tell anyone it was a bad idea to open the door because there was a random banging on the other side. When she listened closely, she could hear the accompaniment of groans through the heavy metal door.

"Has anyone found a map of this place yet?" she asked the squad leader.

He was a short but really broad shouldered young man, and he answered with politeness that was typical of all of Captain Miller's soldiers.

"No, Ma'am. Private McCarthy is trying to decipher something in code that might let us log into one of the computers. First squad says they power up, but they have passwords. There might be information in them about the layout."

She scowled at the young man.

"Please don't call me Ma'am again. You can call me Gibbs, Cass, or even Sarge, but not Ma'am."

He started to say Ma'am again but caught himself in time.

Cassandra wandered around the kitchen checking out the supplies that were stored in different cabinets and on shelves. She couldn't help but wonder about why everything was a wreck in the dining hall, but the kitchen was still largely intact.

She caught my attention and asked for my opinion since I had seen so many different places since the infection began.

"We've tried to reverse engineer settings plenty of times," I said, "but a hundred different things could have happened here. My guess is that the explosion over the main entrance was so massive that it rocked this place. No one knew what it was, so they panicked and ran for the rooms where we've found the infected."

When I said it, it made me realize why some rooms were empty, and some rooms were overcrowded. People trying to escape would have known where the exits were located. Either they were running to designated shelters or running for designated exits. Since they were already inside a shelter, the odds were in favor of exits.

"Cassandra, you're a genius," I said before running off to find the Chief and Captain Miller.

They were still at their table trying to make sense of the room numbering system so they would have some idea how many levels there were, and where the connections were between the levels. There wasn't a clue about how to get the elevators to operate, but they would settle for stairs.

When I explained to them my theory about the dining hall being populated at the time of the explosion, and the people evacuating to specific rooms, they couldn't have jumped up and headed for the first corridor any faster.

The rooms had been cleared of the infected, and a group of soldiers had moved the bodies to storage closets. It seemed like an unnecessary task at first, but the Captain had explained we would need to search the rooms more than once, and we didn't need to be stepping over bodies every time.

The three of us burst into the first room where the infected were found and eliminated. We moved as if we had entered a crime scene. We didn't want to disturb anything more than it already had been, and we needed to see the room through the eyes of frightened people who were trying to escape.

"I wonder how the infection got into the shelter," I said as we stayed glued to a small patch of space just inside the door.

"We may never know that for sure," said the Chief, "at least not until we find out if the infection made it to every level. I'm still hoping it was confined to this level."

"I didn't learn what it was like to be an optimist until you guys showed up and rescued us at Fort Jackson," said Captain Miller. "If you think there are still safe levels in this shelter, I'm willing to believe it too."

From where we stood we could see most of the large office. It was laid out in cubicles down the center, and the surrounding walls all had private offices, presumably for management.

The obvious choice for a hidden exit would be one of the private offices, so we agreed to start our search in them.

"Imagine yourself being employed to work in an underground shelter," said the Chief. "You report for work just like any other job, but the shelter would need tremendous resources in order for all of the workers to live in it."

"They would have to work in shifts just like any other big business," said Captain Miller.

I added, "And some of them wouldn't even know what this place really was. They probably were given a cover story when they were hired."

"Right," said the Chief. "The people who work in the CIA cafeteria have background checks done before they're hired, but no one is going to tell them any secrets."

We each went into the first three private offices and started checking for anything out of place. I knew something was different about the one I entered immediately. It appeared normal, but it didn't feel normal. The desk was positioned off to the left and was facing the entire right side of the office. It didn't feel like a personalized private office.

"Hey Chief, Captain Miller. Do your offices have family pictures and other personal items?"

Rather than answer, they both showed up at the door of the office I was checking.

There was a computer on the desk with the back of the monitor facing us, but it was the rectangular device next to it that drew our attention. It had a slot on it like a magnetic card reader for laminated badges.

We all began concentrating on the wall to the right, and we weren't surprised when we found that a panel of the wall opened easily when we pressed on it. What we didn't expect was the stainless steel wall behind it. There were seams in the shape of a door, but there was no handle, and it didn't budge.

"They were sealed in just like the priests in the pyramids in Egypt," said the Chief.

"That would explain the wrecked rooms. There must have been a crazy panic in here. Maybe the explosion happened first and then the infection got inside," I said. "That would explain why the cafeteria got wrecked."

The screaming and yelling caught us off guard, and even though it was far away, we felt the urgency. It was followed by the unmistakeable bursts of shots being fired in close quarters. We ran from the offices back to the common area just in time to see it all happening.

It was coming from the kitchen and from the area just outside the swinging doors where we saw Colleen go down under the weight of two infected dead. Our view was blocked by furniture, so we couldn't tell how bad it was going to be, but it seemed like our nightmares and worst fears were coming true.

The kitchen doors burst open again, and Cassandra almost literally flew from the doors to the place where Colleen had gone down. She disappeared, and between the bursts of gunshots fired in the kitchen we heard the loud cracking of bones.

The Chief was the first to reach them, but we all saw one of the infected was now lying off to the side. Cassandra had her right forearm under the chin of the infected that was face to face with Colleen. She was pulling back as hard as she could, but this one was stronger than most and not as emaciated.

I thought the Chief was going to run straight through them, but when his left leg planted and his right leg came up in a long arc, I remembered in a flash that I heard a field goal kicker say that you kick through the ball. His size fourteen foot came in just above Cassandra's forearm, and the head hit a wall at least six feet from them.

Cassandra pulled the body aside, and we all held our breath as she helped Colleen to a sitting position. It wasn't like either of them to cry, but this was one of those times.

Hampton came over a pile of tables to get to them, and the fear was written all over his face. He wanted to ask her to say she wasn't bitten, but he didn't want to hear the answer. Colleen threw her arms around his neck, and it seemed like forever before she stopped sobbing.

While they were holding each other, Cassandra was checking her arms and neck. She gave us an expression that said she hadn't found a bite, but she would need to be checked more thoroughly.

The shots inside the kitchen began again, and we realized something had gone wrong enough for the men inside to need help. We left Hampton to take care of Colleen, and went through the doors.

Someone had opened the loading bay door, and it had been standing room only on the other side. The soldiers had done a good job stopping the advance of the infected, but without our firepower, they would have been overrun while reloading. We joined in, and eventually we were shooting at the infected that had been at the back of the crowd.

We carefully stepped over what had been a horde of infected that had been a crowd of employees trying to get in the door when the infection had reached them from behind. The corridor behind them curved off to the left, and there were still shadows approaching the turn as we advanced. We waited until they came into view before shooting again.

"There's something different about this corridor," said the Chief.

I saw it, too. There was a slight downward slope to it as it curved out of sight. We started crossing the pile of bodies. Kathy, Tom, and Jean came in behind us and followed. None of them asked what had happened because it was obvious, but everyone was ready to do battle. A part of me gave in to the knot in my stomach, and I assumed it was because they had already seen Colleen outside the kitchen.

The knot seemed to move to my throat when I saw that Cassandra had joined us, and she was flat out furious. I thought I was going to be sick.

Someone sniffed behind me, and I glanced backward into Colleen's face. She was being slightly supported by Hampton, but she was even more angry than Cassandra. Seeing her made me stop where I was.

We made eye contact, and she said, "I'm so sick and tired of running into those things."

She had a big lump on her forehead where she had slammed into something, but she wasn't wearing any bandages.

"No bites?" I asked in a voice much higher than normal.

"No bites," she said, and her voice was shaky.

When we started forward again, everyone showed in their own way that they were relieved to see we weren't going to lose one of our family, but there was a feeling that the game was finally on. The corridor had no openings at all, and was definitely making a wide spiral downward. What we had assumed was a loading bay door was actually a door to a lower level. It might do nothing more than get us there and leave us with the puzzle of finding the next door, but it was better than sitting still on the cafeteria level. We moved forward with more anger than I had ever felt in our circle of friends.

******

Tunnels have a way of making people feel the weight of the world above. Whether it's a tunnel under water or buried by the ground, if the tunnel is long enough, it will eventually cross a person's mind that the only thing separating them from death was a man made ceiling.

Finding the way station wasn't as good as finding the final destination, but to Garrett it felt close. His enthusiasm was contagious, and his quicker pace seemed to energize the crew of Executive One.

They began chatting with each other instead of just shambling forward on tired legs. It had gradually sunk in that the goal they had hoped to reach on the very first day of the outbreak was now within their reach almost two years later. It was really happening, and they were free of the airport that had been both their shelter and their prison.

Their eyes had adjusted to the darkness so well that none of them noticed at first when there was less light than before. They had begun a lively conversation about what they would say to the President when they found his bunker, or whatever they called it. Some of them were in favor of speaking their minds about what they had been put through after serving their President, while the others argued that they didn't want to trade hot showers, food, and safety for a few moments of verbal payback. Mike made the comment that eating crow wasn't the worst thing in the world if it was cooked right, and he would be glad to beg if he had to.

"How long have the lights been out?" asked Jon.

"Not long," said Garrett. "They stopped working about fifty yards behind us."

Everyone pulled out their flashlights and played the beams in different directions, and the conversations changed to whispered concerns. It was amazing how a dark tunnel that echoed voices caused them to feel like someone was listening.

Addison tripped over something but stayed on her feet. She aimed her flashlight at the tracks and saw a decayed body. When she let out a small gasp, everyone stopped and began shining their flashlights around at the ground. There were several more bodies, all in advanced states of decay.

"The good news is, there aren't any rats down here, or those bodies would be gone," said Sim.

Susan answered, "Funny how good news has changed from winning the lottery to not having rats."

"Right now I'll take no rats over the lottery," said Anne. "No place to spend the money anymore."

"How the bodies got here is what I want to know," said Mike. "These people had to come from the shelter, so this can't be good."

"Only one way to find out," said Garrett.

Garrett started walking again, but now they were aiming their flashlights more toward the floor instead of straight ahead. They passed more bodies, some obviously burned, and some appeared to have been destroyed by the concussion wave of an explosion.

It was so dark in the tunnel that they almost walked right into the rear end of a subway type train that was sitting on the tracks. A landing was on the right side level with the doors, so they began helping each other up. When the last of them was on the landing, they all saw that Addison was shining her light on a huge wall mural of the Presidential seal. There were murals of scenic landmarks surrounding it, but some of them were blackened as if someone had started a fire near them.

"I think we're here," she said.

They saw that the train wasn't actually sitting on the tracks. Something had lifted it and then sat it back down a foot or so to the right. That was why it was right up against the landing. The front end was also blackened, and the glass was missing from the windows.

"Are these bullet holes?" asked Susan.

She was shining her flashlight around the door of the train.

"I think someone was shooting at the passengers as they got off the train."

Garrett had already walked up ahead of the train and his flashlight was illuminating a massive pile of rubble. The debris was stacked so high that it reached the ceiling of the tunnel. It wasn't hard to imagine what caused such a collapse considering the scorched walls, bodies, and the train.

When he moved his flashlight over the debris he saw the gap between the devastated tunnel and the wall on the right. He did a closer inspection, and the distinctive curve of a huge vault door took shape.

"Jon, give me some more light over here," he called out louder than he wanted to. The whole place felt like a tomb, and it didn't seem right to be loud in a tomb.

Jon joined him and saw why he needed the light. There was a dark gap between the vault door and the steel frame, and the door was blocked open by the body of a man and several large chunks of debris.

They cleared away the debris, and a quick search through the tattered remains of the body revealed the man had been a Secret Service agent.

They didn't need to talk about what to do because going back meant walking miles just to reach the way out of the tunnel. If they weren't going to find what they had come for, they would at least need to try to find another exit.

Everyone lined up at the narrow gap between the vault door and the wall and Garrett stepped through into the darkness of the Presidential shelter.

It was quiet, but there was a faint tingling sensation in Garrett's hand when he leaned against a wall. It was a vibration that hinted at either mechanical or electrical activity somewhere inside.

Once they were clear of the entrance the surface of the walls changed texture under their fingers, and Addison walked right into something that was protruding at an upward angle from the left side.

"Is this brick?" she asked. "And what is this stupid thing for?"

When they aimed their lights at it, they saw it was a lantern, or at least a facsimile of an old style lantern. To the right of the lantern was an oil painting of Ulysses S. Grant. Addison reached up out of reflex and turned the small switch on the lamp, and they all stared at it in disbelief when it turned on.

A scraping noise from the dark hallway ahead told them they weren't alone, and they all drew their knives. Guns in such a small area would be difficult to manage.

The first infected stumbled into view, and Garrett waited to see if it was alone. A second one was just coming into view behind it, so he gave it a hard shove instead of aiming for its head. When it fell backwards it collided with the second infected and revealed two more had come up from behind them.

Addison had a blade attached to a pole, and she passed it up to Garrett. He quickly stabbed each of the infected in the head, and then they just listened.

There were no sounds, but there was a dim light coming from somewhere up ahead. It wasn't a difficult decision to go in that direction, but as they passed two other openings in the wall on the right, they shone their flashlights into ink black darkness.

The light was coming from another lantern just like the one Addison had turned on, but this one sat on a desk in a small replica of the Oval Office. A very realistic wax figure of President Grant sat at the desk.

Addison said, "I wish I had never read Alice in Wonderland. This has got to be the rabbit hole."

Mike was shining his light on a wall where a bronze plaque was attached. When he finished reading it, he asked Sim, "Didn't you say something about a tunnel built under the railroad tracks in downtown Columbus?"

Sim nodded and said, "North High Street. A tunnel that was sealed off and never reopened. The entrances at neither end were ever located."

"This sign says we're in that tunnel. I hope it doesn't just get us to the other side of the tracks."

"How could that lamp still be on after all this time?" asked Susan.

The question made everyone uncomfortable. Either someone was expecting them, or they had done something to make it turn on.

Addison took the lead again and twisted the little switch on the side of the lamp. Instead of turning off, lights turned on everywhere. Recessed ceiling lights lit the brick hallway, and brighter lights turned on in the dark corridors they had passed. They stepped back to the previously dark void and stared in wonder at the beautifully decorated hallway. There was a security checkpoint complete with a metal detector, but beyond it were rows of doors. The hall became wider at the end, and they could see an atrium in the distance.

"Well, this is what we came here for. Might as well take the tour," said Garrett.

The first door on the left had a small sign on it that said Secret Service Dormitory One.

"Sim, time to use your navigation skills to memorize our movements so you can draw us a map later," said Jon. "Let's pass that door and come back to it. I'm a bit worried about what might be inside."

Sim gave a nod, already constructing a map in his mind.

The first door on the right was unmarked, so Mike tested the knob. It opened easily, and he found that the light switch worked.

An infected stood in the far corner of the room, and Susan thought he was vaguely familiar. Then she remembered she had seen him board Executive One with the President. Jon and Mike stepped past Susan and disposed of the former White House staffer, then checked the rest of the room.

"This room was lived in for a while. I would have to guess the infection got inside after they got here," said Garrett.

"Maybe because that explosion made the door stay open," said Anne.

"That's one way, but someone may also have been bitten but didn't tell anyone," said Susan. "I think we all saw how well they took care of themselves but not others."

There was general agreement that they shouldn't expect a warm welcome if they found someone alive in the shelter. As a matter of fact, they should expect the opposite.

As they moved further into the complex that was the shelter for the command and control of the entire country, their hopes of finding it functional grew more and more dim. Sections were without power, and there were pockets of infected dead scattered throughout the rooms.

Where they could, they eliminated the infected, but some rooms were so crowded with them that they just marked the doors by cutting a big X into the wood.

They reached the atrium, and it stretched several hundred yards away in all directions. It had a curved dome for a ceiling that made it feel like the structure belonged in Washington DC. The center of the atrium had a doublewide spiral staircase that descended to the main floor, but it circled around an aluminum cylinder that was at least ten feet wide. They couldn't miss the row of buttons on the side.

From the railing of the staircase they could turn and take in the panorama that spread out below them. Unknown to them, other shelters existed that offered similar amenities, but not quite as upscale.

"Is that a Starbucks?" asked Addison.

"It sure is," said Susan. "I'm sort of torn between finding the President and getting a cup of coffee. Any chance we could get our coffee to go and then search for people?"

"I don't see why not," said Garrett. "I could use a cup myself."

Behind the rest of the group, Mike was inspecting the buttons on the shiny aluminum cylinder. There was no door visible to him, and the buttons weren't labeled. They were just red, green, and yellow in two parallel rows of each color. He pressed the green button, but nothing happened. It occurred to him that he would have to push a sequence of buttons to get something to happen, so he walked away.

The rest of the group had picked up speed in pursuit of a promised cup of really good coffee, and they had their backs to the cylinder when it turned. Mike had only reached the top of the spiral staircase, so he couldn't miss it. Out of the corner of his eye he saw the open door rotate into view. He couldn't tell if the door had opened, or if it was open already and the cylinder had turned it to face him.

Mike leaned over the railing and saw that his friends had already reached the Starbucks and were going inside. He wanted to get his own cup of coffee, but he was worried the door wouldn't come back. It didn't take a moment for him to decide to step inside the elevator to press the stop button. He stepped inside, but the walls were smooth. His confusion lasted just long enough for the door to shut in the blink of an eye, and he couldn't tell if he was going up or down, but he was moving.

The coffee machines still had power and water, and Susan was well versed in the operation of the equipment. As a matter of fact, it wasn't that different from the equipment they used on their Boeing 737. It was only a few minutes before the aroma filled the room.

"Where'd Mike wander off to?" asked Sim.

Everyone turned around as if they had to verify he wasn't there. The reaction only took seconds, but it seemed longer to them. They spread out from the door of Starbucks yelling his name and backtracking toward the spiral stairs.

Moving out from the stairs they started going into all of the other stores. The place was like any other mall, but some of the displays were wrecked, and blood streaks were dry, black patches on the otherwise shiny floors.

They found bodies in some of the stores, especially the ones that had emergency exits. Strangely, the bodies seemed to be closer to the exits, and some of them appeared to have been shot. No one would ever know what had happened when the end came, but it had played itself out a thousand different ways inside the shelter.

A pair of infected were found trapped in a restroom, but Garrett and Jon had been fast enough to finish their miserable existence.

Addison was caught off guard by one when she sat down on the pedestal of a floor display in a clothing store. It had been standing stock still behind the mannequin, and it reached through to grab a handful of her long blonde hair. She screamed, but her fear quickly turned to anger. She was frustrated by the constant threats and the disappearance of Mike.

Despite the fact that her head hurt where the hair was being pulled, she backed away and yanked her head downward. The infected was forced to fall over the pedestal onto the floor. It didn't let go of her hair, but now she was looking down on it instead of the other way around. She drove her knife straight through its left eye.

Addison had to pry the hand out of her hair, but as soon as she finished she started making sure there were no more infected in the store.

Sim backtracked all the way to the security station and then came back toward the atrium. He was trying to think like Mike, and it didn't take him long to think about the rows of buttons on the aluminum cylinder.

He studied the buttons and thought back to a Psychology class in college. Western cultures read from left to right, and green is seen as a more positive color than yellow or red, so he pressed the green button on the left row.

Nothing happened at first, but since he was standing close to the cylinder, he felt a vibration in his feet.

"Hey people, I think I've got something up here," he called out.

They came running as fast as they could, and they were all standing at the cylinder when the door opened so quickly they couldn't really tell where it had gone. The chamber inside was like a round elevator, so they all got inside together. There was plenty of room for everyone, so they all got their weapons ready. They didn't know if they would be facing safety when the door opened or if it would be hell.

The door closed and there was a faint feeling of motion, but when Anne asked if they were going up or down, everyone just shook their heads and said they didn't know.

When the faint movement stopped, there was another long pause before the door opened. It was hell.

It was another level of the shelter that was similar to the main dining areas of any large hotel, and apparently the majority of the shelter's occupants had been dining when the infection had gotten inside. Hundreds of infected dead were converging on one end of the dining room trying to reach the top of a small platform.

The dining hall must have doubled as an entertainment club, and there was a spotlight attached to the platform. Mike was sitting on the platform just out of reach from the infected. He was holding his right arm against his stomach, and it was covered with blood.

21 CONVERGENCE

The door to the strange elevator didn't close, and in the time it took for the door to open onto the chaotic scene of the dining hall, Garrett had concluded it was probably operated by personal remote controls carried by each individual. The remote would only give an individual access to preprogrammed floors. Garrett quickly told the others that he had read an article about security in the Pentagon, and a new feature was the remote controlled elevator.

Knowing that the elevator door was just as likely to stay open, it seemed like their only choice was to get out before the horde of infected noticed their arrival. The decision to get out became a moot point when Addison screamed for Mike to stay where he was.

There was little doubt that the two youngest members of the group had become emotionally attached to each other, but Addison's outburst was unexpected and more than enough to draw some of the infected away from the crowd.

"Everybody out," said Garrett. "Stay in a group and follow my lead. I think I see a way we can get to Mike."

Garrett went through the door and cut to the left instead of the direction where the infected were gathered below Mike. Garrett had his eye on a door outside the dining hall that could be a stage door, and if it was, it would at least put them four feet above the crowd of infected. A couple of them had gotten up onto the stage, but the height would allow them to dispose of those easily just by pushing them off the stage again.

As they ran past the dining hall a few of the infected broke away from the crowd and came in their direction.

"Don't bother with them," yelled Garrett. "We can outrun them."

They made it to the stage door, and it was unlocked. They went through and pulled it shut behind them. They were at the bottom of a short set of steps leading up to the stage. As soon as they went up, the infected on the stage turned toward them, and a few others tried to climb up from the dining hall floor.

Sim and Jon met them head on and did it the easy way. They just grabbed them by their outstretched arms and gave a shove in the direction of the groaning crowd at the front of the stage.

Anne saw an interesting switch on a panel with a big sign on it. It said to be sure the area around the orchestra pit was clear before opening it.

"What orchestra pit?" she said out loud.

Susan heard her and realized what the sign was for. She flipped the switch upward, and the infected along the back of the crowd disappeared. The roof of the orchestra pit retracted into the stage in a wide curve, and the crew of Executive One was able to stand back and watch them fall. As the pit filled, more of the infected tried to walk forward, and the dining hall gradually emptied.

The pit held hundreds of bodies when they were in a prone position, and since the infected don't know the difference between falling and walking, they landed like sacks of flour and became entangled with the others. Even as the pit filled close to capacity, they wouldn't be able to climb out.

There were a few stragglers at the back of the dining hall that were being slow to approach, so they used their guns to get rid of them.

Mike was trying to climb down from the platform on his own, but his right arm was useless. He had also gotten blood on the rungs of the ladder, so he kept losing his grip. The bottom of the ladder stopped two feet from the floor, but that only left about one foot of stage for him to stand on with his back to the orchestra pit.

Addison ran over to the ladder to try to help him, while everyone else was screaming for them both to wait. Garrett was the closest to them, and he tried to get there in time, but he wasn't fast enough.

Addison got herself in position directly at the bottom of the ladder to catch Mike if he slipped, but Mike outweighed her by over one-hundred pounds and was much taller. He tried to reach with his foot for the floor that was two feet below the bottom rung of the ladder, and not finding it, he reached too far and made his left hand lose its grip. It wasn't a fall. It was more like a backward step, but it was too far.

Mike's left hand shot out at the last second and grabbed the bottom rung. Addison's hands both grabbed the back of Mike's jacket and dug in. Together the two of them were hanging backward at an angle over the orchestra pit.

For the second time in one day, Addison's long hair became a tempting target, and as Mike's feet slid forward under the ladder, it lowered Addison closer to the pit. A pair of hands reached up from the pile of bodies in the orchestra pit and grabbed her hair.

It seemed like slow motion, but it was actually very fast. Garrett, Jon, and Sim all started pumping rounds into the infected that was holding onto Addison's hair, but even as the infected stopped pulling, its hands were so tangled in her hair that its weight kept pulling her backward.

When Mike's feet slipped one more inch he lost his grip again, and when he let go, both of them fell backward into the squirming mass of bodies. Their screams were more than Anne could take, and she collapsed against Susan. They were well back from the stage, and the only blessing was that they were too far back to see what was happening to Addison and Mike, or what had to be done.

There was only a two second, unspoken exchange between Garrett and Jon, and both of them redirected their aim toward their two close friends. The screaming stopped, but so did their suffering.

They had made it so long and so far without losing a member of their crew, and up until now they had still looked forward to seeing the President safely protected in some remote part of the shelter. Now, they only felt the anger they had kept inside when they were abandoned by him. Even though they had gotten him out of Washington DC safely, they were left to survive on their own, and yet they had never let themselves give in to the resentment most people would have felt.

All of them were crying. Even the men were wiping at the streams of tears, and they turned away from the orchestra pit in silence. They were only five now, but they had lost their youngest friends. That hurt more because Anne and Garrett in particular felt like parents toward Addison and Mike.

Garrett and Jon both went to the two women still huddled together on the stage and put their arms around them. Sim felt like the fifth wheel, but the only reason he didn't join them was because he had something to do first.

He walked over to the switch that had opened the orchestra pit and flipped the switch in the opposite direction. As the floor extended out from the stage and covered the mass of infected, the great dining hall became quiet. The only sound left was the crying on the stage.

******

There had been the sound of gunshots. Rifles or pistols were fired somewhere in the complex, but the way sound carried, the combined force of Captain Miller's soldiers and the Mud Island survivors could only keep moving forward. There was no way to tell if the shots came from inside the spiraling corridor they were following or from one of the many levels.

They had been progressing steadily downward for almost an hour, but they hadn't come to a single exit through the metal walls.

Captain Miller held up a fist calling for the entire squad to come to a halt, and everyone took a minute to catch some rest. They stayed on guard, though, waiting for him to let them know why they had stopped. He was talking with a soldier who was in radio contact with the first squad. First squad was still in the process of calling all of the phone numbers throughout the shelter.

"First squad reports that McCarthy has hacked the password into the main system. She has a map of the facility and has our approximate location," he told the Chief.

"Are we on a wild goose chase down this corridor, or are we heading in the right direction?"

"It appears the answer is both. This is a resupply tunnel that leads to a motor pool under the shelter. The motor pool connects to a series of tunnels under Ohio State University a few miles away."

"How does that help us? We need to get into the main complex and find the President."

"McCarthy says there's an elevator that is operated by remote controls. If POTUS gets into the elevator, the remote sends a signal to the elevator to send it to the correct floor. The Secret Service detail communicates with the computer operator."

"So the remote control is actually an authenticator," said the Chief. "It verifies that the Secret Service detail is making a real request instead of someone forcing the President to go somewhere against his will."

"Even better," said the Captain. "It keeps a log of where he went the last time, and POTUS has only been allowed to visit different levels by using the elevator."

"Does that mean he's still alive?"

Captain Miller shook his head and let out a long breath.

"It means he was alive when the last entry was made in the log."

"When was that?" asked the Chief.

"A year ago, assuming that the computer logs are accurate."

"How far to the garage, Jim?"

Captain Miller spoke over his headset with McCarthy, and she estimated they could reach the motor pool in ten minutes at a trot. Since there were no exits from the tunnel, it wasn't likely that they needed to be quiet. The gang that had been at the door into the kitchen must have been from the motor pool. They couldn't use the elevator without someone operating it from a computer terminal, so they had tried to reach the upper levels at the kitchen.

The Captain informed the squad that there was no need for stealth, and they were going to be moving fast. The soldiers on point were to extend their lead on the rest of the squad. If they had to stop in a hurry, he didn't want the squad to rear end them.

On his command, they began running down the tunnel over a mile underground. It was a brisk workout, but everyone in the group could have done more, even the civilians.

The tunnel came to an end in a garage that resembled an Army motor pool. There were several armored personnel carriers they recognized as Strykers. Kathy was excited when she saw them because it meant they would have transportation back to the helicopters, and on the way they would be able to hunt down a few thousand of the infected.

I noticed all of our group and the soldiers were sizing up the wheels. If the tunnels were clear, they could drive back without losing anyone.

"Where's the elevator?" asked the Chief.

"McCarthy says it's a central shaft straight up through the heart of the shelter, and you aren't going to believe this, but there are one hundred and twenty levels in this thing."

"I would say I don't believe it except for the fact that I think we just ran down most if not all of them."

We found the elevator, and the advanced technology of it was a big surprise. The door could open and close so fast that you almost didn't see it happen.

Captain Miller picked six soldiers to stay behind and see if the Strykers were in operational condition. The motor pool had a small dining area in a side room, and it was well stocked with

MRE's. Two of the men stood guard while the other four got a hot meal. They promised the Captain working vehicles before he needed them.

The Mud Island family always appreciated the attitude of the soldiers under the command of Captain Miller. He managed to keep their morale high even though everyone had lost someone close to them. They also liked to be professional in front of us because most of them were there the night we had helped them escape from Fort Jackson. They wanted to show us just how good they really were.

The rest of us gathered around the elevator and split into two groups. The elevator couldn't carry all of us at once, so we would have to make two trips.

We were just about to send up the first group when McCarthy radioed the Captain again. He listened for a minute, then he told her to send the elevator to the floor she had just told him about.

When he turned to the Chief and Kathy who were standing by the open elevator door, he didn't know where to start, but he managed to get it said.

"The computer logs show that the elevator has been used twice today. Both times it went to the same floor. It's high enough up that it could be where we heard the gunshots. McCarthy will send the elevator to that floor then right back down to here for the second group."

Half of us got into the elevator and got down low to the floor. If there was any shooting, we wouldn't present an easy target. The door whisked shut, and I assumed we were going up even though I couldn't feel the movement.

When the door opened, there was the unmistakeable smell of weapons having been discharged recently. Of course there was also the smell of rotten flesh. Nothing moved in our field of vision, and we spread out wherever we could find cover.

The elevator door closed, and if it left our floor, I couldn't tell, but there was another sound coming from somewhere on the level. It was the sound of a woman crying.

Jean was in my group, and I got her attention. I pointed at my ear and gave her a questioning frown. She nodded, and then did the same toward Cassandra and the soldiers who were with us. Everyone listened and then nodded. There was also general agreement that it was coming from an open door only about twenty yards away.

When the elevator door opened again, I intercepted the Chief and Captain Miller and whispered that we could hear crying, and I pointed in the direction of the door.

From our angle at the elevator, we could see across a large dining hall, and there was a stage at the end of it. Judging by the amount of debris and red blood, this place had been a battlefield. The color of the blood meant it had been recent. We could see a ladder that went up to a spotlight, and someone had lost a lot of blood on that ladder.

We pointed at the open door near the end of the stage. Kathy and Jean told the Chief they wanted to be on point. If it was what it sounded like, there would be one or more very frightened women on the other side of that door.

Captain Miller agreed with the Chief when he pitched the idea to him, so Kathy and Jean moved along the wall as quietly as they could. The rest of the squad moved into cover behind them. If they came back out of that door under fire, they were going to have enough cover to get them through the gates of hell.

Kathy laid down on the floor by the open door and peered around the corner. There was a short row of steps just inside the door, so she had to lift her head higher to see inside. There were two women sitting on the floor. They were holding each other and sobbing deeply.

Kathy whispered something to Jean, and then we were all shocked when she put her rifle on the floor. We felt a little better when she took her Glock from its holster and tucked it into her waistband at the small of her back. As she eased into the open door, Jean stood with her Glock in both hands and aimed at the floor. She would be listening for Kathy to ask for help.

We couldn't see Kathy, but Jean peeked around the corner and gave us a signal to hold where we were. She saw Kathy walk calmly up the stairs and approach the two women. They glanced up at her, but they were too shattered by something to even care that there was a stranger walking toward them. After the glance they just went back to holding each other and crying.

Kathy slowly knelt down beside them and put her arms around them.

"It's going to be okay. You're going to be okay now."

Kathy couldn't imagine what had happened to break these women so much, but she felt them lean into her. Whatever it had been, they had reached their limit, and she hoped that they could be brought back from a sorrow that was a very dark place.

Jean tucked in her Glock and walked into the room. We immediately moved in to see what was happening, but we stayed back far enough to keep from being seen. Jean had joined the women from the other side as if she and Kathy were shielding them from something.

After a few minutes, I could see that Kathy and Jean were both talking with the women. They had stopped crying and were answering questions. I was sure they were asking a few of their own, too.

Kathy motioned in my direction and held up three fingers. Then she pointed off in another direction. It was just enough of a gesture for me to understand there were three more people somewhere, and if they had been doing the shooting we had heard earlier, we had to be careful when we found them.

I went back to the Chief and Captain Miller and told them what was happening. They talked about it for a minute to decide how we would find them, but it was likely to end with someone getting shot if we managed to surprise three armed people.

Colleen, Cassandra, Tom, and Hampton got our attention. Tom spoke for the group.

"Someone just unloaded some heavy firepower on this level. I don't see a lot of bodies, but I have a feeling that whoever these people are, they have survived just like us. If we surprise them, someone will die on both sides."

"We were just saying that," said the Chief. "Do you have any ideas on how to get this done without anyone getting hurt? How do you reach out to three armed people when they find out they have about eighteen people in their neighborhood that they didn't expect?"

Hampton smiled at the Chief and said, "We need the women to help, but they can start by giving us some idea where the other three went and who they are. If we can call out to them, they might not shoot at us."

Colleen and Cassandra went to join Kathy and Jean. Seeing two more women would reassure them without overwhelming them. They sat down and talked for a few minutes, and then the two women came out of the door with them.

Anne and Susan both stopped and stared in disbelief at all the people. It was the largest group of living people they had seen since the day when so many were dying at John Glenn International Airport. None of the guns were pointed at them, and a part of them knew life was just about to get better. It was just too bad that it couldn't have been an hour or two earlier.

Kathy brought the women over to meet the Chief and Captain Miller.

Anne gazed up at the Chief and even though her eyes were red rimmed and sad, she asked, "Are you married? With a man your size around, I would always feel safe."

The Chief was usually on the other side of situations like this. He could put you on the spot without any effort, but it was his turn to be at a loss for words.

Anne smiled and added, "He's shy too. I like that."

Captain Miller came to his rescue and asked if she could tell him about their companions and where they might have gone.

Anne told him they were the pilot, co-pilot, and navigator for the flight crew of Executive One, and that they had gone to the President's room.

******

Garrett Carson, Jon King, and Terrance Simmons had been professionals in their line of work. They were well thought of by their families and friends, and frequently recruited by competing airlines. That's what they had been. Now they were three angry men who wanted the President to tell them to their faces why there hadn't been room for them in his precious shelter. Even though things had worked out better for them in the long run than they had for the people who were allowed inside, they wanted to hear the man say he was sorry.

After they had lost Addison and Mike, they began searching the bodies of the infected for any clues to the whereabouts of the President. They hit the jackpot when they realized the Secret Service details wore special star shaped pins on their jackets. They concentrated their searching on the bodies with the pins, and they found one with a keycard that bore the Presidential seal. The best part was they were already on the right level. They told Anne and Susan to stay where they were and went in search of the Presidential quarters.

When they found themselves standing in front of the door that would give them access to the most powerful man in the world, they didn't rush in for two reasons. They didn't know if there would be agents still alive to protect the President, and they didn't know what they were going to do if the President didn't want to cooperate with their request for an apology. The fact of the matter was that they didn't know if they wanted an apology anymore, or if they wanted him dead.

"What now?" asked Sim.

Garrett held the keycard in his hand, but he couldn't bring himself to use it.

"We didn't think this through," he said.

Jon asked, "Do you think?"

Garrett gave him a scowl that didn't need explanation.

"What if we just knock?" asked Sim.

"If you do, I'd step away from the door and wait for the bullets to stop punching holes in it," said Jon.

Garrett took a deep breath and let it out loudly.

"I feel like I'm back in the fourth grade again. I'm on the playground with two morons trying to work up the nerve to tell Sally Wentworth I like her."

"Thanks, Boss. I needed a good lecture right now," said Sim. "I feel all motivated again."

Despite the situation, Sim grinned at him.

"What is it about times like this that makes men say stupid things?" asked Jon.

"I don't know," said Garrett. "It's just the way men are wired."

Without another word, he slid the keycard into the slot, and a green light lit up the card. He gently pulled on the door, and it opened without a sound.

There was no rain of bullets, there were no Secret Service agents yelling to freeze, and there was no President sitting in a recliner with a brandy snifter in his hand. Of course it was a suite, and they couldn't see all of the rooms, but it was very quiet. There was one thing they could see from the door, and that was a suit jacket on the arm of a sofa that had an American flag pin on the lapel. The President was rumored to prefer them over the Presidential seal, even though he had been seen wearing both.

Without a sound, the three men walked into the suite to see if the President was home.

******

McCarthy was definitely earning her pay. Captain Miller planned to promote her when they got home. She had searched the shelter database until she knew exactly where the Presidential suite was located, and the computer log told her the lock on the door had been opened with a keycard just thirty minutes ago.

It only took ten minutes for them to be in place surrounding the Presidential suite, and the plan was simple. Kathy would go in with Anne. No one felt like the men would casually shoot an attractive blond who happened to show up with one of their closest friends.

The door had drifted shut behind the men when they had entered, but once again McCarthy worked her magic by remotely unlocking it.

Kathy and Anne silently walked inside.

Kathy wasn't sure what she expected, but it wasn't what she saw. Anne stood beside her, and the two women didn't know what to say.

Sim was sitting on a sofa with a glass of bourbon. Jon and Garrett were in separate recliners. Both were in the process of pouring themselves another round.

They weren't aware of the two women at first, probably because their senses were somewhat dulled by the bourbon, but they almost dropped their drinks when they realized the women had come in so quietly they hadn't even heard them. Then the reality sank in that the other woman wasn't Susan.

Kathy and Anne were still staring at the main attraction in the room. The men could have jumped up and shot her, and she wouldn't have been able to react in time.

The President of the United States was sitting on a straight backed chair facing them. Actually, he was tied to the chair, and he was infected.

What had been the President was now a corpse with the ability to groan, and if set free from the ropes holding him on the chair, the ability to kill.

Kathy walked over and sat down on the sofa next to Sim. She reached over and picked up a glass and held it out to Jon so he could fill it with bourbon. She took a fair sized swallow and let out a sigh.

"My name is Kathy, and I found Anne and Susan on that stage where you left them. There are a lot of people outside waiting for me to come out with good news. I'm not going to be able to tell them our President is alive, but it's important for me to know that you guys didn't do this to him. Some of the men out there are US Army, so he's their boss, or rather he was."

Garrett said, "I'm Garrett Carson, pilot of Executive One. We flew him and his family out of DC and then transferred him to Air Force One in Pittsburgh. We found him like this."

Garrett gestured toward the infected dead tied to the chair.

"You found him tied to a chair?"

All three men were shaking their heads at the same time.

"No, we tied him up," said Sim. "Even though he's, you know, already dead, none of us felt like we had the right to finish the job. We've been sitting here trying to decide what to do."

Jon added, "It's a symbolic thing, like properly disposing of an old flag. There must be some kind of ceremony even if he did abandon us after we got him and his family out of DC."

Garrett said, "Sorry we left you and Susan for so long, Anne. We've been kind of stuck."

Despite everything they had been through to get to this day, Kathy felt their sadness. They would have been happy to find the President alive and well in the shelter.

442

"There's an Army Captain in the hallway. Why don't we turn it over to him. He'll make sure that the President is properly honored and receives proper burial."

They weren't too steady on their feet when they got up, but they followed Kathy to the door the best they could. When they stepped into the hallway, the first person they saw was the Chief. There was something about his strong presence that made them feel like they could finally get some rest. He shook their hands and told them they would be safe from now on.

"So, you're a flight crew. We're going to be needing flight crews if we want to take back our country."

"If you don't mind, Chief, I'm going to go to International Falls, Minnesota and take up ice fishing," said Garrett.

The Chief whispered to Kathy, "Is he serious or drunk?"

"Both, I think."

******

Leaving the shelter in Columbus, Ohio was not like leaving the other shelters. We were striking back at an uncaring enemy, but the Columbus shelter was exactly what the flight crew of Executive one had thought it should be. It was a symbol. The President was a symbol. Both were gone, and it was going to be a long time before we would know who was next in line to be President. We didn't even know who was still alive so we could put them in charge.

We spent the next two days going through the shelter and moving supplies to secure areas. We found pockets of infected throughout the levels, including the President's family. His son wasn't with them, so we either couldn't find him or he didn't make it to the shelter in the beginning.

Anything that may be needed in the future was locked away in places that would be hard to access. If we came back to Columbus, it would be great to have survival gear nearby. Weapons were loaded into Strykers, and we would take back as much as we could carry in the helicopters. As for the Strykers, we decided to drive them up inside a garage and try to cover them well enough that they wouldn't be found. They would be nice to have on a return trip, too.

Our only problem was finding out how to get them out of the underground garage. We were stuck with that problem until someone discovered that the north wall of the garage was fake. A Stryker could drive right through it.

Kathy and Captain Miller took a small squad with them in a Stryker, pushed down the wall, and began exploring a maze of tunnels that were most likely intended to keep anyone from ever finding themselves on the other side of that fake wall. As a matter of fact, they wondered how many of the dead-ends they came to were really dead-ends. We had to give Uncle Titus and his friends some credit. They knew how to build some unusual shelters.

They checked in every time they made a turn, but about an hour after leaving the garage, they radioed in that they had found this shelter's equivalent of a houseboat or village on top. There was a hollowed out cavern that held a dozen mobile homes. One of them was stocked full of canned foods and sealed cases of MRE's. They had running water, and electrical cables snaked away down a dark tunnel.

No one was living in the mobile homes, and it didn't appear that anyone had ever found them. Maybe the rats had been responsible for that, or maybe it was just the bad luck of the survivors in this part of town that they didn't find the mobile home park.

Whatever the reason, Captain Miller told us he thought they were somewhere near their exit because the so-called distraction villages and houseboat were all somewhere near the shelters. He was surprised how right he was when he saw they were at the end of the tunnel before he even ended the report back to us.

This time it was a simple garage door. The squad took up positions where they could avoid another fiasco like the one in the shelter kitchen, and they raised the door.

The rest of the radio call didn't make sense at first, but we had been tracking their movements based on their turns and had been drawing their path on a map of Columbus. Sim had been showing us his skills as a navigator by creating a map we could use when we all left the garage, or for when we returned.

"Captain, this is Sim. Did you say your path is blocked by steam pipes and ductwork?"

"That's right. There was a big garage door, but when we opened it, the thing isn't wide enough for a vehicle. There must be another exit."

"No, Sir. The map I've made of your trip puts you directly under the campus of the Ohio State University. The pipes are fake, and I think you can drive right through them."

Captain Miller talked it over with Kathy, and they both had their doubts until Sim told them that the building he figured they were under was reconstructed with modern heating, air, and plumbing around the same time the shelter had been built. He had been talking with McCarthy about shelter construction files she had found on the computer.

"So, we should just drive right through the pipes?" asked Kathy.

"I guess so," answered Captain Miller.

They closed up the Stryker for safety and drove into the tunnel of pipes. The cardboard plumbing and ductwork parted as easily as tall grass, and when they came to the end of the tunnel that only had a regular door in the wall, it wasn't hard to figure out that the wall was made to make people think it was the end of the road. It was actually framed wood, and the Stryker went right through it.

Kathy reported that they were sitting on a snow covered lawn facing something that had to be a park. She wasn't sure, but it was shaped like a football.

"They call that The Oval," said Sim. "You're in the heart of the campus, and I can navigate you to the highways that will bring you back into Columbus. I got pretty familiar with the roads when I was out there on my own."

Now that we knew how to drive out of the garage under the shelter, we could send out raiding parties to eliminate the infected. They mostly occupied the massive hotel that sat on the rim of the collapsed overpass that hid the shelter. Further from the city, the rats that had swarmed through the streets, the suburbs, and the noble university had been thorough.

We didn't want to waste ammunition on the infected, so Captain Miller told his men to come up with a creative idea that would guarantee they were disposed of in large numbers and as quickly as possible. He also told them to find a solution that presented the least amount of risk.

I went outside to watch the operation when they said they were beginning, and it was creative, effective, and safer than setting the whole building on fire, which seemed to be the most offered suggestion.

Hooks were thrown over balcony railings and then pulled by ropes attached to a Stryker. The railings around the balconies were easily pulled away. Once every balcony was cleared, the soldiers scaled the walls and shattered the glass doors as they went. The infected walked out of the rooms and dropped to the ground below.

One of the soldiers suggested it would be quicker to rappel down from the rooftop, but the obvious flaw in that thinking was that they would be dodging the skydiving infected before they rappelled to the bottom. Captain Miller said he didn't want any of his men to be crushed by bad luck or good aim when the infected fell.

It rained bodies for over an hour, and while they were clearing the rooms, another squad started at the top floor and went down the stairwells, propping open the doors as they went. The infected trapped in hallways took the opportunity to follow. Before long they were piled up on the landings, and when they crawled free of the tangle of bodies on one floor, they fell another flight into the pile on the next landing.

It took another two days to be sure all of the infected were properly destroyed, and Captain Miller had asked his men to be sure to do a headcount. They found that between the shelter and the hotel, there had been over two-thousand infected that had escaped the swarms of rats.

We considered that a slow start, but if we attacked the infected dead when they were worn down by the elements, we could gradually take back our homes outside of the shelters.

On our final day in Columbus, we assembled for a special service in the section of the shelter that had been discovered by the crew of Executive One. It seemed fitting that the last known President of the United States should be laid to rest in a place designed to honor his predecessor, Ulysses S. Grant.

The decision about how to properly dispose of the infected dead that used to be President Freeman was resolved privately and with as much dignity as possible. After all of the times that the Mud Island group had destroyed the infected, this felt singularly different. The crew of Executive One had killed the infected by setting their heads on fire, but as much as they had come to dislike President Freeman, they too were unable to bring themselves to take part.

Captain Miller said that martial law was still in effect and ordered all civilians to leave the section of the shelter that held the private quarters of the President. An hour later a group of his soldiers arrived at the shelter with a coffin they had removed from a funeral home. They returned from the Presidential suite with a flag draped over the coffin.

Later that day we found ourselves standing in the small museum intended for President Grant, attending the funeral of President Freeman. It was simple, but it was honorable.

22 INTERNATIONAL FALLS

The Chief did his best to convince Garrett Carson to agree to return to Charleston with us. He even threatened to kidnap him and his crew, but Garrett said he already knew what kind of man the Chief was, and he wasn't the type to force them to do anything against their will.

We went to work on the rest of his crew, but the only one we recruited was Sim. Terrance Simmons would be an asset as a navigator on future trips away from Mud Island, but the main reason he wanted to come back with us was that he was from the south, and he hated the snow. He also said you could get the best sweetened iced tea in Charleston. That much we could promise him, but we also noticed him taking an interest in Cassandra. He wouldn't feel like the odd man out around her.

There was plenty of room for our new friends in the helicopters, and we debated whether or not we should fly them to International Falls and just drop them off, or if we should fly all of the helicopters north. The fuel was an issue, but Sim told us he knew where the fuel trucks were parked at John Glenn

International Airport, and he even knew which ones had the special blend they needed in their helicopters.

In the end it was decided that all of us would go because we didn't really know what we would find that far north. We knew what the rats had done, but there were other animals. We needed to see for ourselves if there were larger predators and if the infected had survived the cold.

We also didn't know what the local population would be like. If they had survived the epidemic, they may not welcome strangers. If that was the case, a show of force would be a good idea.

It was snowing when we lifted off from the tops of the parking garages. It had been a long drive through the maze of tunnels to the Ohio State University and then back to the city above ground, but there were enough Strykers to carry everyone. The ammunition and the weapons had been transported back the previous day, so all we had to do was leave.

Once the engines were warmed up enough, we lifted off with snow flurries blown by our rotors and banked away to the east. Fuel would be first on the list, and then it would be nonstop to International Falls.

From the warmth of the passenger cabin of the Sikorsky, Garrett and Anne stared out at the terminal that had been their home for almost two years. Kathy asked them what it felt like to see it again, and we were surprised to hear them say it was like seeing a prison where they had been incarcerated, but it was also like seeing home again because it had saved their lives. The rest of us couldn't take our eyes off of the tail of Air Force One still protruding from the hangar where it had parked so long ago.

Anne pointed out the plane that had been known as Executive One, and we could see an almost loving softness in her eyes. Garrett was also glued to the sight of the plane.

Fueling the helicopters was routine because there was so much ice and snow. Other than a few falls, there were no problems because the infected were virtually nonexistent. Between the rats and the cold, no one would know what was out there to fear until everything thawed.

The airport faded away below us and was lost in a cloud of gray mist. It was a wet snow that would freeze hard through the night. It was cold, but we were going somewhere colder. We expected the temperature to be between minus six degrees and twenty degrees Fahrenheit. Sim had even volunteered to wait in Columbus until we got back, but we assured him he would stay warm in the helicopter. He was riding with the Army in one of their Navy helicopters, but we made sure they had plenty of coffee on board.

The trip was about the same distance as it had been from Charleston to Guntersville and then to Columbus, so we settled in for the ride and got to know our new friends a little better. We were going to be pretty far from each other, but maybe that was how we would survive the infection and not become extinct. We had already seen what happened when too many people got put together in one place.

Garrett and Anne told us about Addison and Mike and how much they missed them. Jon, Sim, and Susan were undoubtedly reliving their experiences with the Army crews in the other helicopters. The soldiers all felt drawn to the small group that had beaten the odds with no outside help.

We tried more than once to get the other four to change their minds, but we were not surprised by their will to get as far away from it as they could. We were surprised, though, that they knew exactly where they wanted us to leave them.

International Falls only had a population of just over six-thousand people, and they were definitely spread out, but our friends didn't want to be near them at all. They had pored over our maps and the maps in the shelter, and they found what they considered to be the perfect place.

The area was dotted with lodges along the banks of Rainy Lake. Most of them were on the United States side of the border, and all of them would be comfortable. On the Canadian side of the border they had found their home. It was one lonesome lodge on the southern banks of Last Island.

When they told us, our reaction was that it was a fitting name because it was so remote. It was also so similar to our home, Mud Island. The exception was that the island was surrounded by ice for much of the year, and anything that tried to walk out to Last Island was likely to freeze before it got halfway.

We came in low over the city of International Falls. Straight streets were covered in snow, and it was obvious that no one was alive. There wasn't a single trail of smoke from the hundreds of chimneys. The were no lights on in any buildings, and no roads showed signs of recent traffic.

Hampton said, "Georgetown of the North. The infection would have taken hold very slowly here. It was already cold when the epidemic started, so it must have been spread from within. Someone was bitten and didn't tell anyone. Either that, or they thought it was just a bad sickness that would pass. This place must have been cut off from the outside world in a hurry."

"There's another reason you can tell this place died from within," said Kathy. "There aren't any wrecks in the streets that would block traffic. This place died slowly."

"I don't know why it surprises me, but there's a Walmart down there," I said.

I could have been pointing out the Great Pyramids judging by the reactions of my friends. Everyone tried to spot it out the windows before we passed it, as if they had never seen a Walmart before.

We banked east across Rainy Lake, and the Chief spotted our destination. There was a highway crossing the lake just north of the island, but otherwise it was extremely remote. There was a clearing to the right of the lodge, and the helicopters descended toward it.

We had to admit, while we were helping Anne, Garrett, Jon, and Susan get settled into their new home, we were a bit envious. The place was deserted, it was comfortably warm with a new fire roaring in a large fireplace, and it could be easily defended. Our whole group was just a little weary from fighting the infected dead for so long, and the idea of escaping from the fight was attractive. In the end, we agreed that we could always come visit when we were ready to take a break. I think we all took that offer seriously.

One of the Navy helicopters had circled the island, and the part that wasn't wooded showed no signs of the infected or the living. There were more cabins, but once again, no smoking chimneys.

We stocked the storerooms in the lodge with enough nonperishables to last a couple of years. Captain Miller had his men make short work of replenishing the supply of firewood. The Chief insisted on helping, saying that it reminded him of the place where he did his cold weather training as a seal.

We also helped to set up a series of early warning signs along the edge of the forest, but there was little doubt that wild game would trip the wires.

With a long trip home ahead of us, we decided to spend the night at the lodge. It had been a long time since we had slept above ground without needing to worry, but we worried anyway. There was that inescapable feeling that we were forgetting something. Whether it was the infected or the living, not many places were completely safe, so Captain Miller did what any good commanding officer would do and posted a watch.

After a supper consisting of the military version of comfort food, we told the five remaining survivors of Executive One some of our stories. There was a lot to tell, but Garrett and Jon seemed to really enjoy hearing about the stunt the Chief had pulled when he tilted the Sikorsky forward and put the rotors into a horde of the infected.

"I didn't think that could be done," said Garrett.

"I was there," said Kathy. "It can be done. I think it's unbelievable because no one ever thought it would be a great way to kill zombies."

The Chief knew he was being needled, so he just grinned.

The subject eventually got around to how Cassandra had joined us, and how the infection had gotten into the food chain.

Garrett was very concerned because he wanted to use fish as a big part of their diet. We just didn't know what to tell him. The cold weather would undoubtedly suppress the virus, and the fish in Rainy Lake weren't bottom feeders like the blue crabs and ghost crabs. Still, we told them they should boil their drinking water, and if they do eat the fish, always make it well-done.

The following morning wasn't a tearful goodbye. If anything we were happy for the four who were staying behind. They would be able to settle into their life of isolation, while we would be going back to work trying to save our little corner of the world. We still had another stop to make on the way home. The people we had encountered in Guntersville would be wondering if we were going to come back by now, but we said we would, and we planned to keep our promises.

Sim hugged his old friends before climbing into the helicopter. He really hated the cold, and everyone was teasing him about his craving for iced tea when he couldn't feel his fingers.

The helicopters all started warming up, and a few minutes later we lifted off. A part of me said I should ask Jean if we should bring our son up here to live, but when she saw me glance her way, I knew what she was going to say.

"It's time to go home to Mud Island and Charleston. They need us there."

ABOUT THE AUTHOR

Bob Howard (1951-) was born in New Jersey to an Army Sergeant from Ohio and a mother from Romania. He was moved from one Army base to the next, and before he began high school in Huntsville, Alabama he had lived most of his life overseas in Germany and Okinawa with brief stays in Maryland and North Carolina. He credits his imagination to his exposure to different cultures and environments at an early age. He began reading science fiction and fell in love with post apocalyptic novels. He still has an original copy of the first one he read in 1966, The Furies by Keith Edwards. He joined the Navy after high school and continued to move from one base to another, including a submarine base at Holy Loch, Scotland. He eventually stayed in one place when he got stationed in Charleston, South Carolina. He graduated with a BS in Psychology from the College of Charleston and married his wife of 32 years. His son still lives in Charleston, but his daughter has married and made a home in Ohio where the Howard family has its earliest known roots. Through the years he has had one burning passion that he has wanted to fulfill, and through The Infected Dead series he is getting to live that passion. Creating a book is something so many people want to do but never have the opportunity, and after writing these books he believes the sky is the limit. He plans to write for the rest of his life because it is enjoyable beyond his wildest dreams. As for the zombie genre, he saw Night of the Living Dead when it originally hit the theaters, and he believes until recently it didn't receive the attention it deserves.